THE
DUNKIRK
DIRECTIVE

The Dunkirk Directive

DONALD RICHMOND

STEIN AND DAY/*Publishers*/New York

First published in 1980
Copyright ©1980 by Donald Richmond
All rights reserved
Designed by Louis A. Ditizio
Printed in the United States of America
Stein and Day/*Publishers*/Scarborough House
Briarcliff Manor, N.Y. 10510

Library of Congress Cataloging in Publication Data
Richmond, Donald.
   The Dunkirk directive.

   1. World War. 1939-1945—Fiction. I. Title.
PZ4.R53155Du [PS3568.I3515]   813'.54   79-65119
ISBN 0-8128-2687-6

For Lisa

Book One

CHAPTER 1

Captain Pohl's headache was growing steadily worse. He closed his eyes in an attempt to shut out the pain and the unpleasant awareness that the dog was lying so close to him.

"*So odor so,* Pohl."

It was almost a whisper and indistinguishable to the preoccupied officer even in the silence of the Chancellory study. He moved forward a pace and was about to speak, but then thought better of it. He waited as Adolf Hitler leaned farther over the map, continuing to study it through a large magnifying glass.

"Yes, Pohl. One way or the other!" Hitler repeated as he brought his free hand heavily against the marble-topped table, shattering the stillness of the room. The sudden noise brought the Alsatian to her feet, teeth bared, and growling.

"Sit, Blondi," Hitler ordered, pausing only briefly before returning to his scrutiny of the map. The dog hesitated, watching the officer back behind the corner of the table. The frightened captain froze when the animal began to move toward him in a slow, stalking crouch.

"Sit!" This time Hitler's command was sharper, but he was smiling faintly. The dog sat reluctantly, inclining her head toward her master while her eyes remained fixed on the other man. Her low growl continued. Hitler stroked her head. "Blondi doesn't seem to take to you, Pohl."

"I can't understand why, my Führer. I'm very fond of her," the captain answered in a nervous, high-pitched voice. He looked down at the dog, trying desperately to convince both the animal and the master of his sincerity. When their eyes met, the Alsatian tensed.

Hitler watched the exchange. "She may think you're a member of the General Staff, Captain. That would certainly be enough to make her wary."

He turned from the table, leading the dog by its collar, and walked to one of the doors of the new Chancellory study. He opened it and spoke to someone not visible to the uncomfortable captain. The dog looked back and growled again.

Hitler laughed. "Erich, take Blondi to the garden. She and Captain Pohl seem to make each other uncomfortable."

The Führer closed the door and returned to the map. "Come over here, Pohl, I have a job for you," he ordered. "What is it? You don't look well. Are you ill?" Hitler drew back perceptibly.

The captain was well aware of his Führer's morbid fear of illness. He answered quickly, "Oh no, my Führer. A slight headache . . ."

Hitler raised a hand to silence him. "This is no time to be ill." He pointed to the map. "A full week ago, the army moved into France. Here is where they are today. As usual, the General Staff gave me numerous reasons why the attack was doomed to fail. I had faith in my field commanders and the German soldier. And now we are advancing sixty miles farther west every day. Within the week France will be cut in two. Then Paris, and when Paris falls, France falls. But we could have a problem here." He smashed his hand against the table. "England!"

Pohl's head throbbed painfully. He waited as Hitler gazed thoughtfully at the large window near the table and then continued.

"I have ordered a special force of personally picked men to France, under the command of General Kellner. Second in command will be Colonel von Maussner, one of our best tank training officers. What do you know about them?"

Captain Pohl, unaware that he was staring transfixedly at the map, was jarred by Hitler's voice. "What is the matter with you, Pohl? You were not brought here to memorize this map. Pay attention. General Kellner and Colonel von Maussner," he repeated slowly, the schoolmaster to the dunce.

The captain answered hesitantly. "I know General Kellner quite well, my Führer. He seems rather ordinary." He paused, unsure of his ground. "He shows no interest in politics. His main topic of conversation seems to be food. I am usually wary of self-indulgent men, but he seems . . . harmless."

Pohl hoped that he hadn't gone too far. Hitler merely nodded; so Pohl continued, "Colonel von Maussner is a field officer and, from what I've heard, a good one."

Again Hitler nodded. "These men have been chosen to prepare an operation that could shorten the war in the west. Perhaps even finish it. Security will be handled by a special detachment of the Grossdeutschland Division. The S.S. will not be involved. General Kellner has been given his orders and will leave for Cambrai tomorrow morning. I must return to Münstereiffel, so you will be my personal representative at the base. You will accompany Kellner."

Pohl was momentarily elated at being given the opportunity to further ingratiate himself with Hitler but wished that it might be accomplished at a less dangerous place. He decided to risk a question. "May I ask, my Führer, why the preparations are being carried out in France? Surely . . ."

"That's enough, Pohl. I gave you the rank of captain because it gives you entrée to military circles denied to a civilian and even the S.S. But don't equate the uniform with the ability to make military judgments. Perhaps you're worried about your own safety? Is that it?"

"Not my safety, my Führer, only the possible danger to the operation," Pohl lied.

Hitler moved to a desk at the far end of the room. "Pohl, bring that chair over here and sit down."

Captain Pohl felt sweat on his face as he carried the chair to the desk.

"Within a day of your arrival," Hitler began, "Colonel von Maussner will arrive by motor convoy with the twelve men who will undergo a period of intensive training. It will last a week, or possibly a bit longer since it depends largely on the progesss of the Panzer divisions, but I would say that you can expect to be back here by the beginning of June. I have impressed on all of the men concerned that I will accept no excuses for failure. Your presence will serve as a constant reminder of my personal interest. You've been known to unsettle a few of my officers in the past. That is not your purpose on this assignment. Observe, but do not interfere. Is that clear?"

He did not wait for the captain to answer. "England must be convinced of the foolishness of the recent declaration to fight to the finish. Herr Churchill must be shown that England's only hope of survival as a nation lies in alliance with the Reich. He talks of tears, sweat, and blood. I'll give him more than enough of each if I must. The twelve men that I've carefully chosen are going to help the Englishmen make up their minds before it is too late for them."

"How, my Führer?" Pohl asked.

"We are going to invade England."

"Invade England? Now?" Pohl was unable to hide his astonishment.

"Yes, Pohl, now. Twelve of our best men should be enough, don't you think."

As the command car topped a slight rise in the road, Colonel Heinz von Maussner stood up, brushed futilely at the dust that clung to his field gray uniform, and stared ahead at the village beginning to take shape through the haze of smoke far ahead. A man of carefully cultivated imperturbability, the colonel was able to hide his uneasiness as he watched the Stuka disappear into low clouds to the northwest. The dive bomber had attacked something almost directly ahead of the column.

Von Maussner had made clear his concern about crossing such a recent battlefield and was uneasy despite the precautions he had insisted upon: a motorcycle escort to range ahead and investigate anything that might provide cover for ambush; the Arado observation aircraft that were to fly over the route and direct covering fighter bombers to anything considered too dangerous for the security troops to handle; the two light-scout Fieselers that were to alternate above the column during the trip, in constant touch with the ground escort's portable radio; and finally, the isolation of the air space above the vehicles to prevent inadvertent attacks by overzealous German pilots.

As he searched the horizon, the colonel was somewhat reassured by the quiet sky. Apparently the Stuka had managed to destroy whatever it was that might have threatened the column, since no covering aircraft were rushing in to continue the brief attack. He decided, however, that it would be best to let the motorcyclists look into it further. He turned to the driver beside him. "Slow down, sergeant," he ordered, while raising an arm to signal his intent to the three half-track infantry carriers in line behind his car. "Watch for any signals from Lieutenant Krause," he added.

The driver acknowledged the order, inwardly cursing the wary officer. He was angry at being forced to creep through the destruction and death that had surrounded them since they had left Cambrai. The smell was making him sick to his stomach, and yet he was thankful that it was only the dead who surrounded the column.

The four vehicles and their escort had passed the forward units of German infantry an hour earlier and were traveling through the vacuum left by the rapid advance of the Panzer spearheads. During that hour they had seen nothing of the enemy . . . alive. Discarded equipment lay everywhere: helmets, packs, and rifles. Many of the weapons had been stacked and crushed beneath the treads of German tanks on the orders of the more methodical commanders. Artillery of all calibers stood abandoned on or near the road, some apparently still in firing condition, left for the German arsenals by French soldiers unwilling to take the time to render them useless. Occasionally, massive Char B and lighter Souma tanks were seen scattered among the military and civilian vehicles that dotted the fields on either side of the road. Some had been destroyed, others simply abandoned when they had run out of fuel.

Colonel von Maussner stared in mounting disbelief at the evidence of the demoralization of an army that had been thought to be one of the best in the world. Clusters of dead lay at intervals along the road, brought together by a mindless herd instinct and then mingled in death by the strafing Luftwaffe or the high explosive shells of advancing German tanks. Von Maussner removed his hat, ran a hand through graying, closely cropped hair, and said to the two young officers seated in the rear of the car, "Remarkable, isn't it, gentlemen. Nothing but evidence of retreat." He turned to the driver. "How far have we come, Sergeant?"

"Nine and eight tenths miles, Herr Colonel."

The colonel smiled at the preciseness of the reply. "I would guess that we are at least six miles ahead of our infantry—with the leading Panzers who knows how many miles ahead of *us*. If the French had the stomach to fight, this could be a dangerous area for a morning's ride."

The Fieseler scout plane passed low, close to the right of the column. Its pilot, clearly visible through the jutting bow window, dipped the airplane's wings in answer to the men's waves. He made a few tight orbits around the vehicles, then turned away to the southwest, toward the ruins of Villeverte. The colonel watched its progress for a moment.

"The heavy gunfire you hear to the north," he said to the officers, "is that of General Rommel's command attacking the British at Arras. When it falls, the Englishmen will be forced to retreat to the northern coast. Unless French reluctance is catching, they will fight all the way, giving us the time we need. Incidentally, it was near Arras that the British tanks you will use on your mission were captured." The colonel saw the quickening interest of his two passengers. "But I don't have to tell you about British tenacity since you are virtually British yourselves." Von Maussner waited confidently for a reaction and wasn't disappointed. One of the young officers answered with barely concealed anger.

"Not British, Herr Colonel, German. We may have been forced by circumstances to live in England, but we are still German."

Von Maussner raised a hand placatingly. "No offense intended. Actually, those circumstances were precisely why you were chosen for this important enterprise."

The Fieseler was orbiting above the village ahead. Von Maussner saw that the escort commander had ordered part of his force out into the fields, flanking the ruins. "Apparently there is no enemy in sight," he said. "But there are times when it's best to take nothing for granted." He spoke to the driver. "Keep your eyes open, Sergeant."

The column began to bear due west, moving into the fringes of the gently rolling plains of Artois. An occasional farmhouse stood out in sharp relief against the horizon. White cloths hung from the windows of some in gently fluttering testimony to surrender. Gunfire echoed distantly to the north and south as the vehicles moved along a secondary road that was relatively clear of the now familiar litter left by the retreating French. The colonel was looking to the rear at the half-tracks, when one of the young officers in his car stood up and pointed in the direction of the vanguard.

"Something ahead, Herr Colonel."

Von Maussner swung around in time to see the Fieseler making violent maneuvers above the road ahead. The colonel could see the forward escort racing toward what seemed to be an endless mass of uniformed troops filling the road. A motorcycle raced back to the command car and the waiting von Maussner. "What is it?" he demanded.

"Unescorted French prisoners, Herr Colonel. Lieutenant Krause asks that you slow down again, and to please have your men stay alert. They seem to be all that's left of the garrison at Albert. They came out of those woods ahead. Even the Fieseler pilot didn't see them until they began to move onto the road."

"Very well," von Maussner said. "Tell Lieutenant Krause to clear them off the road as soon as possible." He watched the motorcycle roar away. "Go tell the others what that man said, Lieutenant Schiller." He raised a hand, and the column slowed as the young officer dropped from the car and hurried back toward the half-tracks.

The vanguard blocked the road and began herding the French into the fields to the right of the column. The prisoners obeyed immediately. They carried no weapons and were careful to keep their hands visible while passing the wary escort.

The escort commander, Lieutenant Krause, had taken a French officer into the sidecar of his motorcycle and was edging forward through the milling troops still remaining on the road, leaving the shouting of orders to the Frenchman. There were now hundreds of French in the field alongside the column, and the sight of so many enemy troops made von Maussner understandably uneasy. Even without weapons they could be dangerous. He was deciding whether to order the vehicles into the fields to the left when he saw the French at the far end of the mass ahead suddenly begin to break their ragged but orderly lines and begin to run wildly in all directions. He saw the French officer stand abruptly in Krause's sidecar and attempt to leave it, only to be pulled down violently by Krause. Then von Maussner saw the reason: a formation of aircraft, flying low and headed directly toward him.

A chain reaction of panic had spread down the lines of prisoners, and their entire formation was now in violent motion. Some of those nearest the vehicles began to run across the road, through the column. The rear guard of the escort had raced up and began firing their machine pistols into the air, and then into the French as they threatened to engulf the column. The firing only increased the prisoners panic, but they began to turn away when the soldiers in the half-tracks added their fire-power. Von Maussner recognized one soldier, a huge sergeant of the special force, who was standing upright and firing into the French with obvious pleasure.

"Protect the vehicles," von Maussner called sharply to the escort. "Everyone out! Take cover!" He saw the special force sergeant glance calmly at the oncoming aircraft and then smile at him. "Siegler," he yelled angrily, "Take cover!"

The colonel waited until his order had been obeyed, then jumped from the car and ran to the ditch at the side of the road. The firing had stopped. Von Maussner turned to look for the planes. Before he could focus on them, the Fieseler—which he had forgotten about completely—flew over the column from behind, toward the oncoming formation. He saw the treads of its tires clearly as they grazed the windshield of the command car, causing one wing to almost touch the ground, but it recovered and raced ahead barely above the road. Once past the column it began to dip its wings violently to the right and left. Within seconds the sky above the light plane was blotted out by the undercarriage of a large, twin-engined fighter as it pulled up in an abrupt power climb. Von Maussner had begun to duck his head when he saw the black crosses on the undersides of its wings. Three other fighters followed the first skyward.

Von Maussner was angry when he rejoined the young lieutenant, already waiting at the command car. He looked at the half-tracks and saw that all of the men had returned to their seats as quickly as they had vanished at his order. He was impressed by his charges' calm. Then he saw the muscular sergeant Siegler watching his approach, still smiling. The smile had nothing to do with good humor, and the colonel felt that his order to take cover was being judged by the sergeant. Von Mausner knew that Siegler's record had been exemplary since he had returned to Germany from England to join the Wehrmacht, but a close study of it had proved to the colonel that the man was obviously an opportunist and not the sort of man he would have chosen for a mission where close teamwork was necessary for any hope of success. But Hitler had chosen the sergeant personally, and it was out of his hands. His anger showed when he spoke to the lieutenant.

"Despite all of my precautions this sort of thing happened. Those Messerschmitt 110s look much like British Blenheims from a distance. I wasn't able to see the twin tail through the dust." He paused, angered further by his attempted justification. "But even though they proved to be ours, causing us to be thrust into the midst of hundreds of panicking French is inexcusable."

"They must have seen the French and thought we were in trouble, Herr Colonel," the lieutenant answered.

"Even if their intentions were good, they were a bit late, weren't they? If those French had been armed. . . ." Von Maussner paused and called to a sergeant of the escort, "Get that rabble out of here at once! When you've seen to that, get forward and tell Lieutenant Krause that if we meet any more French, he's to detach men to keep them out of our way. They're to shoot if necessary. Now, get on with it." The sergeant saluted and hurried away.

A score of French dead lay around the vehicles. The colonel looked at them briefly and said: "A few more Frenchmen who got their wish for a little corner of France." He beckoned to the lieutenant he had sent back to the half-tracks earlier. When the officer had taken his seat in the car, the column was ordered ahead. Von Maussner watched the escort herding the prisoners well away from the road, then sat down and stared beyond them to the north, where sounds of the distant battle were intensifying.

Lieutenant Walther Dietrich watched the herding of the French with interest from the back seat of the command car. Nietzschean theories of a master race had never interested him greatly. He was confident enough to have no doubt that he was superior to the enemies he had met so far.

Physically, he was a close approximation of Nietzche's ideal Aryan. Blond hair, blue eyes, and an untainted German ancestry. But even more important than the accident of appearance was his complete dedication to Hitler and a firm belief in the army's personal oath to their Führer. As a tank corps officer in Poland, his dedication had led to a transfer to the special forces and his participation in the glider attack on the bridges of the Albert Canal on the first day of the invasion of France. He had then been called back from leave for his present assignment as a personal choice of Hitler. The coming mission filled him with a feeling of expectation. He knew England, having lived there for most of his twenty-four years, and knowing, had little fear of it.

His fellow officer, seated beside him, was not quite as impatient to begin. Lieutenant Friederich Schiller was a head taller, but otherwise a virtual carbon copy of Dietrich. Outwardly they were enough alike to have been mistaken for brothers, but the similarity ended with their physical appearance. Where Dietrich was extroverted, Schiller was introspective and often withdrawn. His successes as the commander of a PzKpfw III in the east of Poland left little doubt of his bravery, but he lacked the unquestioning dedication to the Nazi cause that motivated Dietrich. Schiller, too, had spent most of his life in England, and even though much of his youth had been devoted to pro-German, anti establishment causes in London, he had found himself caught up in a dichotomy of conflicting emotions and had maintained a guarded respect for the British people. As a member of Oswald Mosley's Blackshirts, Schiller had lived for a time at the infamous Black House in Chelsea, only to find that Mosley's adherents seemed to be mostly misfits who would have adopted any cause. His disillusionment led him to look elsewhere for fellow idealists, but he was to learn that all Edens are flawed.

When he returned to Germany in 1938, Schiller became a zealous army officer but a reluctant follower of the Nazi credo. A bloody nose resulting from a street rally in London was a far cry from the bloody pool beneath the body of a Jewish merchant impaled on the shattered glass of his shop window. He found that the opportunistic Blackshirts of England were in no way comparable to the highly regimented thugs of the *Schutzstaffel*. He was careful to keep his disillusionment to himself, but the thought of returning to England as an enemy soldier made him wonder how he would react.

Sergeant Wilhelm Siegler had none of Schiller's doubts. As were all of the men of the special force, he was the offspring of a German family that had left their defeated homeland some years after the war of 1914-1918 to emigrate to England. The nostalgic reminiscences of his father and the lack of opportunities available to him in the class conscious and largely homogenous society of England had led him to return to Germany when war seemed inevitable.

His acceptance of the National Socialist cause was complete, and he used all of his considerable guile to assure that he would be noticed in a German army that was guardedly suspicious of returned emigrants who seemed more English than German. An act of carefully considered bravery in Poland had led to his present rank, his transfer to the elite special forces, and two personal decorations by Hitler. Siegler's self-assurance, outspoken flattery, and poster-Aryan appearance had impressed Hitler, who had even been heard by jealous members of the entourage at a decoration ceremony addressing the young soldier as "Wilhelm." The Führer's personal interest virtually assured an unlimited future for the ambitious sergeant, but that ambition, now reinforced by his idol's attention, only increased Siegler's tendency to flaunt lower echelon authority. He recognized no master but Hitler.

The column crossed a rail line that stretched unobscured to the northern horizon. Near the crossing they began to see the first German soldiers since their crossing of the Canal Du Nord, west of Cambrai. An engineer company worked on the tracks, guarded by armored cars and anti-aircraft guns that could be transported by their Krauss-Maffei tractors along roads now virtually untouched by allied aircraft. The armored cars were placed at intervals along the tracks. Their guns menaced French refugees, keeping them far from the working area. Those few who blundered unwittingly into the forbidden zone were fired upon. The occasional bursts from the heavy machine guns had the desired effect, driving the French farther and farther away, allowing the column to move quickly.

Finally, the Fieseler flew low alongside the column for the last time. The pilot saluted them with wing dips, and then turned back to the east toward his base at Cambrai. Colonel von Maussner watched it for some time, then said to the two officers with obvious relief, "We'll be at the base shortly, gentlemen."

CHAPTER 2

After passing alert perimeter guards and following an isolated, unpaved road for nearly three miles, the column and its escort turned into a heavily guarded lane that led to a large brick and stucco farmhouse. The house was undamaged, as was the imposing barn that stood just beyond it. The men in the vehicles saw two 38T tanks and several 88-mm. flak guns in camouflaged positions near the buildings.

In the fields to the west, a Fieseler Storch airplane sat partially covered by camouflage netting. Still farther to the west there was visible activity around another, smaller, building. The heavy tractor of a tank transporter could be seen through the partly open doors of the barn. Soldiers moved busily around the buildings.

"They *must* consider this post important to keep those guns away from the line," Dietrich said.

"They may need them," Schiller said, looking toward the farmhouse. Attached to the roof was a huge regimental flag. "That swastika can be seen for miles from the air."

"There are few enemy planes in this area," Colonel von Maussner said. "The flag was placed there to protect us from our own aircraft."

The colonel stepped from the car as they were greeted by a tall, efficient-looking infantry captain, who wore the distinctive shoulder patch of the elite Grossdeutschland regiment.

"Welcome, Herr Colonel—gentlemen. I am Captain Schaeffer, commander of the guard detachment. General Kellner has asked me to tell you that he will see you as soon as he is free. While you wait, sir, your men will be fed in the mess area at the rear of the house. The general asks that they remain together until they are called for the initial conference. If your officers will see to the men, sir, I will direct you to your quarters."

"Thank you, Captain," von Maussner said. "Take over, Dietrich," he added, then said to the captain. "Is there any possibility of arranging for some hot water? I'd like to clean up a bit."

Lieutenant General Manfred Kellner watched the arrival of the

13

column from the window of a room on the second floor of the farmhouse. After Colonel von Maussner had been led out of his view by the infantry captain, he continued to study the two junior officers as they moved toward the half-tracks. He could see that the new arrivals stood out even among the elite troops of the Grossdeutschland guard. He was alone in the room, but said aloud, "They might just do it—if there are such things as miracles."

The general was much too heavy for his medium height, and his bulk nearly filled the window. A round, unlined face nestled beneath sparse gray hair carefully combed over a pink scalp. Flesh protruded over the collar of his custom-made shirt, and he touched it occasionally with dimpled hands that protruded from well-filled sleeves. And yet he moved lightly, without the plodding self-consciousness of compulsive eaters. Kellner enjoyed his dissipations and had the rare ability to inspire condolence in his peers when, smiling with the contented expression of a benign Buddha, he would describe his condition as glandular. At that moment, however, he was not smiling. Turning from the window, he walked to a highly polished table, shining in tribute to the housekeeping abilities of the absent mistress of the farmhouse, and rummaged through the contents of a briefcase lying on it. He removed a large envelope and returned to the window where the light was better. For a moment his attention was disturbed by the thumping cadence of the flag on the roof above him. The general was well aware that the large red rectangle, with its black swastika vivid in a circle of white, made an inviting target—and that he was standing directly beneath it.

It was getting warmer. Kellner opened the window and stood breathing deeply through a prominent, rubescent nose that was a monument to the finer restaurants of Berlin. He usually savored the privileges of his rank, but at that moment he was thinking it an abuse of that rank that he, a general of the regular army, indeed a staff general, should be in France to pass along the grand strategy of a man who had once attained the exalted rank of *Gefreiter*—a regimental messenger. The plan seemed ridiculous and his part in it degrading. He was, after all, a man who had served with the giants, von Hindenburg and Ludendorff, during the victorious Russian campaign of 1914-15.

He leaned heavily against the window frame, his jowls moving in indignation. And yet, the general mused angrily, Hitler had been 100 percent successful thus far. Ten days earlier there were those in the high command who would have bet that the army would never cross the Meuse. Three days later they had learned how wrong they were—and Hitler made sure they realized it.

General Kellner turned away from the window and lowered his ample bulk into a comfortable chair, after placing it so that the light was on his back. He removed the contents of the envelope and rustled through them until he found what he was looking for. Then, placing the remaining papers on his lap, he began to reread his orders.

The Führer and Supreme Commander of the Armed Forces	Headquarters
Lieutenant General Manfred Kellner	20 May 1940
Most secret	3 Copies

Designated staff officers only
By hand of officer only

Directive Twelve

1. In accordance with my verbal orders, Lieutenant General Manfred Kellner, accompanied by Captain Theodor Pohl, will proceed to Cambrai France on my personal aircraft Horst Wessel, arriving no later than 1300 hours, 20 May 1940. Transportation has been arranged to point T. (Training)

2. There must be no repetition of the Reinberger incident. Until the training period commences, all orders connected with this operation will be verbal, and relayed to the special force only by my personally designated representatives.

Kellner yawned mightily and skipped through the next pages of the directive. Pausing at section twelve, he ran his eyes quickly over the preface, and then concentrated on the list of the men of the special force.

Walther Dietrich	Lieutenant—Commanding
Friederich Schiller	Lieutenant
Wilhelm Siegler	Sergeant
Gunther Keller	Sergeant
August Thyben	Sergeant
Gerhard Richter	Sergeant
Ernst Priller	Sergeant
Rudolph Becker	Sergeant
Reinhold Falck	Sergeant
Karl Bohling	Sergeant
Eugen Schemke	Corporal
Hans Knoedler	Corporal

These men have all been personally chosen for this assignment. Each man is highly qualified in the specialty required of him. All have been decorated for previous service to their country, even beyond that which is normally expected of a German soldier.

The general skimmed over the next pages, and then paused, scowling at a subheading.

Captain Theodor Pohl will remain at point T until the completion of the training period. His duties are those of historian and observer. He will take no direct part in the training of the special force, or in the operation of the post.

Thank God for that, thought the general. He turned to the last page.

... the success of operation Havoc could be of inestimable value in concluding the war in the west. General Kellner will deliver my personal good wishes to the men of the special force. I am confident that they will continue to justify my faith in their abilities.

Adolf Hitler

Kellner frowned as he closed the directive and leaned back into the soft chair. So, he mused, I arrive on an airplane named to honor a pimp, accompanied by a bastard. The slovenliness and bad manners of Captain Theodor Pohl were familiar enough in Berlin, but now the man seemed determined to surpass himself. Kellner was revolted by the captain, but was also prudent and well aware of the man's power, so he managed to disguise his loathing. Captain Pohl, however, reacted to guarded friendship by becoming even more obnoxious.

The sun was warm on his back and Kellner began to nod. His eyes closed, and the papers fell from his hand and lap. Some minutes later he awoke abruptly. When he saw the scattered sheets at his feet, he bent over laboriously and picked them up, then rose and went to the door. The sentry outside came to attention as the general spoke sharply. "Inform Captain Pohl that I wish to see the special force officers in the map room at 1:30."

The guard hurried away, and Kellner closed the door. The contents of the envelope were still in his hand. He crossed the room and threw them on the table, then thought better of it and replaced them in his briefcase. He was angry at having fallen asleep. The man in Berlin would take a dim view of his messenger boy sleeping on the job while one of his precious directives lay on the floor. Berlin, he smiled in thought, the sooner he got this over with, the sooner he could return to civilization—and the young, buxom Hannelore, who had recently been making the daily pressures bearable. The daydream made him feel better. He resisted the inviting chair and began to pace the room, mentally arranging what he would say to the men at the initial briefing. An occasional smile showed that his mind was not engaged exclusively on that enterprise.

Colonel von Maussner had completed the bath that had been prepared for him in an old-fashioned portable tub and sat on the edge of the comfortable bed, feeling satisfied. His room was at the rear of the house, and he could hear the men laughing as they ate their midday meal at the tables that had been set up in the area below his window. Von Maussner shook his head in wonder. Two hours ago they were shooting at Frenchmen, and now—a picnic! His musing was interrupted by a knock. Reaching for his freshly brushed jacket, he went to open the door.

The man who stood outside wore the uniform of a captain. He was thin to the point of emaciation. The pinched face above an ill-fitting collar was covered in sweat, and his deep set eyes never seemed to settle permanently on the colonel. Von Maussner knew Captain Pohl well enough to despise him.

"General Kellner will see you and the other officers in the map room at 1:30," Pohl said, not bothering with the usual civilities. "While you're waiting, I've arranged for a meal to be brought here to the room. Is there anything else you wish?"

The captain's curt tone annoyed von Maussner, but he managed to answer with less evidence of anger than he felt: "No thank you, Captain. Have my men been seen to?"

"The officers have been assigned rooms and are being fed now. The troops will be assigned billets after the conference," Pohl answered.

"That will be all, Captain. Thank you," von Maussner said with an icy politeness. He closed the door just as Pohl began an ostentatious Nazi salute. "Easy," the colonel mumbled to himself as he moved back into the room. "That little swine can be dangerous."

Captain Pohl wasn't particularly surprised to find himself staring at the colonel's abruptly closed door. "Prussian swine." he mumbled. Von Maussner's avoidance of his salute would figure prominently in his report to the Führer. The thought pleased him.

The men of the special force had finished their meal and had begun the satisfying ritual, common to all soldiers, of speculation. Sergeant Bohling spoke from the far end of the table.

"Did Lieutenant Dietrich tell you anything, Willi?" he asked.

"No, I don't know anything more about it than you do." Sergeant Willi Siegler pushed at the few scraps of food remaining on his plate, dropped his fork, yawned, and stretched his muscular arms above his head. "We volunteered for a raid into England. All of us are tank men. The colonel who came with us from Cambrai is a tank training specialist, and there's a covered tank on that transporter in the barn. Figure it out for yourself."

"Three crews for one tank?" another man questioned.

"We'll need at least twelve men to hold it up when we swim over with it," Siegler said. The others laughed.

"I can't swim," Corporal Schemke said, still smiling.

"Throw him in the well," Siegler said. "You'd be surprised how quick you'll learn, Eugen."

"Let me fill my canteen first," Bohling said. "I saw him squatting in the grass when those Frenchmen were running around, and I don't think he took his pants down."

Siegler poured a glass of water from the pitcher on the table and drank from it. "You'll never know the difference, Karl." He took another drink, spat it out, and yelled, "Jesus! He's already been in it!"

The laughter was interrupted by the sudden appearance of Captain Pohl. The laughter died, and they stared at him with undisguised amazement. Pohl was angered and disconcerted by their reaction. In Berlin he was protected by his position in Hitler's court; here it was different. Facing him were men who made no attempt to hide their feelings, and he had no idea how to handle it.

Sergeant Siegler stood up and looked down at the profusely sweating captain. He broke wind loudly. "Sorry, Herr Captain," he said with exaggerated correctness. There was choked-off laughter from the end of the table.

Pohl attempted to force his voice lower, but was unable to maintain it. He squeaked, "You will all remain here. Within the hour you will be called to a meeting with General Kellner. I don't want to have to look for you. The general doesn't like to be kept waiting—and neither do I." He blanched at the look of curious amusement on the men's faces, then hurried away abruptly. Once around the corner of the house, he paused to listen.

The storm troopers sat quietly for a moment, and then Corporal Schemke asked of no one in particular, "What the hell was that?"

Captain Pohl listened to the inventive answers for some time, then, flushing angrily, moved away toward the front door of the house.

Colonel von Maussner, picking at his meal, heard the sudden increase in the volume of laughter and went to the window to investigate. He watched the storm troopers for some time and found their good humor contagious. He went back to his meal and began to eat with new interest.

"Come in, gentlemen."

General Kellner was standing at the end of a large, rectangular room on the ground floor of the farmhouse. The French family's furniture was piled carelessly at the far end of the room and replaced by unmatched chairs lined up in its center, facing a heavy, ornate table. An armed sentry stood behind a large metal box that stood in the center of the table. Three windows faced the fields to the east, lighting the room adequately enough to accentuate the dust motes that moved visibly in the musty air. Captain Pohl led Colonel von Maussner and his two young lieutenants to the waiting general.

"It's good to see you again, Heinz," the general said to von Maussner and then turned to Dietrich and Schiller. "I apologize for not meeting you earlier, but duty must come before manners. Colonel von Maussner and I are old friends, and he understands my problems with an operation such as this. But I did want to meet and talk with you before we call the men."

After ordering the sentry to wait in the hall, the general spoke to Captain Pohl. "Would you be good enough to bring the colonel's men to the front yard, Captain? Take charge until I send for you."

Pohl sensed that he was being eased out of the conference, but seeing no way to question the order, left the room reluctantly. Kellner brightened as Pohl closed the door, and von Maussner understood how he felt.

"Now, gentlemen," the general began, "sit down and I'll tell you the aims of this operation and our method of accomplishing them. When I've finished, I want you to discuss any flaws you might find in our reasoning. Generals do listen occasionally, so take advantage of the opportunity." He smiled briefly and rubbed the side of his spectacular nose. "Shortly after our breakthrough at the Meuse, intelligence reports showed that the English were beginning to explore the possible need to withdraw from France. The Führer immediately recognized an opportunity to use that withdrawal in a daring way." The general paused and walked over to a large map pinned to the wall behind the table. "Come over here, gentlemen."

Von Maussner and the two lieutenants joined the general, who used a pair of brass dividers to point to a spot in northern France.

"This is where we are now," Kellner began. He then moved the dividers in a rough U, starting at northwestern Belgium, down and through Arras, and up again to the Straits of Dover. "Our enemy is trapped within that area and will soon have little option but evacuation. The steady progress of our army leaves them only one possible port for such an undertaking." He stabbed at the map with the dividers. "Dunkirk—a mere forty-five miles from Dover and ideal for our deception. When our forces have isolated them in the Dunkirk area, and shortly after they've begun their evacuation, you men will embark on a captured Dutch ship, which is being carefully prepared, and join their exodus. We will land you as close to your target as practical under the circumstances of the time. You will be British soldiers in British tanks, and we are therefore hopeful that you will have no trouble landing. You will proceed to your target and destroy it. Plans are now being completed for your retrieval and return." The general noticed that the two young officers were showing no visible emotion and remained impassive as he continued. "Your target is the Vickers-Supermarine Spitfire factory at Woolston, opposite Southampton and situated at the confluence of the Itchen and Test rivers. Your departure could come in a week, possibly less. From now on, you and your men will be required to learn the operational techniques of the British Mark 2 infantry tank, and to absorb all of the information on the terrain and the attack contained in that box on the table. You are all proficient tank soldiers, but it won't be an easy job. I understand that some of you are already familiar with the target area, and that should be of great help.

"From this moment on, we will speak to each other only in English. I want all of you to get back into the rhythm of the language. You will have no trouble doing so. I will, but I trust you will bear with me. You will be supplied with excellent papers. With your backgrounds, they should have no reason to be suspicious of you. Actually, from the nonsense we find in their newspapers, they will be too busy looking for parachutists dressed in nuns' habits, or furtive Germanic types wearing false beards, leading dachshunds, and nibbling on sausages, to notice you at all."

The officers laughed, and the general was pleased with their reaction. "Now, before we discuss this, I'd like Colonel von Maussner to tell you a bit about the British tank."

Von Maussner nodded at the general and then faced Dietrich and Schiller.

"Perhaps you noticed the transporter in the barn when we arrived," he began. "It holds a fully operational British Mark 2 infantry tank. We will have the use of only one during our training period, but the three you will use on the mission are being brought to top condition at a repair depot not far from here and will be taken to the coast to wait for your orders to leave." Von Maussner motioned for the young officers to sit down. "The Mark 2 is an excellent machine. It weighs twenty-six tons, and has the heaviest armor of any tank in service in any army: 78 mm. at some points. It mounts a 40-mm. cannon, one coaxial 7.9-mm. machine gun, and a portable .303. In a tank-to-tank battle, *it* would be the one most likely to survive. I tell you this mainly to show that the original owners will have difficulty in stopping you, should it come to that. Even our heaviest tank cannon will not penetrate the Mark 2.

"It has a three-man turret, with the driver in a separate compartment in the nose, and the similarities to our own tanks should help make our training easier. But now to the drawbacks. They're slow, a top speed of fifteen miles an hour—perhaps a bit more with the governors removed. Their range is a mere seventy miles across country, and that is something we are correcting at the repair depot. We can't have you stalled a few miles from your target for lack of diesel fuel. Diesel, not petrol, and difficult to find if you should run out. The most important drawback to your mission is that the cannon fires only armor-piercing shot, not high explosive, and that is not acceptable. The gun can cause a lot of damage, but for this job you will carry our new hollow-charge explosives as well as incendiaries, and they will have to be placed by hand at the target while the tank provides covering fire. So you see, it's not simply a case of getting to the factory and firing on it. It must be completely destroyed." Von Maussner paused to give the point emphasis. "After the attack you will destroy the tanks. Under no circumstances are you to allow any remaining hollow-charge explosives to fall into enemy hands. Then you will be met by our agents. The escape phase will be gone over thoroughly during our training. The major point in your favor is your ability to pass for Englishmen.

"Lieutenant Dietrich will command, and you, Schiller, will be second in command. Sergeant Siegler will take the third tank. He is qualified and, I might add, has been recommended for a commission by the Führer. All of you have been chosen for your competence, but I'm going to be rather hard on you for the next few days. When we've finished here, you and the men will report to the barn, and we'll begin."

"Well, gentlemen," Kellner said. "What would you like to ask us?"

Dietrich came directly to the point. "How are we going to get past their navy, sir?"

"There are a quarter million British and as many French surrounded there." Kellner pointed to the map. "A serious attempt to rescue that many men will require every ship they have, both naval and civilian. They'll hardly have the time to investigate every returning vessel. It's the

Luftwaffe's job to see to it that no ship is given the time to stop you, and as an added precaution, there will be no less than seven U-boats assigned to the west Channel to keep an eye on you. Your ship will be under our surveillance constantly until you land."

Dietrich hesitated for a moment, then said, "I know that coast, sir. We certainly can't land at Southampton, and the south coast has few ports with a harbor capable of handling anything larger than a yacht. They'll be closely guarded. If we thought of this plan, they must have considered the possibility themselves."

Kellner began to pace. "The reason this operation was even considered is that the circumstances that caused its inception are absolutely unique. Never before, and possibly never again, will there be an opportunity such as this. The British did not allow themselves to believe that the French could be routed in so short a time. They've had months to prepare their coast since they declared war, but I can tell you that little has been done. Intelligence shows that there are miles of completely unprotected coast. They will soon devote all of their effort to sealing their island. But, during the confusion of a major evacuation, their full attention will be concentrated on that formidable task. During those few days they will be vulnerable."

Dietrich sat down, and Schiller rose.

"What do we do if one or more of the tanks should break down on the way to the target, sir?"

"The reason you're being deprived of the use of the other tanks during your training is that we are well aware of the possibility you've mentioned. At this moment all that German technology can accomplish is being applied to the machines you will use on the mission to see to it that the situation never arises. It may seem a lame answer, but you men are in a dangerous business. The tanks will be in top condition. The captain of the ship that will take you over has been as carefully chosen as you and the others. We will get you there, then it's up to you."

Kellner had moved to the window and stood, his back to the others, looking out. "And now, gentlemen . . ." he paused abruptly. He was frowning when he turned away from the window. "We'll have to postpone this. Lieutenant Dietrich, you'd better go out and bring your men in here. Captain Pohl has had no experience in dealing with storm troopers. He looks uncomfortable to say the least."

Dietrich hurried to the door while Colonel von Maussner went to join the general at the window, a worried expression on his face.

CHAPTER 3

Lieutenant Dietrich led the soldiers into the room and directed them into the chairs lined up in front of the table. Captain Pohl followed, moving to the corner of the room near the map where he stood with his back to the wall, glaring venomously at the men as they sat down. But if they noticed the look of hatred directed at them, they gave no sign. All their attention was focussed on the map pinned to the wall. Von Maussner looked first at the soldiers and then at Pohl, wondering what had happened to cause Pohl's obvious agitation. General Kellner glanced briefly at the captain, then turned to the men.

"Good afternoon, gentlemen. I am Lieutenant General Manfred Kellner, and have come here not only to acquaint you with the job you've volunteered for, but also to bring you the personal good wishes of the Führer. Of all the men available in the Wehrmacht, he has chosen you for this operation. Your records are well known to him, and he has instructed me to inform you of the confidence he places in your ability to conclude this mission successfully. I haven't met any of you before, but I have read your records carefully and fully understand why you have his confidence."

General Kellner tapped a finger on the map. "Your objective, gentlemen." The men leaned forward expectantly as he continued. "The Vickers-Supermarine factory at Woolston, on the Itchen River, opposite Southampton." Kellner turned to face the troops and began to repeat what he had told the officers earlier. He saw that his attempt at drama caused no change in the intent expressions of the soldiers and noted that they actually seemed excited by the prospect. He began to relish his discourse, making frequent trips to the map and punctuating his points with staccato taps of the dividers.

When he finished and asked the men for questions, Sergeant Siegler stood. "Why don't we do it right and take Eastleigh airport too, Herr General?" Siegler had recognized an opportunity.

"Airport?" Kellner was puzzled.

"Eastleigh airport is where the airplanes built at Woolston are finally assembled and tested, Herr General. It's less than four miles north of the factory. I lived in Eastleigh and worked in Southampton. I passed the airfield every day."

"You worked in Southampton? That *is* convenient. Did you actually see the airplanes?"

"The day before I left for Germany I counted ten Spitfires on that field," Siegler paused. "Have you ever been to Southampton, Herr General?"

Kellner was momentarily flustered, not used to being questioned so bluntly by a noncommissioned officer. "I've been through the port, Sergeant, but I am not as familiar with it as you must be, having lived there."

Siegler looked at the general calmly. "Then you're not familiar with the location of the factory in Woolston?"

"Not personally familiar."

If Siegler was aware of the menace in Kellner's voice, he gave no sign. "Do you have a map of Woolston here, Herr General?"

The others watched expectantly and were disappointed when the general merely looked briefly at Siegler, and took a large-scale map from the metal box on the table. The sergeant towered over the general as he pointed.

"This is lower Southampton, and just across the river . . . Woolston."

Siegler's gall fascinated Kellner. "I *am* that well informed," he said. "Get on with it."

"The factory is here, in this small triangular area near the floating bridge, with the river on one side of the buildings and Hazel Road on the other. Opposite the factory buildings there's a block of civilian houses, and farther down Hazel Road is a steep embankment with the railroad on top."

Von Maussner looked at his watch. "Get to your point, Siegler," he said.

"We'll probably approach on the Portsmouth Road, it's the only easy way in. Once we turn into Hazel Road, I think three tanks in that enclosed area will only be in each others' way. . . ."

Captain Pohl interrupted with angry vehemence. "You what? How dare you question the Führer's orders?"

"Stay out of this, Captain," Kellner said angrily, forgetting the caution he usually practiced with Pohl. He turned back to Siegler. "Well?"

"Once we get to Woolston, nothing can stop us from destroying that factory. One tank, in that confined space, could do it easily. Two, and there's no doubt, especially if the British tanks are as good as the colonel said they are. The factory building are flimsy hangars, lined up beside each other facing Hazel Road, and in the rear, they're only yards from the river. It's a civilian factory with no grounds to speak of. Crash the fence and you're at the buildings. There's no place they could have a field of fire for any heavy guns. The only big building is the office block. A few incendiaries and it will go up like a torch. It will be all over before they can call in any help."

"You make it sound quite simple," Kellner said sarcastically. "But I assume there's more."

"Yes, Herr General." Siegler planted a finger on the map. "This is Eastleigh airport, less than four miles to the north. We'll be approaching from the southeast. We could stay together for the trip up to this point—a quarter mile east of Lowford. Two of the tanks proceed along here, to Woolston. The other could continue along the A27, cross the upper Itchen, here at Mansbridge, move about half a mile to this road, Wide Lane, turn right and in another half mile be at the hangars."

Kellner leaned over the map, impressed by the young man's enthusiasm. "What you say is interesting, Sergeant, and worth considering under other circumstances. But my orders are to prepare this force for an attack on the factory at Woolston. . . ."

Siegler interrupted vehemently. "As long as we're there, why not do as much damage as possible. We destroy the factory, and they'll move production to Eastleigh if it isn't destroyed, too." He paused. "I think the Führer would agree."

Kellner felt his anger rising, but before he could answer, Pohl broke in.

"You think! You are here to follow orders, not to question . . ." he was shouting.

Kellner raised a hand to silence him. "I will handle this, Captain.!"

Pohl persisted. "This man is . . ."

"Later, Pohl," the general said with finality. "Go over it again, Sergeant."

While Siegler spoke, Kellner looked at von Maussner. The colonel nodded slightly but remained silent, knowing that the general had made up his mind at Siegler's first mention of the Führer. If Hitler learned that the suggestion of attack on the airfield had been dismissed summarily, he might possibly consider it as another example of staff timidity and a direct disobeyal of his orders to report everything that occurred on the base. When Siegler finished repeating his plan, adding further embellishments, Kellner questioned Dietrich and Schiller. Both officers agreed in principal with Siegler's logic. Both had seen the Supermarine facilities at Eastleigh and agreed that they could be used to continue production of the airplanes, even if the factory at Woolston was razed.

"Very well," Kellner said to Siegler. "The German army is not run by consensus, but in this rather special situation perhaps we should make an exception. Please take over here, Colonel. Come with me, Sergeant, and we'll put your suggestion to the Führer, if he chooses to listen. If he doesn't, then I don't want to hear another word about it. Is that understood?"

"Yes, Herr General," the elated Siegler said.

Colonel von Maussner took the general's position in front of the map. As he began to continue the briefing, he noticed that Captain Pohl had followed the general and Siegler from the room.

The special frequency radio connection to the Führer's headquarters at Munstereiffel was made with surprising rapidity. Kellner had made the call with some trepidation, and his nervousness mounted as he went through numerous aides, most of whom were the leader's cronies and personally distasteful to him. Finally Hitler spoke. "What is it, General?"

"Good afternoon, my Führer. I'm sorry to interrupt you at this time, but your orders were to contact you at once if the situation warranted it."

"Trouble already, General?"

"No, my Führer, on the contrary, an interesting development has occurred concerning this assignment. One of the men, Sergeant Wilhelm Siegler, lived in the target area. He states that the Spitfires built at Woolston are assembled and tested at an airfield less than four miles north of the target. During our briefing he brought up the interesting suggestion that production would be moved to the airfield even if the primary target is destroyed. I thought it was important enough to bring to your attention."

"I'm glad that one of my staff officers can follow orders. Arrange for me to speak with Siegler at once."

"He's here with me now, my Führer." Kellner was surprised at Hitler's use of the man's name. He beckoned to Siegler, who was standing near the door. "The Führer wishes to speak with you, Sergeant."

Showing no reaction, Siegler took the earphones calmly. "Good afternoon, my Führer."

"Wilhelm," Hitler said, "tell me about this airfield."

Siegler began to talk. Kellner watched him, amazed at the young man's imperturbability and his own damp palms. Siegler spoke clearly and directly, and even Kellner found his presentation compelling. He listened in further amazement as the young sergeant began an exchange that was obviously bordering on argument . . . with Hitler! It was incredible.

Kellner noticed Captain Pohl standing near the end of the bank of wireless equipment, staring at Siegler in amazement. "What are you doing in here, Pohl?" he demanded.

"I wish to speak with the Führer," Pohl answered. For once his tone was almost that of a plea.

My God, thought the general, he's jealous of Siegler. "Wait," he said curtly.

"The Führer wants to speak with you, Herr General," Siegler said.

As Hitler began to speak, Kellner realized that Siegler had apparently convinced him to do more than just consider the attack on the airfield. He made notes of Hitler's rapid orders, and then said, "I will see to it, my Führer." He paused as Captain Pohl moved over to stand beside him. "One more thing, my Führer. Captain Pohl wishes to speak with you." Hitler's reply caused a smile to pass fleetingly over Kellner's face. "Very well, my Führer, I will tell him." He removed the earphones and handed them to a waiting technician. "I'm sorry, Captain, but the Führer said he hadn't the time to talk to you."

Pohl looked as if he had been struck, and Kellner was suddenly disgusted by the pleasure he felt at the captain's obvious shock. He transferred his attention to Siegler.

"I hope you thought this over carefully before you spoke up, Sergeant, because if it is accepted, it will be your command. You seem to have made quite an impression on the Führer. We will have our answer tomorrow, but as he points out, an attack on the airfield could create problems with your escape. There might not be time to make new arrangements."

"Eastleigh is my own back garden, Herr General. We won't have any trouble escaping," Siegler said confidently.

"Very well, let's get back to the others. Are you coming, Captain?" Kellner saw Pohl look at him with such intense hatred that any feelings of sympathy he had begun to feel vanished instantly. He turned away and left the room, followed by Siegler. Pohl stood for some moments looking at the radio and then moved slowly to the door.

The sentry who stood at the partly opened door to the general's room looked at Captain Pohl as he reached the top of the stairs. He noticed that Pohl was staggering slightly and watched as he leaned against the wall, his hand to his head. He rushed to the captain's side. "Can I help you, sir?" he asked solicitously.

Pohl winced and said nothing. He raised his hand in an abrupt gesture of dismissal and brushed past, entering his own room, which was directly opposite the general's. He placed trembling hands over his eyes for a moment, then went to a low table by the bed. He opened a small bottle, shook out two tablets, and quickly gulped them down. His thoughts raced wildly as the energizing drug entered his bloodstream. He had been unable to think of any way to get back at the soldiers without endangering the mission. He knew the importance Hitler placed on the destruction of the factory, so they would have to wait. But Kellner was another matter. He could, and would, destroy the general for his insults. The thought pleased him, and he decided to return to the conference.

The hall was empty. Suspiciously, Pohl moved to the general's partly opened door and listened for signs of the sentry's unauthorized movement inside. He pushed the door open fully and saw that the room was unoccupied. He was about to turn away when something caught his eye, lying almost beneath a heavy chair near the window. After a furtive glance down the hall, he entered the room and went quickly to the chair. He bent down and picked up two sheets of paper. As he began to read them, Pohl was suddenly transported to a state as close to happiness as was possible for him. "The Führer and Supreme Commander . . . Headquarters . . . Most secret." Pohl's mind began to race. With pure joy he read. "There must be no repetition of the Reinberger incident."

He remembered Hitler's monumental rage when a paratroop officer—a Major Reinberger—while on an unauthorized flight to Cologne with another officer had been forced by engine failure to land near Michelin, in Belgium, carrying a briefcase brimming with top-secret papers outlining in detail the Luftwaffe's plans for the invasion of the Low countries, ultimately causing postponement of the invasion that had originally been planned for January 1940. He could imagine how the Führer would react when he told him of finding a personal directive on the floor of an unguarded room in enemy France. Pohl thanked whatever God it was that allowed the adventitious discovery and was mumbling happily to himself when General Kellner entered the room.

"Pohl? What are you doing in here. The sentry said you were ill." Kellner then saw the papers in the captain's hand and knew immediately what they were. He remembered his inadvertent nap and the hasty gathering up of the fallen directive. God! he thought, I must have missed those . . . and this swine had to find them. "What do you have there, Pohl?" he asked.

The startled look on Kellner's face caused Pohl to groan happily. "Top secret papers, you fat fool!" The general moved quickly to the door and closed it as Pohl continued, "On the floor! You look surprised. Is it because I found them? Maybe there were others—left for the French to find or the British? They would be very glad to know why we're here.

Perhaps they already know?" Pohl's voice was rising with each statement. "I want to use the radio and transportation to Cambrai immediately. I will return to Berlin and see that you're removed permanently."

Kellner listened in shocked silence, his mind working furiously. He watched Pohl push the hastily folded papers under his ill-fitting tunic and decided on attack. Pohl was obviously insane, but it wasn't wise to treat him lightly. It was time to establish a few accusations of his own.

Pohl mistook the look on the general's face as one of defeat. "The Führer will also want to know what you've told your whore. I know all about her," he lied, carried along further into his growing, drug-induced fantasies. "Is it possible that she's more than a simple whore? Maybe she likes the information you deliver to her? What else could she want from a fat pig like you?"

Pohl's characterization of Hannelore stunned the general, and the thought of what could happen to the satisfying young woman who was his mistress of the moment caused whatever indecision he felt to evaporate. He turned away with the calm of decision. Pohl's strident voice followed him as he moved to the door.

"It won't do you any good to run. Order the transportation at once!"

"I suggest that you return those papers to me before this goes any further," Kellner said, easing the door open.

"You suggest? Order the transportation! You won't be looking down that ridiculous nose at me much longer," Pohl shouted.

As the door opened the sentry heard the captain's remark about the general's nose and suppressed a smile. The captain was right, but he must be crazy he thought as the general beckoned to him.

"Come in here, Corporal," Kellner ordered. "I want you to watch this officer until I return with Captain Schaeffer. Watch him carefully. Captain Pohl is under arrest. He's not to leave this room until I give the order. Is that understood?"

"Yes, Herr General." The sentry looked at the captain. God! he thought, he'll be foaming at the mouth soon. He unslung his machine pistol as Kellner left the room.

"Stop him!" Pohl shouted. "I'm giving you an order! That swine is ..." Pohl started for the door. The sentry stepped in front of him, pointing the machine pistol at the captain's stomach.

"Why don't you sit down in that chair over there, Herr Captain?" the soldier said.

Pohl backed away, his eyes fixed on the barrel of the gun. "I'll have you all shot!" he said ominously.

Colonel von Maussner left the men in the map room when he was called into the hall by Schaeffer. He found the general waiting, his face pale.

"Ah, Heinz," Kellner said. "Come with us, will you? I'd like you to be a witness. I'm afraid Pohl has finally gone around the bend. I've just found him in my room, reading top secret papers, a Führer directive, to be precise. One, I might add, that only three officers of the Wehrmacht are authorized to read—and Captain Pohl is not one of them. When I questioned him, his response was a tirade of puzzling, incoherent accusations as to my loyalty." He turned to Schaeffer. "Pohl may be the Führer's personal representative on this post, but that does not excuse his strange actions. You would have no reason to know that the captain has never been considered particularly stable, but he now has gone too far. The papers are hidden in his tunic, and I want them back, Captain. When you've seen to that, I'd like you and Colonel von Maussner to verify that they are indeed part of a highly sensitive directive. The unfortunate creature is obviously ill, but I want our report to be precise."

"How did he get into your room, Herr General? My men have strict orders . . ." Schaeffer paused when interrupted by the general's upraised hand.

"Don't blame your sentry, Schaeffer. He saw a German officer stagger up the stairs—a man who was on the verge of collapse—and reported it. My door was open, left that way by me. I personally told him that he could leave his post until I returned, but he reminded me of your orders. I was impressed, both by him and by you."

"Thank you, Herr General, but I don't understand why Captain Pohl was in your room, and where did he get these papers?"

"You seem to have forgotten that Captain Pohl is the Führer's personal representative. He's been in and out of my room constantly since we've arrived." Kellner smiled when Schaeffer took the bait.

"Is anything else missing, Herr General?"

"Not that I know of. But once you've retrieved my papers, I want the captain's room searched by you personally. If you find anything other than his belongings, inform me immediately."

Von Maussner listened with growing anxiety. "Did you say he accused you of disloyalty, Herr General?" he asked

"I wasn't able to make much sense of it, Heinz. Something about my wanting the French and British to learn of this operation. I was going to handle the situation differently, until he began to make outrageous personal attacks on me. I was forced to place him under arrest for his own good, and he's to remain so until I've contacted the Führer."

Captain Schaeffer didn't see the worried look on von Maussner's face as they followed the general up the stairs.

They entered the room to find the sentry watching the still angry Pohl, who was leaning against the wall in a dark corner of the room. Schaeffer went directly to him. "Place your hands above your head, Captain," he ordered.

As Pohl made no move to obey, he suddenly found his arms raised for him by the muscular officer.

Pohl seemed to notice what was happening for the first time. "What are you doing?" he screamed. "What lies has that traitor been telling you?"

Schaeffer ignored the outburst and held the squirming Pohl with one hand, while opening the buttons of the tunic with the other. The papers fell to the floor. Schaeffer released Pohl, picked up the papers, and brought them to the general.

"Look at the heading carefully, Schaeffer," Kellner said. Then, as an added touch to show his dedication to security, he added, "Just the headings. I simply want you to identify them to your own satisfaction. When you've done that, pass them to Colonel von Maussner."

When the two officers had finished, the general glanced at Pohl, who remained in the corner, glaring at them venomously. Kellner beckoned to the sentry. "Come over here, Corporal." He showed the papers to the fascinated soldier. "Do you know what this is?"

"No, Herr General."

"Glance at the headings and then read this line."

"Führer Directive Twelve, Herr General."

"Very well," the general said. "You saw Captain Schaeffer remove these papers from Captain Pohl—the officer you've been guarding—did you not?"

"I did, Herr General."

"That will be all, wait outside." When the door had closed, Kellner said, "Captain Schaeffer, I want this officer confined to his room under guard until we get to the bottom of this."

"You will regret this," Pohl said, "All of you."

When he was alone, General Kellner placed the rumpled sheets of the directive in an envelope and placed it carefully in his briefcase. Then he sat down to ponder the events that were threatening his previously uncomplicated existence. After a few minutes he rose and made a circuit of the room, concentrating on the floor beneath all of the furniture. Finally satisfied, he left the room, pausing to look at the sentries at Pohl's door. He shook his head sadly, and when he was certain that all of the soldiers had noticed his concern, he went down the stairs.

After escorting Pohl from the general's room, Schaeffer had ordered the sentry to hold the prisoner in the hall, and he entered the room alone to begin his search. He went over the room carefully and found nothing but the captain's meager belongings. He was about to leave when he saw the bottle of tablets on the table by the bed. He had ignored it earlier, but now decided to look at it more closely. He read the label, and his expression changed from one of concern to one of understanding. Pervitin! No wonder! The drug could be poison to some, and the captain's actions were classic examples of its nasty side effects. Schaeffer put the bottle into his pocket, went to the door, and motioned Pohl into the room.

"I would suggest that you lie down for a while, Captain, it will do you good." Schaeffer was uncomfortable, uncertain how he should treat the Führer's personal representative, and decided to say nothing about the pills. He had seen similar erratic behavior in many line soldiers who had relied on Pervitin when circumstances forced them to function for long periods without sleep. He would let the general decide what action should be taken. "I'll have dinner sent up to you," he continued. "I'm certain that all of this will be straightened out tomorrow." He turned to leave.

"Wait, I want to talk to you," Pohl said curtly.

Schaeffer bristled at the tone, but waited.

"I've checked on you, Schaeffer. Apparently you're a good officer. It would be foolish of you to continue to follow the orders of that fat traitor. I want you to arrange for me to use the radio."

"We'll talk about that tomorrow, Captain, when I'm sure you'll see things differently." Schaeffer then said carefully, "Please don't attempt to leave this room. The sentries have orders to stop you, and they will remain outside this door until the general orders them to leave."

"You're making a fatal mistake," Pohl shouted as Schaeffer shut the door firmly behind him.

Pohl sat down on the bed. He hadn't really expected help from the infantry captain. Only the general could authorize use of the communications room, but Schaeffer would soon learn that.... A wave of dizziness swept over him, and Pohl reached absently for the bottle of Pervitin. It wasn't on the table! Captain Schaeffer became the prime focus of his growing paranoia until he remembered the packet of the drug he always kept in his pocket and was somewhat reassured.

CHAPTER 4

After the incident with Captain Pohl, von Maussner returned to the map room and the waiting men. They rose to their feet respectfully.

"At ease, gentlemen," von Maussner began. "The general will be occupied elsewhere for a short time, and we're behind schedule. But we'll make up the time. Very shortly, Lieutenant Rau of the Grossdeutschland guard will show you where you will sleep. Fortunately this is a large house, with room for all of us. The infantry guard, and the other men connected with the operation of this post, have their quarters in an extension at the rear of this building, or in a smaller house across the fields to the west." He motioned for them to sit, then continued, "You are free to move within the inner perimeter of sentries, but conversation with them is to be kept to an absolute minimum. Under no circumstances are you to discuss your mission or your destination with anyone. During the rare instances when you are left to your own devices, you will remain in the immediate area of the house. The security here is absolute, so let's not have anyone shot by mistake. You have your own tables in the kitchen, or you may eat at those outside, whichever you prefer.

"As for now, Lieutenant Rau will show you to your quarters and then escort you to the barn where I'll give you your first look at the British Mark 2 infantry tank and assign the crews.

"We expect the British uniforms to arrive tomorrow. When they do, we'll interupt our training, and you will return here to be fitted. We had quite a few to choose from and have managed to pick those that were as close to your measurements as possible. When they have been altered, they should fit as if they had been issued in England . . . perhaps better." The colonel smiled briefly. "They may not be too clean. There may even be a tea stain on a tunic or two." He waited for the laughter to fade before continuing.

"The details necessary for the preparation of your papers and paybooks—also genuine—will be taken care of at the same time. Then we'll be free to concentrate on our job. When you . . ." Von Maussner was interrupted by a knock at the door. Schiller opened it to admit Lieutenant Rau.

"When you're ready, Herr Colonel, I'll take your men."

"Thank you, Lieutenant. We're finished here for the time being. I'd like the officers and Sergeant Siegler to remain for a few moments," von Maussner said.

Siegler watched the others file out and when the door closed, he looked at the colonel questioningly. He was wary, not knowing what to expect.

"Our force consists of three tanks, Sergeant," Von Maussner began. "The lead tank will be commanded by Lieutenant Dietrich, the second by Lieutenant Schiller. The third command is yours. You are now a lieutenant in the British army, and when you return from this mission, I think I can safely assure you that it will not be to a sergeant's uniform. So you may as well begin to conduct yourself as a *German* officer. Lieutenant Dietrich is moving into Lieutenant Rau's room. You will billet with Lieutenant Schiller. From now on, you will join us at all officers' conferences."

Siegler was too stunned to react with more than a nod of understanding.

"One more point," von Maussner said. "General Kellner has placed Captain Pohl under house arrest. It is a private, serious, and delicate matter. The reason for the general's decision is no concern of ours, and I don't want the special force involved in any way. When it's straightened out, and if Captain Pohl should remain here, it will be the responsibility of all three of you to see to it that the men of your crews behave in a military manner toward the captain at all times. I trust I've made my point."

From the window of his room, Captain Pohl could see one of the 38T tanks, and knew that the other was somewhere on the other side of the house. There was activity around the other farmhouse across the fields to the west; but, he decided, it was too far away to present any problem when night came. He shifted his attention to the shed below his window and estimated that its roof was no more than five feet below him.

A startled Pohl turned away guiltily from the window when Captain Schaeffer entered the room, followed by a soldier carrying a tray. He was enraged that they had entered without knocking. He was suddenly aware that an unannounced bursting into his room was something he would have to consider while completing his plans.

"I've brought your dinner, Captain," Schaeffer said. "If there is anything else you require, the sentries will let me know."

Pohl forced himself to answer calmly as the soldier placed the tray on a table near the door.

"Schaeffer, you seem to have forgotten that I was sent here by the

Führer. I want you to send this man back for that tray in half an hour. Then I'm going to bed, and I don't want to be disturbed until morning. Until morning, do you understand? I'm not used to having people burst into my room unannounced. You're playing a dangerous game. I also find that you've taken it upon yourself to remove a bottle of medication from this room. I want it returned immediately."

Schaeffer had certainly not forgotten that the captain had been sent by the Führer. "I removed the Pervitin for your own good, Captain," he said. "Those tablets can cause problems. I've seen it with combat troops. In your present condition, I'm afraid they can be dangerous. If you wish, I'll have our doctor look in on you."

"I don't need a doctor," Pohl said with quiet menace. "I want you to get out and keep everyone else out. When that man comes back for the tray, make sure that he knocks and then waits for my permission to enter. All of you will have enough to answer for, Schaeffer, so I warn you, it would be very foolish of you to antagonize me further. Now . . . get out."

An angry but cautious Schaeffer said curtly. "You'll not be disturbed again, Captain." He left and closed the door quietly.

Pohl studied the tray of food with suspicion and decided that it was unsafe to eat. He remembered the look on the general's face when he had mentioned the woman. He took a soiled shirt from his suitcase and scraped the food onto it, then folded it carelessly and pushed the soggy mass under the bed. Despite the continuing pain in his head, he managed a smile at his deft handling of the infantry captain.

The canvas covering had been removed. The tank lay exposed on the bed of the transporter, lighted theatrically by a single spotlight trained on it from the corner of the barn. It was imposing, and starkly threatening, its shadow, magnified by the light, covering the wall of the barn.

A soldier made a final adjustment of the light, then left at a signal from Colonel von Maussner. The colonel climbed up to the bed of the transporter and looked down at the men gathered below him, shielding his eyes from the harsh glare of the powerful light.

"This, gentlemen, is the British Mark 2 infantry tank that you will be taking to England. You will learn how it works tomorrow."

Von Maussner began at the sloped rear of the tank and moved slowly forward, explaining the finer points of the tank. It took some time, but he was gratified to see that the men listened with intense interest, and he answered their probing questions with an intensity of his own. He could see that the men were impressed with the machine. It was important that they had confidence in the equipment on which their lives would depend.

Finally he turned his back to the offending light and removed a sheet of paper from his pocket. "The lead tank will be commanded by Lieutenant Dietrich, who will also be in command of the mission. His team will be Richter, Falck, and Schemke.

"Tank number two will be Lieutenant Schiller's, and his team will be Thyben, Priller, and Bohling.

"Tank three will be commanded by Sergeant Siegler, and his team, Becker, Keller, and Knoedler.

"That will be enough for today. You may return to your quarters, with the exception of the tank commanders. You will report back here at 0530, and we'll begin in earnest."

The men left the barn talking excitedly. Colonel von Maussner followed, leading the tank commanders through the dark farmyard, back to the map room.

From the time of the Czechoslovakian crisis, when he had returned to Germany and joined the army, Willi Siegler planned to be more than just another soldier. Normally, he might have been destined to serve out his enlistment being tolerated with some suspicion and not being thought of as suitable for more than minor promotion. It had taken the attack on Poland to provide the opportunity that he had been certain would come.

While advancing south out of east Prussia with the Third Army a few days after the invasion had begun, Private Siegler and the rest of his company were pinned down by a well-concealed Polish artillery position. The Germans were quickly ordered back to the dubious protection of low, hilly ground, when eight men were killed in the first salvo.

Siegler had no intention of lying face down among a target too inviting to ignore. The field in front of him was in violent motion as the Polish gunners raised their sights. The shells crept forward with each salvo, and he knew that the company would soon have to retreat farther.

Siegler raised his head carefully, looking out into the inferno, judging his chances of getting to the lone German Mark 3 tank—its crew apparently dead—that lay exposed between the company and the enemy guns. He knew that the tank was the only reason the Pole's full firepower wasn't directed at the infantry company. They wanted it burning first, since its cannon, Siegler noted, seemed undamaged and was certainly more of a threat to an open gun position than foot soldiers.

Private Siegler decided it was worth a try. He jumped up and ran through the smoke of exploding shells to the tank, and threw himself down behind it. The metal was reassuringly cool, and he was able to distinguish the sound of the engine, still turning over. Siegler climbed cautiously up to the turret. An officer lay half out of the turret hatch, head hanging down, his blood covering the metal beneath him. Siegler crouched by the turret, and was about to pull the body from the hatch when he heard the man moan, and speak weakly. "Help me. I'm bleeding to death." A shell burst well to their right. Spent fragments struck the superstructure below Siegler and the wounded officer.

"Put your arms around my neck and hold on, I'll pull you out," Siegler shouted.

"I can't. I seem to be paralyzed," the officer said.

Another shell landed, closer this time. "They're finding the range," Siegler said. "It's better for me to hurt you a little now, than for both of us to be dead." He stood up and placed his powerful arms beneath the wounded officer's armpits, lifting him easily from the hatch. The officer groaned as he was carried over the engine covers to the ground. Siegler laid the captain on his stomach, between the treads where he would be protected from all but a direct hit. The officer stirred. "Thank you for coming for me," he said, and Siegler recognized an opportunity.

"I couldn't let them get you without trying to do something about it, Herr Captain. But as long as I'm here I'd better try to do something about those bastards, or the medics won't be able to get through. Does the cannon still work?"

"I think so," came the weak reply.

Siegler climbed back up on the tank as the ground in front of it erupted violently. He felt the heavy machine lurch beneath him. They were getting closer to zeroing in. He climbed quickly to the turret hatch, slippery with the captain's blood, and lowered himself inside. Two dead crew members, unmarked except for traces of blood at their ears and mouth, made it impossible for him to move freely in the fighting compartment. He forced one body and then the other up through the hatch and out of the tank.

The gun seemed undamaged. Siegler rammed a 37-mm. shell into the breech, then sat in the gunner's seat. He lined the cannon up on a muzzle flash of the Polish artillery, and pulled the trigger. The noise was deafening and at first he thought the gun had exploded, but he then remembered the open turret hatch. He looked up at it; a stray bullet or shell fragment entering the tank would ricochet until its force was spent, and . . . He shrugged fatalistically and turned back to the ammunition storage.

Siegler loaded, aimed, and fired the cannon until the remaining shells were gone, and then turned his attention to the heavy machine gun. It was then he noticed the silence. He climbed to the turret hatch and raised his head cautiously above the rim. The Polish guns were no longer firing, and he saw his company moving out into the settling dust of the now quiet field. His lieutenant waved at him; Siegler beckoned to the officer urgently. When he saw that he had been understood, he dropped to the ground and knelt beside the wounded captain.

"You did well, Private," the officer said. "What is your name? Were you ordered to save me?"

"No, I wasn't, Herr Captain. My name is Wilhelm Siegler."

"I've good reason to remember that name, Wilhelm. I owe you my life—at least the chance to die in Germany."

Siegler seized his opportunity. He spoke quickly of his desire to enter the tank corps and said that his company commander had refused to consider the application.

He lied easily. The tank corps had never entered his mind, but it would certainly offer more opportunity than that available to the faceless foot soldier. "Could you help me, Herr Captain?" he concluded.

"In my upper pocket," the officer said. "A notebook and pencil. Write your name and number in it, and put it back. If I live long enough, you'll get your wish."

Siegler had replaced the notebook carefully when his lieutenant reached the side of the tank.

"Good shooting, Siegler. They..." he paused abruptly when he saw the wounded man and recognized him as a member of General Kuchler's staff. "Get the medics. Hurry it up!" he ordered.

Willi Siegler ran.

The captain survived. Three days later Willi Siegler was removed from the line and transferred to the Panzer school at Wunstorf in northern Germany. Poland was being quickly overwhelmed, and the armor training was soon returned to its prewar thoroughness. Siegler had no trouble adjusting. The officers at Wunstorf, aware of the circumstances of his transfer, singled Willi Siegler out for special attention. When his training period was over, he had mastered the skills required to operate and maintain the available German tanks so well that he was assigned to the school as a temporary instructor.

Remaining at Wunstorf did not suit Willi Siegler's plans at all. He began to look for a way to change the situation. Guarded references to storm units, small groups of men who landed by parachute or glider behind enemy lines, intrigued him. Siegler knew that decoration and promotion would come rapidly to anyone who survived such operations. Since he had every intention of surviving, the storm troop seemed to be the possible key.

Fate again intervened for Willi Siegler, now a corporal. While toiling discontentedly at Wunstorf, he was ordered to report to Berlin. He had been recommended for decoration by the captain he had pulled from the tank in Poland, and was to receive it from Adolf Hitler personally.

Corporal Siegler stood carefully at attention as Hitler moved down the long line of men receiving the Iron Cross, second class. When his turn came, he remained calm as the decoration was placed over his head to rest on his shoulders. Hitler stepped back, and asked, "What is your name, Corporal?"

"Wilhelm Siegler, my Führer."

Hitler looked at the distinctive—and favored—uniform of the tank corps. "I'm proud of you men of the Panzers? I know that you and your comrades will continue to serve your fatherland in the future, just as gallantly as you did in Poland. We have much left to do."

Siegler fumed inwardly. It was apparent that Hitler thought he had served with the Panzers in Poland. Hitler was about to move on to the next man, when Siegler spoke. "I think I could serve you even better, my Führer, if I were allowed to transfer to the special storm troop."

Hitler stopped and turned back. He looked up at the resolute expression of the imposing corporal. The audacity of the statement had momentarily stunned the officers of Hitler's entourage. A colonel began to recover and intervene, when Hitler said, "Hesitant men aren't the sort we decorate for bravery, Colonel. Tell me, Corporal, why do you think that you would be useful in the special forces?"

Siegler matched the questioning stare, knowing that he had made it over the first hurdle. "Your new concept has revolutionized warfare, my Führer," he emphasized the word *your*. "I am strong, German, and want to be part of it." He kept the answer brief, and without a trace of pleading, and began to sense victory when Hitler looked pleased.

"Where are you stationed now?"

"Wunstorf, my Führer."

"Don't you consider that an important assignment?"

"Yes, my Führer, but . . ."

"Siegler," Hitler said, interupting. "Wilhelm Siegler. Aren't you the man who disregarded Polish artillery to save the life of Captain Brecht?"

"Yes, my Führer," Siegler answered with feigned modesty.

Hitler looked closely at the muscular soldier, at the Iron Cross on his chest. It was a long moment for Siegler. "You deserve your chance for what you did in Poland, Wilhelm. I happen to be very fond of the officer whose life you saved. He's recovering, thanks to your bravery. I think the armor school can do without you for the time being." He turned to an aide standing at his elbow. "See to it that this man is transferred to assault detachment Koch at once."

"Thank you, my Führer," Siegler said. Hitler moved on to the next man in line. Siegler felt the sweat running down his back.

At 0430 on May 10, 1940, Willi Siegler and eighty-four other men of the Koch assault detachment "Granite" embarked in eleven DFS 230 gliders from Ostheim, near Cologne, under orders to attack and secure Eben Emael, considered the most powerful fort in the world and one of the keys to the defense of Belgium. Newly completed in 1935, Eben Emael lay three miles south of Maastricht, near the Belgian-Dutch border. Situated on a hilly plateau, the triangular fort extended 1100 by 800 yards, protected on its southern side by a 20-foot wall and tank ditches, and on the northeast by a 120-foot drop to the Albert Canal. On the northwest, a canal cut provided a similar barrier. All outer walls were dotted with concrete pillboxes, teeming with antitank and heavy machine guns. The fort's top was the natural surface of the plateau, again dotted with heavily armored rotating cupolas and bunkers, enclosing 120-mm. and 75-mm. as well as antiaircraft and machine guns. Honeycombed beneath the emplacements were more than three miles of underground tunnels.

At 1315 the following day, Eben Emael surrendered to the Germans. Only six men of the attack team had been killed and twenty wounded. Willi Siegler was unmarked.

Adolf Hitler had been very much aware that the fortress of Eben Emael was not only the keystone of the defenses of the Albert Canal but that it had to be taken quickly to insure the success of the main flanking thrust through the Ardennes. Hitler wanted a confrontation with the Allies in the north as quickly as possible to keep them occupied and their attention away from the flanking Ardennes force entering France to the south. With this in mind, it was Hitler who ordered and personally directed the planning of the attack on Eben Emael and, at the same time, the bridges of the Albert Canal. The assault teams had succeeded, allowing the Wehrmacht to advance quickly into Belgium while the French and British were still moving confidently into their positions. It was this handful of German soldiers who were ultimately responsible for the fall of France.

Hitler was jubilant as he greeted the men of storm group Koch. While awarding Siegler the Iron Cross, first class, he said, "So, we were both right, Wilhelm. You did well. We'll have other jobs for you." He put his hand on Siegler's shoulder. "You have an unlimited future," he leaned closer, and added conspiratorially, "I'll see to it."

Willi Siegler knew he was on his way to the realization of his limitless dreams.

CHAPTER 5

Captain Pohl waited with angry impatience until the last of the off-duty guards left the outdoor tables and sought the warmth of the house. It had seemed an interminable vigil, but finally he saw the comet arc of the last cigarette thrown carelessly into the night, and the yard below him was empty. He waited another five minutes. No light came from the house and heavy, racing clouds covered the sky, so he no longer saw even the occasional star he had cursed earlier.

Now it was quiet, so quiet that Pohl was afraid his efforts to open the window would be heard by the sentries. As he struggled, he frequently looked over his shoulder at the chair he had placed at an angle under the doorknob. It might stop the soldiers in the hall from surprising him, should his warning to Captain Schaeffer be ignored, but it would also warn them that he was planning escape. Once committed, he would have only one chance. He returned to his task, driven by the conviction that General Kellner was even then planning a way to get rid of him.

His efforts were finally rewarded by a loud creaking as the warped window began to move upward. It seemed impossible that the sentries hadn't heard, so he moved quickly to the door and listened intently. There was only silence. He groped his way back to the window; it moved more easily now, and with great care he edged it farther up. Cool air blew into the room as he leaned out cautiously and looked into the quiet night, wishing that he had taken the trouble earlier to learn the limits of the inner perimeter guard posts. Another thought worried him, the 8-mm. flak gun crews. They would be on duty throughout the night, and at least one gun was within easy sight of his side of the house. But, he reasoned, they would be watching the north where the only real danger from the enemy lay. When he found that he couldn't see the gun he decided that it was unlikely that its crew would be able to see him against the bulk of the house.

Pohl put one leg out of the window and sat straddling the sill. Then he pulled the other leg up and out, turning cautiously until he was facing back into the room. He began to lower himself, as slowly as he could manage, toward the roof of the shed below. When he reached the limit of his upstretched arms he felt sudden panic... his feet still hadn't touched the shed roof. Could he have misjudged the distance so badly? His thin arms were tiring, and he was forced to grit his teeth and let go of the sill. He dropped no more than a few inches, but the sudden contact caused him to fall backward and sit down with what he imagined was a noise loud enough to wake the entire house. Pohl called upon a God he had abandoned years earlier, and fought to control his heavy breathing.

There was no movement in the shed beneath him where he knew the off-duty guards were sleeping. He heard the reassuring sound of a man's loud snores as he crawled to the edge of the shed roof and then dropped to the ground. He had decided earlier to make his way south, away from the dangers to the north. Crouching down, he moved across the seemingly endless open space between the house and the road. When he saw the vague blur of one of the 38T tanks well to his left, he dropped to his knees and crawled away from it.

He reached the ditch at the side of the road and slid down into the hardened mud at its bottom. Pohl's heart and head were pounding. The overwhelming need of his addiction was something he could not deny. He reached into his pocket and found that it was empty. His need for escape was now even more urgent.

Pohl crossed the ditch and peered less than cautiously over its edge to study the road. Once across it and into the blackness of the fields beyond, he would be miles away before they even discovered he was gone. He listened and heard nothing but the insistent beating of his heart. He climbed up to the road and ran across it, stumbling noisily into a similar ditch on the other side. He had hardly landed at the bottom when he heard someone running along the road toward him!

Pohl clawed his way up the side of the ditch, and ran out into the field. A distant voice called, "Halt." He ran faster, ignoring the pain the effort caused in his head, deeper into the covering darkness and its promise of freedom.

He heard the stutter of a machine pistol and was thankful for the night since no bullets seemed to be coming anywhere near him. Pohl didn't actually feel the series of heavy blows across his back. It was only when he tasted the dirt that he realized he was lying face down on the ground. He felt no pain and decided angrily that he had tripped. The machine pistol was no longer firing, and there was only the comforting darkness. He decided it was safe to get up. He raised himself on an elbow, pushing against the cold ground, and in the sudden pain realized that he had been shot. Someone was running across the field toward him, and he made a last determined effort to rise. He made it to one knee, choking feebly on the blood that was filling his mouth, and then fell over on his back. He died, staring with disbelief into an indifferent darkness.

After leaving the barn, Colonel von Maussner and the tank commanders continued to discuss the mission in the map room. The young men showed no signs of fatigue, but for the colonel it had been a long day, and the days to come would be even longer. However, there was still the opening of the first operational order to be seen to before they could all get some sleep. He had sent Captain Schaeffer to the radio room, where General Kellner was waiting for an answer to his report about Pohl, to find out when the general would be available to open the order officially. While they waited, von Maussner went to the window, opened it, and inhaled the cool air deeply.

"There is nothing startling in the order, gentlemen," he said, "but we do have to wait for the general before opening it. Since I was one of those who prepared it in Berlin, I can tell you that it contains the timetable for our training program. This business with Pohl has set us back a few hours, so we'll have to bear with the delay. Arras will not stand much longer, and the British will soon be concentrating on their retreat to the northern coast, so despite this minor delay we will have to work diligently to see to it that you're ready to leave when the time comes. As for Pohl. ... You were with the men outside, Siegler, do you know what caused the angry looks the captain was directing at all of you earlier?"

Siegler remembered the first confrontation with the captain, and the men's jokes. Maybe he had heard? Suddenly his future seemed less secure, but he lied with what he hoped was convincing sincerity: "I have no idea, Colonel."

"Well, if I know Pohl, we'll find out soon enough," von Maussner said. The cool air was now beginning to annoy him. He shut the window, remembering the laughter he had heard below his window earlier. He was convinced that Siegler's innocent expression wasn't as genuine as it seemed. In one way or another, all the thoughts of the men in the room were on Captain Pohl when they heard the sustained burst of the machine pistol.

General Kellner was seated uncomfortably in a chair too small to contain his imposing girth when Captain Schaeffer entered the radio room. Kellner had been waiting an hour, growing progessively more anxious, for an answer to his carefully worded message to Hitler about Pohl.

Captain Schaeffer, thinking the general was asleep, spoke softly: "Herr General?"

"What is it now?" Kellner said irritably.

"Colonel von Maussner has asked me to inform you that he and his officers will wait in the map room for your arrival before opening operational order one."

"Very well, Captain. I'll join them in a few more minutes. What about Pohl? No more trouble?"

"No, Herr General. He ate his meal and then went to bed. I think that it was a wise move on his part," Schaeffer took the bottle he had removed from Pohl's room and handed it to the general. "He seems to have been taking too many of these. Overuse of Pervitin can cause remarkable personality changes. I took the precaution of removing them from his room."

"Very good, Schaeffer," the general beamed. He took the bottle and studied the label with carefully concealed happiness. "This explains everything. I want you to have the doctor look in on Pohl at once. Wake him if necessary. I want a professional opinion on his condition since he may be more ill than we think." He placed the bottle in his briefcase and worked his way out of the chair. He no longer felt it was necessary to wait for the reply from the Führer. "Come along, Captain," he said. "You see to the doctor, and I'll get along to the map room."

The two men were almost to the door when they heard the chatter of the machine pistol, sudden and ominous in the quiet night. Schaeffer placed a restraining hand on the general's arm briefly, listening. No further sound came from outside.

"It was probably one of my men firing at shadows," Schaeffer said. "But I would like you to remain in this room until I find out, Herr General."

"Do what you think best, Captain." Kellner turned back to the chair. Then they heard the unmistakable sound of a tank engine starting, and Captain Schaeffer ran from the room.

At the first sound of firing, the commander of the 38T stationed near the road ordered the engine started and then began to move out into the fields across the road. When it became apparent that the base wasn't under attack, the tank's powerful road lights were switched on. The driver saw a soldier running across the field, pointing ahead of him, and turned when he was ordered to follow.

The running soldier stopped abruptly and, when the tank had pulled to a stop behind him, the tank commander saw that the soldier was staring at a body lying on the ground at his feet. The officer jumped from the tank, pushed the stunned soldier aside, and looked down at the lifeless body of Captain Pohl. "My God," he said. "What have you done?"

Captain Pohl's body lay on the superstructure of the tank behind the turret, covered with the tank commander's tunic. The 38T began to move slowly back toward the farmhouse. The sentry who had shot Pohl was ordered to report to Captain Schaeffer and left to walk back to the house under the watchful eye of his sergeant. The sentry was frightened.

"I had to fire. He wouldn't stop," he pleaded. "How could I know it was a German officer? You can't see more than a few feet out here. I ordered him to halt, and he couldn't have helped hearing me. He came up out of the ditch and ran across the road. At first I thought it was an animal."

"Save the explanations for Captain Schaeffer," the sergeant said impassively. "That was the captain who came here with the general, and he's supposed to be a friend of the Führer's. If you had to shoot an officer, it's too bad it had to be that one."

After ordering the three tank commanders to wait in the map room, von Maussner hurried outside where he found Captain Schaeffer at the front of the house, watching the 38T move across the road toward him.

"What is it, Captain?" von Maussner asked.

"I don't know yet, but it would seem there's no danger." Both men walked toward the tank as it neared the house. "They're carrying a body," Schaeffer said. "What happened?" he called to the tank officer.

"I'm afraid it's Captain Pohl, Herr Captain," the man replied. "According to the sentry he was shot while running across that field, away from the road."

"Where is the sentry?" Schaeffer asked.

"He's being brought here now, Herr Captain."

The yard was filling with hastily aroused guards as von Maussner and Schaeffer stared at the tunic covered body. Finally, Schaeffer looked up at the tank officer. "Have some of these men carry the captain into the house. Put him in the empty room on the ground floor and post a guard. Then see to it that the man who did this is brought to me immediately."

Von Maussner was shocked, but at the same time he was surprised by Captain Schaeffer's calm. "How did he get out there, Captain?" he asked. "There are supposed to be four sentries within sight of his door. And I must say I don't understand your apparent indifference to all of this."

"Psychosis caused by overindulgence in Pervitin is predictable, Herr

47

Colonel. If Captain Pohl had been one of my own men, and not an officer under direct orders of the Führer, I would have had him confined to a hospital under the constant observation of a doctor. The general had ordered me to have our doctor look in on the captain when we heard the shots."

"I'm not quite sure I know what you're talking about, Captain," Von Maussner said. "But I suggest we report this to General Kellner at once."

"It's not starting well, Herr Colonel." Schaeffer said.

Von Maussner, knowing that Schaeffer was unaware of Captain Pohl's power in Berlin, remained silent. The two men followed the soldiers carrying the body into the house.

"Lieutenant Schiller!"

Schiller opened his eyes reluctantly and saw Siegler standing alongside his cot.

"It's nearly five. The colonel expects us outside at 0530," Siegler said.

"Ask the colonel to postpone everything till noon," Schiller said sleepily.

"I have some news that will wake you up," Siegler said. "I just learned that Captain Pohl was killed last night by one of the sentries."

Schiller sat up and placed his feet on the floor. "Captain Pohl?"

"One of the cooks just told me. He was shot out in the fields to the south."

"In the fields?" Schiller repeated, not fully awake. "How could he have gotten out there? The colonel said he was under arrest."

"I asked the same thing. The cook didn't know. Maybe the colonel will tell us this morning. At least he doesn't have to worry about the captain any more."

"I wonder why he didn't tell us last night?" Schiller said, standing up and moving toward his toilet kit and towel, preparing to leave for the latrine.

"He looked worried when he came back. That's why I asked the cook. They know everything that happens on any post."

"When you get to be a colonel in charge of a base where the Führer's personal representative is killed by one of your own men, you'll look worried too, Willi."

Captain Pohl no longer interested Siegler. He went to a mirror on a bureau near the door, settling his beret at the correct angle. He studied his reflected image with the lack of vanity common to a man long aware of his good looks, but who had never allowed it to become predominant in his plans for the future: light brown hair, even features, and light blue eyes that women found attractive until they looked into them too closely and were frightened without knowing why. "What do you think our chances are?" he asked as he turned back to Schiller.

"Chances?"

"England. The mission. Do you think we'll be able to get in and out as easily as the general thinks we will?"

"I don't know. A lot will depend on where we land. There aren't that many ports to choose from along the south coast."

"The last time I drove along it there was one port after the other," Siegler said.

"Suitable for yachts," Schiller said, "but not for ships large enough to carry three tanks. No matter where we go in, we can't simply leave the ship and disappear into the countryside, we have to take three twenty-six-ton tanks with us. The British can't have too many tanks left over here. I'm wondering how they'll react to the sudden appearance of three functioning ones, manned by twelve well-fed, unwounded men. We'd better have the answers to the questions they're going to ask.

"If we do get in and are allowed out of the port, and manage to get to Woolston and destroy the factory, our problems may have just begun. We'll be deep in enemy territory, isolated from our own army and airforce, surrounded by water, and unpopular to say the least."

Schiller's response was hardly reassuring to Siegler. "The colonel said they have a plan to get us out."

"I wouldn't worry too much, Sergeant," Schiller said. "If they can get us in, they'll find a way to get us out."

Siegler thought he heard a certain condescension in Schiller's answer. "I lived an England long enough not to be frightened by Englishmen," he said angrily.

"I wasn't intimating that you were frightened," Schiller said. "A man who didn't worry a bit under these circumstances would be a fool. It helps keep him on his guard. Lieutenant Dietrich has told me enough about you so that I know you're not easily frightened. But as for myself, I must admit concern about the points I brought up. Not fright, concern."

Placated by the lieutenant's calm response, Siegler said: "My only worry about England is my mother and father. They still live in Eastleigh. When the army lands. . . ."

"Your parents live in Eastleigh now?" a surprised Schiller asked.

"Row house, back garden, all that shit," Siegler said. "They aren't citizens, but they're as English as the worst of them."

"I've seen it happen to others."

"Did it happen to your family?"

"No, but my father hadn't wanted to go there in the first place. My mother influenced him, and he went to please her. He was an engineer and had no trouble finding work, but he never allowed himself to become Anglicized. When my mother died, it was too late for him to return. He died soon afterward. I took him back to Hamburg and stayed to join the army. Do your parents know that you joined the Wehrmacht?"

"I don't know. They probably guessed after . . ." Siegler paused and laughed harshly. "One night I made some remark—I've forgotten what it was—about that ass Chamberlain, and my mother slapped me. Hardly five feet tall, but she reached up and slapped me as if I were a child. Damned hard too. But I couldn't help laughing. Two old people yelling at me in German about my lack of respect for the Prime Minister of England. I was supposed to be thankful that the bastards had thrown me out of school at fourteen, forcing me to work at menial jobs with little chance of ever improving myself. Thank God for the Führer. I had somewhere to go. I left that night, and as I went out the door I could hear my father coughing from the effects of a gas shell that exploded near him twenty years ago in France. A shell fired by his good friends the English.

"You'd better get dressed, Lieutenant. The colonel is having the tank taken off the transporter, and from the way he's looking at his watch, I'd say he's getting impatient."

CHAPTER 6

Colonel von Maussner spent most of the morning in the Mark 2's fighting compartment, explaining to each man in turn the similarities and differences between the British tank and those of the German army. Outside, the others were being instructed in the intricacies of the separate driving compartment.

Siegler is the last man, the colonel thought with relief as the sergeant climbed down to stand beside him. The padded grip that fitted around his shoulder and under the armpit had begun to rub his skin raw as he demonstrated the raising and lowering of the cannon to each of the men. He noticed that while they were all respectfully attentive, they also seemed slightly amused. Damned foolishness, he thought. A fifty-five-year-old senior officer attempting to show these young men a job that they probably know better than I do. Von Maussner lay his forehead against the padded periscope bracket, lined up the cross hairs on the general's camouflaged Fieseler sitting in the field beyond the farmhouse, and pressed the trigger.

"So much for the general's airplane," he managed to say lightly. "It's lucky this gun isn't loaded. So far I have shot at everything visible on this post, including two cooks." The colonel struggled out of the gunner's seat. "You take over, Siegler. When you're ready, traverse to your right, line up on the 88 and fire. Luckily, they've been ordered not to fire back, they *have* ammunition."

"Yes, Colonel," Siegler answered. Again von Maussner noticed the amused smile as Siegler dropped easily into the seat. The young man didn't hesitate, the colonel noted. He traversed the turret smoothly, stopped it, and pulled the trigger. He turned to von Maussner with a self-satisfied grin. "Six gunners, and an 88 added to your two cooks, Colonel."

Von Maussner smiled. More proof of what I've been thinking. They should be instructing me. This man operated the gun as if he'd done it hundreds of times before. But the colonel persisted, and finally completed his instructions.

"That was excellent, Sergeant. You men have all taken to the operation of this machine very well. Tomorrow we shall see if you are able to hit a target with live ammunition. I should have known that this machine would present no real problems to any of you. I don't think we need waste any more time in here. Let's get outside. I want to stretch my legs and see if I can manage to breathe real air again."

Once outside, von Maussner called to Lieutenant Dietrich, who was standing with the rest of the men listening to a sergeant-major explain the subtleties of the tank's steering levers.

The colonel leaned thankfully against the rear of the turret, and spoke to the expectant Dietrich: "As soon as the sergeant-major is finished with the men, dismiss them for their meal. At 1300 we'll return here, and move this machine out into the fields. We've had enough theory for today. Practical experience is what you need, and the sooner we get started the better. I want all of you to spend some time in the driving compartment, while the others concentrate on the interior. Nothing we've shown you seems to be a mystery, but within a few days you will have to prove that by taking it over a rather tortuous course we've laid out in the fields to the south."

"Herr Colonel, a few more hours to familiarize ourselves, and I think we could try your test this afternoon."

"A few hours? Your optimism is commendable, Lieutenant, but don't get carried away by youthful overconfidence. This tank is sixteen-thousand pounds heavier than our heaviest machine and has quite different handling characteristics. You will see to it that your men apply themselves with diligence. Nothing is to be dismissed with a snap of the fingers. After lunch, one of the 38Ts will join you in the fields so that the radio operators can familiarize themselves with the British set. The 38T will also provide a moving target for your gunnery practice."

Dietrich saluted. "I didn't mean to imply that I was taking the training lightly, Colonel," he said.

"Good, Dietrich. I don't want to dampen your enthusiasm, Lieutenant. I merely want you to be aware that one seemingly minor point forgotten could conceivably kill all of you. I don't want that to happen."

"Neither do I, Colonel," Dietrich replied.

When von Maussner arrived in the map room after leaving the men, General Kellner was pacing the room angrily and hardly waited until the colonel had closed the door before he said, "I curse the day when that revolting little man was born. I thought when he was killed I'd be rid of him at last. Instead, Hitler is raving. He's ordered me to send Pohl's body to Cambrai in my Fieseler where it will be transferred to his own airplane, complete with honor guard, to return him to Berlin. An honor guard for that swine! Hitler apparently blames me for Pohl's death. Me! I was working on that Austrian madman's wild scheme when that fool Pohl climbed out of a window and went running across a field crawling with sentries he knew had been ordered to shoot at anything that moved. My God! What has Germany come to? We've surrounded by maniacs."

Von Maussner held up a restraining hand. "Please, Herr General, I would respectfully request that you lower your voice. I don't think that many of the common soldiers share your opinion of Adolf Hitler, particularly since we seem to be winning so handily."

The general's face was red, his nose surpassing even its former brilliance. He slowly sat down, breathing heavily. "You're right, Heinz. Pohl has already caused enough trouble."

"When Hitler digests all the facts, he'll realize that Pohl was responsible for his own death."

"I hope you're right, Heinz. As a Wehrmacht officer, I shouldn't be bothered by Himmler's snoopers, but I'm no longer even certain of that. I doubt that he'll be satisfied with an Abwehr investigation."

"You're allowing your anger to make you imprudent, Herr General. Unguarded references to Hitler as a madman serve no purpose here and can only endanger you and many of your fellow officers, including myself. I don't understand your reaction to this affair with Pohl. Did he actually discover something incriminating about you?"

"Of course not," Kellner replied impatiently.

"I'm glad to hear that. Still, if there was something, it might be best if you told me before we're faced with *any* investigation."

"I told you there is nothing," the general snapped. "Do you think that I would allow myself to be compromised by a drug-addicted idiot like Pohl."

"Then you believe he was addicted to Pervitin?"

"I should be an expert, considering how many of the Austrian's cronies are involved with the filth, but I'm relying on our doctor's opinion."

"All this will pass, Herr General," von Maussner said. "Meanwhile, we must see to it that the men are ready to leave in a few days. I may share some of your doubts about this operation, but if it fails, we must be certain it isn't through any dereliction on our part. Wild scheme or not, Hitler has a way of proceeding over the objections and doubts of the High Command—and succeeding—and that makes our plans for him doubly difficult to accomplish."

"We're never allowed to forget his successes, are we? I wonder if it will remain so when the inevitable mistakes begin?" Kellner rubbed his forehead with a handkerchief and changed the subject: "How did it go this morning?"

"After seeing how the men took to the British tank, and my observation of their general attitude, I think we're both being too pessimistic about their chances of getting to the targets. Unfortunately, I'm not quite as optimistic about getting them out afterward."

"It's a shame that missions such as this require the participation of the best men," Kellner said. "If the British fail to cooperate and it becomes necessary to mount a full-scale invasion, then we shall need all of the good men we can find."

"It's worth attempting."

"Is it? Hitler seems to feel that the fall of France and the defeat of the British expeditionary force will make England anxious to concede. I prefer to leave the wishful thinking to him and deal with reality. If we don't destroy the British army here and then invade their island immediately, I'm afraid we won't find the English Channel as easy to cross as a French border river." Kellner rose and walked heavily to the map. "There's something else I haven't told you, Heinz. Among the more intelligible of Hitler's comments was that latest information shows that the British have built another Spitfire factory near Birmingham, well to the north. Luckily it isn't operational yet, so perhaps our adventure is worth attempting. If the men do manage to halt production of the Spitfire before the other factory is ready, then *perhaps* we'll gain the time we need. And I'll be the first to admit that Hitler was right, distasteful as that would be for me."

"What you've just told me is all the more reason for us to see that these men are well prepared," von Maussner said. "I've ordered them to work with the tank in the fields this afternoon, if that doesn't interfere with your plans."

The sound of the Fieseler's engine suddenly broke the stillness of the room.

"Apparently they're ready," Kellner said. "I must now assume a suitable expression of concerned sorrow, and escort the late Captain Pohl out to the airplane. By all means have the men work with the tank wherever you see fit. We'll have our scheduled briefing later this evening."

"I'll await your orders, Herr General."

Von Maussner walked to the door, but turned when the general asked softly, "What do the men think of Captain Pohl's death, Heinz?"

"They've already forgotten him, Herr General."

"I wish I could say the same." Kellner picked up his hat and joined von Maussner at the door. "When I've seen our friend Pohl off to his hero's welcome, I'll get back to work. Hopefully, a few uninterrupted hours should get me back on the projected schedule. Let us hope that there are no more . . . incidents."

Six hundred yards east of the British tank, the 38T was throwing huge clods of dirt into the air as it maneuvered at high speed. Its commander ordered a sudden turn to the left, to begin a sweeping arc around the Mark 2. He cursed angrily when he found that he was unable to keep the other tank's cannon from following his every move with unfaltering consistency.

"Turn right . . . sharply!" he called to his driver through the headset and clutched the turret rim as the eleven tons beneath him began to slew around, its outer tread tearing a deep trench in the soft ground. He watched with disgust as the Mark 2's gunner followed him through the maneuver without a lag. His own turret was still turning as he shouted into his microphone to the gunner, "Are you asleep, Hans? The enemy is behind you! It's lucky we're only playing games. Listen to my commands, keep your eyes on the bastards, and start traversing as soon as I order a turn!"

In the open cupola of the Mark 2, Dietrich laughed as he watched the 38T's commander through his binoculars. It had gone that way for most of the afternoon. Dietrich leaned down into the fighting compartment. "Call them, Schemke. Tell them we're breaking off to change crews." He stood up in the cupola, noting that his cannon still remained fixed on the 38T. "Let's get back to the road, Falck," he said to his driver. "We'll let Schiller take over and let his team show our disgusted friend over there another example of how we British chaps handle our tanks."

The tank began to turn. Schemke pushed open the turret hatch and looked over at the 38T. "That chap should learn that we'll not rest until we've hung our wash on the Siegfried line." he said in an exaggerated English accent.

Dietrich laughed. "You've got the wrong war, Schemke," he said.

Lieutenant Schiller and his crew were not quite as successful as the others had been, being last. The commander of the 38T, anxious for revenge for his earlier humiliations, began to use his tank's high speed to keep the late afternoon sun behind him and shining into the eyes of the men in the Mark 2. Sergeant Priller, in the gunner's seat, often lost the 38T completely when the sun reflected in his periscope lens. Sergeant Bohling, both hands busy with the steering levers, had similar trouble with his driving goggles.

But Schiller was well satisfied with his crew's performance, despite the difficulties. All of his orders had been carried out promptly and efficiently. He was formulating a plan to lure the 38T toward him when he focused his binoculars on the distant tank and saw that von Maussner, in a signals vehicle, was keeping pace alongside the 38T. As he watched, both stopped. Schiller then saw Colonel von Maussner turn and gesture at him vigorously.

Sergeant Thyben called from below: "Orders from the colonel. We're to pick up the others, and return the tank to the barn. He's worried about the steering clutches."

"I'm not surprised," Schiller said, watching the signals vehicle begin to move back toward the farmhouse. Earlier in the afternoon, both he and Dietrich had been worried about the same thing. Dietrich had magnanimously allowed Siegler and his team to take the first turn in the tank. It had been a mistake that Dietrich was unlikely to make again. They had watched as Siegler ordered the tank through violent turns and kept its diesels at top speed throughout his entire mock duel with the 38T. It was obvious that the sergeant didn't like to lose—even a game.

Schiller ordered the tank back to the road where the other crews were waiting. It was moving in a slow, grinding turn to the south, when Schiller saw a lone vehicle approaching along the road from the east. He spoke to the gunner. "There's an armored car coming toward us along the road. They must be bringing uniforms. Track him while I call ranges. We may as well take advantage of a target we can see." He followed the car with his binoculars as the turret began to turn, not believing what he saw. The armored car increased speed, and two men standing in its rear were training a mounted machine gun—toward him! His hand went to his headset button as he watched the gun kick, and begin to fire. "Get your head down, Bohling! Close your hood and turn hard right. Those bastards are shooting at us."

Schiller crouched low in the cupola until he saw the armored hood roll down over Bohling's head. Geysers of dirt spouted well ahead of the tank and crept toward him as the range was adjusted. The tank lurched into a turn, and he dropped into the turret, pulling the cupola hatch closed. Bullets began to strike the heavy armor, only to bounce off harmlessly.

"That car is German," Priller said from the gunner's seat. "What the hell's happening?"

"The morons must think we're English. Thyben, contact the 38T. Tell them a German armored car is shooting at us."

"You're right, Lieutenant. They are morons. Take a look, they went into the ditch," Priller called.

"Stop, Bohling," Schiller ordered through the headset, then went to the commander's periscope, focused, and found the car. It now lay in the ditch on the side of the road closest to him, the front end down in the crevice, the rear wheels standing in the air, still spinning. There was no movement of the men in the wreck. Schiller climbed up to the cupola, opened the hatch, and raised his head cautiously. He focused his binoculars on the armored car, but swung the glasses away toward the sound of straining motors coming from his right, and held them on the signals vehicle until it came to a stop near the wrecked car. Both von Maussner and the sergeant-major were standing upright in the front seat, alongside an obviously hunched down driver. Schiller heard his gunner say, "They better get their heads down, something's moving in the ditch."

Schiller saw the 38T approaching him at high speed across the field, then turned back to see the second German guard tank pulling up behind the colonel's car, its horn blasting continuously, apparently attempting to remind the colonel of his danger.

After silencing the horn with an angry gesture, von Maussner stepped down from the signals vehicle and waited for the two infantry half-tracks that pulled up behind the tank. He motioned one forward, his arm moving in what Schiller took to be punctuation of rapid orders. Armed soldiers leaped from the half-track to surround the colonel protectively, while those from the other fanned out in the fields. Von Maussner stood with his hands on his hips, watching a man climbing slowly from the ditch, followed by two others carrying another man who was either unconscious or dead. The guard soldiers made no move to assist them. The first man reached the road and stumbled to the colonel, swaying visibly, and raised his arm in the party salute. Von Maussner ignored him and turned away to speak to the sergeant-major who then dropped into the ditch to inspect the wreck.

Schiller turned his attention to the swaying man, now in animated conversation with the colonel. He saw that the man had been injured. Blood streamed down the side of his face and soaked his collar, almost obscuring the two runic flashes of silver of his tunic's emblem.

At that moment the 38T that had raced across the field in answer to Schiller's urgent summons pulled alongside, its 37-mm. gun pointed menacingly toward the road. The turret hatch opened and a man's head appeared slowly above the rim. The officer looked over at Schiller.

"How did you manage to do that," he pointed at the wreck, "without ammunition?"

"They didn't need any help from me, they did it to themselves."

"How could they have gotten past our perimeter guards?"

57

Both men's attention was diverted by a motorcycle vanguard, preceding a small column of lorries, raising the dust to the east.

"That would be the supply column from Cambrai," Schiller said. "They must have come in with them. As for the perimeter guards, I doubt that the men who fired at me would pay much attention to them."

"What do you mean wouldn't pay attention to them? If I had been near you, they certainly would have learned to pay attention to me before they died."

Schiller answered the angry officer quietly: "They make their own rules, my friend. They're S.S."

The distant chatter of a heavy machine gun, and then the muffled sound of grinding metal, brought General Kellner to the window of his room in the farmhouse. He saw the dust raised by the signals vehicle as it roared up the road, followed closely by one of the 38Ts and two infantry half-tracks. His eye was caught by the distant British tank moving away from the road, and the second 38T approaching it rapidly from the northern side of the field. Thinking it part of the exercise, he was about to turn away when he noticed that the 38T was moving with an urgency that didn't seem required.

Kellner rushed from the room and hurried down the stairs. At the front door he collided with Lieutenant Rau, who was just entering. The general was a formidable obstacle, and the young lieutenant was barely able to keep his footing.

"Forgive me, Herr General," he said. "I was just coming in to report to you."

"What is happening, Lieutenant?"

"An armored car, Herr General. It fired on the British tank. I don't think they hit anyone."

"That you don't think is abundantly apparent. I'm beginning to have serious doubts about you and your men's abilities. Are you telling me an armored car simply drove through our perimeter guards, past all of the men in your detachment, and fired at one of our tanks? You allowed the French . . ."

"It wasn't French, Herr General. The car is one of ours. It was most likely ranging ahead of the supply column from Cambrai. I don't know yet why they fired on the tank, or why they ran into the ditch. Colonel von Maussner is out there now."

Kellner looked at the junior officer with disbelief. "Do you mean to tell me that there was a possible enemy out there, and the colonel personally went charging out like an Uhlan?" Lieutenant Rau wisely decided to remain silent, and the glowering general continued: "I'll be in the map room. Ask Colonel von Maussner to report to me there with whomever was in charge of that car. And, Lieutenant, find out if any of the special force was injured . . . immediately!"

CHAPTER 7

General Kellner's ponderous bulk was quivering with rage as he paced the map room. Captain Schaeffer stood at attention near the table while Colonel von Maussner stood looking out of the window, watching the British tank enter the courtyard. Von Maussner turned when the general stopped in front of the uncomfortable Schaeffer and said ominously, "What are the S.S. doing on this post? What the devil do they mean, shooting at that tank, Captain Schaeffer? I thought I had made clear our need for inviolable security. Yet, incident after incident occurs. I don't see how I can keep from expressing my displeasure with you in my reports. The Führer's order was clear: No one is to enter; no one is to leave, without my permission. This post is supposed to be sealed. Is that so difficult to understand? You and your men were chosen for this assignment because you were supposed to be the best available. If you . . ."

"Herr General," the harried Schaeffer said, "they had authorization from Reichsführer S.S. Himmler."

"Do not interupt me, Captain. The Führer's order states that no one is to enter, he did not exclude S.S. snoopers. They should have been held at the checkpoint while I was informed. You haven't followed either my orders or the Führer's. I want no more excuses. In the future you will follow your orders to the letter. Even if Himmler himself should try to enter this post, he is to be stopped. Now, when those intruders have been seen to by the doctor, I want you to bring them here at once. They are to remain under guard, and not talk with anyone on this post without my permission. In the future, Captain Schaeffer, leave the interpretation of your orders to me. You are an officer of the Wehrmacht, not a Jewish shopkeeper. You will see to it that your men are not intimidated by outside authorizations of any stripe, Himmler's included. If they allow as much as a stray dog to enter this post, they will face court martial. Now, go and see about those men."

Schaeffer, grim and silent, saluted and left the room. Kellner joined von Maussner at the window.

"You can't blame the sentries too much, Herr General," the colonel said. "You can imagine how our S.S. friends acted at the perimeter. The secret of their success is their ability to intimidate. They're obviously here about Pohl."

"They should have been stopped, Heinz. How did the guards know the order was really signed by Himmler? Good God, your own men are going to enter England with papers that will appear genuine. Let us hope the English are as foolish as Schaeffer's sentries. As for this S.S. major and his fellow cutthroats, they have no authority to investigate Pohl's death. The man's commission was in the army," Kellner shuddered at the thought, "even though he was an obvious S.S. spy. His commission in the army puts any investigation under the jurisdiction of army intelligence. These fanatics try continually to overstep their authority."

"Please allow me to give you some advice as a fellow officer and a friend," von Maussner interrupted. "Even though they have no authority here, why not get their investigation out of the way now? It will do our future plans for Hitler no good to antagonize Himmler to the point where he's having us watched out of spite. I'm afraid that the moment we began to engage in plans to rid Germany of Hitler we became too vulnerable to treat the S.S. lightly. Would you like me to handle this situation, Herr General?" he asked worriedly.

"No thank you, Heinz. I will attempt to control myself. Actually, I'm anxious to hear what they have to say."

"I don't think we should have any trouble with them. If they had succeeded in killing one of the men in that tank, Hitler himself would have had them shot. There are no standby replacements for this mission."

The noise of lorries brought both men back to the window.

"The uniforms at last," von Maussner said and began to move to the door.

"I'd prefer that you were here when I talk to the S.S. major, Heinz. I'm still a soldier under orders and will do nothing to endanger this mission. But I'd like you to remind me by your presence." He looked out of the window again. "I'd rather the S.S. didn't see the unloading of those lorries. They apparently know nothing about the purpose of this post, and I'd like to keep it that way. Why don't you go and have the unloading postponed for a bit and then return here. We'll get this over with as quickly as possible."

The maps had been removed from the walls. General Kellner leaned both hands on the bare table and spoke to the disheveled S.S. officer.

"Are you badly hurt, Major?"

The officer touched the bandage on his head gingerly and glanced down at the bloodstains on his field gray uniform. "No, I was lucky." His tone was curt.

"Lucky? Were you?" the general said. "I wonder if you will feel that you were so lucky when they learn in Berlin that you entered a top secret installation without my specific permission and then had the effrontry to fire on men who are here under the personal orders of the Führer."

"A British tank was training its gun on me," the major answered unemotionally. "I fired in self-defense. I had no way of knowing it wasn't attacking this post."

The general looked down at the triangular emblem on the major's sleeve.

"I see that you are S.D. and not field S.S. But policeman or not, I suggest you take the trouble to learn something about your enemy's weapons before you enter a battle zone. You could have fired at that tank all afternoon and not have made a dent. But you might have gotten lucky and hit the man in the turret or the driver. If you had, I would have had you shot immediately. Now, what do you want here?"

"I am under the orders of Reichsführer S.S. Himmler to investigate the death of a Captain Theodor Pohl, killed on this post."

"And what interests the S.S. in the death of a Wehrmacht officer?"

"I don't question my orders. The Reichsführer has his reasons, I'm sure." The major's bloodstained face showed complete unconcern for the general's rank or his own wounds. Kellner, his anger rising, looked at von Maussner and saw the slight shake of the head.

He straightened up and said, "This is a top secret post established on the personal orders of the Führer, which I'm sure you will have learned, had your superiors bothered to check before sending you to blunder in without proper clearance." Kellner locked eyes with the tall, broad major. "You'll conduct no investigations here. I don't know how you found out about the regrettable death of Captain Pohl. I hope for your sake that it was come by through proper channels. A full report is in the hands of the Führer. If he feels it requires further investigation, then I'm confident he will notify the proper agency: army intelligence."

The major remained unimpressed. "You may be making a mistake, General. The Reichsführer S.S. feels that the circumstances of Captain Pohl's death require our investigation. I don't think he will appreciate your lack of cooperation."

Seeing anger rising in the general's face, von Maussner quickly interrupted. "In your zeal, Major, you seem to have forgotten that you are speaking to a lieutenant general of the Wehrmacht. You have had the effrontery to avoid the normal courtesies of address expected from a junior officer. You're treading on dangerous ground."

"My orders state . . . ," the major began.

"Quiet!" von Maussner shouted. "Since you seem incapable of conducting yourself like a gentleman, we shall have to deal with you on your own level. Your orders—if they are genuine—were signed by Reichsführer Himmler, not the Führer. We've received no signals concerning you or your men. Until we do—with your permission, Herr General—you will be confined to one of the buildings on this post. When we have received clarification from Führer headquarters, and confirmation of your identity, then, and only then, will we discuss this further."

The S.S. major looked at the two senior officers with undisguised anger. "So, you find it necessary to involve the Führer in this? A few hours' cooperation would have cleared it up, but since you insist on placing obstacles in our path, it might be wise for us to go into the matter more thoroughly. I wish to inform my own headquarters at once, and then we'll see how long you are able to detain us."

"That will be enough, Major," the general said coldly. "Save your threats for the civilian population. You are under arrest. Your rashness has already caused the wreck of your vehicle and injury to yourself and your men. I've tried to take into consideration the shock you've probably suffered from your head wound, but now my patience is at an end." He went to the door. "Captain Schaeffer!" he called. The captain, who had been waiting in the hall, entered quickly.

"Herr General?"

"Escort this man and the others to the hospital section of the other house," Kellner ordered. "They are to be considered under arrest and are not to talk to anyone on this post until we receive confirmation of their papers. And, Captain, see to it that my orders are followed without interpretation."

The major studied von Maussner for a moment, then transferred his cold stare to the general. "We are used to interference by the army," he said coldly as he raised his arm in salute. "Heil Hitler!" He seemed satisfied when neither officer reacted as he left the room under the watchful eye of Captain Schaeffer.

When the door closed, Kellner brought the side of a fist down on the table top.

"Impudent bastard! God, how things have changed, Heinz."

Von Maussner, who was still looking at the door, turned back to the general. "There no longer seems to be any doubt that Pohl was working for

Himmler, but I find it difficult to believe that he would order an investigation of Pohl's death without Hitler's permission."

"There's no doubt that Himmler used Pohl, and I suspect he's allowed the loss of an energetic snooper to make him incautious. Think about it, Heinz. Himmler's even knowing about Pohl's death is a point in our favor. I believe Hitler will be quite interested to learn that the major's orders were sent from Berlin shortly after I reported Pohl's death. Hitler said nothing about it when I spoke to him. Either our Austrian is being devious or Himmler will have some explaining to do. If Hitler didn't tell him, and if our corporal Führer has any brains at all, then he'll begin to wonder how his friend Heinrich knew about Pohl's unfortunate accident. If Hitler did tell him, then I suspect the major would have been Gestapo, not S.D."

"So Himmler has other Pohls planted in Hitler's headquarters?"

"I wouldn't be a bit surprised, Heinz."

"Then we may have opened another can of worms, Herr General."

"Perhaps. But the contents won't bother us this time, and we shall have to be suitably shocked at the opening. It's the future I'm thinking about. We can't tell where Himmler has men planted, and I'm suddenly afflicted by the need to look over my shoulder. Treason inevitably leads to paranoia."

"Himmler's spies are easily recognizable, Herr General."

"Are they? If we continue to win, I wouldn't be too sure, Heinz. Now, before you see to the lorries, I'd like you to assign a work party to remove the flag from the roof of this house before it gets too dark. I find it impossible to concentrate or sleep with the constant tapping above my head. They can put it on the barn tomorrow."

"I'll see to it at once, Herr General."

Sergeant Siegler held the officer's hat at arm's length and studied it. The silver death's head grinned emptily against the surrounding black leather. Siegler rubbed it with his sleeve, then, removing his beret, he tried it on and found that it fit perfectly. Earlier, Schiller had given him an idea when he had said, "You had to land on top of a Belgian fort to earn a stripe, Willi. In the S.S. a man like you would be at least a captain by now."

The remark had caused Siegler to look at Schiller narrowly and search for any hidden implication. But Schiller had already passed on to another topic, unaware of the sergeant's suspicious scrutiny, so Willi decided that it had been meant as merely a statement of fact—one with which he agreed heartily.

Siegler, Dietrich, and the men of their crews had been watching the tanks' tracking exercises when the armored car had opened fire. They dived quickly to the ground and watched the car slew off the road to land in the ditch. They then saw the arrival of the colonel and the guards and watched his confrontation with a groggy, bloodstained officer who staggered up from the wreck.

After the four occupants of the armored car had been helped into one of the half-tracks and taken away, the storm troopers watched the remaining half-track maneuver into position to pull the wreck from the ditch. As it was pulled onto the road, Siegler's eyes were attracted by the hat. He clambered down into the ditch and picked it up.

Dietrich was waving at the British tank which stood alongside the 38T far out in the field, but as he watched, both vehicles began to move west toward the farmhouse.

"We'll have to make our own way back," Dietrich said. "Schiller seems to have forgotten about us." He had then noticed the hat under Siegler's arm. "Collecting souvenirs, Willi?" he asked.

Siegler shrugged.

He had kept the hat with him during the hastily ordered lecture that the colonel had set up with the sergeant-major before entering the house to report to the general. After the lecture they had watched the maintenance crews load the two-pound, armor piercing shot into the fighting compartment in preparation for the next day's firing drill. They soon tired of the inactivity and were glad when Captain Schaeffer ordered them to the map room, where the next hour was spent in being fitted in the captured British uniforms.

Dressed again in their own uniforms, the storm troopers left the map room and went to their waiting dinner. While the three tank commanders were eating, Schiller had them laughing at his description of the 38T-officer's rage, and his quick reversal when he learned the intruders were S.S. It was then that Schiller had made the remark that had led Siegler to think about what *he* might accomplish in the S.S.

Later, he left the others still talking at the outside table and went up to the room he shared with Schiller. Placing the hat carefully on a chair, he lay down on his cot to mull over his next move. He had heard that the major and his men were billeted in the farmhouse across the fields to the west, and he decided to find time on the following day to return the officer's hat, using that as an excuse to question him about the opportunities available to a dedicated officer of the S.S. before he approached Hitler with another request for transfer. But it would have to be thought over carefully. It suddenly occurred to him that if he made the request, and Hitler agreed, he might end up in the Führer's personal guard; a prestigious but dead-end assignment. He began to have second thoughts about his plans. It would do no harm to talk to the major, but he would wait until he returned from the mission to make any further decision. His musing was interupted by Schiller's entrance.

"Colonel von Maussner wants to see you, Willi. A light plane just landed behind the house. There was an Abwehr officer in it, and he was taken directly to the general, so I suspect he's brought the answer you've been waiting for."

When he was told that Hitler had agreed to the attack on the airfield, Siegler was elated. To have convinced the Führer so easily was staggering and infinitely promising. He stood alongside von Maussner and pointed to the map while the colonel leaned over his notebook.

"When I turn into Wide Lane—here—the entrance to the airport is less than half a mile to the northeast. There are very few houses near the road, only fields on either side."

"The hangars begin just inside the entrance and stand alongside the road, as shown on this map?" the colonel questioned.

"Yes, Colonel. No more than a few yards from the fence."

"If this installation is a test center, it certainly doesn't seem to have been planned with ground defense in mind. The other side of the field would seem to be the logical area for hangars, empty land and a double river barrier behind it, easily defended."

"It was built as a civilian airfield, Colonel, but even if it hadn't, I doubt they would have changed anything. No Englishman believes an invading army could land, much less get as far as Eastleigh."

"Considering the exposed locations of both our targets, I believe you may be right, but the reconnaissance photographs I showed you confirm that the field is now an R.A.F. station, and they also show three antiaircraft guns clearly."

"What good will they do them, Colonel?"

"Antiaircraft guns can be utilized as a very effective antitank weapon. The British have shown no inclination to use them as such so far, but they might just have learned something from our success in using 88s against their tanks here in France."

"If we get as far as the targets, it will be because they think we're British. If not, we'll have to fight before we get anywhere near them. I'm assuming we've gotten to the field and they think we're what we seem to be. They won't have time to react. I'll be in and out before they think of firing, and even if they did, they'd be helping us to do what we came to do, since the hangars will be between the guns and the tank. When we've finished, we'll crash the fence here, cross Wide Lane with what's left of the hangars at my back, and into the fields on the other side. We cross the rail line and Monk's Brook, and continue due west to Stoneham Lane. Here, at the corner of North Stoneham Park is where I'll destroy the tank. Right here," he drummed the map with a finger, "is where the car should be waiting. It's deserted. No houses, and less than half a mile from where we crash the fence. They won't have time to react, Colonel."

Von Maussner was impressed. "You seem to have given this a great deal of thought. Very well, Siegler, let's go over it once again. The officer who brought this material is waiting to deliver my notes to the Führer. Luckily, an Italian emissary to London is available to contact our agents in England and prepare them for our change of plans."

"We trust the Italians with this?" asked Siegler.

"You're lucky we still have entree into England. The information will be coded. The Italian will be a messenger, nothing more. Now, if you want that car waiting for you, we'd better get on with it."

CHAPTER 8

Colonel von Maussner was working in the map room when the general entered, waving a sheet of paper animatedly.

"Hitler has received intelligence that the British are building components of a prototype heavy bomber, four engines and a three-thousand-mile range, at the very factory your men are training to destroy!" He handed the paper to von Maussner. "As far as we ourselves are concerned, it would seem that Hitler no longer gives a damn about Pohl. I've been ordered to hold the major and his fellow louts for security reasons, and have been told in no uncertain terms to keep them out of your hair," Kellner smiled broadly. "Can you imagine what he said to Himmler after learning about the new British bomber and then hearing that his own S.S. had been shooting at the men he's hoping will destroy it? God, I'll wager Heinrich wishes he was back on his chicken farm tonight."

Von Maussner finished studying the statistics. "This is unpleasant information, Herr General. Do we have anything comparable to this bomber in production?"

"Unfortunately, no. Since Kesselring stopped the development of the Ural bomber, which was to have characteristics remarkably similar to this new British plane, we've transferred all of our priorities to dive bombers and fighters. It now seems that that decision may prove fatal."

"Fatal, Herr General?"

"Yes, fatal. Even now we are beginning to find that our soldiers quickly advance beyond the range of our existing aircraft, causing a dangerous lag in air cover while their bases are being moved forward. The Ju 88, our best bomber, has a range of only fifteen hundred miles, and is proving to be weak defensively. If Hitler continues with his plans to conquer the world, he'll need a better airplane than the Junkers to help accomplish it. I'm now in complete agreement with our corporal Führer. Development of that British bomber must be halted now, before we look up one day and find the sky full of them."

"Why doesn't Hitler forget this raid nonsense and order an air strike against the factory?" von Maussner asked.

"Apparently he still has hopes of persuading the English to become an ally against Russia."

"Does he really believe our twelve-man invasion is likely to convince them?"

"Come now, Heinz, for once he's being realistic. Bombing at the limits of range over a defended target with enemy airfields only minutes away is hardly likely to be 100 percent effective. In this case, bombing Woolston would only serve to alert them. They'd guess we've learned of this new bomber and transfer their research to another, less vulnerable facility. But, if our men *are* able to plant explosives in that factory, we can be quite certain of the results. If they fail, and the British decide not to accommodate us by conceding, then I've no doubt we'll attempt to use our bombers."

"Attempt, Herr General? Do you mean that the Luftwaffe is incapable of destroying a factory less than one hundred miles from the French coast?"

"One hundred miles when we take southern France. It's half again that distance from Calais. The bombers would have no trouble getting there, but the limited range of the fighters would allow little time over the target." The general could see von Maussner's shock. "These problems will be seen to quickly, Heinz, but at present, Hitler wants to avoid bombing British cities. It demands retaliation, and once the cycle has begun it's impossible to stop. Prototype or not, that British bomber is as dangerous as the Spitfire. It would be a remarkable feat if we could cancel out both at the same time. Your men will attempt to do just that in the next few days."

"Do you have any idea when they will leave?"

"Hitler hinted that it would only be a matter of days," Kellner gestured at the wall behind him. "Our forces are even now at the gates of Calais. The trap is closing. Reconnaissance, and the broken British naval code, tells us that they're gathering naval and civilian vessels at the English southern ports. They're getting ready, Heinz, so we must see to it that we, too, are ready."

It had been a long, tiring day and General Kellner, having finished his own remarks, watched drowsily as von Maussner continued the briefing. The general sat near an open window, preferring the cool air to the cloud of acrid smoke generated by the French cigarettes of which the men seemed to have an endless supply. How can they stand those foul smelling things, he wondered, with the selfrighteousness of the nonsmoker. He held a handkerchief to his nose. It didn't help, so he edged the chair closer to the window where he was rewarded by an occasional breeze. As he watched the men, Kellner found himself thinking of the remark attributed to the Duke of Wellington in 1809: "I don't know what effect these men will have on the enemy, but, by God, they frighten me." The general made an effort to listen to the colonel.

"Lieutenant Schiller has brought up a point worth considering. Twelve unwounded soldiers returning in three comparatively undamaged tanks would, under other circumstances, call for considerable explanation. However, at the time you'll be landing—during the confusion of a mass retreat and evacuation—I don't think anyone will stop to think about incongruities. After all, wounded men would not be chosen to man heavy infantry tanks. But that or other questions might occur, so I suggest that you act accordingly. Conceal yourselves in the tanks as quickly as possible and leave conversation with authorities to the officers. Does that satisfy you, Lieutenant, or do you suggest we shoot a few of you to add authenticity?"

Schiller laughed with the others. "No, Colonel, but perhaps a few bandages?"

"I don't think so. Better to risk a question or two than a well-meaning attempt at medical assistance in the port."

Schiller sat down as Corporal Schemke stood and was acknowledged by the colonel.

"What if the British decide to wait for confirmation before they unload the tanks, Colonel?"

"They won't be given the time for such decisions, Corporal. The vessel we've chosen to transport you is a small coastal freighter. It's being equipped with specially reinforced booms capable of unloading the machines without help from the shore. The tanks will be carried on the deck, beneath the booms, and should take little time to remove. Once they are down, it will be up to your officers to evaluate the situation. The method of disembarkation will be gone over both here and aboard the ship. You men have proved that you don't panic. We will prepare you as well as we can, but the rest will be up to you."

The men's voices were having a hypnotic effect on the general and despite a valiant attempt to stay awake, his head began to drop slowly into the fleshy folds of his neck, only to jerk upright as if controlled by invisible strings. Von Maussner watched the general's struggle and found it disconcerting. Finally, he walked over to the table and brushed against the lid of the heavy metal box, causing it to drop shut loudly. Kellner awakened abruptly, uncertain at first of his surroundings.

"It's almost 2300, Herr General," von Maussner said. "You asked me to remind you?"

"Ah yes, Colonel, thank you," Kellner said thankfully. "It's almost time for my report to the Führer. I'll leave you to continue." He rose from the chair with effort. "I'll be occupied for some time, so I'll say goodnight." The men stood up respectfully as he left the room, closing the door quietly behind him.

Von Maussner was expressionless when he faced the men to continue the briefing.

It was still dark when Lieutenant Rau woke Dietrich. The infantry officer left the room immediately afterward so Dietrich, aware that he might doze off again, forced himself to put his feet on the floor. He rose and went to the open window and breathed deeply, contemptuous of the chilly air. When he was fully awake, he gathered up his clothes and left for the latrine.

The colonel had kept them in the map room until nearly two in the morning. It was during the latter part of the briefing that von Maussner had told them about the British prototype bomber. Dietrich had seen the look on Siegler's face when the colonel spoke of the airplane's dangerous potential. Willi's sorry he talked himself into the Eastleigh attack now, Dietrich mused.

Walther Dietrich was not without ambition and had his own plans for the future. By early 1938 there was no doubt that war was inevitable, and he would soon have to choose between military service in England or return to Germany. His mother and father were both dead, and his only other tie to an England he was not interested in was his sister, Liesel, who was married to a London restaurant owner he despised.

Adolph Hitler fascinated him. He had spent most of his holidays in Germany, watching with uninformed pride the obvious changes in the German economy as the Führer outmaneuvered the world leaders who were attempting unsuccessfully to contain him. He finally made his decision.

He bought, and learned to use, a Leica camera, his plans for the future formulated. He quit his job and began a month-long trip covering the coastal and northern industrial areas of England, photographing, and taking notes on, as many of the military installations, airfields, and potential war factories as he could safely approach. Finally, beginning to become nervous about the growing and potentially damning film record, he withdrew his savings, took the Dover ferry to Ostend, and then the train to Germany. In Berlin, he turned the film and notes over to the Abwehr and was rewarded by an appointment to officer's training school by a grateful Admiral Canaris.

As a newly commissioned second lieutenant, he entered the tank corps, where his efficient handling of a PzKw IV soon became apparent to the senior officers who had been ordered by Canaris to look for potential in the young man.

It was at Hildesheim, the secret base in western Prussia, that Dietrich met other men who had left England to fight for their fatherland, and who had also sought the most dangerous assignments to prove their dedication.

On May 10, at 0430, the assault teams were airborne in forty-one canvas-covered 16-cwt gliders, towed by trimotored Ju 52s. Rendezvousing south of Cologne, they moved above a string of ground beacons stretching forty-five miles to Aachen, where they were to unhitch and glide silently above an unsuspecting enemy. Dietrich had been assigned to a ninety-six-man detachment, whose target was the high, concrete bridge that spanned the Albert Canal at Vroenhoven. The others were to attack the nearby bridges at Veldswezelt and Kanne and the fortress of Eben Emael.

Dietrich's unit landed among the pillboxes guarding the western end of the bridge. Surprise won the day and the bridge was captured intact. They held their precarious foothold until late afternoon, when they were relieved by vanguard units of the advancing German army. With the exception of the bridge at Kanne, which had been destroyed by the Belgians before they arrived, the Germans had achieved all their objectives.

Dietrich and Siegler had met casually at the training base, and they met again at the formal decoration ceremonies.

Dietrich noted that the Führer seemed to be looking directly at Siegler as he ended his brief speech with a favorite quotation from the Edda.

"All things will pass away; nothing will remain but death and the glory of deeds."

Dietrich wasn't surprised when he learned that Siegler had also volunteered for the coming mission to England.

During breakfast, Dietrich ordered his team to be the first to use the British tank for the morning's live gunnery practice, followed by Schiller, and then Siegler. Schiller saw that he had been right in assuming that Dietrich wasn't about to make the mistake he had made the day before. Siegler could expect to be last in any exercise from now on. But when he glanced at the sergeant, to his surprise he saw that Willi looked pleased.

The high velocity cannon presented no problems to Dietrich's crew. They scored hit after hit on the targets that had been set up on the northern edge of the field. Dietrich soon tired of the game. His ears rang from the muzzle blast of the cannon, and he was beginning to cough as cordite fumes rose up through the cupola hatch. He could imagine what it was like in the fighting compartment. He ordered the gun secured and directed the tank back to where the other teams waited in the shade of a fuel lorry. He was greeted enthusiastically by Schiller.

"That was damn good shooting, Walther."

"We didn't leave you too many targets," Dietrich said with a smile. "But what the hell, maybe you'll get a chance at another armored car—but make sure Himmler isn't in it." Both men laughed. "It's a good gun, Friederich, but if we continue to fire it this way there won't be much left of it by the time it's Willi's turn." He looked around, expecting a retort from the sergeant. "Where is Siegler?"

"I let him go back to the house in one of the half-tracks. He forgot his stopwatch. Don't worry, he'll be back in a few minutes. Willi wouldn't miss a chance to play with that gun."

"He'd better not let the colonel see him," Dietrich said. Then Siegler was forgotten as he saw the roof of the farmhouse. "What happened to the flag?"

Schiller climbed up to the turret and squinted at the building. "I hadn't even noticed it was gone," he said.

The infantry private who drove the half-track was a large young man, but he was overawed by the even larger storm trooper sergeant. He had reluctantly agreed to drive Siegler to the second farmhouse, and he waited nervously at the rear of the main house while the sergeant entered to pick up the S.S. officer's hat.

Once back in the vehicle, Siegler attempted to hurry the driver during the detour around the northern edge of the field when he found that the barn blocked his view of the fields to the east and the British tank. He could no longer hear the cannon firing and began to wonder if his trip would prove worth the risk. The colonel wouldn't like him leaving the others; his orders had been clear.

When the half-track finally pulled to a stop in front of the smaller house, Siegler leaped out, ordering the driver to wait.

"If Captain Schaeffer sees me here, I'm going to be in trouble," the reluctant private said. "Can't you get a ride back with someone else?"

"I'll only be a few minutes. Wait," Siegler ordered curtly, thinking, You won't be the only one in trouble, soldier. Why the hell did I come here? I can't learn much in a few minutes.

As he moved toward the house he was relieved to hear the Mark 2 cannon begin to fire again. He climbed the stairs to the porch and was stopped by a sentry who moved in front of the door.

"I want to see the S.S. major," Siegler said, attempting to brush past.

Unlike the half-track driver, the sentry was unimpressed by Siegler's size.

"I have orders that no one is to enter, Sergeant. See the sergeant-major, he's at the back of the house."

Siegler decided against argument. He went back down the stairs and walked quickly to the side of the house. He was watched anxiously by the half-track driver, who shook his head angrily when the sergeant vanished around the corner.

Stationary firing soon proved too tame for Schiller's team. He ordered top speed and moved parallel to the newly replaced targets, seven hundred yards to the east. The diesels whined steadily. At Schiller's order the turret turned, steadied, and had hardly stopped when the gun fired. Schiller watched the target shatter.

"Direct hit," he yelled into the intercom. His smile faded abruptly when he saw an airplane flying from the north no more than five hundred feet above the fields. It banked erratically to turn in his direction, gusts of smoke pulsing from its engine cowling. Schiller crouched low in the cupola and spoke into his headset: "Close your hood, Falck. Schemke! Inform the base, quickly. A single, damaged British fighter is approaching base from due east, flying low." He pulled his beret from his head and crouched lower in the cupola, ready to drop into the turret. He paused when he saw that the plane was going to pass well to the north and was making no threatening move toward him.

The Spitfire seemed to be flying remarkably slowly as it passed five hundred yards ahead of him. Schiller could see the gaping holes in its fuselage and a missing wing tip. The pilot gave him a thumbs up gesture.

The poor fool is headed directly for the house, thought Schiller. If it was yesterday he would have seen the flag and at least tried to take some evasive action. He's probably badly wounded from the look of those holes and so low that Schaeffer's men could knock him down with stones. Schiller watched with fascination as the doomed plane neared the farmhouse.

The well camouflaged 88-mm. flak guns did not fire; there was no need. Twin 7.92-mm. MG 34s, in antiaircraft mounts, sprayed the stricken plane from positions near the house and barn. The pilot was killed instantly as continuous rounds struck the Spitfire from either side. The plane flew on, settling slowly as the engine cowling burst into flames.

Siegler had found the infantry sergeant-major as immovable as the sentry. He decided that continuing to press the matter would only get back to Colonel von Maussner and lead to questions. He abandoned his plans, deciding to wait for another opportunity. He handed the officer's hat to the sergeant-major, and started to return to the half-track.

Lost in thought, Siegler was startled by the whine of the rapid-fire machine guns. Added to their din was another sound that he quickly recognized. He began to run toward the front of the house, keeping close to its side, searching the sky. At the end of the building he looked across the field and saw a blazing fighter, flying no more than a few feet above the ground, headed directly toward him! The half-track driver still sat in his seat, apparently frozen in fright as three tons of blazing metal approached him inexorably.

"Get out of there, you fool!" Siegler yelled.

If the man heard him, he gave no sign. Siegler began to run toward the half-track but stopped abruptly when he saw he had no chance of reaching it in time. He stood suspended between the inevitable crash and the safety of the fields to his right. Suddenly the young driver screamed, and the hypnotic effect of the tableau was broken. Siegler turned and ran away from the house and into the fields. Over his shoulder, he saw the airplane settle to the ground, still in level flight. It touched lightly as if still controlled by its dead pilot, then caromed up and over the half-track, carrying the still screaming driver with it as it crashed into the front of the house.

Siegler dove to the ground and pressed his face hard into the dirt when the Spitfire's remaining ammunition and fuel exploded. Almost instantly the frame house became a torch. The sudden blast of heat forced Siegler to his feet to retreat in a crouch farther out into the field. He could hear the screams of men trapped in the sudden pyre. They lasted only seconds, then all that remained was the roar of the fire.

Siegler sat down to regain his breath. The blazing house was already a shell and beginning to crumble.

CHAPTER 9

"You have endangered the entire mission, Siegler!" said a furious General Kellner. "You were told to remain in the immediate vicinity of the main house when not on duty—and you were *on* duty, which makes this even worse. Apparently you can't obey a simple order and yet you seem to believe that you are qualified to become an officer of the Wehrmacht. I do not share your belief. Under other circumstances I would see to it that you were stripped of your present rank at once. Well? What were you doing at the house?"

The usually imperturbable Siegler was sweating. "I was returning the major's hat, Herr General."

Kellner looked at the sergeant in amazement. "You were what? The rapid completion of our campaign in the west is possibly involved in the mission you're here to train for, and yet you leave an important training exercise to return a hat? Sergeant, you're not a complete fool. You expect me to believe that you left your comrades, traveled two miles across this post in a guard vehicle to return a hat?" The general strode to the window, and glanced out into the fields for a moment, then continued. "Why did you want to see that officer so urgently?" He paused when he saw the cautionary frown on von Maussner's face. "Well?"

Siegler was thinking fast. The hat business did sound ridiculous. He assumed his most penitent expression.

"I returned to this house to get my stopwatch, Herr General, with Lieutenant Schiller's permission. I had forgotten it when we went to the field. My team was last in line for gunnery practice, and I was sure I'd be back in plenty of time. I had no intention of going to the other house, but the half-track driver said he had some errand over there, and since he was my only means of getting back to the tanks, I went with him. I only decided to take the hat since we were going there anyway."

Siegler searched the general's face. He saw only flushed exasperation and decided it was time to whine. "I realize I shouldn't have gone there now, Herr General. I should have walked back to the tank, but I didn't know about your order and only learned about it when we got over there. I thought we were told not to leave the area of this house at night. As soon as

I learned of your order, Herr General, I gave the hat to the sergeant-major and was returning to the front of the house, intending to walk back, when the British plane crashed. I'm sorry." Well, that's it, thought Siegler. Anyone who could possibly contradict me is dead. He lowered his eyes in feigned contrition.

Kellner was about to speak when von Maussner said, "I must admit the sergeant is correct, Herr General. The men were not told of your order against speaking to the prisoners. I saw no reason to include them in the order, since the major and his men were billeted well away in the other building. It certainly doesn't excuse Siegler, but perhaps I wasn't specific enough in defining the off-limits areas and precisely where they could or couldn't go, during daylight hours. Schiller did give him permission to leave the field. It would seem there were extenuating circumstances."

Siegler was surprised by the colonel's defense, until he thought about it. Three tanks, twelve men, and no replacements. He remained at rigid attention, his eyes fastened on the general, and could see that a silent signal was passing between the two senior officers. He was barely able to suppress a self-satisfied smile when the general said, "Very well, Siegler. If it happened as you said, then perhaps it was the result of some misunderstanding on your part. Misunderstanding, however, is hardly a recommendation for commission. Twenty-three people died in or around that house, the major and his men, our doctor and his entire staff, and eleven soldiers of the guard unit. You barely missed joining them. Because you seem prone to misunderstanding, I shall be very explicit. From now on you will not leave the training area for any reason whatsoever, unless you are specifically ordered to do so. Have I made myself understood so far?"

"Yes, Herr General."

Kellner searched the sergeant's face for a moment. "Discipline has been lax where you men are concerned. Perhaps I've been wrong in believing it wasn't necessary to remind you that you are German soldiers. Just so you won't take my leniency as a sign of weakness, I want you to know without doubt that any further infraction of the rules will be dealt with harshly—even if it means replacement of an assigned man. If you heed my warning, and continue to remain with us, I trust your performance in England will help erase the doubts I now have about your qualifications." The general turned away. "That will be all, Siegler. Return to your crew—without detours."

"Thank you, Herr General." Siegler was smiling as he closed the door. They had enough trouble finding twelve of them. There was no way he could be replaced, and they knew it.

Kellner went to the window and watched Siegler pass through the yard, striding purposefully out into the fields toward the tank. "What do you think he was doing over there, Heinz?" he asked.

"I don't know, Herr General, but I think I can reassure you. There is nothing in Siegler's dossier to suggest that he's anything more than a rather crude, ambitious and self serving man. Whatever his reason for visiting the major, I don't for a moment think it had anything to do with us, or our" he searched for a proper euphemism—"activities in Berlin."

"I would prefer that you stop treating me as if I were an overanxious fool," Kellner said. "Siegler is not your average soldier. I personally heard the remarkable conversation he had with Hitler. He *told* our Austrian that the airfield should be included in the mission, and when Hitler apparently hesitated, he launched into an argument that would have gotten either of us shot."

"I happen to know a bit more about Siegler than you could be expected to learn from records, Herr General. Siegler met Hitler twice, both times at decoration ceremonies. Coincidentally, I was there on both occasions. Hitler was apparently impressed by a fellow primitive, or perhaps he was struck by the man's bluntness and lack of sycophancy? Who knows what caused him to single out Siegler for special attention, but he did."

Kellner didn't seem convinced. "I suppose suspicion of everything, and everyone, is the price one must pay as a conspirator, and I must admit it's beginning to get on my nerves. Siegler is a lucky man. There will be no mention of his foolishness in my report. The ease with which the S. S. entered this post, their attack on the tank, and now their deaths, will take a bit of explaining. To add that I can't maintain control over one of twelve men would just about do it for me."

"I'd say you're being unduly pessimistic, Herr General. Even Hitler can't blame you for the crash of a British airplane. As for Siegler, in a few days he and the others will be gone. Until then I intend to make certain that all of them are kept too busy for any of them to get into further mischief."

It was late in the afternoon when Siegler directed the tank back into the barn. He dismissed the crew, and remained in the tank with the intention of stripping down the defective exaust fan. Cordite fumes inside the fighting compartment had begun to impair the effectiveness of the men during the firing drill, and he had little faith in the maintenance crew.

He was about to begin when he heard the voices of General Kellner and Colonel von Maussner as they entered the barn. He started to climb up to the turret hatch when he heard the general order to clear the barn, including the sentries. His decision was instantaneous and characteristic. He dropped back into the fighting compartment and switched off the festoon lights, then moved to the turret turntable and waited. If he should be discovered, he would say that he hadn't heard them and hope they wouldn't notice that the tank's interior had been dark for some time.

He knew he was treading on dangerous ground, but Willi Siegler's successes had never been due to caution. He stood below the open cupola hatch, breathing softly. He had no idea why he had decided to wait, but serendipitous information had served him in the past and the opportunity was too good to resist. He began to hear the voices of the two officers clearly as they approached the tank. He jumped guiltily as one of them hit the tread skirt with an open hand.

"Will these treads hold up until the training is completed, Heinz? Only one tank, and they're using it to the limit." Siegler recognized the general's voice.

"Maintenance assures me they will, Herr General. This machine was in excellent condition when it was captured. Our exercises, up to now, have all been in the fields on soft ground without obstacles. The night exercises on paved roads will be controlled until we learn something further about their departure. Frankly, we could manage without it. These men are remarkable."

"Your confidence is reassuring, Heinz."

"It's justified. From now on, apart from the night driving, I think we should concentrate on the attack itself."

"That might be wise, since the time is drawing near for them to leave. This sort of accelerated preparation is hardly fair to these men."

"They were picked because they're up to it, Herr General. I wonder if they realize how famous they're going to be, win or lose."

"Try to see that they live to enjoy it, Heinz."

"I can show them how to operate equipment, though even that is debatable, but I can't inspire the qualities that will make them succeed or fail. I can only say that if any men can do it, these men can."

Siegler was beginning to be sorry that he had decided to wait in the close air of the turret, until he heard the general's next statement.

"That will all take care of itself, Heinz. I sent the men out of here so I could talk to you privately. Even though I've just received a message from Hitler ordering me to remain here and continue with my assignment, I have inferred from our Austrian corporal's tone that, as I suspected, I will have more than a bit of explaining to do when I return. I hope, with luck, to be able to talk my way out of it. But, no matter how well explained, Himmler won't easily forget the death of Pohl or that of the S.S. major. So, for the time being, I have decided to drop all connection with the anti-Hitler group. Overthrowing the leader of one's country is a dangerous business indeed, and the occurrences on this post have made me vulnerable to close interest by Hitler's cutthroat friends. I no longer have any intention of compounding my vulnerability by continuing to meet fruitlessly with men who do nothing but endlessly discuss what has become little more than a dangerous fantasy."

"Herr General, you—" von Maussner began.

"Hear me out, Heinz. I've managed to survive a number of purges of the high command because Hitler apparently looks on me as something of a fool. So be it. If I thought there was a chance our group might act, I might feel differently. But since we both know that talk is cheap, I intend to be very careful from now on. It wouldn't suit me to be retired at this time—and it certainly wouldn't suit me to be shot." The general watched von Maussner turn away and begin to make a circuit of the barn. Puzzled, he asked: "What on earth are you doing, Heinz?"

Von Maussner paused. "What I would have done earlier, had I known that you were going to be so frank."

Inside the turret, Siegler heard the exchange, and immediately guessing what the colonel was doing, he froze, scarcely daring to breathe.

Von Maussner circled the tank, then returned to confront the general.

"General Kellner, on numerous occasions since I arrived I've tried, as diplomatically as possible, to warn you to be more careful with your statements. Forgive me, but you seem to have suddenly acquired an apparently uncontrollable self-destructive urge. Were you absolutely sure this barn was empty before you made your foolish and damning confession? We seem to be alone, so your luck seems to have held. But one soldier, napping in one of those darkened corners, suddenly awakened by his general's voice loudly proclaiming his involvement in anti-Hitler groups, references to the Führer as Austrian corporal..." Von Maussner stopped in mid sentence. He could see that he had made his point. Kellner leaned against the tank, and wiped his face with a handkerchief.

"So, Heinz, again you are forced to remind me that I'm becoming careless." He held up a hand as the colonel was about to reply. "You're quite right. But you see, it proves a point; conspiracy is a younger man's game. Very well, I'll say no more about it, and I ask that you do the same. I shouldn't like to have our friendship strained by too many blunt truths. Now, let us return to the house. I've taken a sudden dislike to this place. What else do we have to discuss?"

The voices faded as the general and the colonel left the barn. A stunned Sergeant Siegler began to breathe deeply in the close air of the turret. What he had heard was the answer to all of his dreams. He began to ponder how he could use the information to his best advantage.

He climbed out of the turret, dropped to the rough floor of the now deserted barn, and moved to the partially open door. After looking out cautiously, and seeing only the maintenance crews beginning to return to the barn, he stepped out quickly and walked toward the road where he could be alone and think.

He immediately dismissed the idea of telling anyone on the post what he had heard. It struck him that even Captain Schaeffer might be one of them, and he might get himself conveniently shot like the little captain. Anyway, he reasoned, they would deny everything and have time to cover their tracks. Even if he did convince someone, the operation would be cancelled, and that was something he didn't want to happen. What they had said was true. Anyone who returned from the British mission would be a national hero.

Siegler stood for some time watching the sun setting behind the still smoking ruins of the house across the field and smiled finally in decision. He would wait the few days until they returned from the mission and he could tell Hitler what he had heard privately. Then they could be watched and the others they spoke of uncovered too. From that moment on Hitler would be in his debt, and there was no limit to what he might accomplish. He turned abruptly and began to walk back to the house and the dinner he knew was waiting. He was suddenly very hungry.

Kellner sat in the darkened room and looked fixedly down at the Luger pistol he held in his hand. Did he hear us? he wondered, or am I allowing guilt feelings to get the better of my judgment?

For twenty minutes he had been sitting in the chair by the window, waiting for the door to burst open and the room to fill with angry, accusing soldiers. Despite his fear, he found, to his disgust, that he was getting drowsy.

When he and von Maussner had entered the hallway of the farmhouse after leaving the barn, they had paused just inside the door while the colonel finished a point he had been making. Then the colonel had moved up the stairs toward his room. The general was about to follow when he glanced out of the door and saw vague movement at the door of the barn. The blood drained from his face when he saw a figure slip through the door and begin to walk toward the road, and when the man passed in front of the house, he recognized him as Sergeant Siegler.

The general went quickly up the stairs to his own room and its window, where he stood and watched the sergeant's progress toward the road. The man didn't seem at all in a hurry, and once at the road, simply stopped and stood staring out to the west. Kellner was puzzled. Siegler's actions were hardly those of a man who had just heard a general confess to treason. Without thinking, Kellner had gone to the table, opened his briefcase, and removed the holstered Luger. He fumbled with the holster catch and finally managed to remove the pistol. He cocked it and moved back to the window. When he saw that Siegler was walking back toward the house, he toyed briefly with the idea of shooting him as he passed below the window, but then dismissed the thought as insanity. The sergeant was whistling!

He began to wonder if Siegler had gone into the barn after he and the colonel had left it. He sat down in the chair with the gun in his lap. He would know soon.

There was a knock on the door. Kellner opened it slowly, the Luger hidden at his side. The young soldier who stood in the hall saluted.

"Your dinner is ready, Herr General. Colonel von Maussner and Captain Schaeffer are waiting in the dining room."

Kellner held onto the door tightly, afraid that he might collapse with relief. He managed to answer calmly, "Thank you. I will join them in a few minutes." He closed the door and leaned against it, the back of his shirt soaked with sweat. "Thank God!" he said aloud.

A much-relieved Kellner ordered night exercises for the storm troopers, mainly to avoid contact with Siegler, and, later, watched from the darkened map room as the two 38Ts and the British tank moved out of the yard. They were to practice close-order driving without lights. The men of the special force had taken over the 38Ts and would alternate in the British tank during the exercise. Sergeant Siegler stood in the turret of the rear German tank. As it passed the house, it seemed to the general, the sergeant looked directly at the window of the map room. Kellner drew back guiltily, certain that he had been seen. In the darkness, the glow of the tank's low headlights gave the sergeant's features a satanic harshness. Uncertainty again overtook him, and for the first time he could remember, General Kellner spent a sleepless night.

The next day passed quickly for the men of the special force, if not for General Kellner. Von Maussner kept them constantly employed with the tank during the morning, and in the afternoon they practiced setting the hollow-charge explosives, using the barn as their target.

Von Maussner watched the exercise critically. He could see that even the highly trained men of the special force were taking too long to assemble and fuse the cumbersome explosives. If British resistance was heavy, the men leaving the protection of the tank would be all too vulnerable, no matter how skillfully the driver used the bulk of the tank to protect them. Perhaps Siegler's plan to enter the hangars at the airfield before setting the charges had more merit than he had at first thought. He jotted that and other thoughts down in his notebook for further discussion.

The storm troopers were not in the least inhibited by the colonel's scrutiny, but the maintenance crew, still working inside the barn, looked upon the drill with understandable nervousness. They knew that one mistake by the seemingly casual storm troopers could destroy the barn and add their number to the growing population of the new cemetery in the field to the south.

The general carefully avoided contact with Siegler during the day, but as the evening's briefing approached he knew he could no longer put it off. He entered the map room, and despite his resolve to ignore the sergeant, he found that Siegler was the first man he looked at, and the man stared back relentlessly. Siegler's expression, something in his eyes, an obvious change in his attitude, told Kellner that what he had feared wasn't imaginary, and he knew he had to get out of the room. Von Maussner sensed that something was wrong.

"Are you all right, Herr General?" he asked.

Kellner answered in a whisper. "Please take over, Heinz. I don't feel well. I'll be in my room. Come and see me when you're finished here." He walked to the door unsteadily.

As von Maussner watched him leave, he noticed Siegler staring at him with an enigmatic half smile. He returned the stare questioningly, and the sergeant looked away. He walked over to the map and tapped it to get the men's attention.

"The general doesn't feel well, and he's asked me to take over." He tapped the map again. "The British abandoned Arras last night." He paused as the men cheered lustily. "They have fallen back fifteen miles—here—to the Haute Duele Canal. From now on it will be flight to the north. They will be surrounded and contained by our forces within a fifteen-mile corridor. I imagine the Panzer commanders are very angry men at this moment. They have been ordered to halt their advance temporarily, and they have no way of knowing the reason for what they must consider an astounding order. *We* know the reason, gentlemen. We can't very well send you to England on your own, can we? If the armor was allowed to continue unchecked, the enemy would be trapped before he could begin an evacuation in any numbers. So, one army is being held and another manipulated for the sake of your mission. The next few days are critical. My own guess is that you will have completed your mission and be back in Germany in less than a week." He noticed that Siegler was still staring at him and wondered why he felt uneasy. "Is there something you want to say, Siegler?" he asked.

"Will you and the general be in Berlin when we get back, Colonel?"

"The general and I will be waiting at the port when you return to personally escort all of you to the Führer. But the German people and, I might add, history will have little interest in anyone but you gentlemen. As a soldier, I envy you."

"I'm sure that you and the general will be remembered, Colonel," Siegler said with a smile that was somehow menacing. He had found out what he wanted to know.

When von Maussner entered the general's room he found Kellner sitting in a chair, his back to the door. "Are you feeling better, Herr General?" he asked.

"He heard us, Heinz," Kellner said softly.

"Who heard what?"

"Siegler. He was in the barn when I made—what did you call it?—my damning confession."

Von Maussner was shocked, but recovered quickly. "I've just left him, and though he did seem to be acting strangely, he made no accusations, and the others seemed perfectly normal. Why do you think he heard us?"

Kellner leaned forward, his head in his hands. "I saw him slip out of the barn just after you left me in the hall last evening. I didn't mention it because I thought that perhaps I was mistaken. But I could tell at the briefing he was there."

Von Maussner looked down at the general disgustedly, attempting to hide his own fear. "I think we should take a walk, Herr General. Whether you're mistaken or not, I would say we've done quite enough unguarded talking."

Kellner obeyed meekly. Once outside, they walked to the road and stopped within sight of the guard tank, but far enough away to be certain they would not be overheard.

"Please tell me everything, Herr General. From the beginning," von Maussner said. "Start with when you saw him leave the barn. What did he do then?"

"I went up to my room and watched him from the window. He walked out here, where we are now."

"Did he speak to the tank crew? And more importantly, did he see you?"

"He didn't speak to anyone. And if you mean, was he aware that I saw him leave the barn, the answer is no. Where could he have been, Heinz? You looked the place over thoroughly."

"The most obvious place. I looked everywhere but inside the tank."

"The tank? Good God, we stood right alongside the damned thing."

"After the exchange I've just had with the sergeant, I suspect that he *was* there," von Maussner said. "But the fact that we're not under arrest now makes me think that I can read his intentions, and I think there may be a good chance we can silence him without involving ourselves directly. He doesn't seem to have told any of the other men. So, if he was listening, then he's keeping it to himself, and I think I know why."

"Why didn't he report to Schaeffer immediately?"

"He's an opportunist, following a pattern. I told you how he managed to ingratiate himself with Hitler. He now has the means to get Hitler's full attention. Anti-Hitler *group,* isn't that the way you put it? I suspect that Siegler now fancies himself being responsible for rounding up half the senior officers in the army. From the look of it, I would say that the sergeant is no danger to us until the British mission is completed. He just made it a point to ask whether you and I will be nearby when he returns. It's my guess that he intends to wait until he can speak to Hitler personally. He knows he has no real proof, and that we'd simply deny everything. A disgruntled soldier, just warned by his general for disobeying orders, would be suspect as to motive, even by Hitler. And, no matter how it went, the mission would be over for him. If I'm any judge of the man, that's the last thing he wants."

"Your reasoning is comforting, but will he keep it to himself when he stops to think that he could be killed in England?"

"I doubt that Siegler believes for a moment that he can be killed. Even if he did, I still believe he would wait. If I am wrong, then all my speculation is unimportant. It's only a matter of days before they leave, and during that time we must not do anything to make him suspect we're on to him. No more sudden illnesses, Herr General. You'll only force him to act."

"He has kept quiet so far, so you may be right. But if he should manage to return from England. . . ."

"We shall have to see to it that he doesn't return, won't we?"

"What?"

"We will allow him to complete the mission, but I think you will agree that it would be best if the sergeant were allowed to die there as a hero, rather than return as one."

Kellner winced. "I surmise that you're suggesting we use our contacts in the English government to warn the British. That might be acceptable to me if only Siegler was involved, but there are eleven other German soldiers to consider, to say nothing of our agents. They don't deserve to die because of us. I haven't sunk to Himmler's level yet."

"And you think I have? Not quite. The escape plan calls for the men to split up after the attack, each crew to proceed independently of each other to different points on the southern coast. The odds of them getting that far are astronomical, but let us assume that some do in fact reach the coast. They'll have a much better chance if all of the British attention is on Eastleigh and Siegler. Granted, it means four men might be caught and perhaps executed. I dislike that as much as you do, but I'm afraid we've no other choice."

Kellner studied the colonel and wasn't particularly reassured with what he saw: another frightened man, using logic to justify his fear. "You will see to it that the others have their chance to escape?" he asked.

"It will be handled very carefully, Herr General."

"Very well, Colonel. Do it your way."

When the initial shock wears off, von Maussner thought, the general is bound to realize that I can't take the chance that Siegler might *not* confide in his comrades when he's faced with the enemy and begins to realize that he may not be immortal after all. None of them could be allowed to return.

CHAPTER 10

The morning of the following day passed interminably for General Killner, but as it progressed uneventfully into afternoon he began to relax. Von Maussner's assessment of Siegler's intentions seemed to be proving correct. Activities on the post moved ahead routinely, and it was increasingly obvious that the sergeant was keeping his dangerous secret to himself.

The general watched from the window of his room as von Maussner ordered the special force on what was to be the final daytime exercise with the British tank. The colonel's calm astounded Kellner. There was no perceptible change in his attitude toward Siegler or the others as he informed them that their remaining time would be spent in night operations and further work with the explosives.

"The order will come any time now," the colonel was saying.

"The enemy knows that the imminent fall of Calais will bring their evacuation port within range of our heavy coastal guns. The Luftwaffe is keeping them under constant pressure, and even though the armor has been halted, the infantry has not. But while we wait, we'll continue to keep busy. You have a long afternoon ahead of you, gentlemen. But I do want to add that you have exceeded even my expectations of your abilities, and I can tell you that the Führer is pleased with our reports and sends you his congratulations."

General Kellner winced at the reference to the Führer but was relieved to see Siegler join the others in an uninhibited cheer before climbing aboard the idling tank.

Earlier in the day, a trimotored Ju 52, heavily escorted by fighters, had flown low over the farmhouse to make a prearranged parachute drop. Discussion of the new information kept Kellner and von Maussner occupied until late afternoon. Finally, when the voluminous papers had been locked away, the general left for the radio room. Von Maussner was surprised when he returned minutes later, apparently anxious to talk.

When he had settled in the one chair he seemed to find passably comfortable, Kellner said, "The Austrian must be overwhelmed by his own genius by now."

"Good news from the front, Herr General?" von Maussner asked.

"Time will tell. The Belgians have withdrawn to the Lys. Only the halt order keeps Guderian from taking Dunkirk." Kellner looked briefly over his shoulder at the wall map. "Can Hitler really believe this mission of ours is more important than the total surrender of the major portion of the viable British army? *If* the mission is successful, *perhaps* they will listen to reason. Yet, if their army were destroyed it would seem they'd have little choice. Herr Hitler may go down in history as one of England's better generals." Kellner stretched his arms in front of him, yawned, and then leaned back, clasping his hands over his ample stomach.

"I must say that you seem to be feeling better, Herr General," von Maussner said.

"Feeling better? Ah yes, you mean Siegler. Perhaps I do. Your estimation of his intentions seems to be proving correct. Actually, I'm beginning to believe I may have been wrong about the sergeant."

"I wouldn't count on it," von Maussner said.

"No, I suppose not. One way or the other, I'll leave it to you, Heinz. I'm afraid I wasn't thinking too clearly last night."

Von Maussner now knew that the general, despite his earlier protestations, had surrendered to the instinct of self-preservation.

The retreat corridor to the sea had become an unrelenting hell as German pressure was brought to bear against the withdrawing allied troops. The few serviceable roads leading to the north were crowded with soldiers who were hindered in their movement by thousands of confused and frightened civilians and the constant attacks of the Luftwaffe. To the northwest, Calais, though isolated and surrounded by the tenth Panzer division, remained in allied hands until the evening of May 26. Boulogne had surrendered on the twenty-fifth.

On the afternoon of May 26 the halt order had been rescinded and the German armor again began to advance, but too late for Dunkirk to be easily overrun. Stopping the Panzers had allowed the Allies time to construct a defense perimeter that ran from western Dunkirk south to Bergues, through Furnes, and north again to the Yser River below Nieuport, reinforced continually by retreating troops.

In the east, von Reichenau's infantry had penetrated French and Belgian lines on either side of Cortrai while von Bock was advancing on Bruges. In the west, German tanks had crossed the northern end of the Canal Du Nord and threatened the entire Allied pocket. They were held only by heroic stands at Ledringham, Cassel, and Hazebrouck.

On May 26 and 27, 7,669 British were evacuated from Dunkirk by the Royal Navy. It was the beginning of the miracle.

And on the twenty-seventh, General Kellner was ordered to report to Berlin on the following day for a final conference on the mission; at the same time, the special force was to proceed by road convoy to Boulogne.

The morning was clear. Colonel von Maussner watched the arrival of the motorcycle detachment that had been assigned as escort for the special force's journey to the coast. He then walked with the general to the waiting Fieseler.

"I'll see you tomorrow, Heinz," Kellner said. "Is there anyone I should see in Berlin to pave the way for what you have to do?"

"No, Herr General. I'll have sufficient time for that." The general seeing anyone at all about Siegler was the last thing von Maussner wanted.

The noise of the idling propeller made further conversation difficult. Kellner shook hands with von Maussner and shouted above the noise: "Goodbye, Heinz—and thank you, my friend."

The colonel stepped back as Kellner was helped into the passenger seat by the sentries that surrounded the Fieseler. The plane taxied to the easternmost end of the field, then bounded forward. Kellner waved briefly at von Maussner, the relief he felt at leaving the base momentarily dampened when he saw the diminishing figure of Siegler standing at a corner of the house watching his departure.

The seat was too small, and Kellner twisted in it uncomfortably. He glanced above him, his eye caught by the fighter escort. He smiled at that manifestation of his importance and settled himself, determined to bear the discomfort stoically during the short flight to Cambrai where the transport to Berlin would be waiting.

Von Maussner watched the Fieseler pass above the wreckage of the Spitfire and begin a climbing turn to the northeast. Then he turned and walked briskly toward the house. His stride faltered only momentarily when he saw Sergeant Siegler standing near the outdoor tables. He walked directly over to him. "You'll be in England soon, Sergeant. How do you feel about it?"

"The sooner we get there, the sooner we'll return, Colonel."

"Assuring your return is the precise reason why the general has just left us, Sergeant. He'll rejoin us tomorrow in Boulogne with the final details of your escape from England."

Siegler brightened visibly. "When do we leave for Boulogne, Colonel?" he asked.

"In two hours," von Maussner said while thinking: The sooner the better.

The men of the special force waited impatiently in the armored transport while Colonel von Maussner said goodbye to the Grossdeutschland officers. Captain Schaeffer, who had been ordered to remain and deactivate the base, was delighted at the departure of his charges. What was to have been a brief, uncomplicated assignment had taken dangerous turns. He stood at attention, mentally urging the colonel to get on with it.

A select group of the guard detachment was lined up in front of the two German tanks. Von Maussner acknowledged their salute, turned and saluted the new graves in the field to the south, and then walked briskly to the waiting command car. The column, ringed by motorcyclists, moved out of the farmyard to the road, and were soon proceeding west at high speed.

It was late afternoon when the column arrived at the double walled city of Boulogne—walls that had been breached by the twenty-pound projectiles of 88-mm. guns, and through which the tanks of the Second Panzer Division had passed even as the Allied garrison was being evacuated by units of the French and British navies.

The vehicles of the column edged cautiously into the city. Light rain had begun to fall as they inched through masses of marching, shirt-sleeved German infantry, into the Rue Victor Hugo. The rain fell harder as they passed Place Dannou and turned into what looked to be a fenced park. The column stopped in front of the imposing Boulogne Casino, a large Renaissance-style landmark of the city. The storm troopers stared at the ruins around them and then looked inland toward the apparently untouched ramparts of the upper city. Such selective destruction was, to them, an indication of the skill of the Luftwaffe and somehow eased their tension at the first sight of the English Channel and the knowledge that England lay just below the horizon.

A waiting guard detachment, supplied by Admiral Canaris, led them through the gardens fronting the casino and into the building. The storm troopers climbed a broad marble staircase to a large reception room where they were met by a colonel, who greeted von Maussner with a handshake, then faced them.

"Welcome to Boulogne, gentlemen. I am Colonel Bruning. This will be your last billet on what is now German soil until you return. I know that you would like to join your victorious fellow soldiers in inspecting the city, but I'm afraid that will not be possible.

"General Kellner will arrive tomorrow with your last-minute instructions from the Führer. So I suggest you enjoy the dinner we've prepared for you and then get as much sleep as possible. Your British uniforms are waiting in your quarters. Change into them at once, and then my men will collect all of your personal possessions. You will find boxes, clearly marked with each man's name, provided to hold everything you're carrying now. They will be taken to Berlin to await your return. Before you go, I would like to add my personal good wishes for the success of your mission."

The Abwehr colonel gestured to a waiting soldier, who led the men from the room. Then said to von Maussner, "It's good to see you again, Colonel. Come, have something to drink and tell me how you'd like security handled."

Willi Siegler watched Dietrich and Schiller, still carefully packing their belongings, and smiled in mild disgust. His own uniform had been thrown quickly and unconcernedly into the box provided him and was already forgotten since he knew he would never wear sergeant's stripes again. He went over to a large window and looked out into the light rain. The seemingly endless English Channel filled the horizon, and beyond it lay Siegler's future.

CHAPTER 11

When General Kellner arrived the following morning he was nursing a monumental hangover. He had barely been able to stifle a yawn during Colonel Bruning's interminable greeting and was relieved when the man had finally left him at the door to the room where von Maussner was waiting. He mumbled an answer to von Maussner's greeting, made for the nearest chair, and sank into it with relief.

"I bring you the regards of your Führer, Heinz," he began. "He was so happy with the progress of the army that when I expressed our regrets at the death of Captain Pohl, he acted as if he'd never heard of the man."

"When will the men be leaving, Herr General?" von Maussner asked.

"Well before dawn on Friday. Everything is ready, even though there are a few complications. The English have arrested all suspected aliens and known sympathizers to our cause. Fortunately, the agents we will use are among those who have kept their feelings carefully hidden throughout the years, preparing for just such a situation as this. Also, reconnaissance tells us the English are beginning to set up roadblocks along the coast, but they are mostly jury rigged and manned by civilians. Hitler feels that the men should leave Friday before the civilians settle in and become more than just a minor annoyance and before Goering destroys the enemy at Dunkirk, as he has been bragging he will do. Meteorological reports are favorable. Rain and fog are expected to continue for the next three or four days and," he nodded at the window "we can see that they may be right, for once. An Abwehr naval commander will be on the ship to brief the men.

"It's all very simple. The men will land in a country surrounded by water, among frightened civilians manning roadblocks, proceed sixty or seventy miles and attack an important factory and an equally important airfield, then simply drive to the seashore, to be brought out to a waiting U-boat, which will surface if it can find a spot not occupied by the British navy."

"This is hardly the time for sarcasm, Herr General. It certainly won't help the men if they sense your lack of confidence in their chances."

Kellner looked at the colonel calmly. "Perhaps you're right. We are committed, so I guess I should make the best of it."

"What are our personal orders, Herr General?"

"We're to fly to Berlin as soon as they leave. I'll see to it that you have ample time to handle our particular problem with the sergeant. And, Heinz, please don't think me so naive as to believe that your plans are confined to Siegler's team alone. Obviously they will all have to be compromised. I regret it, but I'm forced to face the need. Wasn't it Nietzsche who said: 'Man must become better and more evil.' "

"I'm quite certain Hitler will see to it that we succeed in doing just that."

"We obviously need no help from Hitler," the general said.

Willi Siegler was wide awake. He turned restlessly and heard the regular breathing of Dietrich and Schiller, asleep on their cots across the room. He looked at his watch, then shut his eyes in another attempt at sleep as he reflected on the general's briefing. The Dutch ship, *Van Hoorn*, flying the British flag, would leave a protected anchorage a few miles south of Boulogne and proceed to a position outside the harbor entrance. The special force would be taken out to the ship on an MTB. What happened after that was apparently up to the ship's captain.

What they were told of the escape arrangements seemed acceptable to Siegler, particularly when it was confirmed that a car would be waiting for him at Eastleigh. Siegler watched the rain strike the window.

A short while later he rose from the cot and decided to explore the huge building. He opened the door quietly and stepped out into the deserted hallway. There were no guards in the casino. Even the kitchen workers had been withdrawn after preparing the evening meal to assure the complete isolation of the storm troopers.

Siegler prowled casually along dark, spacious corridors, looking into each room he passed. What was obviously a reading room didn't hold his attention. He moved along the hall and entered a large, mirrored salon, where he stood looking out of one of its many windows at the sea. It was then he heard voices, faint and muffled. He opened the window fully and leaned out. At first he was unable to tell where the sounds were coming from, but finally, by concentrating all his attention, he decided they came from the long terrace jutting out above him. He recognized General Kellner's voice and knew that he must be speaking to von Maussner. Siegler smiled. Listening to another unguarded conversation seemed to be a profitable way to spend an otherwise monotonous evening. He might even get some clue to the identities of the "others" they had spoken about at the base.

He left the mirrored salon and retraced his way along the dark corridor to the stairway. At its top, he paused to orient himself and then walked silently down a corridor similar to the one on the floor below. He stopped at the first door and opened it slowly. The voices were louder now but still too muffled to understand. Siegler eased his way into the darkened room. Far down its considerable length he saw a large, glass-paneled door standing open, leading to the terrace that ran the length of the long rectangular room facing the sea. Its size made it obvious that it was a formal ballroom, and many similar doors led to the seaward terrace. Siegler opened one of them and silently moved outside. He flattened himself against the damp outer wall. The General and von Maussner were in earnest conversation no more than thirty feet from where he stood.

The westerly wind pushed miniature breakers onto the barely visible beach at the edge of the casino grounds. The rain had stopped, but Siegler was momentarily startled when a single raindrop struck his cheek as he edged closer to the two officers. They stood looking out over the water as they talked, and Siegler could now hear their voices clearly.

"Hitler's hesitation about war with England was certainly expressed in *Mein Kampf*," Kellner was saying. "Behind us, on the ramparts of the upper city, Napoleon contemplated our unseen enemy with much the same thought. Are you familiar with the museum here, Heinz?"

"No, Herr General," von Maussner answered.

"A plaque on its main staircase rather presumptuously states 'France and England, well united, could defy all the world.' When France has been fully defeated, will England attempt to stand alone?"

"We'll know soon enough, Herr General. Man for man, our army is the best in the world," von Maussner said. "But the last war proved that time can be the most important ally of our enemies."

"Very true," Kellner replied. Both men stared out into the darkness for some time. Von Maussner wasn't aware that the general looked over at him nervously from time to time. He turned only when the general spoke again. "I'm sorry that I won't be in Berlin to hear of the success of this mission. I would have liked to be there to hear the end of *all* our problems, but I trust that you will keep me informed."

"You won't be in Berlin? I don't quite follow you, Herr General."

Sergeant Siegler, who had begun to get bored with the conversation and was starting to move cautiously back to the door leading to the ballroom, listended with a new intensity.

"It would seem the Führer is pleased with my handling of his pet mission. As a reward, he's sending me to Rome." Kellner said.

"You didn't mention that earlier, Herr General. I thought you said our orders were to proceed to Berlin?"

"And so we shall. But I'm to leave shortly after we arrive. To be frank, I don't report all of my private business in detail . . . even to friends."

"Of course, Herr General."

"Come now, Heinz. Spare me your anger. I should think you would be delighted to have me out of Berlin. You certainly haven't hesitated to point out my shortcomings recently."

"How long will you remain in Rome?'" von Maussner asked.

"I don't know. Mussolini has been watching our sweep across France with understandable envy and has just about convinced himself he's ready to join us. I'm to be part of a delegation to help him make up his mind."

"I'm afraid that Hitler may find the Italians to be more of a liability than an asset," von Maussner said.

"Most likely," Kellner agreed. "But the tactical advantages make Hitler feel otherwise. Spending some time in Rome is hardly a distasteful assignment for me. I'm always quite happy there. There is also the comforting thought that neutral Switzerland is somewhat easier to get to from Rome than Berlin." He saw the look on von Maussner's face and was quick to add, "Come now, Heinz, I was joking. I have neither the intention, nor the ability, to clamber about on the Alps."

Neither von Maussner—nor the eavesdropper—believed the general had been joking.

Sergeant Siegler didn't wait to hear more. He reentered the ballroom, made his way to the corridor, and went quickly down the stairs to his room. When he was convinced that both Dietrich and Schiller were still sleeping soundly, he moved to the chair where he had hung his uniform jacket. He felt for and removed the Enfield pistol from its holster. Picking up a towel, he made his way silently to the door and retraced his steps to the ballroom and the terrace.

General Kellner was standing alone, leaning on the balustrade and looking contentedly out at the sea. Good, thought Siegler. Two of them, and I would have had to shoot. He held the revolver by its barrel and placed a steadying finger through the reversed trigger guard, then wrapped his hand in the towel.

Widely spaced raindrops began to strike the terrace, and General Kellner decided that he had had enough sea air for one evening. He yawned, and as he turned to enter the ballroom, he saw Sergeant Siegler bearing down on him. He opened his mouth, but no sound would come. He stood frozen with fright as the towel wrapped pistol descended. The last image that registered on his brain was the look of intense hatred on Siegler's face. He fell heavily.

Siegler quickly pushed the pistol into his belt and wrapped the towel around the general's head. He felt for a pulse and found none, but he couldn't be sure. He rolled the body over, placed his hands under the chin and twisted the head backward violently. The sharp crack as the neck broke was astoundingly loud. Siegler stood up and looked carefully over the balustrade at the stone promenade below. He saw no sentries and heard nothing but the moan of the wind. He pulled the body upright, removing the towel as he did so. Finally, the head, arms, and upper body were hanging over the balustrade. He reached down, grasped the legs and slowly forced the body over the stone railing.

There was no outcry after the body struck the ground, only the sound of the wind and the sea rolling up on the beach some few hundred yards away. Siegler picked up the towel and began to look for bloodstains. He abandoned the search as heavier rain began to blow onto the terrace, knowing that it would remove all traces, and went quickly through the ballroom. The corridor was quiet, and there were no sounds of activity on the floor below.

Once on the lower floor, he moved stealthily to the boxes of personal belongings still piled up at the end of the hallway, and opened one carefully after checking to make certain that it wasn't his own. He removed the neatly folded uniform, placed the bloodstained towel at the bottom of the box, replaced the uniform, and resealed the lid. It was the one place they would be unlikely to search. But if they do, Siegler thought with a smile, Knoedler would have some explaining to do.

Minutes later he was back in his room. He replaced the Enfield in its holster, removed his shirt and pants—relieved to find they were hardly damp—and hung them up carefully. He pushed his shoes well under the cot, after checking them thoroughly. Satisfied with his precautions, he lay down and pulled the blanket up. It wasn't long before Willi Siegler was asleep.

Colonel von Maussner listened to the Abwehr officer question the sentry who had been on duty at the southeastern corner of the promenade when the general had died. The frightened man lied well. Actually, the intermittent rain had driven him from his quiet post to the protection of a room on the lower floor of the building. At first he had stood at the window, watching more for his sergeant than possible intruders. But finally an overwhelming desire to smoke had caused him to move to an inner door to the dark corridor of the hallway. If the sergeant should find him, he would simply say he had heard a noise and. . . .

He hadn't heard the general's body hit the stone promenade and didn't discover him for twenty minutes, when he had decided that it was time to get back outside.

"Tell us again, Heiss." Colonel Bruning said.

A general! God! the sentry thought as he forced himself to relax. "I was walking my post, Herr Colonel, when I looked up and saw the general leaning over the railing. He seemed to be looking at the quay. I turned to look, too. The next thing I knew, he hit the ground. It happened so fast—one minute he was up there, and the next, he was lying on the ground, I ran over to him. I could see his neck was broken—it was twisted—I knew he was dead, so I ran and got the sergeant."

"Was the general alone when you saw him leaning over the railing?"

"Yes, Herr Colonel."

"He made no outcry, before or as he fell?"

"No, Herr Colonel."

"Is it possible he jumped rather than fell?"

"I don't know. He seemed to be looking at something, and he was leaning out pretty far."

"The general was a rather heavy man. How could he lean out far enough to fall over a waist high railing?"

"Whatever he was doing, it looked dangerous to me, Herr Colonel. He was hanging over, far out . . . " The private paused, knowing he was overdoing it.

"And you're quite certain that he was alone?" Bruning persisted.

The sentry glanced briefly at von Maussner, glad that he had been alert earlier. "I saw this officer talking to the general, but he left long before the general fell."

Colonel Bruning looked at von Maussner with some embarrassment. "Forgive me, Colonel, but I'm sure you understand the reason for my question." Von Maussner nodded briefly, and Bruning said to the sentry, "So, the general was alone, and made no outcry."

"He didn't make a sound, Herr Colonel."

"Very well, Heiss. It would seem that it was an unfortunate accident," Bruning said, then turned to von Maussner. "Is there anything you would like to ask?"

"One or two things, thank you, Colonel," von Maussner focussed his attention on the uncomfortable private. "Is there any way for any unauthorized person, or persons, to enter this building from the outside?"

"None that I know of, Herr Colonel."

Colonel Bruning seemed annoyed. "This building was searched thoroughly just before you and your men arrived, again this morning, and again this evening just before my men were withdrawn—at your request—for the night. We are as safe here as if we were in the Chancellory, I assure you, Colonel."

"And yet this man seems to be our only witness to what happened," von Maussner said.

"There is no possible access to this building except from the sea, and the beach is more than adequately patrolled. The northern and southern perimeters are blocked by high fences, guarded by men chosen by Admiral Canaris himself and backed up by armored cars, constantly on the move."

Von Maussner looked at the private closely. "How long had you been on duty before the general fell?"

"Nearly three hours, Herr Colonel."

"What are the limits of your post?"

"From the west end of the wing to the center door, Herr Colonel."

"You said the general seemed to be looking at something on the quay?"

"He was looking at something, Herr Colonel."

"Not on the quay. How could he see it? The wing of the building completely obscures the quay from the terrace. If the general was leaning out over the railing, he must have been looking at something in the wing. And yet, that section of the building is damaged and sealed. What could have been so interesting there to have caused him to lean out far enough to fall?"

"I don't know, Herr Colonel."

"You said you had been on duty for nearly three hours walking your post. I was informed shortly after you reported the general's death. I went to the room where you and your sergeant had carried him. I then went outside to inspect the promenade and remained there for perhaps five minutes. It has been raining, rather heavily at times, for at least four or five hours. Why is it that your uniform seems comparatively dry?"

Private Heiss tried to hide the shock he felt. "My uniform, Herr Colonel?" he said, playing for time.

"Why is it that you've been outside in the rain for nearly three hours and are drier than I am?"

Frightened, the private didn't stop to think. "I stood in the doorways when it was raining, Herr Colonel."

The soldier's guilty sincerity disarmed von Maussner only momentarily. "I see. Precisely where were you standing when the general fell. In which doorway?"

"In the middle of the wing. That's why I could see him."

"And when you saw him fall.... Wait now, didn't you say you turned to look where he was looking? How could you have done that if you were standing in a doorway?"

"I—"

"Did you run over to him immediately, when you saw him fall?"

"Yes, Herr Colonel."

"Was it raining at the time?"

The private hesitated, trying to anticipate the trap. "No, Herr Colonel."

"Then why were you standing in a doorway. Why weren't you walking your post?"

"It ... stopped. It was raining hard, then it stopped, and the general fell."

"So, General Kellner was looking at something, leaning dangerously over the balustrade, during a heavy rain? That will be all, Private."

"That will not be all from me, Heiss," Bruning said ominously. "I will speak to you later." He knew as well as von Maussner that the man was lying and was probably asleep in one of the lower rooms when the general had died. He watched the stunned soldier leave the room, then said, "That was neatly done, Colonel. You should be with the Abwehr. I will see to it that Private Heiss gets what's coming to him, but other than the fact that you so deftly proved that one of my men was derelict in his duty, what is it that bothers you? I trust you will not complicate an already sticky situation with suspicions of Frenchmen sneaking past my sentries and calmly throwing the general off that terrace, without a sound. Heiss wasn't the only man patrolling that promenade. I've questioned the others; none of them saw or heard anything unusual, including the officers. I can assure you *they* do not doze off in doorways."

"I'm not questioning your competence, Colonel Bruning. But I couldn't let that man's story stand in view of the obvious inconsistencies."

"I hope you don't equate me with Private Heiss," Bruning said. "As soon as the general's death was reported to me—even as I sent a man to wake you—I had a complete search made of the building. I even checked personally on your men, minutes after the death was reported. All of them were sleeping peacefully."

"You say you checked them personally?"

"I did. Come now, von Maussner, surely you don't suspect your own troopers?"

"Of course not, Colonel. Since they know nothing about this misfortune, I ask you to have your men keep it to themselves. There's nothing to be gained by telling them of the general's death. I want their minds on the mission, not clouded by another accident. Please have the general's body removed from this building immediately, and then, if you will, see if we can get the investigation cleared up tonight."

"I'll give the necessary orders at once."

Von Maussner turned to look at the window. He was frowning as he watched the steady tattoo of the rain against the pane.

It was early morning before Colonel von Maussner was able to return to bed. The terrace had been gone over thoroughly, as were the building and the grounds. Sentries were again interrogated. In the end, they found nothing to indicate that it had been anything but an accident. Von Maussner accompanied the body to the Boulogne morgue and some time later listened to the senior doctor's report with growing suspicion and anger.

"And so, Colonel, I would say the general was dead before he reached the ground. I suppose he could have struck his head on some projection of the building, but, off the record, I think you have enough unanswered questions in this case to order an immediate autopsy."

"Thank you, Doctor, but I've been ordered to return the body to Berlin when I leave. Please have a copy of your official findings ready for me in the morning."

Two hours later, in his room at the casino, von Maussner finally fell into a troubled sleep.

Willi Siegler woke early and waited for the inevitable questioning, but nothing happened. He and the others had breakfast and were then told to return to their rooms. After the midday meal, they were taken outside and allowed to walk in the casino grounds within an isolated area, under the watchful eye of an Abwehr officer. When it began to rain, they were again ordered back to their rooms.

Siegler had watched for any unusual activity in or around the casino but had seen nothing out of the ordinary. The rain had stopped, and occasional shafts of sunlight burst into the room only to disappear abruptly as heavy clouds raced above the building toward the east. Soon his curiosity became impossible to contain. Dietrich and Schiller were napping again when he left the room.

After noting with satisfaction that the personal property boxes had been removed from the hall, Willi Siegler forced himself into a casual posture and strolled through the ground floor, pretending interest in the rooms he inspected. He met no one. Moving to the upper floor, he abandoned his hesitation and went directly to the ballroom. The empty room seemed much larger in the daylight. He crossed it to the door he had used the night before, opened it, and stepped out on the terrace. He was closing the door behind him when he was startled by a familiar voice.

"Doing a bit of exploring, Siegler?" von Maussner said, hiding his own astonishment at the sergeant's sudden appearance. "I should think that you would be taking advantage of the isolation we've provided for you to rest. You'll have little opportunity for it in the next few days."

"I couldn't sleep any longer, Colonel. I thought I'd take a look around."

Von Maussner noted that Siegler's eyes were on the middle of the terrace as he spoke, the spot where he and Kellner had been standing last night. "As long as you're here you may as well join me for a few minutes, Sergeant. Look out there. It's difficult to believe that a few days ago our Stukas sank a French destroyer while it was evacuating enemy troops. Four days, ago, French and British were standing here where we're standing, admiring the same view."

This damned fool is nattering like a bloody tourist guide, Siegler thought. What the hell happened? He moved with what he thought was sufficient indifference to the balustrade. Von Maussner walked with him. He now had no doubt that Siegler had been responsible for the general's death. Guilt and puzzlement were written all over him. Why? Switzerland! That was it, the fool had mentioned Switzerland and this time his unguarded talk had proved fatal. Siegler came through that door with complete familiarity. He'd used it before—last night. Von Maussner couldn't help but be thankful that he had left Kellner when he had. He had no doubt that if he had remained he would have joined the general in his fatal plunge.

The colonel watched Siegler pull his head back almost imperceptibly when he saw the sentries—now increased to four—patrolling the promenade below. Enjoy your victory, von Maussner thought, you have little enough time left to gloat. He forced control into his voice. "Now, Sergeant, you've seen the view, and I have work to do. I want you to return to your room and at least try to rest. Early tomorrow morning we will board the MTB for the trip out to the ship, and it will begin for all of you."

Willi Siegler needed no prodding. He was anxious to get away and think. This one didn't even mention the general. They must think he jumped, and are keeping it quiet. God, what luck, he mused as he turned to leave. But finding it impossible to hide his elation, he faced von Maussner again. "Heil Hitler." he said, smiling happily.

"Heil Hitler," the surprised colonel answered. You impudent bastard, he fumed to himself.

Heavy rain soaked through the thick British uniforms as the men of the special force ran across the Quai Gambetta to the waiting motor torpedo boat. Von Maussner boarded last.

The three-shaft MAN diesels roared powerfully as the eighty-six tons of potential destruction crept past the twin moles of the inner channel entrance and into the outer harbor. After a sudden turn to the right, the MTB steadied for a short time, then executed another sharp turn to the left and passed through the outer harbor entrance into the choppy waters of the English Channel. Once outside, the captain ignored the violence of the rain and ordered the speed increased to an economical twenty-two knots, the bows pointed toward their unseen rendezvous.

No one had spoken to the men of the special force, no one had offered to lead them to shelter. They crouched together on the open deck behind the bridge and clung to any handhold they could find. It was crowded and wet. It seemed to the men that the small ship was under the waves more than over them. The bows struck surging swells, burrowing beneath them and flinging heavy curtains of water over the open decks.

"This thing is a goddamned submarine," Siegler yelled. "Why is he going so fast?"

"This isn't fast for this boat, Willi," Schiller said. "He can make thirty-five knots when he has to."

"Tell him I'll take his word for that," Schemke said unhappily.

"Tell him to stop and let me off," Richter said.

Von Maussner backed down the short ladder from the bridge to the deck and stood above the crouching men. "It won't be long. You can dry out on the *Van Hoorn*. We don't want those uniforms to be too neat, do we? The captain tells me the ship is in position not far ahead."

"Couldn't these madmen let us wait inside, Colonel?" Richter said. "They must have a cabin somewhere on this matchbox."

"A little rain won't hurt you, Richter," von Maussner said, feeling more than a little uncomfortable himself.

"I don't mind the rain, Colonel. I just don't want to throw up all over my nice new English uniform," Richter answered.

The diesel's roar died suddenly, and the MTB slowed. The men crowded to the side of the narrow boat and looked forward. A break in the driving rain allowed them to see the sweep of bows looming above them, and they watched as the pitching torpedo boat was maneuvered skillfully alongside an embarkation ladder that was hanging from the freighter's deck to the water's edge.

"Please get your men off quickly, Herr Colonel." The MTB's captain called over the roar of the idling diesels. He watched impatiently as von Maussner shook hands with each trooper, who then waited for the upward swell before stepping onto the swaying ladder to begin the perilous climb to the freighter's deck. The three tank commanders were the last to leave. Siegler grasped the ladder, then turned to the colonel with a look of confident amusement on his face.

"Goodbye, Colonel. My regards to the general."

"Good luck, Siegler," von Maussner managed to answer calmly.

After appropriate words Schiller followed Siegler up the ladder, and von Maussner said to Dietrich. "So, Lieutenant. From now on it's up to you."

"I'll do my best, Colonel," Dietrich said.

"I've no doubt of that, Walther. Auf wiedersehen."

Dietrich saluted and then climbed the ladder effortlessly.

As soon as the deck was clear, the MTB's diesels roared and the small boat pulled well ahead of the freighter. At a safe distance, the captain slowed and then stopped. They drifted, now safely away from the larger ship.

Von Maussner heard the muffled ring of an engine order telegraph and saw the water begin to churn at the *Van Hoorn*'s stern. The freighter began to move slowly ahead and finally disappeared into the mist and driving rain.

Moments later the MTB leaped forward into a tight turn and raced toward the coast. Colonel von Maussner, oblivious to the discomfort of his rain-soaked, once impeccable uniform, turned to stare at the churning wake impatiently, his thoughts on Berlin and Sergeant Siegler.

Book Two

CHAPTER 12

In London, on Wednesday, 29 May 1940—the afternoon of the third day of the evacuation from France—Brigadier General Viscount Arthur Fox interrupted his intent discussion with the young major seated opposite him and showed obvious exasperation at the gentle knock, and subsequent entrance, of a Wren officer:

"What is it, Connor?" he asked, dropping his pen to the cluttered table.

The girl ignored the scowl bravely. "I'm sorry to interrupt, Lord Fox, but this dispatch was just delivered. It's marked urgent, I thought that you would want me to bring it in at once." She felt on safe ground, knowing that the tall, sandy haired, ruddy-faced brigadier was not the ogre he attempted to make his subordinates believe he was. But she also knew, from his present expression, that it was best she not tempt disillusionment. She handed him the envelope and turned to leave.

Brigadier Fox smiled. "Thank you, Connor. I didn't mean to growl."

The girl looked back at him, her confidence justified: "You're welcome, sir," she answered with more than the trace of a brogue and closed the door quietly behind her.

The brigadier grunted briefly and removed the seal of the envelope. He spent some time studying its contents. When he had finished, he removed his glasses and spoke to the young officer.

"This is the latest, Edward. So far we've managed to remove 72,783 men."

"That is good news, sir," Major Edward Fitzroy answered.

Brigadier Fox agreed. "Remarkably, the Eastern mole is still undamaged, but they have had to switch embarkation to the open beaches temporarily. Jerry is pounding the beaches too, but sand apparently lessens the effects of shells and bombs, so we're managing."

"Anything on ship losses, sir?"

Brigadier Fox referred to the dispatch: "Not too good there, I'm afraid. Goering seems to be throwing his entire airforce at us over there. I imagine he's unhappy to find that the RAF is making that an expensive decision indeed. The destroyer chaps are taking it on the chin since they've been in the thick of it from the beginning, but they're helping to give us the time we need."

"How long can the Dunkirk defenses hold, sir?"

Fox stroked his neatly trimmed mustache thoughtfully. "It's difficult to say from what I have here. I expect that we shall learn more about it this afternoon. Plenty of shelling, infantry attacks, and that damnable Luftwaffe. Still, General Brooke seems to have the retreat situation in hand. I can't understand why the Germans held up their tank attacks when they did, but it was damned fortunate for us, whatever the reason." He paused, pointing to a well-marked map of France. "They were already within medium gun range of Dunkirk, but they simply stopped their armored advance when they might have overwhelmed our defenses in a matter of hours. The Germans are methodical fellows, and usually have reasons for whatever they do. But, with luck, they've given us the time to extricate our army before they spring whatever it is they've planned."

"We've made a good start, sir."

"Yes, with God's help, the British navy, and our civilian sailors."

Major Fitzroy leaned forward, hesitated, then spoke. "May I speak frankly, sir?"

"Of course, Edward."

"My yacht, sir. I'm certain you'll agree that the *Seraph* could help with the job at hand. Unfortunately she's still in Hamble."

"In Hamble? She's just what Ramsay is looking for. Can't you get someone to take her out?"

"I'd like to take her myself, sir."

"I see." The brigadier shook his head negatively. "Sorry. I know you would, but I'm afraid I can't spare you just now."

"I understand, sir. Still . . ."

"I know what you're thinking, my boy. You're impatient. A bit uncomfortable with the fate that made you an aide to an old general while other young men are in the thick of the fighting. I understand and even sympathize with your feelings, but we have important work to do here. You'll get your chance. Hitler will see to that. Surely there are men in Hamble who can man the *Seraph*."

"Under normal circumstances, but I'm afraid she's not quite ready. The auxiliary's dismantled. That's why she's not at Dover now."

"How long would it take to get it reassembled?" the brigadier asked, seeing the young man's disappointment.

Fitzroy shook his head in frustration: "I had it pretty well stripped down. She could run under sail, but that's not much use in this case, is it, sir?"

"No, my boy. This is hardly the time to be sailing to France. It is being done, but the losses are unacceptably large for vessels without power . . . and hardly fair to the troops they pick up."

"I guess that's so, sir. It seems a damned shame though. A forty-five foot yawl, with her beam and stability, could carry quite a few men. Elizabeth will be disappointed too. We were trying damned hard to get it in shape. I imagine she's working at it even now."

"Working at it? Is Elizabeth still at Hamble?" Fox was surprised.

"Yes, sir. When this Dunkirk business began, and I was recalled, I had no time to help close the house. She's staying on for a few days to do it herself."

"I'm sorry we had to interrupt your leave, Edward. Elizabeth is a lovely girl, and I've always been terribly sorry that my brother didn't live long enough to see her married to you. I can only say that he would have approved as I do." The brigadier paused, somewhat embarrassed by his expression of sentiment. "When did you ring her last?" he asked.

"Early this morning, sir."

"I take it you discussed the evacuation?"

"Only in passing, sir."

"I'm sure you're aware that Elizabeth can be rather headstrong at times." The brigadier rose abruptly and walked to the door. "Connor, please ring Major Fitzroy's wife. The Hamble number. Put it through in here." He began to pace the room and didn't notice the faint smile on the major's face.

The connection was made quickly.

"Is that you, Elizabeth?" the brigadier said. "How are you? Yes, I'm well, dear. Edward is fine. He and I are going down to Dover this afternoon." There was a pause while the brigadier listened, and then looked over at Fitzroy knowingly. "The *Seraph*? No, dear, I don't think we'll be able to use her. Yes, I know how you feel, Elizabeth, but I'm afraid the *Seraph* will have to remain out of it. No foolishness, dear, the navy will handle it. Good. Not another word then. I have some news that will please you. When our business in Dover is finished, I can spare Edward enough time to see you back to London. Possibly tomorrow. I'll have him ring you. Please make sure that you are ready, will you? I won't be able to spare him for more than one night, but it's the least I can do for interrupting his leave. Yes, my dear? Am I? Well thank you. Goodbye." He replaced the receiver, reddening slightly. "It isn't every day that a general is told that he's a perfect lamb," he said to the major, smiling.

Fitzroy laughed: "I don't imagine it is, sir."

"Forgive me for butting in, Edward, but since the death of my brother, the suddenly meddlesome Uncle has become used to acting like a Father. I seem to have forgotten that she's quite grown up."

"Elizabeth loves you very much, sir." Fitzroy hesitated, then continued, "She wanted to tell you herself, but we're going to have a child. I don't think you need worry about her attempting a trip to France."

"What marvelous news." The brigadier beamed. "When, Edward?"

"Early January, I should think. We've just learned of it ourselves."

Brigadier Fox dropped his pen and leaned back in his chair. "I shall show appropriate surprise when she tells me herself. I shan't tell anyone, not even Lady Fox. I think we can leave the rest of this paperwork for the time being. Time enough for it on the train." He looked down at the large pocket watch lying near his hand. "I must be off to my appointment at Admiralty House. We'll meet at my club at one. Yes, I think that we may even have a small bottle of wine with lunch. Your news seems to demand it. A child . . . marvelous!"

Elizabeth Fitzroy studied her reflection in the mirror that hung above the telephone table as she spoke to her uncle. It wasn't vanity that made her pleased with what she saw. She accepted her beauty as a fortunate gift and had never allowed ego to override her warm, friendly personality. While brushing an errant wisp of blond hair back from her forehead, she studied the reflected face: blue eyes, the nose perfect above a mouth that a hopeful suitor had once described as sensual. She assumed her schoolgirl *femme fatale* pose while suppressing a laugh. Her Uncle Arthur was being so serious. He's such a darling, she thought. He actually thinks I might try to take the *Seraph* over to France. Under other circumstances I think I might have tried, but now I wouldn't dream of it. As she talked she moved away from the table to the limit of the telephone cord, turned sideways and stood on tiptoes to study the profile of her well-formed body in the mirror, searching for any visible signs of her pregnancy. No, nothing yet, she decided.

Her uncle had not only taken the place of her dead father but had been responsible for her present happiness. Poor old dear, she reflected, while remembering how angry she had been with him when her mother had told her that he was bringing his new aide to dinner. She resented being manipulated. At twenty she was hardly the age to be considered under the cloud of possible spinsterhood, yet since she had returned from school she soon began to resent the seemingly endless parade of pale young men herded before her by her mother, and now her uncle seemed to be joining in. On the night of the dinner she prepared herself to be civil.

When her uncle had come into the room, followed by Edward

Fitzroy, she had looked up resignedly with every expectation of disappointment. She looked into the young officer's eyes and found that she was far from disappointed. It was remarkable that a man with all of the prerequisites necessary to suit her mother should also be tall, almost handsome, palpably masculine, and as completely at ease with her as she immediately felt with him.

During dinner she had managed to remove her concentration from the young man and glance at her uncle and her mother fondly. She saw her uncle's puzzled smile and realized that it hadn't been a contrived meeting. He was as surprised as she was at the intensity of their attraction.

Eight months later, she and Edward Fitzroy were married.

When her uncle said goodbye, Elizabeth hung up the receiver, straightened the mirror needlessly, and then crossed the room to sit in one of the large wing chairs near the fireplace. She studied the comfortable room and remembered the evening that she and Edward had sat together in the same chair, reassured by the headline of the *Southern Echo*: "Germans held in check at Sedan."

Now, only thirteen days after that reassuring headline had appeared, the British army was evacuating France, many of them in vessels no larger than the *Seraph*. It seemed unbelievable.

"Some tea for you, my girl," she said aloud, "then we've work to do." She left the parlor and busied herself in the kitchen while the kettle boiled. After she poured her tea, she moved to the window and looked out at the quiet blue of the Hamble River and was comforted by the familiar view.

The train exited suddenly from the tunnel through the coastal cliffs into the Dover harbor area, and stopped. Brigadier Fox attempted to concentrate on his papers while they waited nearly ten minutes as another train, crowded with troops, crept past on the London-bound track. When it had passed, they began to move slowly ahead along the curving approach to the marine station, an imposing structure rising on the Admiralty pier, directly alongside the inner harbor.

During the approach to the station, Brigadier Fox and the major moved out of their compartment into the narrow aisle and stood looking out at the feverish activity on the countless ships lining the piers, moored two or three abreast. The two men watched in stunned silence until the train moved beneath high arches into the station proper.

Brigadier Fox and Major Fitzroy stepped off the train into an incredible mass of remarkably orderly men, who were already beginning to line up to board the train the two officers had just left. The brigadier paused occasionally to speak to groups of soldiers—many blanket-covered, still wet from the crossing and the ordeal of the beaches of Dunkirk—as they drank tea and waited as calmly as they waited on the beaches. Groups of French, somewhat less sanguine than the British, stood together with their interpreters, uncomfortable, but visibly relieved.

An armed lieutenant, followed closely by two alert military policemen, approached the brigadier and politely asked for identification. He complied instantly. At a nod from the brigadier, Major Fitzroy allowed a thorough inspection of the bulky briefcase he was carrying and then presented his own papers. The lieutenant apologized. "Sorry to subject you to this, sir. Orders, I'm afraid."

"No such thing as being too careful, Lieutenant," the brigadier replied.

"May I help you, sir? Is there someone in particular you wish to see?"

"No, Lieutenant. We're expected by Admiral Ramsay, but I wanted to see something of this operation for myself before proceeding to Dover castle. Now I can see that you have quite enough on your hands without the added interruption of uninvited visitors. Our car will be waiting at the pier gate. Perhaps you would be good enough to have someone accompany us there. Save extra work for your security men, I daresay."

"We *are* a bit jammed up here, sir. Two more destroyers will tie up alongside at any moment, one rather badly damaged, quite a few dead. If you and the major will excuse me, I'll arrange for an escort to the gate."

By late afternoon the initial conference was over. Major Fitzroy, waiting for the brigadier in Admiral Ramsay's room, stood looking out of the castle window at the ships lined up alongside the Admiralty pier. The sky was angry and seething. Mist flowed around the upstretched arms of huge dock cranes. Fitzroy's eyes moved past the outer entrance into the Straits where patrolling destroyers cleaved the water, bow waves white in the growing darkness. A light rain struck the window. As Fitzroy watched, a sudden gust blew a wall of heavier rain inexorably across the inner harbor, momentarily obscuring the clock tower at the landward end of the Prince of Wales pier.

A door behind him closed abruptly. Fitzroy turned to find Brigadier Fox walking toward him, his expression grim. He joined the major at the window. "Thank God for the rain, Edward. Thankfully, it's even worse over there." He gestured at the unseen coast of France. "It will be a busy night in this harbor. Unfortunately, Admiral Ramsay now feels that we may soon have to halt rescue operations at Dunkirk."

"Does that mean we may have to abandon half our men, sir?"

"No decision has been made yet, but as it stands now, more than half. There are thousands of French manning the perimeters with our troops. With luck, this weather will alter the circumstances. Let us earnestly pray that the rain continues. Some time this evening General Brooke will be evacuated from France by destroyer. Ramsay hopes to get a firsthand account of the situation over there from him early tomorrow morning. I shall need you here with me until General Brooke arrives, and during the morning conference. Then you can take the afternoon train to Hamble. You and Elizabeth can spend the night there and take the morning train to London."

"This doesn't seem quite the time for personal leave, sir," Fitzroy protested.

"There's nothing you can do for the men in France, Edward. That job belongs to the navy and air force. Our turn will come soon enough. If the Germans overrun the rest of France as easily as they seem to have done in the north, then we may be in for a rather nasty time, so take advantage of this opportunity. I can spare you until Saturday afternoon, no longer."

"Thank you. I . . ."

"When you've finished calling your wife, please join me in Admiral Ramsay's office. I have some notes I'd like you to unscramble."

Major Fitzroy sat down at the desk and watched fondly as the brigadier closed the door to the inner office. He had always felt somewhat uncomfortable being an aide to a close relation. The possible inference of nepotism by others had been bearable since his appointment as aide had taken place nearly a year before his marriage. Now, with the country at war, he was certain that the brigadier had also begun to feel a bit uncomfortable with the arrangement and was becoming more receptive to his requests for transfer to active duty. A sudden gust of rain struck the window, rattling the pane angrily and bringing him out of his brief reverie. He picked up the telephone and placed his call to Hamble.

Elizabeth hummed softly as she packed the guest linen into cardboard containers. She had begun the task somberly that morning, but since the telephone call from her husband, confirming his arrival on Friday night, even thoughts of the uncertain future hadn't been able to dampen her good humor. The brief rapping of the front door knocker interrupted her concentration. She dropped the blanket she had been folding and hurried down the stairs.

Her smile was one of recognition when she opened the door. An elderly man stood outside, ramrod straight, ruddy complexioned. He removed his hat, exposing full, white hair that matched the neat mustache and well-trimmed beard. On his sleeve he wore an armband bearing the letters LDV.

"Good afternoon, Mr. Peters," Elizabeth said.

The old man bowed slightly. "Afternoon, Ma'am. Sorry to bother you, but would you mind if I inspected your air raid precautions? Sand, water buckets, curtains, and such. Being on the river as you are, the blackout is doubly important."

"Please come in," Elizabeth answered. "Would you like some tea?"

"No thank you, Ma'am. If you don't mind I'll just look things over and be on my way. There are four more stops I have to make before I go back on duty. Truth is, this isn't really my job. I'm with the LDV, and feel more at home with a shotgun than a torch, but so many folks here have been evacuated, or moved north, the wardens are having trouble keeping up with the home checks. I thought I'd give them a hand."

"I can imagine how difficult it is for you," Elizabeth said.

"Glad to do it. I'm sorry to hear that you and the major are leaving too, but it's best, I imagine. With the major away, this house is a bit isolated for a young woman alone."

"I'm afraid so, Mr. Peters."

"Won't be long before you're back. Well then, with your permission, I'll get on with it. Will it be all right if I start with the parlor?"

"Yes, certainly."

He followed her into the comfortable room and began a careful inspection of the blackout curtains. "Something here, Ma'am. This little table being so close to the window might just interfere with the curtain. Would you mind if I moved it back a bit?"

Elizabeth led him through the rest of the house. His inspection was quick and thorough. Elizabeth felt a great affection for the old man, glad that the war had given him a new sense of purpose. There had been many times when she had stopped to speak to him and his wife as they sat on the promenade overlooking the Hamble River, accepting the retirement years with pleasant resignation. The challenge of war had changed that, and she was proud of the race that had produced men of such adaptability. When he had finished his inspection, she led him back down the stairs, saying, "Are you sure that you won't have some tea, Mr. Peters?"

"No, thank you, Ma'am. I should be getting on. Oh yes, the list shows that you'll be leaving on Saturday?"

"Yes. I'm not quite certain when, but my husband will be here tomorrow evening if there's something you need to speak to him about."

"No, Ma'am, just give him this please." He handed her a carefully folded paper. "New regulations. I don't want to be a bother, but when a house is unoccupied there are a few rules: Water, gas, and electricity turned off, curtains left open, and the telephone disconnected. Please give my respects to the major and tell him if he hasn't the time to see to all of that, I'll be glad to do it. And don't you worry, I'll be keeping an eye on this house personally until you and the major return." He saw Elizabeth's smile and knew that its warmth was genuine. "I'll say goodbye then, Ma'am. All my best to you and the major."

"Thank you, Mr. Peters. I love this house, and shall feel ever so much better knowing that you'll be watching over it."

The elderly man gave her a half salute, and walked over to a bicycle resting against the house. Elizabeth watched as he removed the gas mask container from the handlebars, placed it over his shoulder, and rode steadily down the driveway.

Chapter 13

From the confining deck of the MTB the freighter had seemed huge and undamaged. It wasn't until the men of the special force had climbed aboard that they were able to see some of what had been done to the ship to prepare her for the voyage to England.

The 3,000-ton, shallow draft *Van Hoorn* was slightly more than 325 feet long, had been carefully maintained by her former owners, and was just entering her third decade of service when illegally interned two weeks before the invasion of the Low Countries. Now the German soldiers saw that little of her upper deck—at least what was visible to them in the disorienting darkness—seemed to remain untouched. It was riddled with ragged holes blown through the planking into the thick deck plate beneath, exposing glimpses of emptiness below.

The men had been stopped at the top of the embarkation ladder by a working party, one of whom introduced himself in excellent English: "Welcome aboard. I am Commander Loesner and have been attached to this vessel by Admiral Canaris to serve as your briefing officer. But I have also been asked by our captain to take charge of this working party, so you men will have to wait here until I see that the ladder is secured."

The commander turned away to give unintelligible orders to the smoke-stained, unshaven, and generally disreputable-looking work crew. But any doubts that the storm troopers may have had were erased by the efficiency of the obviously well-trained sailors. The embarkation ladder was raised quickly and carried forward by two men, while others replaced the open section of life railing. Moments later their attention was diverted by a muffled roar out in the darkness as the MTB's engines throbbed to full power. The troopers heard, rather than saw, their last link with France as it moved away into the rain. Sergeant Siegler was the last to turn away from the sound.

They felt the hull shudder as the *Van Hoorn* began to turn and pick up speed. As the freighter settled on its new course, a horizontal, wind-driven torrent struck them with its earlier intensity, racing down the narrow, exposed deck between the superstructure and the rail. The ship's crew paid no attention to it. When the commander completed his inspection of the rail he dismissed the work detail and turned to the special force. The storm troopers fell in behind him as he beckoned for them to follow.

Above decks, the *Van Hoorn* was divided symmetrically into thirds: the forward section was an open cargo deck, over which an upright boom towered. Just behind the open deck, the centercastle rose three cabin decks, and above them, the bridge and funnel. The after section was like the forward, open, with another cargo boom jutting above it.

Commander Loesner led them to a ladder at the after end of the centercastle. As they climbed, Dietrich looked back at the stern. The imposing cargo boom reached up into the low fog racing past its projecting spars, creating an illusion of incredible speed. Beneath the boom lay a vague shape covered with tarpaulins lashed efficiently to the deck. They climbed a second ladder to the next deck level, and the motion of the ship became more noticeable.

At the top cabin level, they again moved forward and up a final ladder to the bridge. Loesner ushered them into the wheelhouse, which ran across the entire width of the centercastle and seemed comfortably large. In the center of the bridge, dim green light was reflected from a large compass onto the face of the helmsman. Behind him, along the after bulkhead, a few weak red instrument lights appeared and disappeared as figures moved busily in front of them.

Commander Loesner directed the soldiers to an unoccupied corner where they stood dripping on the steel deck.

"Welcome aboard, gentlemen."

They turned in the direction of the deep voice to find a large man looming in front of them who was as disreputable looking as the rest of the crew. "I am Captain Brinker. Hans Brinker, but despite the name, I skate rather badly," he said pleasantly in German and laughed boomingly. "I'm afraid that this ship is not the *Europa* by any means, but at least you won't have to dress for dinner." Again his laugh echoed in the enclosure. "Come now, gentlemen, don't look so glum. The damage that you have apparently noticed as you came up here was done deliberately, and carefully, and in no way interferes with the operation of this vessel." He studied the soldiers for a moment, then continued. "I asked Commander Loesner to bring all of you here so that I could take what may be my only opportunity to wish you luck in your enterprise. I will be kept busy until we arrive. Now, Commander, please take the men below and get them settled in. The officers will remain here. I will only keep them a short while."

When the men had gone, Captain Brinker directed Dietrich, Schiller, and Siegler into a chart room located behind the wheelhouse. "Gather 'round here," he said, pausing by a chart table.

They looked down at the chart expectantly and saw the single, erratic line penciled on it that led to their destination. The name was clearly visible: Newhaven, approximately seventy miles from their targets. Captain Brinker directed their attention along the pencil line with a substantial finger: "Here—Boulogne. Our present course, almost due west." The finger moved. "Here—we turn north, preceded by minesweepers, around Cape Gris Nez, then northest to Calais, keeping as close to the French coast as possible. From Calais, we will proceed to a point below the sandbanks off Gravelines, where we will wait for a while behind some very convenient wrecks to confuse the British radio direction finders. We are not yet certain of their range and can't be sure that they aren't taking interest in a ship moving into the Straits after having proceeded from an occupied port. Our wait will hopefully cause them to transfer their interest elsewhere, and in the north we will be just another ship among many. At dawn we will move into the southern route around the sandbars. Most British captains have learned to stay away from Gravelines, since the route leads them within range of our coastal guns at Calais, and Gravelines itself. Some still try it at first light. We will join the more adventurous, slip out and hopefully cross their picket lines . . . about here."

"Why wait for dawn, Captain?" Siegler asked. "A night like this should provide good cover."

"For a very good reason. At first light our air force will be above us to keep occupied anyone who might become too interested in us. The Luftwaffe plays an important part in our deception. They will waste quite a few very expensive bombs in apparent attempts to sink us. They will miss, but they will not miss anyone endangering us. Also, it will be comforting to be able to see any mines we might come upon. The Channel is full of them, to say nothing of spent torpedoes and floating wrecks. And most important, we will rendezvous with seven submarines in the deep water southwest of Gravelines. They'll need light to take over our protection, particularly if this weather doesn't clear and the air force is unable to fly."

"Why so many U-boats, Captain?" Dietrich questioned.

"The submarines will perform a dual function. Protection for this ship on the way over and back, and then as the vehicles of your escape from England."

"How do we get to the U-boats after we've finished, Captain?"

"Commander Loesner will go over that with you." Brinker opened a drawer in the chart table and removed another chart. "This is Newhaven harbor," he said as he spread it open. "I will dock here, as close to the harbor entrance as possible. Reconnaissance tells us that these docks were empty as of sunset tonight. Let us hope they stay that way. The first two tanks are beneath the booms, ready to be unloaded immediately, and should be down before the English can begin to question us. The third is in the after hold, but will be ready to lift as soon as the one on deck is down. My crew has been vigorously trained, and their time for unloading this particular cargo is rather remarkable. So, within minutes you and your machines should be on the pier, and you will be on your own. We all know what's happening at Dunkirk. The English can't be removing many tanks from France, so our arrival might be something of an event. I will attempt to leave before the port authorities descend on me."

"They're going to look us over closely if you do that, Captain," Dietrich said, uneasily.

"Your credentials are as close to perfect as could be managed, as are mine. If they should manage to stop me, my actions will be put down to the impatient act of a headstrong Dutchman. Believe me, the eventuality has been explored, and no matter what should happen, you and your men will not be endangered."

"You're going to have to turn around to get out, Captain," Schiller said. "I'm no sailor, but it looks damned narrow on that chart."

"I don't intend to turn. I'm going to back out."

"Back out? That should be something to see," Siegler said.

"I wouldn't wait to watch, if I were you. I would advise you to get out of the port area as quickly as you can. Now, come with me, gentlemen." They moved out of the chart room and followed the captain along a narrow passage leading to a surprisingly spacious sea cabin. "Come in and sit down anywhere. Don't mind your wet clothes." Brinker closed the door, drew a curtain across it, and switched on a bulkhead light. Both portholes were sealed by heavy deadlights. "Forgive me for staring, gentlemen. It isn't often that I get to entertain three enemy officers in my quarters."

He went to a safe built into the bulkhead above a small desk, twirled the dial expertly and soon had it open. He removed an envelope and placed it on the desk. "This is for the officer in command. Take it when you leave, and open it in the presence of the commander." His hand disappeared into the safe and then reappeared holding a bottle. "From the look of you, I imagine that you can use a drink of this," Brinker said as he poured. "It's only Steinhager, but it will warm you. When you've finished I will have someone direct you to the wardroom where the commander will be waiting." He handed a glass to each man, then held his own up in a toast. "To your success, gentlemen. Heil Hitler."

The storm troopers rose to their feet. "Heil Hitler," they echoed and drank the clear alcohol.

Their glasses were being refilled as a bulkhead phone buzzed angrily.

Brinker reached for it, suddenly businesslike: "Yes?" he asked. The storm troops heard a staccato humming from the receiver. The imposing, gray-haired captain motioned for them to drink as he listened and then poured what remained in his own glass into a small sink near the phone. "Very well, I'll be right out." He replaced the receiver and put his empty glass down on the desk. "It's time for me to leave, gentlemen. In a few minutes we will be turning north. My place is on the bridge, and it's time for you to join Commander Loesner." He locked the bottle back in the safe. "Finish your drinks. I'll send a man to guide you to the wardroom.

"Incidentally, until we arrive in England the only languages that you will hear spoken aboard this ship will be Dutch and poor English. You will follow our example." There was no questioning the authority in the voice. "I doubt that any of you speak Dutch, few of you British do . . . or would if you could. So, remember, no German, even to me. I will see you gentlemen later."

Commander Loesner was alone when they entered the wardroom. He sat at a long table behind neatly stacked papers placed with precision at the edge of the inevitable map. Sighing unhappily, he watched the young men enter the cabin. The commander's last sea duty had been aboard the cruiser *Deutschland*, a spotless ship manned by immaculate officers and crew, and the storm troopers' rumpled appearance caused him to think of his own. Lifelong habit was difficult to set aside, even temporarily. He adjusted his tie, waved the soldiers to seats at the table, and offered them coffee, pointing to a large silver pot standing on a tray near him. Loesner watched as they poured, prepared to save his papers and map from manners he was afraid might be as casual as their appearance. But they managed to pour without mishap, and when they had settled in their seats, he began.

"Pass me that, Lieutenant," Loesner indicated the envelope now lying alongside Dietrich's free hand. He opened it carefully and removed a sheaf of papers. He studied them briefly, chose three, and handed one each to the soldiers. "Read this carefully, gentlemen. It tells you the location of your escape rendezvous points on the British coast, and your means of arriving at them."

When the soldiers had finished they sat back and looked at Loesner expectantly.

"Well, what do you think of our preparations?" the commander asked, with apparent satisfaction.

Dietrich answered without the enthusiasm Loesner had expected. "They seem adequate, Commander."

"Adequate?" the naval officer was jarred.

"Who are these people who are going to help us get to the coast, Commander?"

"Germans. Their present availability is the result of the foresight of Admiral Canaris, who some years ago decided that since some of our countrymen apparently chose to emigrate from the fatherland, it would provide an excellent opportunity to plant agents in various countries. England was the primary target of that foresight, and you are reaping the benefits. One of the men you will deal with actually works in a British government department, which is certainly a tribute to his ability. Another owns the fishing boats that will be used to transfer you to the U-boats."

"And you're certain that they can be trusted?" Dietrich asked flatly.

"Without question. They will supply you with civilian clothing, money, ration books, legitimate identity cards, and transportation to your rendezvous. I doubt that you would have much chance of escaping the British after your attack without them," Loesner said angrily.

"We're not used to depending on civilians, Commander," Dietrich said.

"These men are as much soldiers as you are, Lieutenant."

Dietrich shrugged while the commander fumed.

"What about photographs for the identity cards, Commander?" Schiller asked.

"There are no photographs on British identity cards."

"Then what good are they?"

"I am not qualified to discuss British reasoning," Loesner replied, his anger continuing to rise. "Be thankful that they seem to find them sufficient."

During the exchange, Sergeant Siegler continued to pore over the order, further infuriating Loesner. "What seems to be worrying you, Sergeant?" he demanded.

"It says here that we split up after the attack," Siegler said.

"For obvious reasons. You are proceeding to three different rendezvous."

Siegler looked at Loesner steadily: "I understand that, Commander, but it also says that only the officers are to know the locations of the rendezvous. Why?"

"Originally that clause was put in as a precaution. The reasoning was that if a man, or a team, is captured, they would be unable to give away the destinations of the others."

"Or the locations of the U-boats?"

"Sergeant, your enemy is the British, not me," Loesner said coldly. "Save your temerity for the battlefield, and listen. If I had been allowed to continue uninterrupted, I would have told you that the clause you seem to find so devious is subject to each team commander's discretion."

The briefing continued and, despite occasional baiting by Siegler, Commander Loesner managed to cover the logistics of the attack and escape thoroughly. He illustrated his presentation with aerial photographs and frequent references to the map. Finally, he reached into his briefcase and removed carefully folded papers, which he handed to Dietrich and Siegler, and said: "Your orders, authentically British, and excellently forged. They cover a number of contingencies, so study them carefully before you land. Once you have reached your targets, I want to impress upon you again that all of the equipment you enter with is to be destroyed with the tanks after the attacks. For your own safety you must follow the instructions of our resident agents without question. I am forced to stress that since you, particularly Sergeant Siegler, seem to show a propensity for debate. The agents will not have the time for argument. Your safety will require immediate compliance with their instructions. Is that understood?" When they had answered affirmatively, Loesner rose and began to gather up his papers. "Now, if you will follow me, we'll join your men in the dining room and go over it again."

CHAPTER 14

Dietrich, Schiller, and Siegler left the men and followed a steward to the bridge in answer to a summons from the captain.

"Christ," Siegler said, "Look at that!" The three men paused on the outside ladder to the wheelhouse. Ahead, the sky pulsated with reflected fire, punctuated by the sudden brilliance of a parachute flare. Off to their right, from the unseen shore, the thunder of heavy guns followed flashes of white against low, racing clouds. They resumed their climb, awed by the evidence of the obvious hell that glowed in the distance.

They saw Captain Brinker standing on the bridge wing, silhouetted against the distant fury. He heard their approach and said, "I sent for you because I thought you should see this," he gestured at the horizon. "I doubt that any of us will ever be in a position to see anything like it again."

"Is that Dunkirk, Captain?" Schiller asked.

"What's left of it."

Schiller shook his head in wonder. "And they're still able to take out troops through . . . that?"

"They are, Lieutenant. So far."

"How close are we going to Dunkirk, Captain?" Schiller asked.

"Not much closer. We've begun to slow down already. Another few miles and we will anchor between the sandbanks, where we'll wait until it's time for us to start across. Mines are being swept now. Unfortunately, it's our own magnetic mines that are the most dangerous. I've been told where they're supposed to be, but—" He paused meaningfully. "As you men know, all life is a gamble. I can assure you that we will proceed cautiously. Luckily we have plenty of time."

"We do?" Dietrich asked.

"This ship can make a bit over thirteen knots. We could be at Newhaven in about six hours, but we won't attempt the landing until approximately one hour before sunset tonight."

"Why, Captain?" Schiller asked.

"For a number of reasons. To allow for the possible interference of our British friends, the mines I've mentioned, and most important, the tide. Sunset is approximately an hour after high water at Newhaven. I need enough water and light to get in and out of that harbor. With luck, all of us should be on our way before it gets dark."

"What happens if you can't get out, Captain?" Siegler asked.

"I'll get out. I won't give them the time to stop me, but should something happen to prevent me from going all the way, this ship will sink, conveniently, in the harbor entrance. It won't look good on my record, but fortunately, that is as counterfeit as my present identity."

Ahead, bursts of tracers rose into the violent sky as a sailor hurried from the wheelhouse and spoke to the captain who listened, his back to the storm troopers, and then explained to them, "We have a wreck ahead, gentlemen. The escort has ordered a change of course." The *Van Hoorn* began to swing away from the gun flashes to the right, and the soldiers could feel the ship tremble as speed was reduced. An E-boat of the escort raced out of the darkness, passed below them, and disappeared along the *Van Hoorn*'s original course. It wasn't long before the captain pointed. "Over there, gentlemen."

"I can't see a bloody thing," Siegler complained.

"I see something," Dietrich said. "Jesus! Is it a submarine?"

"Look closer, Lieutenant," Brinker said. "It's what's left of a ship—capsized—upside down. What you see is her hull. If we had struck that, your trip might have ended right here."

Siegler squinted into the darkness. "What the hell is that sticking out of its side?"

The captain raised his binoculars and studied the wreck. "It's a paddle wheel. She's probably one of the Isle of Wight excursion boats. Red funnel line. They seem to be risking everything that floats at Dunkirk."

They watched the wreck disappear into the murk behind them. Soon Brinker returned to the wheelhouse, and the *Van Hoorn* began to turn slowly back toward the angry arc of horizon to the east.

Shortly before dawn the sea was calm. The rain had stopped, replaced by dense banks of intermittent fog. A light wind blew from the northwest as the *Van Hoorn* got underway, moving slowly into the Strait of Dover. Occasionally the fog would disperse, opening like a theater curtain to reveal the smoke and flame rising above the distant agony of Dunkirk, now some twenty miles behind the ship. To the right the heavy coastal guns at Calais continued their song of death.

Captain Brinker stood on the starboard bridge wing, his eyes fixed ahead. The ship was barely moving, but a light wind moaned in a high-pitched whine as it passed through the boom rigging. Brinker listened to the sound gratefully. Wind should clear the fog. A voice came from within the wheelhouse.

"Bow lookouts report that they can now see the escort on station ahead, Captain."

"Good." Brinker moved to the entrance to the wheelhouse. "Anything from the escort yet?"

"No, sir."

Brinker returned to his vigil. The ship moved steadily forward, isolated in the channel between the sandbanks of Ridens and Dyck. The captain watched the dense fog with troubled eyes.

His second in command joined him on the wing. "It's not pleasant to be blind in these waters, is it, sir."

"We'll soon be out of it," Brinker said.

As if in answer to his statement, the fog lifted suddenly to a thinning mist. Ahead, the stern of the escorting E-boat was now clearly visible.

"We're out of it, Captain."

"It would seem we are, Pieter. Nothing to worry about now except mines, the British navy, air force and . . ." As he spoke, three twin-engined Messerschmitt 110s appeared above the clearing fog to their left and flashed over the *Van Hoorn,* causing the two officers to duck. The first officer ran to the door of the wheelhouse and called angrily, "Tell those lookouts to stay awake."

His anger was directed at a seaman wearing a headset, who said, "Three aircraft dead ahead, sir."

The first officer quickly rejoined the captain on the wing. "Lookouts report . . ."

"I heard, Pieter. More 110s," Brinker said as the fighters passed above the escort and banked away to the right.

"Three aircraft on the port quarter, Captain," came a voice from the wheelhouse door. The two officers turned in time to see the Junker 88 bombers climbing in the gray sky to the west.

"Our lookouts have regained their sight, but apparently they can't count. There are four of them," Brinker said. "Tell the forward lookouts to keep their eyes on the sea. The aircraft are comforting, but they won't be of much use to us if we hit a mine because those men are gawking at them."

The *Van Hoorn* was overtaking the escort, which lay stopped near a pitching buoy. A signal light began to flash from its low bridge. Brinker read the message as it was transmitted: RETURNING TO BASE. INDEPENDENT COMMANDS COVER YOU NORTH AND SOUTH. AIR COVER NOW ABOVE. GOOD LUCK.

He turned to the signalman, now standing beside him on the wing. "Send: UNDERSTOOD. THANK YOU."

The E-boat acknowledged the reply. Then, with a sudden burst of power, the smaller ship moved past the *Van Hoorn*. Figures on its bridge saluted them as it vanished into the thin mist of fog astern, back toward France. Brinker entered the wheelhouse and beckoned to the first officer. "I'll take the watch, Pieter. There are a few things I'd like you to handle. I want our passengers out on deck. I want them visible if we meet any British ships. It won't stop anyone from wondering why we don't have a deckful, but even a few should reassure them. All hands will wear lifejackets, particularly our passengers. Have the bos'n start the smoke. It's time we began to play our part, but don't let him overdo it. I'd rather not attract every sympathetic captain in the area."

"Let's hope they stay sympathetic, Captain," Pieter said.

"I believe they will. One good look at this ship, and there isn't a sailor alive who wouldn't feel sorry for her."

"This thing is on fire," Siegler said anxiously. "If I had gotten a good look at it last night I think I would have preferred to swim over."

Dietrich laughed: "We're not there yet, Willi. You may still have to swim over."

Pieter was amused at the soldier's apparent distrust of things nautical, as he preceded them on the now familiar ladder to the bridge. Captain Brinker greeted them heartily. "Enjoying your trip, gentlemen?" he asked, ushering them into the wheelhouse.

"Your ship is on fire, Captain," Siegler said.

"It's only smoke. All part of our preparations for deception."

"The damage looks as if it was really caused by shell fire and bombs, Captain. How did you manage that?" Dietrich asked.

"The bomb effects were achieved by explosives experts. The shell holes are real. They actually fired armor-piercing shot into us. It was an interesting few days. After the engineers virtually rebuilt the power plant, the army moved in and did their best to blow the top decks to hell."

"They damn near succeeded," Siegler said.

Brinker's laugh boomed. "They did, didn't they."

"British aircraft ahead, sir," the sailor wearing the headset called nervously.

"You've arrived just in time, gentlemen. Outside with me. Hurry," Brinker ordered. On the wing, he raised his binoculars and studied the horizon.

"More to your left, Captain," Siegler shouted. "Six ... just above the water."

Brinker focussed on the shapes, rapidly growing larger, and calmly said, "Hurricanes. Now we'll see."

They watched, fascinated, as the fighters approached, flying no higher than the ship's bridge. When they were dangerously near the *Van Hoorn,* they began to climb, and passed above them without apparent interest. Then, one broke away from the tight formation, banked sharply, and turned in a tight circle to again approach them from the front. The Hurricane slowed visibly and flew past them at bridge level. The pilot waved. Brinker answered the wave vigorously and, after a slight pause, the soldiers joined in. The British fighter increased speed and soon disappeared in the direction of the others.

"Where the hell are our planes?" Siegler asked.

"Our air cover is with us to guard us against attack, and those British pilots were extremely friendly," Brinker said. "Well, gentlemen, we seem to have passed our first test."

"Won't they report our position, Captain?" Schiller asked.

"Most likely, and it won't be the last time today, particularly when we begin to bear southwest toward Newhaven." Brinker's binoculars swept the horizon as he spoke. The storm trooper officers saw him tense and lean forward, steadying his arms on the rail.

"Small boat on the starboard beam!" Pieter called.

"I see it." Brinker studied the drifting boat. It was a thirty-foot, demasted private yacht dangerously overloaded with uniformed British soldiers. A man in the stern, wearing civilian clothes, waved vigorously. "Nasty place for a breakdown," Brinker said, while returning his glasses to another sweep of the horizon.

"She's settling, Captain," said the first officer.

"Damn!" Brinker fumed. "I wanted to avoid something like this, but now I have no choice."

"What are you going to do, sir?"

"Pick them up, of course." Brinker lowered his binoculars. "And worry about that smoke out there." He pointed over the bow.

A man rushed out of the wheelhouse. "Masthead reports a British destroyer on the starboard, forward of the beam, sir."

"Get the masthead lookout down, Pieter, and send someone to get those soldiers to the rail. I want them visible." He pointed to the noncoms of the special force sitting on the deck, forward of the centercastle. As the first officer moved hurriedly into the wheelhouse, Brinker followed, raising a hand to Dietrich, Schiller, and Siegler to remain where they were. "Starboard ten," he bellowed.

The *Van Hoorn* began to swing slowly toward the closing destroyer.

"You're still going to help that boat, sir?" Pieter asked.

"I want to convince the destroyer's captain of our good intentions. But I want him to think I'm having trouble doing it."

"The destroyer is signaling, Captain," a sailor called.

"Signalman!" Brinker yelled, moving out onto the starboard wing.

"Right here, sir." The signalman wrote rapidly, his eyes fixed on the distant flashing light. "WHAT SHIP—WHERE BOUND,"

"Give them our name," Brinker said. "DESTINATION DOVER. Send it slowly; you're a bit too efficient for a civilian vessel."

"Yes, sir." The signalman was encouraged by the compliment. He used a hand blinker to tap out the code laboriously.

Brinker moved to the wheelhouse door. "Starboard ten. Come to course three-zero-zero. Don't settle on it too smoothly. Let her swing past, and overcorrect. I want them to think we're having trouble controlling our turn . . . understood?"

"Yes, sir," the helmsman answered, his attention on the compass.

Brinker returned to the wing and watched the destroyer's answering signal, flashing rapidly from her bridge. "Their man is showing us how efficient *he* is. Ask for a repeat—slowly."

The answering signal came immediately, much slower: "ARE YOU AFIRE? DO YOU REQUIRE ASSISTANCE?"

Brinker, not waiting for the signalman's translation, said, "Send— FIRE OUT. MINOR STEERING DAMAGE. NOT SERIOUS. REPAIRING. DISABLED YACHT AHEAD OF ME. TROOPS. ATTEMPTING RESCUE."

Captain Brinker released pent-up breath as he read the destroyer's answer. "I'LL TAKE OVER RESCUE. KEEP CLEAR. RESUME YOUR COURSE IF POSSIBLE."

"Acknowledge," Brinker ordered. He beckoned to the army officers, still waiting on the port wing. They followed him across the wheelhouse to the starboard. Outside, Pieter looked questioningly at the captain.

"We aren't out of the woods yet, Pieter. Even if they aren't particularly suspicious, they will certainly look us over closely after they've picked up those men on the yacht. If they insist on escorting us to Dover—Pieter, tell the engineer to build up more turns while they're still occupied, but slowly. I don't want them noticing any sudden increase in speed."

The destroyer was now well behind the *Van Hoorn*, on her starboard quarter. Brinker nodded reassuringly at the army officers and then returned to his scrutiny of the warship, which was now edging cautiously alongside the floundering yacht. They all heard the sudden, whining pitch of a diving aircraft's engine. Before they could locate the source, they saw the water erupt in a mast high spout close to the starboard side of the destroyer as a Ju 88 passed above it and began to climb, followed by intense fire from the warship's guns. The yacht was flung high into the air, tumbling back almost lazily as toy-like figures of men—already dead of concussion—fell into the churning wake of the destroyer as it leapt into forward motion. Another plane followed the first. Suddenly, a huge geyser of flame rose from the stern of the turning warship as a one-hundred pound bomb exploded on its upper, after turret. The destroyer faltered, and then churned into an even tighter turn, her antiaircraft batteries filling the air with the black bursts of shells and machine gun tracers. The dull thud of the guns echoed angrily.

Another Ju 88 approached the destroyer in a flat dive, dangerously low, firing into the open bridge. Tracers converged inexorably on the plane, and one engine began to trail smoke, followed by a sudden, billowing flame that seemed to envelop the bomber. The nose suddenly dropped as its canopy disintegrated in a storm of 20-mm. shells. The remains of the Ju 88 passed above the destroyer's forward turret, its left wing shattering the bridge, as the fuselage was flung sideways into the sea. The severed wing clung momentarily to the bridge, then dropped to the deck below, its Junker engine burning brightly.

Now obviously out of control, the destroyer heeled over in a skidding turn as another bomb fell near its stern, obscuring it behind a wall of roiling water and oily smoke.

On the *Van Hoorn,* Captain Brinker's concentration on the duel was broken by a voice from the wheelhouse.

"Two 110s approaching us from the stern, Captain."

"Very well. Now it's our turn, gentlemen," Brinker said to the others. "Not quite so violent, I hope. Everyone into the wheelhouse. The alarm, Pieter, and let's hope that the British were too occupied to wonder why we didn't think of it earlier. Move quickly!"

The raucous, insistent clanging of the alarm sounded, causing Dietrich to yell, "My men are on deck, Captain."

"Your men are in no danger. We're being attacked by our own planes for the benefit of the men on that destroyer . . . the survivors, that is."

They entered the protection of the wheelhouse and heard the heavy machine guns of the 110s as they streaked along the length of the *Van*

Hoorn. Brinker called, "Helmsman. Make it look as though we're taking evasive action. But use only five degrees of rudder. We don't want to confuse those pilots into a mistake."

Two bombs exploded in rapid succession in the sea close to the starboard side. The *Van Hoorn* lurched as the concussive shock wave rang against its hull. Brinker cursed angrily, moved out on the wing, and clutched the rail as he watched a Messerschmitt pulling away in a climbing turn. Off to the starboard, another 110 sped toward the ship. The captain saw the muzzle flashes of the two 20-mm. cannon in its nose, followed by the eruption of the water near the port side of the ship. Part of the port rail disappeared as a cannon shell struck a stanchion and exploded. He ducked hastily as fragments peppered the boom, while others struck the forward superstructure. Brinker stood up and gestured angrily. The Messerschmitt passed below the level of the bridge and banked away. Brinker thought he saw the rear gunner wave. "You bastard," he roared and then called to the wheelhouse, "Pieter! Have the bos'n check the damage on the forecastle."

The Messerschmitts gained altitude and sped away into the low cloud. The mock attack was over. Brinker looked over the wing rail and saw that the shell hadn't caused any fire, and that the bos'n had already arrived with a damage control party. He returned his attention to the destroyer, now moving in and out of its own smoke in an apparently aimless circle. Its remaining operational guns were still firing. Flames blossomed from the upper turret aft, which was now glowing redly, Through his binoculars, Captain Brinker saw figures fighting the fire and realized that no bombs had fallen for some time. He swept the sky and saw the remaining bombers flying off to the southwest. Why had they abandoned the attack? He moved the lenses back to the destroyer and a movement behind the floundering ship caught his eye. Two E-boats were approaching from the port side of the listing ship.

They roared in confidently, but even a wounded destroyer can be a highly dangerous weapon. A hail of 20-mm. Oerlikon shells reached out for the attackers. One exploded in a sheet of flame and stopped dead in the water, burning furiously. The other was obscured by the listing bulk of the destroyer. Brinker assumed that it, too, had been hit and was searching the smoke for it when the explosion came, tremendous and deafening, The destroyer slewed sideways, flung to starboard almost casually by the force of the blast, while nothing remained of the E-boat.

As Brinker watched, the warship rolled over to its starboard rail, then slowly recovered, only to lurch over to an angle of forty-five degrees on its port side, the superstructure hanging barely above the water. The destroyer lay unmoving, enveloped in smoke and flame.

The remaining E-boat burned furiously and was slowly sinking just beyond the destroyer. Captain Brinker watched it vanish in one brief instant as flame reached the ammunition and primed torpedoes. The new holocaust shook the floundering warship. Her foremast toppled, again she was thrown over on her opposite beam, and again, incredibly, recovered.

A loud voice from behind him broke Brinker's almost hypnotic concentration on the violent scene. "British aircraft on the starboard beam, sir."

He shifted his binoculars to the sky and counted six Spitfires racing toward the destroyer. He moved quickly to the wheelhouse, shouldering past the storm trooper officers standing in the door. "Ahead full," he ordered, moving to the helmsman.

The first officer spoke: "But the course to the Varne light is . . ."

"Not just yet, Pieter. We'll wait until we're clear. Those British fighters will look us over soon. We'll remain on the course to Dover for the time being."

The *Van Hoorn* was trembling with the increased demands on her engine. Brinker again brushed past the soldiers, returning to the wing. The crippled destroyer was almost obscured by heavy smoke. The Spitfires orbited above it, and there was no sign of German aircraft. His glasses swept the horizon. "My God! Another one." he said as Pieter called. "Warship bearing three-three-zero, sir."

"Port twenty," Brinker ordered. The *Van Hoorn* began to swing away from the clearly visible bow wave of the approaching destroyer.

"British aircraft approaching from the stern, Captain," Pieter called.

Brinker gestured to the storm troop officers. "Come out here and help me greet them. No hesitation this time. Wave like hell."

Three of the sleek fighters roared past them, bridge high. Brinker and the soldiers waved vigorously. One of the pilots waved back.

"Good," Brinker breathed.

The British pilots wasted no time on them. They made only one pass and then turned back toward the burning destroyer now far behind the *Van Hoorn*. The distance between them and the approaching destroyer was also widening rapidly. It made no signal, disregarding the *Van Hoorn* completely, apparently satisfied by the Spitfires' inspection. It never deviated from its dash to assist its wounded sister ship. Brinker waited until he was certain of the destroyer's intent, then entered the wheelhouse and went quickly to the chart room, motioning for the first officer to follow.

"Where are we, Pieter?"

"Here, sir." the first officer said, leaning over the chart and pointing to the end of a penciled line that clearly showed their course and erratic maneuvers.

Brinker looked at the compass repeater above the chart table, and then back at the chart. "Forget the Varne light, Pieter. Work out a course for the North Colbart buoy. I'm going between the Varne and the ridge. It's much too busy here. We have a good excuse for it now. Our deception seems to be working, but luck can change." He gestured at the chart: "I don't know if we can depend on our air support. The British radio direction finders seem quite efficient. You've seen how quickly their fighters show up. Once we're past the Varne sands, we'll rely on the U-boats. Let's get to them as quickly as we can."

CHAPTER 15

Colonel Heinz von Maussner stepped from a trimotored Junkers transport onto the runway in a secluded area of Tempelhof airfield. It had been a melancholy trip for him seated in the forward section of the aircraft with the overly solicitous Abwehr colonel—whose assignment in Boulogne had ended with von Maussner's—while in the rear of the compartment lay the flag-draped coffin of General Kellner.

Von Maussner had wanted solitude, time to think. Instead, he was forced to listen to Colonel Bruning's platitudes throughout the five-hundred-mile flight from Boulogne. He had been glad to learn that the Abwehr colonel had his own transport waiting at Templehof. At least, when they arrived, Bruning would go his own way, and von Maussner knew that he could look forward to a quiet drive from the airfield to central Berlin.

Now, minutes after the transport had landed, von Maussner stood on the rain-dampened runway and said goodbye to Colonel Bruning, who regarded him sadly.

"Would you like me to see to the transfer of the remains?" he said.

"Thank you, Colonel. I would appreciate it," von Maussner replied.

"I understand, Heinz. It is difficult to lose a friend. I hope that the next time we meet it will be under happier circumstances."

They shook hands, and the Abwehr colonel moved away toward a group of soldiers waiting at the edge of the runway. Soon, the coffin was removed from the Junkers and placed in a waiting military ambulance. ."

"The train is waiting, Herr Colonel," the major said with When it was moving away, von Maussner walked briskly toward the staff car assigned to him. He was surprised to see that the driver, standing at attention at its side, was dressed in the uniform of the S.S. As the colonel neared the car, the rear door opened and an S.S. major stepped out.

"Colonel von Maussner?" the officer asked.

"Yes," von Maussner answered warily.

"Welcome, Herr Colonel. I am Major Voelkner. The driver will see to your luggage. I have been sent to escort you to the Führer's private train.

You leave in one hour for Hildesheim. The Führer is waiting at the Fellsnest."

Von Maussner was stunned by the major's statement. "So soon, Major? But I must stop in Berlin. I have reports to prepare and . . ."

"Your original orders no longer apply, Herr Colonel. The reason you are not being flown to Hildesheim is to allow you the time to prepare for your conference with the Führer."

"I need . . ."

"The train is waiting, Herr Colonel," the major said with finality and stepped away from the door. "Please get in. The Führer's orders require you to be available to meet with him early this evening. We have no time for stops."

Von Maussner stepped into the car and sat down, his thoughts racing. Obviously Hitler wanted an immediate personal report on the status of the special force's operation. I'm a fool, he mused angrily. I should have known that Hitler might decide to remain at Hildesheim. It was now frighteningly apparent that the storm troopers could conceivably complete their mission and be on their way to the U-boats—even on their way home—before he would have the opportunity to transmit a message to the British. It would seem that Siegler had won after all. At the thought, von Maussner was suddenly tired. He leaned back in the seat resignedly and stared at the mist rising from the runway, hoping that General Kellner at least would be buried with dignity before. . . . Von Maussner was startled as his body shuddered involuntarily. Fright was not an emotion he was accustomed to.

After the noon meal with the storm troop officers, Commander Loesner placed his knife and fork on his plate with conspicuous precision and turned his attention to Lieutenant Dietrich. "Captain Brinker will take this ship as close as possible to the seaward end of the east wharf," he began. "When the tanks are off-loaded, I will presume that your orders are imposing enough to allow you to clear the harbor area and its roadblocks. And having gotten that far, I will also assume that you have managed to move the tanks across the swing bridge, through the fringes of Newhaven, and to the Brighton Road." Saying it out loud brought home the incredible difficulties inherent in his presumptions.

"After the climb to the top of the heights overlooking the harbor, you continue on a downgrade to the sea level and the coast road. Tell me, Lieutenant, how do you feel about taking three tanks along what must be a heavily guarded road, through a number of cities? If you have any reservations about the route, now is the time to express them."

Dietrich looked at the commander steadily, certain that Loesner was expressing his own doubts, seeking justification in him. "No reservations, Commander. The coast road isn't only the easiest, it is also the safest for us. If we're stopped, we have our papers. There's no other way, actually. Inland, the roads are a maze, particularly in the blackout. I'm more worried about this ship getting into the harbor."

"Captain Brinker will get us in, Lieutenant. Supposedly we have been chased by E-boats and attacked by aircraft, justifying our present position. Near Newhaven, one of our submarines will show itself if necessary, giving us even more reason to seek sudden entry into the port."

"What if one of these destroyers we've been meeting insists on escorting us to Portsmouth?" Dietrich persisted.

"Most of their forces are well occupied at Dunkirk. Those left in this area will be kept too busy by our submarine escort to have time to escort a single vessel, particularly when there is a perfectly suitable port miles to the east of Portsmouth. We have made provisions for every confrontation we could think of in the time given us. Do you have any idea what it took to resurface heavily bombed, virtually useless airfields in coastal areas occupied only days earlier? How many transports were diverted from provisioning our Panzers to deliver the fuel required to keep our air cover flying? And the U-boats . . . ."

Loesner was interrupted by a seaman who had entered the dining room. "Orders from the captain, sir. All passengers are to show themselves on deck, starboard side. The captain asks that you take charge, Commander, and direct them to cover if the general alarm rings."

"What's going on?" Siegler asked.

"We've sighted another British destroyer," the seaman answered.

"I thought they were all at Dunkirk," Siegler said.

Loesner glared at Siegler. "Follow me," he said, starting for the door.

The *Van Hoorn* had rounded the northern Le Colbart buoy and was now steaming between the midchannel hazards of the Varne and the Ridge. The ship crept ahead slowly, her engine producing barely enough turns to maintain headway. Brinker watched the destroyer and read the message being transmitted by a flickering light on her bridge. The warship was staying well away to starboard, the warning buoys of the Varne sands between her and the *Van Hoorn*. He dictated his answer to the waiting signalman. "Give them our name. No destination unless she insists. Radio out. Attacked by E-boats and aircraft, give him the position. Destroyer aiding me sinking at same position."

The captain waited for the answering flicker of the destroyer's aldis. "DO YOU REQUIRE ASSISTANCE."

"Send: NEGATIVE. MINOR STEERING DAMAGE. REPAIRING." Brinker turned to his first officer. "That's getting to be a familiar message, eh, Pieter?"

The signalman called, "Destroyer answers, GET BACK INSHORE AS SOON AS POSSIBLE. YOU ARE IN DANGEROUS WATERS."

"Acknowledge," Brinker said as he watched the destroyer pick up speed and begin to race ahead.

He smiled at the first officer: "Simple, isn't it, Pieter?"

The first officer looked puzzled: "I don't understand it, sir. We send a simple message, and they move away. Why don't they show more interest in us, particularly since we're under Dutch registry?"

"The *Van Hoorn* was on all of their recognition lists long before we left Boulogne, Pieter."

"On the lists? How did we manage that?"

"I took more than four hundred rear echelon troops into Dover on the twenty-seventh—from Dunkirk. It was quite an experience. Too bad you hadn't joined the ship yet."

The first officer was dumbfounded. "British troops? To Dover?"

"I should have told you earlier and saved you some anxiety. Supposedly I escaped from Ostend and heroically stopped at Dunkirk, where I was asked to transport troops. At Dover, they were so glad to see me—gallant Dutchman that I am—and so grateful, that when I demanded to be allowed to return for more of their precious troops, they were kind enough to supply me with a substantial amount of fuel and send me back in company with a sea full of ships that same night. When we arrived off France, the E-boats and our aircraft kept the escort busy. I managed to slip away and moved down the coast to Boulogne, where I picked up the special crew. The rest you know."

"What if you had been sunk at Dunkirk?"

"Then the navy and Luftwaffe would have been in serious trouble with the Führer. They were warned. It was a calculated risk that was justified as you can see from our recent encounters. But we haven't won yet. If the confusion at their ports isn't all I've been led to believe, I may have a bit of trouble explaining where this ship has been for the last four days. Now, Pieter, I want you to contact all of the lookouts personally. One of the U-boats should let us know he's on station at any time now, and we don't want to miss him. We'll stay out here in deep water as long as we can, but I imagine that someone will be out to chase me inshore soon, for our own good, and then the U-boat's part in all of this will begin."

"Yes, sir." The first officer moved quickly down the bridge ladder.

Lieutenant Commander Maurice Pierce, RN, watched the *Van Hoorn* recede behind him thoughtfully. Finally, he said to his executive officer. "*Van Hoorn*. That ship is familiar, number one. She has army aboard, but I can't understand what she's doing down here."

"I checked the lists, sir. She was in the group we escorted from Dover to the Dunkirk roads last Monday. Looks as if she's had a rough go since."

"Yes, that's it, but there's something else I can't quite put my finger on."

"She's listed as presumed sunk, sir."

Commander Pierce turned to look back at the receding *Van Hoorn*. "Damned shoreside fumblers. How do they expect us to keep on top of things when they can't keep track of a ship that size?"

The noncoms of the special force stood on the main deck and watched the now distant destroyer.

"Every time one of them comes near us, they take one look at that captain up there and run like rabbits," Sergeant Richter remarked.

"They had their guns trained on us," Knoedler said grimly.

"You're wrong, Richter," Sergeant Thyben said. "They probably saw Knoedler. Wouldn't you want to get away as fast as possible?"

"You may be right," Knoedler said. "I do seem to have that effect on the enemy."

"On the enemy? You have the same effect on me," Priller laughed.

"I'm sorry to hear that, Ernst," Knoedler said, feigning a hurt expression. "I thought you were a man of good taste. I was even going to allow you to be the first to hear that there is a bomber heading straight toward us right now, but you've hurt my feelings." He pointed. They all turned.

"It's one of ours," Priller shouted. "It's on fire."

They watched the Ju 88 bomber closing from the northeast, smoke billowing from one engine. Barely above the water, it dropped lower with each passing second. Less than a mile away it caromed off a swell, bounded back into the air, and then fell, nose first, disappearing in a fountain of spray. Moments later, figures appeared on the partially submerged wing and abandoned the aircraft in a rubber life raft.

"Only two of them made it," Sergeant Richter said.

The life raft bobbed on the swells. The two survivors sat motionless, watching the *Van Hoorn* as it began to turn toward them. They did not look back when the airplane's tail rose, and the wreck dived in its final dive to the bed of the Channel.

"The damned fools," Brinker said. "Why did they have to seek me out?"

"I don't understand, sir?" Pieter said.

"Three fighters. Port beam, sir."

"Now do you see what I mean, Pieter?" He studied the approaching planes. "Hurricanes. British, damn it! Every contact reduces our odds. Port five!"

The *Van Hoorn* turned erratically, slowly reversing her course.

"Small craft on starboard quarter, sir. Torpedo boat!"

"Stop engine," Brinker yelled. "Get over to the starboard wing, Pieter. Ask them to take over the rescue." The first officer moved away quickly.

Brinker leaned over the wing rail and watched the British fighters flash above the life raft. The *Van Hoorn*'s bows with her engine stopped settled for a time on the English coast, and then began to slowly edge back toward her original heading.

"Patrol boat answers affirmative, sir," Pieter called.

"Good."

The British fighters left their low orbit above the *Van Hoorn* and flew away to the north as the patrol boat roared past the bows in a violent turn and approached the life raft.

Pieter rushed up behind the intent Captain Brinker. "Three of our aircraft approaching on the port beam, sir."

"Damn!" Brinker said. He rushed through the wheelhouse to the port wing. He saw them immediately. Three twin-engined fighters, flying close to the water. He ran into the wheelhouse and pressed the emergency alarm button, while yelling, "Signalman! Inform the patrol boat. Enemy aircraft."

The signalman hesitated, "But they're ours, sir."

"Send it at once!" Brinker snapped. He saw the first officer's stunned look and shouted, "They're supposed to be on our side. Do you want someone questioning why I didn't warn that patrol boat?"

The German fighters began firing long before they roared over the *Van Hoorn* and angled down toward the patrol boat. The water near the larger ship's hull erupted as each fighter passed above it, their carefully aimed cannon shells striking uncomfortably close. The patrol boat was hit on the first pass. Smoking at the stern, it began to circle the *Van Hoorn* protectively, antiaircraft batteries angrily seeking out the attackers.

One German fighter banked into an angled dive toward the stern of the *Van Hoorn*. The men on the bridge wing watched its cannon fire, waiting for it to turn away. But the pilot had been trained to hit targets and, despite his orders, he miscalculated. A short burst of 20-mm. shells cut an explosive path across the *Van Hoorn*'s after working deck. The tank beneath the stern boom was mostly hidden by the superstructure. Brinker ran out to the far end of the wing, which provided the only unobstructed view of the boom. Smoke rose from the deck, and it seemed to the captain that the canvas covering the Mark 2 was smouldering.

Brinker cursed angrily and was about to order a damage control party when he saw that the efficient bos'n had taken charge. Men were already running aft. Hoses were soon connected, and a steady stream of water played over the smoking deck.

"Get on the phones, Pieter. Have the bos'n report damage as soon as possible," Brinker called as he moved back to the wheelhouse.

"Yes, sir. Lookout reports six aircraft on the starboard beam. It looks like the Hurricanes are coming back."

As the first officer spoke, the twin-engined German fighters suddenly broke off their attack. Climbing under full power, still followed by the tracers of the patrol boat's guns, they disappeared into the low cloud, closely pursued by the Hurricanes.

Brinker returned to the wing to watch the patrol boat circle the stern and make its way to a position below the *Van Hoorn*'s bridge, and he saw a figure on the open bridge gesture with a megaphone. He walked to the far end of the wing to look down on the damaged boat.

"Thanks for your warning, Captain," a young officer called.

"Thank you for your protection," Brinker responded.

"Where are you bound, sir?"

"My destination was Dover, but I was driven down here by E-boats and aircraft, so I'm proceeding to Newhaven."

The lieutenant glanced at the patrol boat's smoking after deck. "The jerries are giving us hell today."

Brinker, too, was looking at the heavy, oily smoke. "Do you wish to transfer to this ship, Lieutenant?" he asked.

"No thanks, sir. I think we'll manage. As soon as I get that fire out, I'll escort you in."

A sudden gout of flame rose from the patrol boat's stern. "That fire is beginning to look dangerous for both of us. I'm moving ahead, Lieutenant." Brinker turned and called, "Ahead full!" then returned his attention to the small boat. "Don't you think you'd better jettison those torpedoes?" he yelled, as the *Van Hoorn* began to surge forward.

"Not just yet, Captain. Terrible waste." The lieutenant saluted, yelled an order, and the patrol boat turned away from the churning wake of the larger ship.

Brinker rushed to the wheelhouse door. "Ahead emergency. I want as much distance as possible between this ship and . . ." Had he been watching, Captain Brinker would have seen the pall of smoke rising from the patrol boat's stern suddenly blossom into an orange flower of flame, reaching hundreds of feet into the air. The explosion was followed by a shock wave that threw the captain heavily to the deck. The *Van Hoorn* shuddered but continued her headlong dash. Stunned, Brinker slowly pulled himself to his feet and looked aft. Nothing remained of the patrol boat. High above, an angry, churning mass of smoke was already dissipating. He rushed into the wheelhouse.

"Did we blow up, Captain?" the helmsman asked.

"The patrol boat," Brinker answered shortly." Watch your helm. Stop engine."

He turned to the dazed first officer. "Tell the engineer what happened. Ask him to report damage." He moved to the helmsman. "Does the helm answer?"

"Yes, sir."

Brinker watched Pieter as he spoke into a headset. "Well?" he said impatiently.

"Engineer reports no damage, sir, except to his ears. He says he would appreciate it if you would try to avoid such incidents in the future."

Brinker laughed loudly. "I can imagine what that sounded like down there. Ask him if I can resume speed." The question was answered affirmatively. "Very well. Ahead two thirds," he said. "I want to put some distance between us . . . and that." He gestured behind him at the now quiet sea.

CHAPTER 16

The *Van Hoorn* moved slowly on a west-southwest course, passing the promontory of Dungeness in midafternoon. As the ship passed its tip there was a moment of minimum sighting possibility from the shore. It was at that moment that a U-boat surfaced briefly, close to the seaward side of the *Van Hoorn*, and then dived to rejoin the others on their staggered stations along the ship's course.

Brinker adjusted his already slow speed in deference to his unseen, but infinitely comforting, consorts.

The ship steamed on. Once past the promontory they remained nearly ten miles from the indented coastline, still within the normal inshore shipping zone, and yet remaining on the edge of the deep water necessary to their underwater escorts. An occasional coastal freighter passed far to starboard, hugging the shore. Other than that, the normally heavily trafficked sea was startlingly empty.

An hour later, Dietrich, Schiller, and Siegler stood on the bridge with Captain Brinker looking at the smoke on the horizon, far behind the *Van Hoorn*.

"I have ordered my bos'n to have the tarpaulins partially removed from your tanks," the captain said, "enough for you to look them over briefly and to test their engines. Do it quickly. What you see overtaking us back there," he gestured astern, "is the same destroyer we passed earlier. She's now escorting a hospital ship. They should reach us in somewhat more than an hour."

"You seem glad to see him, Captain," Dietrich said with surprise.

"More than you know, Lieutenant. It simplifies things enormously. Our U-boats no longer need show themselves. I've told them about the air attack, and the loss of the patrol boat, and I imagine their captain is feeling a bit guilty about abandoning us."

"I see we're no longer on fire, Captain." Siegler said.

"The smoke has served its purpose. I don't want them descending on me with fire fighting apparatus when we come alongside the pier."

"Will the destroyer follow us in?" Dietrich asked.

"I think I can safely say that she will be otherwise occupied. As soon as you are finished with the tanks, I will reduce speed and allow them to overtake us even more quickly, and then things will begin to happen. So get to it, gentlemen. You have twenty minutes."

They were back on the bridge well within the captain's twenty-minute time limit. All engines had started easily, and they had assured themselves that the tanks were ready. Brinker called an order to the man on the engine order telegraph. They soon felt the ship take on a subtle shudder as it slowed.

"In approximately an hour they should be within a mile of us, and we will be passing Beachy Head. The timing is perfect. Now, I want you to join your men in the wardroom. One of you will remain near the phone at all times. Keep your men together and ready to follow orders instantly. I've decided that I want you inside the tanks when they're lowered to the pier," Brinker said.

"Inside?" Siegler repeated, incredulously.

"Yes. The sooner you are able to get moving once you're down, the better it will be for all of us. There will be inquisitive people on the wharf, I'm sure. If you are all inside the tanks, only the officer in command need deal with them, and you will be in a position to defend yourselves should something go wrong."

"It sounds like a good idea to me, Captain," Dietrich said. "Just try not to drop us."

"I didn't bring you all this way to drop you, Lieutenant. The booms have been carefully tested. The ship's relation to the pier should make it less than a twenty-foot ride. One of my men will be on the outside of each machine, ready to release it as soon as you're down, and that should be only a matter of minutes for all three. Any questions? No? Then I wish you good luck." Brinker shook each man's hand. "Give my best wishes to your men. When you return, I hope that you will all be my guests at a celebration of the success of our joint enterprise. So, auf wiedersehen and Heil Hitler."

"Heil Hitler." they all echoed.

His Majesty's destroyer *Hereford* kept station slightly ahead of the hospital ship *Saint Michael*. Alert lookouts scanned the sea's surface while asdic operators listened for the underwater contact that would change the warship's contained, protective posture into the hunter she had been designed to be.

On the high, open bridge above the wheelhouse, Lieutenant Commander Pierce divided his attention between the hospital ship and the *Van*

Hoorn, while speaking to his first lieutenant. "What's our ETA, number one?"

"Approximately 2030, sir. It depends on the *Saint Michael*. The jerry shells didn't do her power plant any good."

"That Dutch ship seems to be leading a charmed life," Pierce said. "You did say that we have her down as presumed sunk? What date?"

"Sorry, sir. I'm afraid I didn't notice. I'll check at once."

Pierce shook his head. "Not now. We'll clear it up in port. Amazing that she's lasted this long. At least she doesn't seem to be afire any longer. When will she be able to get inshore?"

"Her captain says that their steering problem will be cleared up momentarily, sir."

"He said the same thing earlier, didn't he. Well, I hope he's right. She's hanging on the edge of deep water. Be a shame to lose her now. There's little we can do until we get *Saint Michael* past Beachy Head and into safe water."

"*Van Hoorn*'s flashing, sir. Yeoman!"

"FIFTEEN - MINUTES - TO - COMPLETION - REPAIRS, sir," the yeoman translated.

"That's the ticket," Pierce said. "Acknowledge. Then send: INFORM ME WHEN YOU CAN TURN." He glanced at the bulkhead clock and said softly, "Come on, captain. Fix your bloody rudder or you'll end up in Cherbourg."

Minutes later, the yeoman called, "She's signaling: REPAIRS COMPLETED, sir."

"Send: PROCEED INDEPENDENTLY TO FALL IN ASTERN OF HOSPITAL SHIP," Pierce said. When the message had been sent, Pierce added; "Make to *Saint Michael*: MAINTAIN SPEED. CARGO SHIP WILL FOLLOW YOU IN. NO WIRELESS. ASSUME CON BY ALDIS."

He stood on the starboard gratings and watched the *Van Hoorn* edge north as the hospital ship closed on her rapidly from the beam. "Worked out fine, number one. We'll see them in and..." He paused abruptly at the sudden, unmistakable change in the rhythm of the asdic's electronic signal. A buzzer sounded angrily. "Asdic-bridge. Contact red nine-five, sir. Range five thousand. Opening."

The first lieutenant's glasses were instantly on the bearing, as the asdic buzzer sounded three rapid *P*s, the signal for torpedoes to port. "Torpedo tracks on the port beam, sir," he shouted, as his sighting was confirmed by the masthead lookout.

Pierce leaned to the voicepipe. "Hard-a-port. Ahead full both. Depth charge stations." His eyes were on the torpedo tracks as the ship turned.

"Midships, meet her, steady as you go." One track passed slowly, well to starboard, and another far to port. Pierce turned and gave rapid orders for the *Saint Michael* and *Van Hoorn* to proceed at their best speed into Newhaven as the *Hereford* raced ahead, its electroacoustic transducer, housed in a dome suspended beneath the forward hull, emitting sound waves as it rotated. Alert operators in the asdic cabinet listened for the returning echo of a contact ... fruitlessly.

"Asdic-bridge. Contact lost, sir."

"*Saint Michael* is turning to the entrance approach, sir," the first lieutenant said. "The *Van Hoorn* seems to be shielding her."

"Good. At least they're safe in that water. Now we can concentrate on our ghost. We'll give them another chance at us and try to keep them occupied until our charges are safe in port."

The *Hereford* raced into a sidling turn to port, crossed over her own wake, and then steadied on a northwestern heading. Behind the destroyer, another of the U-boats fired her stern tubes at extreme range. The two torpedoes were set to run shallow, and had virtually no chance of hitting the target, so the disgusted submarine commander didn't wait to watch their progress. He had followed orders that to him were incomprehensible, but he had followed them without question. His only consolation was that the Dutch ship he had been charged with protecting was now proceeding into the English port. He ordered the U-boat to the bottom.

The *Van Hoorn*, throbbing at maximum speed, kept pace alongside the hospital ship. Captain Brinker's full attention was on the task of maintaining safe distance, so he did not turn when he spoke. "What about the destroyer, Commander?"

Loesner focussed his glasses on the distant warship. "They're now heading south under full power, Captain. From the look of their wake, they seem to be running in circles."

"Let me know if they seem to be giving up the chase. Apparently things are going well. I haven't heard any depth charges. The U-boats should begin to draw them west soon."

"I will keep you informed, Captain." Loesner's disappointment was evident in his voice.

"Why so glum, Commander?" Brinker asked. "Under the restrictions of their orders, our men out there couldn't have been expected to make a hit other than by pure chance."

Loesner grunted.

The captain smiled briefly and said to the signalman: "Make to hospital ship: NOW IN SAFE WATERS. AM DROPPING ASTERN OF YOU."

The signalman tapped out the message rapidly, his earlier instructions to slow his transmissions forgotten in the excitement of the moment.

The answering aldis blinked steadily from the bridge of the *Saint Michael*. The signalman read the message aloud as it was being sent, writing on his pad as he spoke. "FOLLOW ME. WILL SIGNAL COURSE CHANGES. YOU ARE CLEARED FOR ENTRY." Brinker was smiling broadly as the man continued, "DISREGARD PILOT REQUIREMENTS. MY HEADING THREE-five-ONE FROM WEST BREAKWATER LIGHT. FIVE KNOTS FROM BREAKWATER. YOU BERTH SOUTH END WHARF BEHIND ME. AUTHORITIES WILL BOARD. THANK YOU FOR ASSISTANCE."

Brinker took the sheet handed him by the signalman, and said to his first officer. "We seem to have done it. Acknowledge this, Pieter. Tell them we're glad we could help."

Brinker's eyes remained fixed on the ship ahead as he said, "Commander, it's time for your men to stand by the tanks. When I pass the word, they are to enter them immediately. Since I've been ordered to dock astern of the hospital ship, it makes our getting the tanks on the pier quickly most important. A hospital ship means even more activity on the pier, so I intend to have them down before the *Saint Michael* is fully tied alongside. Tell the officers to try to move out as soon as they are on the ground. If they are forced to discuss their orders with the military authorities, have them do it well forward of the hospital ship. As I understand it, they carry orders ostensibly signed by General Gort that call for complete secrecy and immediate movement from the port."

"They do, Captain," Loesner agreed.

"Then they should use them vigorously, if at all possible. To me the one weak link in all of this is the low rank of the leader of this force. I hope he can carry it off."

"Lieutenants have a certain anonymity, Captain, less easily identified by others—particularly in a specialized branch like the tank corps. Higher ranking officers, with whom they might come into contact, could hardly be expected to be familiar with all of the lowly lieutenants."

"You've made your point, Commander. Now, please check and see that you have all of the papers and other materials you brought aboard. Then Pieter will take you to the engine room, where you can oversee the burning of my early working charts and your papers," he paused, smiling, "including that obviously German briefcase you carry . . . *particularly* that."

"The engine room?" Loesner questioned.

"Positive destruction of anything incriminating is what I want to be certain of. There will be nothing thrown overboard, nothing burned above the engine spaces. I leave nothing to chance. If they decide that this ship must be searched before I can leave, I must assume the search will be thorough. Nothing must be found to indicate we're not what we seem to be. Even you, Commander, present something of a problem. Your lack of fluency in Dutch forces me to ask you to remain in the engine spaces until we have left the port. My engineer will find a place to keep you out of the way."

"But my English is excellent, Captain."

"A Dutch officer who speaks only English?"

The first officer appeared behind the commander, carrying folded charts. "Ready, sir, The new charts are in place, appropriately marked."

"Then get below and get on with it. Return here as quickly as you can, Pieter, we'll be at the breakwater soon."

"I will, sir," the first officer replied, as he led the unhappy commander Loesner toward the bridge ladder.

Lieutenant Schiller stood on the forward deck near the canvas-covered tank and watched the *Van Hoorn*'s bows swing slowly to the right. Far ahead, the hospital ship edged toward the narrow entrance to the port of Newhaven.

Schiller felt his jaw tighten, and he made a conscious effort to relax. His crew, Sergeants Thyben, Priller, and Bohling, leaned against the forward bulkhead of the centercastle, their faces expressionless, but Schiller knew that they too were fighting the tension that becomes an integral part of the preparation to face danger. It wasn't the fear of action, but the wait for it to begin that annoyed. At least that was what they told themselves, and some even believed it.

The *Van Hoorn* seemed to be barely moving. Off to the left of the bows, chalk cliffs, formed through the centuries by the shells of the minute Foraminifera, rose behind the breakwater. The stone barrier ran curving to the shore to join a promenade that ran for twelve-hundred feet to the east and then turned sharply to form the western side of the harbor entrance. The cliffs ended at the turn, and Schiller could see that their face was dotted with hollowed-out gun emplacements and the summit crowned with an old fort that, he decided, was also manned and mounting guns. His eyes swept past the lighthouse that stood at the end of the entrance. Another breakwater stretched out for less than half the distance of the more formidable one to the west. A green light on its outer top blinked metronomically. Beyond it, the coast arched away to the town of Seaford, nestled beneath the heights of Seaford Head, where the land seemed to end, and the English Channel lay unobscured to the horizon. As his gaze moved back toward the harbor, Schiller saw a train moving along the coast. Nothing seemed intimidating or in the least out of the ordinary.

Priller shook his head in wonder. "I don't know how that captain did it, but we're here, and it looks like it's going to be easy."

"Maybe we can stop at the Crown and Anchor in Shoreham, Lieutenant?" Priller said, smiling. "We'll probably be able to use a pint by then."

"I could use one right now," Bohling said.

Schiller laughed. "I think we'd better wait until we're back home for that. If we stopped at every pub that Priller is familiar with, we wouldn't get to Southampton until December, and the war will be over."

"You're right," Priller agreed. "Not about me, but you can't trust Bohling in a pub. Two drinks and he wants to sing. Imagine how *'Wir fahren gegen Engelland'* would go over in the Crown and Anchor?" He began to sing, "So give me thy hand, thy fair white hand, ere we sail away to conquer Eng - el - land."

They were all laughing when their attention was caught by sudden activity around the tank. Sailors began to remove the tarpaulin from the turret top, and the idling drone of the boom machinery suddenly changed to a business-like roar. The laughter faded, and the soldiers leaned back against the superstructure and waited quietly.

Captain Brinker watched the *Saint Michael* begin to enter the harbor entrance.

"Have the soldiers get in the tanks now, Pieter. And have the boom parties stand by," he ordered.

The first officer rushed to the bulkhead phone and spoke into the mouthpiece hurriedly, then returned to the wing. "The bos'n reports that once the soldiers are in the tanks, everything is ready, Captain."

"Good, Pieter. It's almost time to turn to the final approach. As soon as we're alongside the pier, I want you to go to the stern and take over the phones. I'll need your help to back this ship out. I'll be conning her from the starboard side, you watch the port. Once we're through the narrowest point I'm going to back full astern, so warn me if I'm straying from the limits of the dredged channel."

Ahead, the *Saint Michael* was being assisted by a single harbor tug in its cautious approach to the pier. The *Van Hoorn* crept ahead and passed the lighthouse on the end of the west pier. Soldiers patrolling the promenade waved and called encouragement to the working parties on the *Van Hoorn*'s scarred decks.

When the inner entrance lights were abeam of the *Van Hoorn*,

Brinker called a series of rapid helm and engine orders, and the ship swung slowly toward the pier. Most of the shore activity was centered around the *Saint Michael,* but a handful of civilian stevedores waited to receive the *Van Hoorn*'s lines. Brinker was more interested in the soldiers lined up behind the line handlers and spoke over his shoulder to Pieter, "Inform the tank officers. Thirty soldiers and two Bren carriers on the pier. They look friendly enough."

Schiller felt the jarring impact of the *Van Hoorn*'s first contact with the pier, as the sailor standing outside the turret repeated the captain's message about the soldiers and Bren carriers. "Stand by the cannon, Ernst," he ordered, "Just in case." He looked up as the sailor called, "Get ready. The tank on the stern is starting over."

"I'd like to put in for a leave... starting now," Priller said nervously.

"So would I," Schiller agreed.

"Now!" the sailor yelled.

Schiller held onto the turntable supports as he felt the tank lurch beneath him and then begin to rise upward from the deck.

CHAPTER 17

Despite some minor grating and a gentle bump, Lieutenant Dietrich and his crew were not certain that the tank had reached the pier until they heard the heavy boom hook drop resoundingly against the turret top, followed by a terse, unintelligable grunt from the sailor outside. Dietrich moved quickly. He began the short climb into the commanders cupola. Looking up, he caught a glimpse of the sailor, one foot in the cargo hook, being raised back toward the deck of the *Van Hoorn*. "Start the engines," he said into his headset microphone.

The two powerful diesels were idling steadily as Dietrich raised his shoulders through the cupola hatch. Below him, a young British officer—a second lieutenant—stood staring with disbelief at the tank. The soldiers that Brinker had warned about stood near the officer.

"Good evening," Dietrich said, relieved at the officer's junior rank.

The young man looked up, even more surprised by Dietrich's sudden appearance. "Where in God's name did you come from?" he asked and then suddenly caught himself. "Sorry. Good evening, sir. I must say I wasn't expecting a tank. From what we've heard of France . . ."

Dietrich took the initiative. "Rumors, Lieutenant. Order your men back a bit, will you, while I move off the landing stage." He spoke into the intercom, "Move ahead twenty feet."

The young lieutenant gave the order and walked alongside as the tank lumbered forward.

"Are you the officer in charge?" Dietrich shouted above the tread noise.

"For the moment. Lieutenant Willard is the watch officer, but he's up seeing to the *Saint Michael*. I daresay he'll be along soon enough when he sees you. We hadn't expected a tank. Hadn't expected you at all, actually." The lieutenant paused momentarily and stared ahead at the second tank just touching the pier. "Two of you?"

Dietrich ordered a halt. "Three, Lieutenant." He pointed at the third, being lowered behind him.

"Three?" the young officer repeated. His inexperience showed.

Dietrich smiled. "When were you commissioned, Lieutenant?"

"This is my first day here, sir. Is it that obvious?"

"I only asked because you seem to have little faith in the Royal Tank Corps and our Dutch captain." He gestured at the *Van Hoorn*. "He got us here, and personally, I'm for giving him three cheers."

"I can well imagine, sir." The young officer watched Schiller's tank move off its landing stage. "Your captain certainly seems efficient. I've waited hours for simple hand baggage to be landed from ships not much larger than this one." He turned to watch Siegler's tank moving off its stage. "All this must be something of a record." He shook his head and looked up at Dietrich. "I must say, I don't know exactly what to do with you. I shall have to send a man to fetch Lieutenant Willard. He'll want to inform the CO. How many of our men are aboard the ship?"

"None. We're the lot. The troops we were carrying were transferred to a destroyer this morning. This ship was in some danger of sinking at the time. We decided to remain with the tanks. By the way, I'm Lieutenant George Parker, Seventh Battalion, Royal Tank Regiment," Dietrich said.

"Albert Foster, sir," the young officer replied.

"Nice to meet you, Foster. Now, there's no need for you to send anyone ahead. Why don't you climb up here and have your men follow. We'll all go see your Lieutenant Willard."

"Actually, we should remain here. But since there are no troops aboard..." Foster hesitated, then made his decision. "All right, sir, but I think I'd better lead the way in one of the Bren carriers. Give me a minute to turn the men over to my sergeant-major. They should stay down here. I'll let you know when I'm ready." Foster moved away to speak to an obviously interested sergeant-major and then climbed into one of the Bren carriers, signaling to Dietrich.

"Follow the Bren carrier, Falck. And all of you remember the names on your paybooks. From now on you're British soldiers," Dietrich said into the microphone, while gesturing for Siegler's tank to close up.

A group of men stood on the pier below the *Van Hoorn*'s bridge, watching the tanks. Dietrich saw Captain Brinker, on the wing, waving for him to stop.

"Halt," Dietrich ordered, raising his arm in a warning to Siegler. Schiller was watching alertly from his position near the bows, and his turret swung partly around as he saw the exchange.

An older man, well into his sixties, approached Dietrich. "Good evening. I'm Captain Williamson. Port Captain," he said, his voice surprisingly steady and vigorous.

"Can I help you, sir?" Dietrich asked.

Before the man could answer, Captain Brinker's voice boomed from the wing. "Ah, Lieutenant. I have been trying to explain to your countrymen that my gangway has been destroyed and I am arranging to lower a ladder."

"The chap's English has suddenly improved," Captain Williamson said dryly. "Glad you came up, Lieutenant. Couldn't understand a word he said till now."

"We took a bit of a pasting coming over, sir. I doubt that Captain Brinker has had any sleep for God knows how many days. I'm quite sure he's doing all he can to assist you, as he did us."

"We saw the attack made on you outside this harbor," Captain Williamson said. "Perhaps that accounts for the unorthodox approach your captain used in docking this vessel. But all's well that ends well. You were fortunate that the destroyer was there to help." He placed a hand on the tread skirt. "Incidentally, where have you come from? Certainly not Dunkirk, not with these tanks."

It was the question that Dietrich dreaded. "Nieuport, sir. It was arranged by General Gort for this ship to pick us up just before it was overrun. Then the captain put in at Dunkirk. We left there this morning with troops."

Williamson looked at Dietrich closely before saying, "General Gort arranged for you to be picked up, and yet the captain risked going into Dunkirk?"

"He's Dutch, sir. Rather unpredictable chaps, I understand."

The port captain smiled. "That would explain it. I don't see the troops you spoke of, Lieutenant."

"Transferred to a destroyer this morning, sir. We were sinking, or thought so at the time. We remained with the tanks. Been chased all over the Channel ever since, until that destroyer took us in hand."

"Terrible times for the country," Williamson said. "Well, I'm glad that you lads made it. We certainly can use you. I see young Foster is looking out for you?"

"Yes, sir. We're off to report to the commanding officer."

"Fine. Good luck to you and your men." The port captain looked down the pier. "Ah, there's the ladder. Carry on, Lieutenant."

Dietrich signaled for Foster to move ahead, thinking, old men and green officers. General Kellner had been right. They didn't seem really to know what was happening in France or he would have been questioned more closely about his reference to Nieuport.

Schiller fell into line between Dietrich's and Siegler's tanks, and they moved in single file behind the Bren carrier. It didn't seem possible that

155

their good luck could continue. But it did. On the last day of May, 1940, closely connected chance events conspired with the storm troopers and continued to work in their favor.

On that evening, the security forces at the port were to be reinforced by a Canadian detachment, and the *Saint Michael* had been expected hours earlier. It had been intended that the hospital ship would be unloaded and the wounded enroute north long before the arrival of the Canadians. The reinforcements were, however, arriving at the port on a troop train at the very moment that Dietrich's tanks were moving away from the *Van Hoorn*, and that required the presence of the commanding officer of the port's security force. Thus, Major Brian Sancroft, who was understandably anxious to disembark the reinforcements and clear the tracks for the waiting hospital train, was unaware of the *Van Hoorn* and the tanks.

Lieutenant Albert Foster had been posted to the security force only the day before and was unfamiliar both with his duties and the rigid requirements for movement through the port. When he arrived at the hospital ship, closely followed by the tanks, he learned that his immediate superior, Lieutenant Willard, was busy aboard the *Saint Michael* and temporarily unavailable. Further inquiry added to his uncertainty when he found that Major Sancroft was at the harbor station and also unavailable. Lieutenant Foster was at a loss as to what to do next.

Another incident aided in the storm trooper's deception. A small fire was discovered aboard the *Saint Michael* as the tanks sat idling alongside on the pier. There was nothing but chance connected with their proximity to the ship when the fire became evident.

The hospital ship had been shelled as it lay alongside the east mole at Dunkirk and had sustained one hit on her upper superstructure and another, more serious, in her engine room. There had been only minor damage to the upper decks, and every available man had been sent below to repair the damage in the engine spaces. They had worked feverishly, knowing that engine room damage at Dunkirk usually proved fatal.

The *Saint Michael* had lain alongside the mole throughout the night. Six hundred wounded had been brought aboard before the shells struck. Unloading would have been a monumental task under the best of circumstances, and Dunkirk provided only the worst. It had taken hours for sufficient repairs to be accomplished, allowing the ship to move out into the rain and fog. The crew was exhausted, and nothing further was done to the upper deck damage. The shell that struck the superstructure had not exploded and had passed through the outer bulkheads cleanly. But electrical insulation had been smoldering undetected throughout the trip from Dunkirk and had finally broken out into recognizeable fire as the ship lay in the safety of the port. Lieutenant Foster had been attempting to get aboard the ship when the fire alarm rang. He was forced to return to the pier when the gangways were closed to all but the intent medical personnel removing the wounded. He made his way back to the Bren carrier. "I'm afraid we'll have to wait here a bit, sir," he called to Dietrich, only to be interrupted by a harried civilian official who had heard what he had said.

"You can't wait here, Lieutenant. Please get those tanks moving. They're blocking the whole pier. Fire equipment's coming in," the man said with authority.

Dietrich saw the young officer's indecision. He dropped to the ground and ran over to him. "We'll have to move these tanks, Foster. Where is your commanding officer?"

"I've just learned he's at the harbor station. We're being reinforced, and it seems the troop train's just arrived."

"Then we'll move up there," Dietrich said.

Foster looked around at the increasing activity on the pier and the ship. "I expect that would be best, sir. It is getting rather crowded, and the station isn't far."

"Have you ever been in a tank, Foster?" Dietrich asked.

"Only the Mark 1."

"Have your Bren carrier move back down the pier out of the way, and you come aboard my tank. We'll move up to the station and look for your C.O."

"I don't know, sir. I was told to . . ."

"No time for that. Give your orders and come with me." Dietrich ran toward the idling tank, not giving Foster time for further discussion.

The Bren carrier was moving past them, on its way back to the far end of the pier as Dietrich leaned down to help the young lieutenant climb aboard the tank. "Just stand there for a bit. I'll let you see what it's like inside as soon as we get out of this mess."

Dietrich clipped on his headset and ordered the driver to move ahead while raising his arm in a forward sweep in signal to the others. The three tanks lumbered forward cautiously through the frenetic activity on the pier, moving close to the cargo sheds when fire trucks passed, their sirens blaring angrily. Dietrich gave orders into the headset at that moment, unheard by Foster who was looking back toward the smoke rising from the upper decks of the hospital ship. Then Dietrich, too, looked back, not at the hospital ship, but at the *Van Hoorn*. It still lay against the pier, and he hoped that the boarding of the port officials hadn't spoiled Brinker's opportunity to take advantage of the confusion and get the ship out of the

157

port. Despite the captain's assurances that his papers covered every contingency, Dietrich was worried about possible questioning of the crew. There was always one man who would say something, even inadvertently, that would... His thoughts were interrupted as the tank crabbed sideways to the right and slowed to cross the complex of railroad tracks that had been hidden by the cargo sheds. Once across, they turned left into the road leading out of the pier area and were now shielded by buildings on both sides. Dietrich beckoned to Lieutenant Foster.

"Better take your look inside while you can, Lieutenant."

Foster climbed eagerly to the turret hatch. "Are you sure I won't be in the way, sir?"

"Not at all. Be careful going down, mind your head. My men will answer any questions you might have."

"Thank you," Foster said as he backed down through the turret hatch.

Dietrich heard the dull thud and waited until Richter peered out of the hatch cautiously. "Well?" he questioned.

"I hit him pretty hard. I think I killed him," Richter said.

"That's what you were supposed to do. Now get back down there and make sure, then stand by the guns. We aren't out of here yet."

The harbor railroad station lay just ahead, blocked from view by the buildings, and the tanks passed the road leading to it unaccosted. Actually, the occasional soldiers who patrolled the street watched them pass with the feigned boredom that hid the basic awe foot soldiers feel when confronted with the heavy, tracked vehicles.

The harbor station was now well behind them, and the sentries were few and far between. Ahead, the road curved sharply to the left, blocking Dietrich's view completely. He ordered the tanks to slow. As they neared the blind curve, an imposing staff car rounded it, saw them, and stopped. It was obvious that there wasn't room for it to pass. Dietrich passed the order to halt and swore angrily at the impasse. He gestured at the car's driver, urging him to move over. He saw the man turn and speak to someone in the back seat, then turn back to drive the car slowly up onto the sidewalk, where it stopped alongside a row of deserted private houses.

"Move ahead," Dietrich ordered.

The tank lurched forward, and as they started to pass the car, Dietrich saw an inquisitive look on the face of an officer who had leaned out of the rolled down window and was gesturing for him to stop. Dietrich saluted smartly as the tank rumbled past the car. The officer continued to signal unmistakably. Dietrich looked ahead and behind quickly. They were shielded on either side by the evacuated buildings, and in the front by the blind curve. Nothing was visible behind. No, he could see a lone sentry behind Siegler's tank, moving toward it.

"Halt," Dietrich ordered, while signaling to the others. He spoke into his headset microphone rapidly. "Stand by the guns. Take command, Richter, and hand me up one of the incendiary charges." He turned and beckoned meaningfully to Shiller and Siegler, and then dropped to the ground to walk back toward the car, the incendiary charge hidden under his tunic.

The driver had opened the rear door of the staff car, and was standing at attention beside it, his back to Dietrich.

As Dietrich neared the car he saw that Schiller was approaching him purposefully and caught a glimpse of Siegler talking to the patrolling sentry. Dietrich jerked his head briefly in the direction of the driver and saw Schiller's nod of understanding.

Dietrich stepped past the driver and faced the officer. "Sir." he said, saluting. Schiller stood beside the driver.

The officer, a colonel, returned the salute, and began to step out of the car, saying: "Where on earth did you come from, Lieutenant? I wasn't informed that any tanks . . ." His eyes barely caught the movement of Dietrich's hand. He felt the blow that struck him behind the left ear, and nothing more. Dietrich pushed the body back into the car as he heard the driver fall behind him.

"I'll put that one in the car. Go and see if Siegler got his man. Send Priller up ahead to watch the road, then get back here," Dietrich ordered.

Schiller moved away at a run, pausing to yell a command to Sergeant Priller who was watching calmly from the turret of the middle tank. Schiller stopped abruptly as Siegler appeared from behind the rear tank, carrying the body of the sentry effortlessly. Dietrich waved them forward anxiously, and said, "Inside with him, Willi. Is someone watching the rear?"

"Becker," Siegler answered, pushing the body of the sentry into the rear of the car.

Dietrich looked over at the row of attached, empty houses alongside the car. "Can you get through the door of one of them, Willi?"

Siegler quickly ran to the closest house. Using a massive fist to break a panel in the wooden door, he reached in and opened it from the inside. Dietrich and Schiller ran around to the other side of the car, opened the door, and immediately began to drag the bodies out. Moments later, Siegler carried the third corpse into the musty interior of the house.

"Go get the other one in my tank, Willi," Dietrich said. "This is as good a time as any to get rid of him."

Siegler hurried out the door, while Dietrich and Schiller dragged the bodies of the colonel and his driver up the narrow stairway to the landing of the upper floor. Then they returned to the ground floor and pulled the dead sentry to the middle of the staircase.

Siegler burst through the door, carrying Lieutenant Foster. "All clear ahead and behind," he reported.

"Take that one upstairs with the others," Dietrich said. "Leave the sentry where he is. Take this," he tossed the incendiary charge to Siegler. "Put it under the stairs. We'll get back to the tanks and cover the road. When you're finished in here, take over Schiller's tank until we get out of here. He'll be using yours to cover the rear. Make it quick!" Dietrich and Schiller ran out the door.

When he was back in his turret, Dietrich beckoned to Priller, ahead at the curve. Priller loped back, calling, "Nothing in sight. It's a double curve."

"Get back to your tank," Dietrich ordered.

It wasn't long before Siegler came out of the deserted house. He climbed aboard the middle tank and raised his hand in a thumbs-up gesture.

"Let's go, Falck," Dietrich said. The tank lurched forward, followed by the others.

When they had crabbed around the second leg of the curve, Dietrich saw the town railroad station about five hundred feet ahead to his left. He glanced back and saw the third tank moving out of the curve. An eerie, white light filled the street behind it.

The attached buildings ended at the curve. The road now ran straight, past the railroad station, to end at a junction with another road, which ran at right angles to the one on which the tanks were proceeding. Where they joined, soldiers patrolled on either side of a temporary roadblock of large farm wagons. To the left, beyond the block, lay the swing bridge that crossed the Ouse. Dietrich watched a British sergeant walking toward him, his hand raised in a stop signal. He spoke into the intercom. "Entrance roadblock coming up. Get ready, all of you. We're almost out."

The three tanks stopped near the roadblock. Dietrich took the initiative, "I think you have a fire back along the road, Sergeant."

The sergeant, a small wiry man with a scarred face and battered nose, looked up at Dietrich, still puzzled by the tank's appearance. He hadn't been told that there was armor in the pier area. "Fire equipment's already come in, sir," he said.

"I'm not talking about the fire on the pier, Sergeant. The evacuated civilian houses around the bend behind me. We saw a bit of smoke.

Apparently one of them is on fire. There was a Humber staff car parked on the sidewalk in front of it. I assume whoever was in it is investigating. Your Lieutenant Foster was with us, but he stayed at the building to see what was happening. Better get cracking, Sergeant, they may need . . ."

They all turned as a sudden roar, followed by flame that erupted skyward in a violent geyser, came from the roofs of the buildings.

"Cor!" the sergeant yelled. "You say the colonel's car was there, sir?"

"A Humber. I don't know if it was your colonel's. Lieutenant Foster didn't say."

The sergeant spun away, running to a nearby guard shack. Dietrich calmly watched as the sergeant shouted into a telephone, then rushed out, calling orders to the soldiers at the roadblock. Heavy smoke was beginning to roll toward them from the blazing buildings.

"Have your men clear those wagons out of our way, Sergeant," Dietrich yelled. "We can't block this road."

"Yes, sir." The sergeant hastily gave the orders and then ran after the men already moving toward the fire. He had made no attempt to ask for Dietrich's orders or authorization to leave. In the confusion of the moment he found no need to question the presence of the tanks, which had obviously come up through the major portion of the security force, and the tank officer *had* mentioned Lieutenant Foster by name.

The farm wagons were moved, and the tanks passed through the barrier, virtually ignored by the remaining sentries who were gazing in fascination at the flames rising above the roofs of the clustered houses. The lead tank turned abruptly to the left, moved cautiously over the railroad tracks, and rumbled slowly across the swing bridge. Once across, Dietrich signaled and the second tank crossed, followed in turn by the third.

They moved past the entrance to another road, which ran along the west bank of the river. Once they were well past it, Dietrich raised his arm in an order to halt and pulled to the side of the road. The others pulled up behind him. Dietrich dropped to the ground, motioning for Schiller and Siegler to join him.

"Make sure the compressor pressure's 110 pounds. We have a hill to climb ahead. I'm going back to make a quick check on the ship. If the captain gets out of the harbor, we're in the clear . . . for the time being. If not, we may have to get ready for trouble." Schiller and Siegler turned back toward the tanks as Dietrich rushed to the bridge, crossing to its center. The fire in the buildings was still raging, but the smoke was being carried east by the wind, so he could see down the river. The *Van Hoorn* lay well out in the harbor, its bow pointed toward him. As Dietrich watched, the water at her stern began to roil, and he guessed that it was starting to back. Satisfied, he pushed his way back through the crowd of civilians rushing across the bridge to the fire and ran quickly back to the tanks.

CHAPTER 18

The *Van Hoorn* shuddered slightly and began to back steadily into the entrance. Brinker watched the stern begin to swing dangerously as the torque of the reversed propellor forced the ship into a yawing motion.

A voice called from the wheelhouse, "First officer reports stern wandering, sir."

"Stop engine," Brinker ordered. "Steady her up easy, Quartermaster."

"She swung off by herself, sir," the quartermaster called.

"I know. We're riding too high to get a decent bite. Put your rudder five degrees to port, no more."

"Rudder is port five, sir."

It was a time for seamanship, and Brinker supplied it. He watched as the stern moved back toward the center. They were in the narrowest part of the entrance, and Brinker's knuckles whitened as he clutched the wing rail and called a series of rapid orders.

The ship's side was barely ten feet away from the concrete sides of the entrance when they backed past the lighthouse. Brinker released pent-up breath but did not relax his concentration, even though he knew the worst was over. Interested soldiers lined the promenade as the *Van Hoorn* backed steadily toward the end of the western breakwater. A blinking light flashed from the lighthouse steadily. Brinker said to the signalman, "See what they want. Read it out," before returning his attention to the stern and the light on the breakwater's tip.

The signalman spoke slowly as he read the message. "WHY BACKING? WHAT AUTHORIZATIION FOR LEAVING PORT? IS PILOT ABOARD?"

"Send: PORT CAPTAIN AUTHORIZED DEPARTURE. FIRE IN PORT DANGER TO MY VESSEL. NO PILOT."

An answering flicker came almost immediately, and the signalman translated: "YOU ARE STANDING INTO DANGER. U-BOATS STILL IN AREA. RETURN PORT IMMEDIATELY."

"Send: I AM NEEDED DUNKIRK," Brinker said.

The breakwater light was now abeam. "Have the first officer report to the bridge and tell the engineer we're out. Commander Loesner can come up now," Brinker called to the wheelhouse.

163

"They're continuing to repeat: RETURN PORT IMMEDIATELY, sir," the signalman said.

Brinker silenced him with a wave and called, "Port twenty. Stop engine." The *Van Hoorn* moved to the west in a backing turn. Finally Brinker called, "Midships. Ahead one third." When the ship began to move forward slowly, Brinker rushed into the wheelhouse and studied the compass. "Ahead full," he ordered.

The first officer entered the wheelhouse, breathing heavily. "You made that look easy, Captain," he said.

"It's not over yet, Pieter. On the contrary, it's just beginning. They want us to return, and I'm ignoring them. They'll have someone after us soon. Let's hope our U-boat escort is still out there."

Commander Loesner had entered while the captain was speaking. "Why will someone be after us, Captain? Have they captured the storm troopers?" he asked.

"If they had, shells from that fort would be falling on us now. You'll be happy to hear that my lookouts reported that all three tanks crossed the bridge before we left the harbor. They seem to have gotten out without trouble. There are two fires in the port, one on the hospital ship, and another somewhere between the pier and the bridge. I suspect your troops had something to do with that one."

"Then we've done it!" Loesner said jubilantly.

"Not quite yet, Commander. We have other problems. The port captain of Newhaven boarded this ship when we were alongside. He was accompanied by three other armed security officials. The port captain immediately began to ask some very perceptive questions, many of which I had no logical answers for. I was forced to detain them and move out without authorization. They're in the wardroom, under guard."

"Then we'll have the entire British navy in this area after us and have most likely compromised the mission of the storm troopers," Loesner said angrily.

"If I had remained, Commander, there would have been no chance at all for the mission ever beginning. We would all be under arrest. Now at least they're in, and they didn't have to fight their way out of that port. I told you that the port captain asked questions I couldn't answer. He knew immediately that I wasn't what I pretended to be. He had been told by your troops that I had embarked the tanks at Nieuport. As good a story as any to the uninformed. Unfortunately, the port captain was well informed." Brinker glared uncharacteristically at the commander. "I began to be uneasy when I noticed his interest in the booms when he came aboard.

When we were face to face, he said that it was his understanding that Nieuport fell on the twenty-ninth. Today is the thirty-first. I tried an incredible tale of heroism, prepared by your department, and absolutely ridiculous under the circumstances." Brinker ran a large hand across his face, rubbing his tired eyes. "He didn't believe it for a moment, and I don't blame him."

"Sorry, Captain. I didn't realize. . . ."

"Let me continue." Brinker said. He moved to the wheelhouse door and stared back at the *Van Hoorn*'s churning wake for a moment. "Why didn't you make for Dover, or an east coast port, particularly with such an important cargo? How much fuel do you carry precisely? To what destroyer did you transfer the troops you are supposed to have been carrying? Why is it they didn't escort you to port? Can you explain why your ship has been listed as sunk since the twenty-seventh? We can be thankful that these questions didn't occur to him until after he had spoken to your men and that he boarded the ship before he alerted anyone else in the port."

"He was seen boarding, wasn't he, Captain? They'll know he didn't leave," Loesner said.

"Most of the people near us were moved up the pier when the fire broke out on the hospital ship. It will take the authorities some time to question anyone who remained. I'm hoping they'll think I'm simply a headstrong Dutchman and not begin to put it together for some time. They've contacted the navy by now. Let us hope they let it go at that."

It was less than ten minutes later when the lookouts reported smoke on the horizon behind the *Van Hoorn*, and only minutes after that when Pieter said, "Masthead reports contact is a British destroyer, Captain, approaching at high speed."

"Only one? Good," Brinker said.

After satisfying himself that the *Van Hoorne* was moving out of the port, Dietrich made his way back to the western side of the bridge, ignoring the roar of the fire behind him. Siegler was leaning against the rear of his tank when Dietrich approached.

"The ship's on its way out. Are we ready to go?" Dietrich asked.

Siegler nodded, then said, "See that old man hobbling down the street over there? He just told me that a general order came through from the government today. All road signs in the country are to be taken down."

"Why is he looking back at us like that?" Dietrich asked.

165

"We had quite a conversation, but when he asked me where we were going, I gave him what for. Loose talk, and all that. He's afraid he'll be arrested before he gets to the pub."

Dietrich laughed. "Amazing what you can learn without trying. Get aboard, Willi, we're moving out."

He moved ahead, stopped to talk briefly with Schiller, then climbed aboard the lead tank and clipped on his headset. A group of interested civilians were talking with Falck, who was standing up in the driving compartment, holding court. The civilians were obviously interested in the shell dents in the tanks armor (sustained before they were captured), and Falck was explaining their origin. "Bloody moths," he said, to the delight of the civilians. He dropped back into his seat when he saw Dietrich and clipped on his earphones.

"Move out," Dietrich ordered.

The three tanks rumbled noisily along the Brighton road and began the climb up Castle Hill. The road rose in a climbing curve to the right and then left in a sharper rise. An occasional lorry on its way to Newhaven passed them cautiously, but otherwise they had the road to themselves. Finally, the rise grew less steep and gradually flattened as they turned to the south. Ahead lay the Channel, two hundred feet below, filling the horizon. They turned west, and had an unobstructed view of the coast, which curved away to the west below them. They were now atop the chalk cliffs that had dominated the view as they had approached in the *Van Hoorn*. Behind them, the port of Newhaven was hidden by the mass of Castle Hill, but the breakwaters were clearly visible. Dietrich saw the *Van Hoorn* well to the east, water churning at her stern. He gave a thumbs-up gesture and settled himself in the cupola, watching the road ahead. Glancing again out over the channel he saw another ship moving to the east. Even distance couldn't hide the sleek lines of the destroyer, or its bow wave.

H.M.S. Hereford cleaved the water gracefully, flinging water back over her raked bows. Lieutenant Commander Pierce stared through powerful glasses at the *Van Hoorn* from the open bridge above the wheelhouse. He lowered the binoculars to his chest, and spoke to the first lieutenant, "Look at her counter, number one."

Lieutenant Taylor studied the *Van Hoorn*'s stern. "I've been looking at it, sir. She's going flat out."

"What in bloody blazes is going on? She must see us," Pierce said.

"They were ordered to return to port, sir. I would say that captain wasn't happy with the order."

"Obviously not. According to Newhaven, they ostensibly left with the permission of the port captain. Old Williamson is not a man to rescind orders without reason. See if you can find out what it is. And see if you can clear up that nonsense about her having backed out."

"Yes, sir. Backed out indeed. I've even felt uncomfortable entering that port bow first."

"Precisely. More shoreside fumbling, I suspect," Pierce said, his eyes on the *Van Hoorn*. "But that Dutch ally of ours is carrying independence too far."

Lieutenant Taylor was about to speak to the wireless room, when he paused. "One more thing, sir," he said. "Her draught."

Pierce focused his glasses. "She is riding rather high. Find out what cargo she was carrying."

Lieutenant Taylor moved away to carry out his orders. Pierce turned to the yeoman, who was continuing in his attempt to get a response from the *Van Hoorn*, tapping out the same message on his aldis continuously. "Anything yet?" Pierce asked.

"No, sir, nothing."

Lieutenant Taylor moved back beside the commander. "We should have an answer directly, sir."

"Damnedest thing I've ever seen, number one. If you were in command of an unarmed, damaged ship, and had finally managed to make a safe port after having been attacked by submarines and God knows what else, would you move back out here?"

"I most certainly would not, sir. But I'm not Dutch."

A buzzer sounded. "Message from Newhaven, sir. VAN HOORN BACKED OUT OF ENTRANCE. PORT CAPTAIN UNAVAILABLE. NO INFORMATION ON CARGO. CHECKING. WILL INFORM."

"Did you hear that?" Pierce asked. "They have no information on the cargo and they've misplaced their port captain! God help us if that's an example of our shoreside efficiency."

"She did back out, sir," Taylor said.

"I'm beginning to wonder if those fools back there know a bow from a stern." Pierce moved to the chart table and leaned over it. "We should overtake her in less than a quarter of an hour, just off Eastdean. I'll have her turn inshore and herd her back to Newhaven."

"They seemed determined to leave, sir. What if her captain refuses to turn back?" Taylor asked.

"In that case, you will board her and take her in yourself, number one," Pierce said, looking at the rapidly growing dusk. "I don't relish the thought of mucking about out here in the dark with that ship."

"She's finally answering, sir!" the yeoman called. "Asking for a repeat."

"Well that's something at least," Pierce said. "Get on with it." He watched as the yeoman tapped out the message and soon saw an answering flicker.

"She says: UNDERSTOOD, sir," the yeoman said.

"That's more like it. I was beginning to think they were all blind." Pierce moved over to the voice pipe and was about to speak to the wheelhouse when he heard Lieutenant Taylor gasp.

"She seems to have stopped, sir."

Pierce focused his glasses on the *Van Hoorn*. "What did you send, yeoman?"

"MAINTAIN SPEED. RETURN NEWHAVEN, sir."

"Find out why they've stopped," Pierce ordered, and waited impatiently for the answer.

"Overheated bearing, sir," the yeoman said.

"Damn it! That's all we need. Send: I AM COMING ALONGSIDE."

Ten minutes later the *Hereford* was closing cautiously along the drifting ship's starboard side. Pierce studied the captain of the *Van Hoorn* through his glasses. Brinker was standing on the wing, holding a megaphone, calmly watching the *Hereford*'s approach.

"He's a cool one, I'll say that, Number One," Pierce said. "Warn all stations to stay alert. I'm going to stop alongside her briefly and see what the man has to say."

Pierce waited until all stations had acknowledged their readiness, then ordered the engines stopped. He took the megaphone handed him by the yeoman and spoke, his voice amplified and metallic, "You've caused us a bit of trouble, Captain. You were ordered to return to Newhaven."

"I was given permission to leave by the port captain. I am out. Why return now? This is a Dutch ship, and I am a Dutch citizen. One I might add, who is attempting to assist an ally. I am going back to Dunkirk," Brinker replied.

"We appreciate your assistance, Captain, but I'm afraid my orders are to see that you return to Newhaven. How long before you can get underway? You must admit your constant breakdowns are endangering your ship and your crew."

Brinker seemed to shrug in exasperation. "Very well. I will return with you, but under protest."

"Noted, Captain. Now, how long will it be until you're ready?" Pierce asked.

"It's not as bad as I had thought. Perhaps twenty minutes," Brinker responded.

"As quickly as you can, please, Captain." Both the audible change in the asdic's pinging and a voice from the bulkhead loudspeaker caused Pierce to spin around.

"Asdic-Bridge. Contact green eight-oh. Range eighteen hundred and closing, sir."

Pierce reacted instantly, even though he was faced with a situation dreaded by naval captains. A crippled ship lay helpless beside him. If torpedoes were fired, and the destroyer escaped them, the *Van Hoorn* would surely be sunk. His only option was to attack quickly and draw the U-boat's fire. He was at the voice pipe immediately. "Ahead flank both," he ordered and then swung back to call to Brinker, "Submarine to starboard. Clear your below deck stations."

"Asdic-Bridge. Contact now green one-oh-oh. Range two thousand. Steady."

"Hard-a-starboard," Pierce called. "Stand by depth charges. Maximum depression all guns. Keep a sharp lookout, number one."

"Asdic-Bridge. Contact now green two-oh. Range twenty-five hundred. She's turning." There was a slight pause, and the Asdic operator's sudden intake of breath was magnified through the loudspeaker. "Sir! We have HE dead ahead!" HE, or hydroplane effect, meant torpedoes!

"Midships. Meet her. Steady as you go," Pierce called.

"Torpedo tracks dead ahead, sir," Taylor cried. "Running shallow. Almost on us."

"I see them," Pierce said. "Steady as you go. It's going to be close. Bastards!"

The destroyer raced ahead. Two torpedoes churned by to starboard, another well to port. The fourth was running directly at the *Hereford*'s bows. Pierce watched its track hypnotically. Further correction of the destroyer's course was now impossible. To turn either way was to expose the entire length of the warship to the torpedo. Pierce glanced briefly at Lieutenant Taylor as the deadly track moved beneath the ship's bow wave, and was lost from view. They braced themselves for what they thought was the inevitable explosion. Seconds passed—nothing.

Pierce sighed in relief, "That was close. How's the *Van Hoorn*, number one?"

"Good God. She's turning to starboard, sir," Taylor said.

"Away from the shore? Are they blind? The man must be mad!"

A voice came from the wheelhouse pipe, "Gunnery Officer reports something struck the hull just outside A magazine, sir."

"Thank you, pilot. It was the torpedo. A dud, thank the Lord, but don't tell him. It might be best that he doesn't know how close it was."

"Asdic-Bridge. Contact dead ahead. Range three thousand. Opening."

"Steady as you go. Stand by depth charges," Pierce ordered.

"What about the Dutchman, sir?" Talor asked.

"The *Van Hoorn* will have to wait. She can't get far," Pierce said.

The noise heard by the gunnery officer in the forward magazine had indeed been the torpedo, but it wasn't a dud. It had glanced off the destroyer's hull by chance, touching only lightly as it sped by, and caromed off to the northeast, still deadly.

Captain Brinker had waited until the U-boat had engaged the destroyer and then ordered flank speed, turning toward the safety of occupied France. To turn inshore or continue the pretense of engine failure would inevitably lead to the capture of his ship and the discovery of his British prisoners. He wondered when the U-boat would fire.

The *Van Hoorn* now moved away from and astern of the destroyer. Brinker cursed as he watched the warship begin what was obviously a high-speed depth-charge run. If the U-boat was sunk, he was finished.

Commander Loesner stood beside Brinker on the wing, his expression strained, as he stared at the destroyer fixedly. Then, something moved in the water to his right, a brief intrusion on his peripheral vision. He looked down and saw nothing. His attention returned to the duel to the west. A pattern of explosions echoed across the water, followed by huge geysers erupting into the air behind the churning wake of the destroyer. Again the peripheral movement caught his eye. This time he saw what he took to be a large fish leaping in and out of the water. He watched it with fascination. Suddenly, his hand reached over and clutched Brinker's arm. "Captain! Torpedo!" he cried.

"What did . . ." Brinker said, beginning a question he was never to finish.

The torpedo struck the *Van Hoorn*'s hull below the centercastle, almost exactly midships. Nearly five hundred pounds of amatol exploded viciously against the flimsy hull. The ship was flung upward and violently torn in half. The stern portion was driven off at an angle for several hundred yards by the still turning propellor, before sinking from sight. The shattered bow stood on end, then, forced under by the heavy boom, it was gone.

The tidal current of the indifferent Channel flowed steadily westward, carrying bits of wreckage with it, but soon even those vanished, and nothing remained to show that the *Van Hoorn* had passed only minutes earlier.

CHAPTER 19

At the time the tanks were passing the town railroad station and approaching the road block, Major Brian Sancroft stood on the platform of the harbor station directing the unloading of the Canadian reinforcements. As commanding officer of the port security force, he had just been informed of the fire aboard the hospital ship. When he learned that it was minor, under control, and presented no danger to the wounded or the ship itself, he returned his attention to the Canadians. He had also been told of the arrival of the *Van Hoorn* and had dismissed it as something unimportant. Unexpected arrivals had been occurring frequently during the past four days, and he knew that Lieutenant Willard would handle it.

Sancroft was moving along the platform, urging the troops to greater effort in removing their gear, when a muffled explosion rattled the train's windows. The overhanging roof above the platform made it difficult for him to pinpoint the sound. He looked anxiously in the direction of the pier, but turned quickly when he heard a group of soldiers at the far end of the platform calling to the others, and pointing at the sky to the north. Sancroft rushed to the end of the roof overhang and saw the flames rising above the buildings near the town railroad station. His first thought was air raid. Then he realized that the sound hadn't been the terrifying crack of high explosives, but more like the whump of a gas oven being lighted, amplified many times. Some bloody fool neglected to shut off the gas in one of the evacuated buildings, he thought, and made a mental note to give the inspection teams what for.

He shouldered his way back to the far end of the platform and out to the road. A troop carrier pulled to a stop just as he arrived, and he saw the roadblock sergeant leap out and rush toward him. "Sir." The sergeant came to attention and saluted smartly, his face and uniform covered with soot.

"I just heard an explosion. What was it, Winkle?"

"That was Colonel Collingwood's car, sir. Bad fire up there. His car was parked on the sidewalk in front of one of the burning buildings. The fire got to it. Went up like a bomb."

"How did the fire start, and what was the colonel's car doing on the sidewalk?" Sancroft asked.

"Can't say about either, sir. The colonel passed through the roadblock half an hour ago, and then the tanks came up. One of their officers told me there seemed to be a fire. Said the colonel's car was sitting near it, and that Lieutenant Foster had left him to investigate. I went to check, but there was no sign of the colonel, his driver, or Lieutenant Foster. Couldn't get near the bloody buildings."

"Good lord, Winkle, you don't think the colonel could have been in one of the buildings?"

"No way to tell yet, sir. I have men searching the entire area around the fire now. Looks bad though. Fire should be under control soon, then we'll know."

"Get back up there, Winkle, and keep me informed. Wait," Sancroft said. "What was that you said about tanks?"

"Three heavy infantry tanks went through the block, sir."

"Three tanks? Where did they come from?"

"Don't know, sir. Came up this road. I thought they must have come from here." Winkle stood waiting for the inevitable question.

"What did their orders read?" Sancroft asked.

"I'm not sure, sir. The tank lieutenant ordered me to get down to the fire. Just then the whole thing went up, so I hopped it when he told me about the colonel's car."

"In other words, you didn't look at their orders."

"No sir. I had them in my hand, but . . ."

"Are the tanks still at the roadblock?"

"I don't think so, sir. The officer ordered me to open the barrier. Said he was blocking the road."

"And you did?"

"Yes, sir."

"As soon as this is cleared up, Winkle, you and I will have a little chat. Until then, I will remind you that roadblocks are erected for what the name should suggest to even the most dim witted—to block roads. Now, get back up there and see if you can locate Colonel Collingwood and Lieutenant Foster. Wait for me at the fire."

Half an hour later, Major Sancroft stood at an open window of the customs house, which dominated the inland end of the pier, and looked out into the growing darkness. He could hear the sound of the hospital train as it moved out of the station. He ran a thin hand through sparse red hair and adjusted rimless glasses perched on a minutely veined nose that jutted out of a pale, prematurely wrinkled face and waited until the sound faded. Then he walked across the Spartanly furnished room to an old, but highly polished conference table. He sat down at one end, facing Lieutenant Willard and a stern looking naval commander, who sat on either side.

"Let's go over it again, shall we?" Sancroft began. "I'd like to have something concrete to say to the intelligence chaps when they descend on us. Lieutenant Willard?"

Lieutenant Willard leaned forward, his elbows on the table. "Yes, sir. As you ordered, I went aboard the *Saint Michael* to expedite the disembarkation of the wounded. While aboard, I learned that the Dutch ship had entered directly behind *Saint Michael*. I sent word to Lieutenant Foster to proceed to the end of the pier with thirty men, all that could be spared, and told him to inform me if she had troops aboard. I told him that all but their wounded should remain aboard the Dutch ship until further orders, since the hospital ship had first priority. Actually, I never saw the *Van Hoorn* enter *or* leave, but it turns out that there were only twelve troops aboard, and we can't even be certain of that. I'm assuming twelve since there were three tanks. Four to a tank, but no one actually saw more than the drivers and the officers."

The naval commander spoke. "You seem to share my suspicions, Willard."

"Suspicions of what?" Sancroft asked.

"The *Van Hoorn* landed the tanks and left shortly afterward. She was ordered to return and refused. Captain Williamson boarded her soon after she docked, and I have been unable to find anyone who saw him leave."

"I understand it was sunk shortly afterward by a U-boat," Sancroft said.

"There is some question as to whether she was attacked or sunk by the fluke hit of a torpedo meant for the destroyer *Hereford*."

"Are you actually implying that Captain Williamson may have been aboard the . . ." Sanford glanced down at the papers in front of him, "*Van Hoorn* when she left?"

"There's no other logical explanation. Not only the captain, but three others boarded that ship. None of them can be located. Now I learn that Colonel Collingwood, his driver, and young Foster are also missing."

"And a road sentry," Willard added.

Sancroft glared at the lieutenant. He was beginning to have his own doubts, but still attempted to rationalize. Headquarters would have his head as it was, since Winkle had allowed the tanks to leave without a check on their orders. "Perhaps Williamson and the others left the Dutch ship and moved directly to the fire in the civilian houses. God knows, I hope

173

I'm wrong, but all of our missing men may have been trapped in those buildings when the fire got out of control," he said.

"I don't understand your reluctance to face facts, major," Commander Whiting said. "You must realize how ridiculous your statement was. Could Captain Williamson and three other men leave the Dutch ship unseen, proceed up the pier past the activity around *Saint Michael*, again unseen, and move half a mile up to houses that must have been well afire before they could get there, even at a run? Would Captain Williamson simply ignore the fire on *Saint Michael*? I for one have had enough of this idiotic speculation."

The commander rose, his chair grating against the floor as it was pushed back vigorously. "I am contacting naval intelligence at Dover, and I suggest that you contact your own headquarters. Obviously they confirmed the tank's movement orders when you first informed them, but it would seem that there are enough grounds for closer investigation." The commander left the room.

Major Sancroft was worried. "The chap seems to be attempting to put this entire mess on my plate," he said.

"May I make a suggestion, sir?" Willard asked, thinking, On your plate—where it belongs. He wondered who his next commanding officer would be since, after Whiting had his say and they found out about Winkle's blunder, the major would be fortunate to retain his commission.

Sancroft was pacing. "What is it, Willard?" he asked, looking at the young man hopefully.

"Winkle said the tanks moved west, sir. They'll be on the coast road, and they move slowly. They can't have reached Brighton yet. We could call ahead and have them detained until this is cleared up."

Sancroft brightened. "Good thinking, Willard. But I don't think we need involve Brighton in this. I want you to take my car and find them yourself. Take as many men as you wish. This is all nonsense and will be explained in no time, I'm sure, but you'd better bring those tanks back here, no matter what their orders read. That should satisfy our intense naval type."

But not headquarters—or intelligence—if Commander Whiting's suspicions prove right, Willard thought as he moved to the door.

When he was alone, Sancroft reached for the telephone. It hadn't been until Whiting had mentioned the assumed confirmation of the tank's orders that he realized he hadn't informed headquarters about the fire or the tanks. Better late than never, he thought.

The exigencies of war had forced the security command at Newhaven on a previously desk-bound, moderately competent supply officer. Unfortunately, it was a command for which Major Brian Sancroft was proving to be totally unfit.

Dietrich listened to the powerful diesels with the characteristic attention to detail of the well-trained tank officer. Once he was satisfied that all was well, he shut the noise from his conciousness and returned his attention to the road ahead. The moon hung in the sky behind him like a shimmering scythe, its glow accentuated by the growing darkness, allowing the drivers to operate without headlights. Dietrich wanted to avoid their use as long as possible, since lights would be seen for miles by anyone watching—or waiting—ahead. They had passed through the coastal hamlets of Peacedean, Telescomb Cliffs, and Saltdean unchallenged. Occasional soldiers and civilians patrolled the road, but they were surprisingly few and far between. Most waved greeting to the tank officers.

Once past the houses on the southwest fringes of Rottingdean the road was straight and deserted. On the left, the Channel lay far below the cliffs. To the right, open downland rolled away to the north. Dietrich watched for the old, familiar windmill he had passed so many times during his civilian business trips. When it loomed ahead on the higher ground to his right, he leaned down into the fighting compartment.

"Contact the others, Schemke. We'll soon be at the edge of Brighton. Warn everyone to be alert. We're bound to run into a checkpoint soon."

The moon disappeared briefly behind a rare cloud, and the darkness was suddenly dense. Dietrich heard Sergeant Falck curse loudly in his driving compartment, and was about to order him to slow down when the cloud passed and visibility again improved. He could also hear Schemke talking into the radio in the dimly lighted turret. Moments later the turret hatch opened, and Schemke's head appeared.

"Siegler reports a vehicle two or three miles behind us, moving this way fast, using headlights."

Dietrich swung around and stared into the darkness. "Well, it had to happen sooner or later. Someone has finally taken some interest in us back in Newhaven, I suspect. Fine, this is a better place than Brighton to find out where we stand. Tell the others to follow me to the side of the road and stop. I'll be back to tell them what we're going to do." Schemke dropped from sight. Dietrich spoke into his headset: "Falck. Pull over to the left. Get well off the road and stop." He watched the moving beams of taped headlights appear and disappear as the approaching vehicle moved in and out of dips in the road.

The three tanks pulled to a halt. Dietrich leaned into the turret. "Keep the engines running. Take over the headset and command,

Schemke. Warn Falck to be ready to close his hood. Stand by the guns, but no shooting unless I give the word. I'm going back to arrange a reception." He climbed out of the cupola and dropped to the ground.

He approached Schiller and Siegler at a run and gave rapid orders. Siegler's crew immediately gathered together at the side of their tank and opened the access doors on the side of the tread skirting plate. Siegler was given the job of dealing with anyone who might remain in the vehicle when it arrived, and he faded away into the darkness behind the tanks. The plan was simple and soon explained. That done, Dietrich said to Schiller, "You'd better take your tank up ahead for a few hundred feet. If anything comes from the west, block the road and keep them occupied."

"This isn't France," Schiller said. "We can hide bodies, but what are you going to do with the vehicle?"

"I don't know," Dietrich said. "We'll have to find a way. Now get going, they're almost here."

Minutes later, a car pulled to the side of the road well behind Siegler's idling tank. Dietrich glanced up from his crouching position alongside the skirt plate. Becker and Keller were working busily at the access doors. Dietrich handed a crowbar to Becker and turned toward the car, his face reflecting feigned surprise in the beams of the taped headlights. When he raised a hand to shield his eyes, the lights were shut off. The rear door opened, and three men left the seat and walked toward him. There was no urgency in their movements, Dietrich noted. Two of the men were soldiers, carrying slung Lee Enfield rifles, and one look told him that they were skilled regulars. The man striding ahead of them was an officer, tall, well tailored, and competent looking. He wore a holstered Enfield pistol like the one Dietrich carried. Test firings in France had proved to Dietrich that the weapon was only useful at extremely close range, and even then it was more apt to wound the man firing it than the one it was pointed at. "Watch for my signal," he said softly to Becker and Keller, and then turned back to the nearing men, assuming an expression of wary puzzlement.

"Glad we caught you so quickly, Lieutenant," the officer said, his eyes watchful.

"Caught me?" Dietrich said. "I don't quite understand."

"I'm afraid you've caused a bit of a flap back in Newhaven. My commanding officer sent me along to fetch you back. But first, I'd like to ask you a few questions." Willard was reassured by Dietrich's voice and manner. He didn't know what to expect after listening to Commander Whiting's implied suspicions. Heavily accented English? Shifty eyes? He suppressed a smile. No German could curse quite so colorfully as the soldier who was fiddling with the tank's treads and had just then hit his hand with the wrench he was wielding. It was pure cockney. "Had a breakdown?" he asked.

"Trying to prevent one," Dietrich answered. "We're making an adjustment in the tread tension. But what's this about a flap in Newhaven?"

"I'll get to that, Lieutenant. First, may I see your orders and identification?" Willard said.

"Certainly—after you show me yours. Sorry, but I'm afraid I don't know you either," Dietrich smiled.

Willard reached into his tunic and the two officers exchanged documents. Willard studied Dietrich's bogus orders carefully, showing no sudden suspicion. "I see you're under the personal orders of General Gort?"

"We are," Dietrich agreed.

"Proceeding to Portsmouth? It's too bad you were forced into Newhaven. You'd have been there by now and avoided all this."

Dietrich scanned the officer's identification, then said, "I'm not complaining, Lieutenant Willard. Frankly there were times when we didn't expect that ship to make it to any port."

"Might have saved yourself a detour," Willard said, "if you had shown these orders at Newhaven."

"I certainly tried. Frankly, I did think it sloppy procedure, but everyone was rather busy with fires. You seem to have more than your share of them," Dietrich replied.

"Not usually," Willard said. "It seems to have been a unique day in many ways. Incidentally, I thought there were three of you."

"I sent the other ahead to prevent anyone from barrelling into us in the dark."

"I see. Well, now I think you'd better finish your tinkering with those treads, and then we'll all be on our way," Willard said.

Dietrich made a movement with his hand to Becker, unseen by Willard. "Surely you weren't serious about our returning to Newhaven, Lieutenant."

"Quite serious, I'm afraid. There are a number of things that must be cleared up before we can let you proceed. We can arrange for transporters to take you from Newhaven to Portsmouth, so you shouldn't lose any time at all. Be a damned shame for you to wear out these treads on a fifty-mile trip over paved road anyway. I'm surprised you didn't think of that."

"My orders don't allow for interpretation," Dietrich said.

"I'm quite certain that General Gort wouldn't consider the saving of a complete refit as interpretation, Lieutenant."

Becker and Keller were on their feet. Becker moved to the end of the treads, holding the crowbar. He was now behind the soldiers, standing together near Willard, watching the exchange between the two officers. Dietrich moved past Lieutenant Willard and knelt at one of the tread access doors, forcing him to turn away from the other men.

"What on earth are these things that must be *cleared up* in Newhaven?" Dietrich asked, apparently busy at the tread bogies.

"A number of missing officers and men. Why the ship you arrived on left the port without permission and was sunk off Beachy Head after disobeying orders of the captain of a destroyer sent to fetch her back. That will do for starters."

"Sunk?" Dietrich said, his surprise genuine.

"No survivors," Willard said. "How long will you be? I don't want to spend the night here." At that moment he heard from behind the unmistakable sound of metal hitting flesh. He spun around in time to see Becker lowering the crowbar, and the two soldiers sprawled on the ground in front of him. Willard had no time for fear. God, he thought, the commander was right. He was reaching for his holster when Keller hit him expertly with his wrench. Lieutenant Willard was dead before he began to fall.

"Keep an eye on the road," Dietrich ordered and waved the car forward. He had seen Siegler approaching the driver when he had given the signal to Becker and Keller. He had no doubt that Willi had accomplished what he had been ordered to do. His confidence was confirmed when the car pulled up beside him, Siegler in the driver's seat, and the body of the driver visible through the rear window.

"What do we do with them? Over the cliff?" Siegler asked.

"On top of the coast watch down there? Use your head, Willi. No, we'll have to hide them, and do it fast. Dammit! I should have found out if they called ahead."

"Why would they send three men after us if they were really suspicious?" Siegler said. "If they called ahead the whole goddamned army would be here now."

"You have a point. They were supposed to bring us back to Newhaven. So that means that we have some time. Is there a radio in the car?"

"No," Siegler said.

"Good. So we have to hide it and the bodies quickly, somewhere out of the way when they finally begin to search for it."

"Burn it. They could have had an accident," Siegler offered.

"A fire would bring everybody out for miles within minutes. No, we have to hide it. They probably won't start worrying about us until we don't show up at Newhaven. Even if we started now that would take the better part of an hour. By that time we should be through Brighton and in a better position to move inland if we have to."

"There was a boarded up petrol station about a quarter of a mile back, near the last road that branched off north," Siegler suggested.

"That's the first place they'd look."

"Why? They'll be looking for the car on the road. If they wait an hour, they aren't on to us. If they are, what does it matter?"

"Becker," Dietrich called, "help Willi with these bodies and go with him." He looked at Siegler. "Do it. And get back here as fast as you can."

Dietrich waited impatiently in the cupola, glancing occasionally at his watch. It was taking too much time, he thought worriedly, and was then angered by his impatience in the face of Siegler's calm logic. Willi was hardly a man to let any hint of indecision pass unoticed.

"They're back," Keller shouted, running toward him, Siegler behind him.

"Keep it down," he said. "Any trouble, Willi?"

"No. There was a shed behind the station full of empty barrels. We piled them around the car and covered it with old canvas. It probably won't be found until the war's over. I was even able to close the padlock again."

"The weak link is that car and the bodies."

"Not much use worrying about that," Keller said. "The way Siegler fixed it, the whole place will go up if they do decide to look in that shack."

"What do you mean?" Dietrich asked, his voice hard.

"The door opens outward. He fixed a string to the pins of some grenades and attached it to the door. He came out through a window. If they open that door they're in for a surprise."

"And if they decide to go in the same window?"

"It was boarded up. Willi replaced the boards after he came out. No reason why they should go in that way."

"You'd better pray they don't," Dietrich said angrily. "If that set-up is discovered, Siegler has made sure that they can't help but connect us with that car. It had better work."

When they neared the tank guarding the road ahead, Dietrich could see Schiller standing alongside it, talking to three civilians. He ordered the tanks to halt. "What is it, Lieutenant?" he asked. He left the tank quickly and walked toward them.

"These gentlemen are manning a roadblock at Rodean Road," Schiller answered. "They've been telling me that they saw lights moving along the road. I've been assuring them it wasn't us."

"Good evening, gentlemen," Dietrich said and then turned to Schiller. "They're right. I saw them, too, and they were rather bright. Damned carelessness, if you ask me. I saw them turn off on a road leading north."

One of the civilians stepped forward. "The blackout's still a bloody mess, sir," he said. It was difficult to tell the age of the man. Well into his sixties, perhaps even seventies, Dietrich thought, but his eyes were alert, and he spoke with a youthful vigor. Two younger men stood behind him. Neither spoke, thinking perhaps how ineffectual they would be, despite their willingness to die in the attempt, against the imposing power of the tanks, had they been an enemy. The older man shifted his shotgun into the crook of one arm as he continued. "Fools still driving like maniacs are killing off people every day. You say they turned off down below, sir?"

"Less than a mile behind us."

"Went up Greenways then. Most likely headed for Woodingdean. Wait till they run into old Denton's block, showin' those lights. Most likely shoot 'em in the arse."

Siegler laughed. "I must say that you gentlemen seem to have things under control here."

"We do what we can, sir," the old man said soberly. "Didn't mean to make it into a joke. I spent three years in France in the last one. Damned Boche didn't try to come across here the last time, but it's in their minds now. We're here to see they have more than a bit of trouble trying."

"All of us appreciate what you're doing, I can assure you," Dietrich said. "Now, what's the drill for passing your roadblock, mister . . ."

"Tom Willis, sir. Sergeant, Royal Sussex, retired. This here's John Riddle, and that's Bob Windsor—no relation to the Duke. As for the block, we'll need to see your identification."

Dietrich and the others complied. "Anything else, Sergeant?" Dietrich asked.

The old man was pleased at the use of his former rank. "That'll be fine, sir."

"Where is your roadblock?" Siegler asked.

"Just past the Rodean School, sir. About half a mile down the road."

"Half a mile? No need for you to walk. Climb aboard the lead tank, and we'll drop you off. We really must get cracking," Dietrich said, then added, "Oh yes, Sergeant, one more thing I should take the time for. Would you mind glancing at our headlights to see if they're correctly taped. We don't want to cause any consternation ahead."

The elderly man was pleased. "Be glad to, sir," he said.

CHAPTER 20

Dietrich glanced to his right. Well off the road, beyond a high, iron fence, the impressive buildings of the Rodean School rose symmetrically against the moonlit sky. Tom Willis pointed ahead. "Be at the roadblock soon, Lieutenant. There she is."

At the western end of the school grounds a road ran down from the north, and was joined by another from the northeast. The triangular junction was crowded with carts and farm machinery, effectively isolating it from the coast road. Dietrich was surprised by the large number of men visible near the barrier. "You certainly have a good turnout there, Sergeant," he said to Willis.

"Couldn't keep 'em away if we tried, sir," Willis answered proudly. Ahead, a man was approaching them cautiously. He cupped his hands and shouted, "Hallo, Jim. It's Willis here." He winked at Dietrich. "Captured three of 'em. A bit embarrassing when they turned out to be ours."

The other man laughed loudly while Dietrich watched with an amused smile. He gave the order to halt. The man below him was unloading an ancient over and under shotgun. He said, "We heard you coming for five minutes, Tom. Thought it was a bloody regiment. Did you find the damn fool who was showing those lights?"

"It wasn't these lads," Willis answered. "They saw 'em too. The lieutenant here saw 'em turn off at Greenways."

The other man smiled up at Dietrich. "Didn't think it was you. Good to see you, Lieutenant."

"Thank you. We really must be on our way, Sergeant," Dietrich said to Willis.

"Right, sir. I already checked 'em, Jim," Willis said to the man below. Then he looked back at Dietrich. "We appreciate the ride, sir, though I don't see how you lads can stand it. I came near to losin' my teeth when we went over the bumps back there."

The man standing on the road laughed. "It wouldn't have mattered, Tom. If the Jerries come, we won't let them get close enough for you to bite."

Dietrich joined in the laughter. The three civilians jumped to the road, and he was about to order the tanks ahead when Willis said, "Likely to meet a few of your mates in Brighton, sir. Saw two tanks down at the Palace pier this morning. Much smaller than these though."

Dietrich saluted the old man and waved to the men at the barrier. Then he ordered Falck to move ahead. As they left the roadblock behind, they were given a rousing cheer by the civilians. Dietrich saw Siegler waving at them vigorously and smiled at the incongruity. He spoke into the headset. "Tell the others. The old man said there are two tanks, most likely light infantry, at the Palace pier. Tell them to stand by the guns just in case."

Dietrich settled himself in the cupola. The outlying buildings of Kemp Town soon filled the horizon to the right of the road. Ahead, lay the unbroken sprawl of Brighton, Hove, Portslade, Southwick, and finally, Shoreham—an eight mile, heavily populated, stretch through which they must pass to get to their next barrier, the Norfolk Bridge over the River Adur. That eight-mile passage could prove the most dangerous leg of the trip. They would remain on the excellent coast road with the Channel guarding their left—preventing a flanking movement from that side—but, until they crossed the Adur, the sea was as much an enemy as a friend. They would be vulnerable and exposed for more than an hour, even if all went well. To their right were the Georgian homes, guest houses, and hotels that lined the road along the seashore. If attacked, their only way to turn would be into one of the roads leading into the maze of Brighton proper. If that should happen, Dietrich had no doubt that they could be easily defeated by the city.

He heard the motorcycles long before he saw them.

"Something ahead. Code it to the others," he said into the headset, then settled back and stared into the darkness.

If it comes to a fight, they would turn back if possible, move over the Downs, ford the Ouse above Newhaven, and attempt to make their way to the nearest alternate target—the direction finder at Beachy Head. Dietrich shrugged fatalistically.

Then he saw them. The two motorcyclists turned smartly into the middle of the road and stopped, their backs to the approaching tanks. Dietrich sighed in relief. "I think we have an escort. Two men, nothing else as far as I can see," he breathed into the headset microphone. "Tell the others."

The two soldiers had left their cycles and stood in the center of the road. One of them raised a white gloved hand in a signal for the tanks to halt.

"Stop, but not too close," Dietrich told Falck. He was able to make out the distinctive badges of a sergeant and a corporal. Both men wore holstered pistols, but neither man made any move toward the weapons, and Dietrich saw that the corporal was yawning mightily. He gave a thumbs-up signal to Shiller and then pressed the intercom button. "Forget what I said, Falck," he said softly. "Move right up to them. Up to them, not over them. They're friendly." He raised a hand in greeting as the tank lurched to a stop.

The British Infantry sergeant saluted. "Evening, sir. The civilians at the Rodean roadblock told us you were coming. My commanding officer, Major McLure, sent us along to escort you to the checkpoint."

"Thank you, Sergeant. Where is it?"

"Just a bit past the Black Rock curve, sir. Not far."

"Lead on," Dietrich said.

Again the sergeant saluted. He and the corporal remounted their motorcycles and waited.

Dietrich leaned into the turret: "Tell Schiller and Siegler that we're being escorted to a checkpoint at the edge of Brighton. Send that clear, then add the code for 'no problem, but caution.'"

The road began a slow downward curve to the left. They followed the dim red taillights of the motorcycles past a fringe industrial area. Then, as the road straightened, they rumbled past the first of Brighton's Georgian townhouses. Moonlight accentuated the crossed white paper tape pasted on the windows of the buildings. Not a trace of light showed through drawn blackout curtains to give a hint of whether they were still occupied. Dietrich began to see civilians edging their way cautiously through the darkness. Many waved and paused to shout good natured greetings to the tanks. Off to the left, beyond the rolled barbed wire on the patrolled beach, the quiet sea rolled in from a barely visible horizon.

Dietrich remembered Brighton as he had last seen it, brilliantly ablaze with light, the promenade crowded with carefree people, the old clinging to yesterday, and the young confident of an unchanging tomorrow. Then he had thought them weak. Now, after his meeting with the elderly sergeant, a man content to wait for the German army behind a wooden cart, armed only with a shotgun and courage, he was no longer certain.

One hooded taillight grew smaller as the rider speeded up and disappeared down the road. The other motorcycle slowed and fell in alongside Dietrich's tank.

"Almost there, sir," the sergeant said. "Please follow me closely. We'll be stopping at Chichester Terrace. It will be to the right. I'll be showing you where."

"At the small public gardens on Kings Cliff, isn't it?" Dietrich said.

"Right, sir. Didn't know you were familiar with it. Major McLure's office is in the post office on Chesam Road."

"Drop back and tell the others, will you, Sergeant?" By the time the sergeant had returned to his position ahead, the three tanks were in line, with less than five feet between them. Dietrich cupped his hands and yelled to Schiller, "We'll be stopping soon. Watch for my signal. Pass it on."

Falck steered the tank close to the curb skillfully, and the two others followed.

"Keep the engines running," Dietrich said into the headset microphone. He then dropped down into the turret and gave rapid orders. "Schemke, you get outside, open the engine covers and look busy. Richter, you show yourself once in a while, but stay in the tank. Both of you stop anyone who tries to get inside. Say it's my orders. I don't want to have to try explaining the hollow-charge explosives to an interested Englishman, He might not understand." He then climbed up to, and out of, the cupola and stood on the outer superstructure. A captain waited on the sidewalk.

"Well done, Lieutenant," the captain said. "I have trouble parking a Minor. Welcome to Brighton. Please come with me. Major McLure is waiting."

Dietrich dropped to the ground agilely, straightened, and saluted smartly. "Good evening, sir," he said formally. "Lieutenant George Parker, sir."

"I take it that you are the officer in charge, Parker?"

"Yes, sir. Shall I call the other officers?"

"I'll meet them later. It's better they stay and see to your maintenance. If you will wait for a moment, I'll arrange for tea, and whatever else we can scrape up, to be brought here to your men."

"Thank you, sir. They will appreciate it."

Dietrich glanced over his shoulder and saw that the men were busily engaged around the tanks, all but the gunners, he noted with satisfaction. He followed the captain around what he remembered as a public rock garden to the end of the street into another that ran parallel to the now hidden coast road.

As they walked, the captain said pleasantly, "Ever been here before, Parker?"

"Yes, sir, I have. Not since the war, but quite often before. Actually, I've sent a number of postal cards from this branch." Dietrich pointed at the post office building they were approaching.

"Really? I never cared much for Brighton myself. People sitting about cooking themselves for two weeks, and all that."

Dietrich laughed. "I hardly sat about cooking, sir. My visits were all business."

"Oh? What firm?" the captain asked, without real interest.

Dietrich was saved further innovation as he followed the captain into the building, passing alert sentries, through a set of double doors and into a brightly lighted interior. Dietrich rubbed his eyes in the sudden brilliance and was led past uniformed men and women who worked at desks, crowded together with little space between them, virtually filling the floor area. Military personnel of all ranks moved through the noisy, but contained, confusion. The captain skirted the edge of the room, made his way to a door, knocked, and then entered, indicating that Dietrich was to follow.

"This is Lieutenant George Parker, sir," the captain said to the officer seated behind a desk.

Major Angus McLure smiled in greeting. He was a craggy, angular man, with red hair that was almost startling. The smile lines at the corners of his eyes were deep, his appraisal was probing, and Dietrich decided instantly that he was a man who could easily fool you, hiding competence behind a good humor not usually ascribed to the Scots.

"Please sit down, Parker," McLure said. "Frankly, we had all better improve our communications and quickly. I had no idea, until we were informed by the civilians at Rodean, that you were going to pass through this command. Where have you come from?"

"We landed at Newhaven, sir." Dietrich hastily reached into his tunic for the orders, then passed them to the major.

"Newhaven?" McLure said. "That would explain something," he added enigmatically as he began to study the papers.

"I imagine you mean the fires, sir." Dietrich watched the major carefully.

"Among other things. Major Sancroft does seem to have more than his share of troubles. Remind me to have a chat with Sancroft tomorrow, Paige," McLure said. "I can appreciate his problems, but fires or not we should have been informed about this." He waved the papers. Dietrich relaxed. Tomorrow. A mild rebuke among fellow officers, and always tomorrow. It was the same in all armies. Captain Paige moved closer to the desk as McLure continued, "This officer is under the personal orders of General Gort and is to proceed to Portsmouth post haste. We can do something to help him, Paige. Please see to it that Lieutenant Parker and his command are provided with an escort to the Norfolk Bridge." He looked at Dietrich, "I was going to offer you some tea, but now I think it best that we don't detain you any longer."

Dietrich was already on his feet. "Thank you, sir," he said.

"Best of luck, Parker," McLure said.

Dietrich was smiling as he followed the captain from the room.

Captain Paige led the way through the darkness back to the tanks. Since they had left the major, a number of gnawing questions had occurred to him. He couldn't help wondering why transporters hadn't been arranged for the tanks rather than subjecting them to the considerable wear and tear of a fifty-mile road trip. And why were they not escorted directly to Portsmouth by the navy? Headquarters must have their reasons, he decided, no matter how incomprehensible they might seem to him. After all, the tanks were here, and those and other questions had obviously been cleared up at Newhaven. But Captain Paige couldn't resist. "Why is it that you didn't continue on to Portsmouth by ship? Why Newhaven?"

"We had more than a bit of trouble, sir. The ship was in danger of sinking. We entered Newhaven where we were informed that we were to proceed overland at once under the contingency section of our orders. They want us at Portsmouth before dawn and there was no time to arrange for other transportation although we will possibly be met by transporters somewhere ahead."

"My men will see to it that you don't have to do more than slow down until you get to the Norfolk Bridge," Paige said, his questions answered.

They were near the tanks now, and Dietrich could see that everything was as he had left it. They edged their way through the crowd of interested civilians who were being contained behind a barrier of military police.

"While you see that your men are ready to leave, I shall make the arrangements for your escort," Paige said.

"Thank you, sir," Dietrich answered punctiliously.

A fine young man, the captain thought as he hurried away.

Dietrich moved quickly to his tank. He gave the order to prepare to leave and then walked back to Schiller, who was waiting on his tank's superstructure.

"We'll move out soon. The commanding officer is providing us with an escort to Shoreham."

"An escort?" Schiller said wonderingly. "You must be a magician."

Dietrich patted his tunic pocket. "General Gort is the magician, not me."

He walked toward Siegler's tank. Corporal Knoedler was seated in his driving compartment talking to Becker and Keller. He saw Knoedler say something to the two men when he spotted Dietrich. They walked toward him hurriedly.

"What are you doing out of the turret, Becker?" Dietrich asked angrily.

"Looking for Siegler. When we stopped he told me to look busy, and I haven't seen him since."

"What?" Dietrich said. "Where did he go?"

Both men shrugged. Dietrich exploded. "Goddamn it! If that son of a bitch has . . ." He paused as Siegler appeared around the rear of the tank. "Where the hell have you been?" he asked angrily.

"I took a walk. I wanted to see what sort of defenses they have here. The Führer will want to . . ." Siegler began.

"Don't ever leave your crew alone again, Siegler."

"I was never out of sight of the tanks," Siegler answered coldly.

"You're in command of this tank . . . for now. If you want to stay in command, don't leave it again unless I tell you to."

Siegler's fists clenched. Dietrich watched him closely. Jesus, he thought, this maniac is actually thinking of hitting me. Twelve men in the middle of enemy territory, and this bastard seems to have forgotten it completely. "Think again, Siegler. We're moving out. We've been given an escort, but keep your eyes on our rear. They aren't just going to forget about us in Newhaven, and they won't forget us here if someone should hear you talking about the Führer."

Siegler glared but said nothing. Dietrich walked back toward his tank. On the way, he saw Captain Paige approaching.

"I've assigned six motorcycles to you," Paige said. "Sergeant Clark, the man who led you here, will be in charge of the escort. He'll see to it that you move ahead sharply. Four of the cycles will take position in front of you, while Clark and another man go on ahead to see to it that the roads are kept clear. Good luck, Parker."

"Thank you, Captain," Dietrich said. He was more thankful than the captain knew.

Ten minutes later they were underway along the Marine Parade behind the motorcycle phalanx. They were soon grinding past the Palace pier. Stripped of its peacetime lights, it lay dark, pointing at France like an accusing finger. Near its entrance, Dietrich saw the light tanks spoken of by the elderly man at the roadblock. Squat and ducklike, they looked more like toys than weapons. A lone figure in one of the turrets waved.

The heavy Mark 2s moved past a barrier of Bren carriers into the gentle curve of Grand Junction, then straightened, and were soon moving steadily at twelve miles an hour along Kingsway. Half a mile ahead, the west pier reached out darkly into the quiet water. Dietrich looked at it while thinking: At this speed we'll be at the bridge in no time. It seemed almost too easy.

Willi Siegler was angry. It had taken all of his doubtful self-control to keep from smashing Dietrich's face in. But even the lieutenant's affront was dulled by hatred of the British. It was an unreasoning hatred that had begun many years earlier and been fanned by what he had just learned.

Young Willi Siegler had always felt that his father was a true German warrior. During his childhood years the boy's obvious hero worship had tended to make the elder Siegler's tales of the Great War progress rapidly from a simple account of the terror and boredom of the average infantry soldier into something of a Wagnerian epic. Soon Otto Siegler began to join in the fantasy he had created for the boy. The well-remembered fear he had experienced for four long years was slowly transformed into pure, heroic self-sacrifice. Plodding gains, measured in yards, became victorious routs of the enemy. Trenches were cleansed of mud and horror. In these fantasies German soldiers seldom died, and when they did, it was gloriously and against terrible odds, inspiring their comrades to overcome seemingly insurmountable obstacles. Their last words always rang with belief in the fatherland and the Kaiser. The final defeat was explained as the subversion of a handful of cowardly politicians who imposed surrender against the wishes of the nearly victorious military. Willi Siegler believed.

Early impressions die hard, and as Willi grew older he became more German while his mother and father grew more Anglicized.

Sensing at last what he had created, Otto Siegler began to regret his earlier exaggeration. In an attempt to soften the effect his stories had had on the impressionable boy he had finally turned to the truth. But Willi looked on the transition from tales of valor to those of fear as his father's final and incomprehensible acceptance of a foreign master. To Otto's relief, the boy soon stopped asking questions. Willi was content with what he remembered. Otto Siegler's second thoughts had come too late.

Willi was thinking of the family he had abandoned as the tanks stopped at the checkpoint in Brighton. He waited until Dietrich left with the captain. Then he climbed out of the cupola and down to the ground. After passing through the cordon of military police and the growing crowd of civilians, he made his way to a telephone kiosk. He deposited one of the English coins issued to each man of the special force and dialed a number. There was no answer. He thought for a moment, finally deciding to take a calculated risk. He dialed again, getting an immediate answer. He pressed the button to complete the connection, and spoke in a voice that was a tone lower than normal. "Hello? Alfred Billings, please."

"'Ew is it?" the familiar voice answered anxiously. "It's not about young Alf, is it?"

"No, madam. May I speak to Mr. Billings please."

"'Old on," the woman answered.

Moments later a man's metallic, but recognizable, voice said: "'Ew's this?"

"My name is Alan Crawford," Siegler said. "I'm with Liberty's of London. I've been trying to reach one of your neighbors, a Mr. Otto Siegler, but I can't seem to raise him. We have a tool case he ordered some time ago that's finally come through. I thought . . ."

"Too late for that," the man interrupted.

"I don't understand, Mister Billings."

"Where in 'ell have you been? Should know from the name the man's a bloody German."

"I still don't . . ."

"Interned. 'E and his wife both sent off to the Isle of Man."

"I see," Siegler said. "Well, thank you. Sorry to have bothered you."

"What'd yer say yer name was?"

"Thank you again," Siegler said and broke the connection. Interned! That's what they get for their great love of England, he thought angrily. Then, as suddenly as it had come, his anger died. They're better off on the Isle of Man. There was no telling what might happen to them when the Wehrmacht landed. He was smiling as he walked across the road and stood looking out over Duke's Mound at the dark water, envisioning a fleet that didn't exist, and an invasion that would never be attempted. Finally he went back to the tanks.

Alfred Billings hung up the telephone and shook his head. Rose Billings looked up from her darning. "What'd the boy want?" she said.

"The boy?"

"That Willi. Old Otto's son."

"I'll be damned, Rosie, did you think it was 'im too?"

"Think? I'd know that boy's voice anywhere—even with a cold. What'd 'e want?"

"I thought it was 'im. Told me some nonsense about a tool box old Otto ordered. Said 'e was callin' from Liberty's store, in London."

"At this time of night?" Rose Billings asked.

"Damn. I never thought of that."

"'E was callin' from a phone box. I 'eard the money drop."

Alfred Billings scratched his head. "If it was 'im, 'ow come 'e didn't know 'is folks was interned?"

Rose Billings snorted. "Don't you remember that man around askin' about the boy? I remember Missus Siegler tellin' me she was afraid the boy 'ad gone back to Germany. That was just before the war."

"I'll be damned, Rosie. Forgot about that. I think I better go down and speak to the constable about this."

"Might be best," Rose Billings said. "But remember, you won't find the constable in the pub."

What a target, Dietrich mused as he looked out at the high smokestacks of the immense power station that filled the narrow strip of land enclosing the eastern end of Shoreham harbor. He was soon smiling as they passed the isolated building housing the Crown and Anchor pub, remembering Priller's reference to it. Around the curve ahead, Dietrich knew, lay the Norfolk Bridge, spanning the headwater of the River Adur. The motorcycles slowed, and Sergeant Clark dropped back to fall in beside Dietrich's tank.

"Seems they haven't anything available here to continue the escort, sir," he yelled. "If you'll stop, I'll check with Brighton. I'm sure Captain Paige will want us to continue on with you through Worthing at least."

"That's fine, Sergeant, but I think we'd better carry on across the bridge," Dietrich answered. "We've been running well so far, and I don't want to risk any of us stalling in the Shoreham High Street. We'll move ahead slowly on the other side, and you can catch us up if you get the word to continue on."

"I'll leave the rest of the escort with you, sir, and get back as soon as I ring in."

"You've been most helpful, Sergeant. I'll see that it's mentioned."

Sergeant Clark showed a gap-toothed smile. "Glad I could be of help, sir. I'll go on ahead and see the bridge is cleared." The motorcycle roared away.

Dietrich spoke into the intercom. "Bridge coming up, Falck. Try not to knock the bloody thing over."

Falck, following the now single file escort, applied the brakes to the left tread and skillfully turned onto the bridge as Dietrich saluted a group of senior officers who stood nearby watching the maneuver critically. They were obviously impressed with the driver's skill. All three tanks crossed without incident.

Once across they began to move slowly along a straight road bordered on either side by attached private homes, rising two stories above deserted sidewalks, that seemed to stretch ahead in an unbroken and endless line.

Schemke's head appeared in the turret hatch. "Siegler reports a single motorcycle coming up behind us. Our escort sergeant."

"Good. If he's alone, we're still all right," Dietrich said and turned in the cupola to watch the road to the rear.

It wasn't long before Sergeant Clark pulled alongside and slowed to keep pace with the tank. "Been ordered to stay with you, sir."

"All the way?" Dietrich asked.

"I'm not sure. I was told to report by phone to Brighton every hour," Clark answered.

"I'd like to get back up to speed, Sergeant," Dietrich said. "Glad you're still going to be with us." He watched the sergeant roar ahead into the darkness. It was going incredibly well.

Book Three

At the Fellnest, during a lull in the constant interruptions of aides and personal bodyguards bearing messages from the front, Colonel von Maussner stood watching Hitler pace the floor. The colonel was tired. Apart from an hour or two of fitful dozing on the train from Berlin, he had had little sleep for forty-eight hours. He listened, with what little attention he could muster, to the familiar, contradictory expostulation that passed for the Führer's rationale of his love-hate feelings for Great Britain.

Von Maussner was barely able to pretend the expected expression of interest in the babble. Earlier, during the interminable and tasteless vegetarian dinner, a report had come in from the command submarine. The special force had apparently landed successfully! Even the later information that the ship used in the mission had been sunk—presumably by a mine—hadn't dimmed Hitler's jubilation. Von Maussner could now see that the Führer was as surprised as he himself had been to learn that the initial phase of the incursion had been so successful. It had obviously started as yet another intuitive caprice, one which even Hitler had little hope would actually succeed. But to learn that the Van Hoorn had not only entered the port of Newhaven, but had managed to disembark three tanks was enough to reinforce a hubris already inflated by constant victory. The colonel knew this would provide encouragement for further adventures by the man who often seemed as surprised by his victories as his enemies were. Now, as he paced, Hitler's good mood continued.

"You've done well, von Maussner. Where do you think they are now? Come show me on the map. When they get to the targets, the noise they make will be heard around the world, and even that fool Roosevelt will have to abandon his attempts to provoke me into war. I can assure you, colonel, we will deal with that miserable mass of immigrants when the time comes."

Now he's beginning to think of the Atlantic Ocean as a river crossing, von Maussner thought as he crossed the room to the table where Hitler was leafing through extensively marked maps. He waited until the proper one was located and spread over one marked "Dunkirk and Approaches."

"Their top speed is fifteen miles an hour, my Führer. Let us assume that they are able to maintain two-thirds of that speed due to the blackout and comparative unfamiliarity with the roads. There must have been changes since any of them were there." Von Maussner made rapid calculations. "They would be somewhere near Chichester—here."

"Chichester," Hitler repeated, savoring the unfamiliar consonants. "That would bring them to the Southampton area well before dawn. Do you realize what I've done, Colonel, despite the timidity of the staff? Where would we be today if I had listened to them?"

"You've done remarkable things, my Führer," von Maussner said quickly. Since he had arrived, he had found himself equivocating, rushing to agreement of anything said, and drained by the almost hypnotic force of the man he claimed to despise. "Obviously I cannot answer for the staff. I'm a field officer. My expertise, such as it is, lies elsewhere."

"I will have to take more advantage of that expertise, Colonel," Hitler said.

"Thank you, my Führer."

"I have need of competent officers." He paused, then added pointedly, "Who can follow orders. You have done that admirably, but there is one thing. I'm not completely satisfied with the explanations of Captain Pohl's death, or that of General Kellner. The reports from the security officer at the base are thorough enough, but I would like to hear what you can tell me."

Hitler moved to a large desk and sat down, listening to von Maussner's detailed account of the incidents that had occurred at the post in France. When he had finished, Hitler nodded.

"That seems to confirm the security reports. Pohl was a foolish man. I had expected much of him. One more thing, the appearance of S.S. on your base."

"They had orders ostensibly signed by Reichsführer S.S. Himmler," von Maussner answered carefully.

"Himmler claims he never signed such an order, and it was not among General Kellner's papers when they arrived here from France—by special plane sent under my orders." It was spoken more as an aside than something requiring an answer, so von Maussner hesitated. He wasn't surprised to learn the order was missing, and was relieved that Himmler's henchmen hadn't discovered anything incriminating about him during their apparent search of Kellner's effects. He was thankful when Hitler didn't seem inclined to pursue the point.

"Don't look so serious, Colonel," Hitler continued. "I have news for you that will show my appreciation of what you accomplished despite all the difficulties. I have decided to give you command of one of the new Panzer divisions. Congratulations, General von Maussner."

Von Maussner was stunned. He realized uncomfortably that his dedication to the cabal was beginning to wane rapidly. "Thank you, my Führer," he said. His new command would allow him to drop all connection with the conspirators. What he had learned of the incredible success of the Wehrmacht since he had arrived at Hitler's headquarters had caused a rapid reevaluation *of his personal fears for Germany's future. It was now obvious that they had won. Thus, General von Maussner began to shed his earlier principles. He had no chance to influence the special force's fate, isolated as he was now, and decided to trust to luck. The storm troopers had gotten in, but it would be a miracle if they got out, whether he managed to contact the British or not. In an instant he discarded what he now considered the visionary impracticalities of resistance to the inevitability of Hitler's—and Germany's—destiny, and decided to concentrate on a Field Marshal's baton. With luck he would live to attain it.*

CHAPTER 21

At Newhaven, Major Brian Sancroft paced the conference room nervously. It had been a bit more than two hours since the tanks had passed through the port, and nearly an hour since Lieutenant Willard had left to overtake them.

Sancroft's nervousness was not caused by any particular worry about either the tanks or Willard. It was Commander Whiting's suspicions, his pursuit of what Sancroft now considered complete nonsense, that was bound to rock the boat at headquarters, and that was something he could ill afford. How to convince the man? At least he had something. Two bodies, both burned too badly for immediate identification, had been recovered from the still smouldering ruins of the burned-out buildings. Dental records were being checked—a difficult and time-consuming procedure—but one Sancroft was certain would justify his theory as to the missing men. He was still firmly convinced that the port captain and all of the others had somehow been trapped in the fire and continued to disregard the commander's logic in an exercise in hopeful self-deception. He was glad that Whiting hadn't yet returned from pressing his suspicions on his superiors at Dover. At least he'd had an hour's respite from the man's paranoia.

Sancroft glanced at his watch and made a decision. He had hoped that Willard would have returned by now, but he knew that the tanks moved slowly and it would take some time for them to arrive. Perhaps Willard had been wrong about the timing, and they had already passed through Brighton. He mustn't wait any longer. Headquarters had to be informed, and he still had a chance to clear it all up before Whiting's call to Dover caused naval intelligence officers to descend upon the post. Sancroft left the conference room and walked quickly to another office down the hall. "Outside please," he said to a Wren who was busily typing at a desk near the door. He waited until she had closed the door before picking up the telephone. "Get me Major McLure in Brighton." His fingers drummed on the desk as he waited impatiently for the connection to be made. "Hello, Angus? Brian Sancroft here. How are you? Good. I'm calling to ask if you and Margaret are free for dinner tomorrow. Say at seven? Fine."

He paused and then plunged ahead. "Well, Angus, did our tanks get to you yet? They did? I've been so damnably busy with a fire in some evacuated civilian buildings, and the arrival of our reinforcements, that I hadn't the time to ring you earlier. . . . Yes, Angus, I agree and I apologize." He listened for some time as McLure took his lead and spoke of the tanks, their orders and the escort, while chastising Sancroft for not letting him know immediately about a unit proceeding under the direct orders of General Gort. Sancroft was both shocked and relieved. He suffered through a few more minutes of small talk and then said, "Thank you for your help, Angus. Then we'll expect you at seven tomorrow. Good bye."

When he hung up, Sancroft realized that he hadn't mentioned Willard and hoped that the young lieutenant would have the sense to phone when he found the tanks under escort and learned of their orders. He was proud of his adroit handling of McLure. He had found out what he needed to know and could now place his call to HQ. He again reached for the phone.

When he returned to the conference room, he found an angry Commander Whiting waiting for him. Sancroft raised a hand placatingly. "Not to worry, George. Major McLure has been informed, and everything was taken care of at Brighton. The tanks are under the direct orders of General Gort and are proceeding to Portsmouth under escort."

Commander Whiting's anger eased somewhat. "Has army headquarters been informed?"

"Of course. I called personally," Sancroft answered.

"Why wasn't I told all of this earlier? I must say, Sancroft, your actions are . . ."

The telephone's ring interrupted the commander's statement. He waited while the major picked up the receiver.

"Sancroft here." It was some time before he spoke again. Then, "And they're quite sure? . . . Yes, I see. How long before you can finish the job? . . . Well, do it as quickly as you can, and keep me informed." He replaced the receiver and turned to Whiting. "That was one of my men calling from the Drove roadblock. They've found two more bodies. One has been positively identified as Colonel Collingwood. Seems he wasn't as badly burned as the others. Two others were found while you were away. We now have a total of four, and the men haven't even finished with all of the buildings. It would seem that my explanation of what happened is proving to be less fanciful."

"Four bodies, Collingwood among them?" Whiting said, looking at the major coldly. "Good Lord, Sancroft, don't you see that there are too many unanswered questions here? I was convinced that something was decidedly wrong when I learned about the tanks, but since their orders have been authenticated, I must admit it eases my mind somewhat. But there are still a remarkable number of coincidences involved in all this, and I don't like coincidence, particularly in wartime."

Sancroft was unable to hide his exasperation. "It would certainly be remarkable if your devious Dutch captain managed to start the fire and arrange for the disappearances of ten men from the bridge of a ship that was leaving the harbor."

Whiting bristled. "Please spare me your sarcasm, Major. Thankfully, this will all be in the proper hands soon. Dover agrees that there are enough unanswered questions and are sending someone to investigate."

"Sorry, George," Sancroft said in an attempt at conciliation. "I do wish that you had waited just a bit longer before having your naval intelligence decending on us. We should have it all cleared up ourselves shortly."

"Not to my satisfaction, Major. I am now acting port captain because Captain Williamson is missing, and I will make my decisions accordingly. You may or may not be pleased to know that it will be your own man you'll have to deal with. Dover is having one of its busiest nights, and our intelligence is occupied with the returning troops, so it will be early morning before anyone can be spared. But it seems that the head of army intelligence is now at Dover, and he will send one of his own men down immediately, a Colonel Blake. I have heard of the man and shall be very glad to see what he has to say about, what you seem to consider, my dubious logic."

Sancroft, too, knew of Colonel Andrew Blake's reputation for investigative thoroughness and did not share Whiting's enthusiasm for his arrival.

CHAPTER 22

Colonel Andrew Blake followed Sergeant-Major Ryan to the mound of rubble spilling out into the road in front of the burned-out buildings. The two men skirted a large steam shovel that stood, one tread on the sidewalk, waiting to begin the final cleanup of the vital road to the piers.

Sergeant-Major Ryan looked up briefly through the skeleton of the houses as he reached the top of the mound, then turned to watch the colonel, ready to lend a hand if necessary, but he found that the older man was surprisingly agile. They scrambled down the opposite side and ducked under the large tarpaulins rigged as blackout shields. They paused briefly to watch the platoon of soldiers working carefully in the ashes under portable lights. Most of the men had tied handkerchiefs across their noses in an attempt to breathe more freely in the still smoky air. Colonel Blake began to root around in the ashes with the tip of a once well shined shoe.

"You'll get covered in dirt, sir," Ryan protested.

"Not the first time, Sergeant-Major," Colonel Blake answered as he moved into the darker recesses of the interior. The beam of his flashlight crossed the remains of the stone dividing wall between the two buildings that had been at the center of the fire. The moving light paused, and Blake studied a portion of the wall intently. Then he worked his way closer to it, pulling charred timbers out of the way with an ease that contradicted his slender physical appearance. Ryan reacted quickly, moving closer to the colonel. "I wouldn't pull things about too much here, sir. This floor is none too steady. Wouldn't want you ending up in the cellar."

"You said you've recovered four bodies," Blake said. "Where did you find them, and where have they been taken?"

"All four were uncovered right about here, sir. They've been taken to the morgue across the river."

Blake continued to study the wall. "From the look of that, I would hazard a guess that the whole thing started right here. This is where the stairs were located, isn't it?"

"Yes, sir," Ryan answered, adding the beam of his own flashlight to that of Blake's. "Have you found something?"

"The fire was hotter in this particular area than any other—hot enough to burn away the walls and then literally fuse the stone behind it. Were there any gas pipes located beneath the stairs? I don't see any trace of them, but it's difficult to tell in this mess."

"I'm not certain about gas pipes and such, sir, but one thing I am sure of, this whole row of houses was inspected and secured more than a month ago and rechecked three times a week since. There's no gas connected up. No coal, no waste paper, not even a loose match left in any one."

"Any chance of an unauthorized person entering here unseen?"

"Not a prayer, Colonel. This port is sealed from Drove Road to the water, and the street patrolled."

"One of the missing men is a road sentry, is he not?"

"Yes, sir."

Blake rubbed his jaw thoughtfully. "Nothing was said before I left Dover about this fire being possible arson."

"Arson, sir?"

"Has the look of it. I'd better get down to the pier and hear what your commanding officer has to say. Meanwhile, I'd like you to have your men search the area near that wall thoroughly. Have them look for anything that doesn't seem to belong, particularly fused metal of any kind." Blake again ran the flashlight's beam over the wall. "Have you ever seen the effects of incendiaries, Sergeant-Major?"

"Do you mean an incendiary bomb, sir? We've had no raid here."

"An incendiary device doesn't necessarily have to be dropped by aircraft."

Ryan stared at the colonel incredulously. "We keep no incendiary devices on this post that I know of, sir."

"Streets patrolled. Port sealed, and yet. . . . Apart from this fire, did anything else out of the ordinary occur here today?"

Ryan thought for a moment. "Well, the Canadian reinforcements arrived on a troop train. Tracks pass just behind these houses actually, but that was some time before the fire. For an hour before these houses went up, only the colonel's car came down the road, and nothing at all went out, except the tanks."

Blake looked startled. "I had no idea you kept tanks here."

"We don't, sir. Three tanks were landed by a ship that came in with the *Saint Michael*."

"Do you happen to know where these tanks came from?" Blake asked.

"France, sir. They were pretty well marked with shell dents."

"Did the tank crews tell you they had just come from France?"

"I didn't speak to them myself. Lieutenant Foster told me, just before he moved up the pier with them."

Blake frowned. "Think carefully, what exactly did Lieutenant Foster say to you."

"He said that the tanks had just come over from France, and he told me he was taking them up to the *Saint Michael* to report to Lieutenant Willard and that I should stand by the Dutchman."

"The Dutchman?"

"The tanks came in on a Dutch ship flying our colors, sir. Docked just behind the hospital ship. Lucky they were escorted by a destroyer. They were attacked by a submarine just outside the harbor."

"They were escorted by a destroyer? That is quite surprising," Blake said quietly, more to himself than to Ryan.

"Ordered them in, sir."

"So they weren't expected?" Blake said.

"If they were, I doubt if Lieutenant Foster would have been sent down without another officer being with him, being his first day on the job and all, but Lieutenant Willard was busy with the fire on the hospital ship, and Major Sancroft and the other officers were seeing to the Canadians." Ryan smiled. "Never seen anything like it, sir. The Dutchman parked his ship like a lorry. Shook the whole pier. And I never saw tanks unloaded so fast either. One minute the pier was empty, next minute three Matilda seniors were standing there with the crews already inside."

Blake began to question Ryan at a more rapid pace. He led the sergeant-major skillfully through the arrival of the ships, the landing of the tanks, the boarding of the port captain and his men, and then to what he knew about the fires. Finally he said, "Thank you, Sergeant-Major, you've been most helpful. Now, while I get down to the piers, I'd like you to go wherever they've taken the bodies you've uncovered here and ask the medical officer to send me a copy of the autopsy reports as soon as possible. He can reach me at Major Sancroft's office."

"Do you think the major will have the answer to that wall, sir?" Ryan asked.

"It's time I found out," Blake said.

Major Sancroft sat stunned as Colonel Blake gave his breakdown of what he had seen at the burned-out buildings and what he had learned from the sergeant-major. Commander Whiting looked at Sancroft with a disgust that was easily readable. "Then you believe that the fire was deliberately set?" he asked Blake.

"I do. I also believe that Captain Williamson and his men could not have been anywhere near that fire. Sergeant-Major Ryan was very exact in his chronology. It wouldn't have been possible."

"Oh, my God," Sancroft said in a low voice.

"Why the sudden shock, Major?" Whiting flared. "I've been telling you the same thing for hours."

"Do you mean that you suspected the fire was arson, Commander?" Blake asked.

"I've been suspicious of everything that has occurred here this afternoon," Whiting said angrily. "I've brought my thoughts to the attention of this officer repeatedly. Very little has been done, I'm sorry to say. My own headquarters was notified immediately, but when the Dutch ship was lost, there was little more they could do, and they are understandably swamped at Dover. But I knew nothing about the tanks until shortly before you arrived."

"There are many unanswered questions here, but the most important among them concerns the tanks. Three heavy tanks arrive unexpectedly, ostensibly from France, but if they did, you've witnessed a rare arrival indeed. I can tell you that during our evacuation from nothern France we've removed no equipment other than the personal rifles of the men. Lucky to do that actually."

"What?" Whiting said, startled.

"This is confidential, gentlemen," Blake continued. "The combined British and French forces in the north are now confined within a perimeter measuring approximately twenty by four miles, and it changes with each passing hour. The troops are wading out into the waters of Dunkirk to reach the small craft that will ferry them out to larger vessels, while under constant shell fire and air attack. Dunkirk is now the only city above the Somme still in our hands. No lorries, heavy guns, and certainly no tanks have been removed from Dunkirk and will not be, I'm sorry to say. The tanks that were landed here must have come from southern France, but if so, why to Newhaven? What did their orders read, and what did they say to you, Major?"

It was Whiting who answered. "It seems that they were allowed to leave this post without even a glance at their orders. Brighton was forced to do this officer's job."

Now Blake looked startled. "You'd better explain, Major."

"I never saw the tanks. I was attending to the reinforcements," Sancroft began. He told Blake his version of the events, damning everyone but himself, and by doing so, making it obvious to Colonel Blake that the army command situation at Newhaven was in the hands of a possibly dangerous incompetent.

When Sancroft had finished, Blake said, "Where is this lieutenant that you sent after the tanks?" He was now a bit more than simply worried about the events of the afternoon.

"He hasn't returned yet," Sancroft answered weakly.

"Hasn't returned yet," Commander Whiting shouted. "More missing men."

Blake raised a hand. "Allow me, Commander. Who did you speak to at headquarters?"

"A Lieutenant Drake," Sancroft answered woodenly.

"Young Howard Drake? You entrusted this to a young second lieutenant? Didn't you ask to speak to someone with more authority?"

"No."

"Very well, Major. You may as well tell me precisely what you said to Drake, I'll find out soon enough."

Sancroft's face was bloodless. "I asked him to confirm the orders with General Gort. Drake said he was unavailable at the moment, but that they would contact him as soon as possible. He said he would get back to me."

"Damn it, man, you're more of a menace than I've always assumed," Whiting said. He would have said more but was quieted by Blake's warning frown.

"I take it you didn't tell Drake why you wanted the orders confirmed, or that the tanks were no longer at this port."

Sancroft answered by his silence. He saw his career tumbling around him.

Blake persisted. "You said that Brighton confirmed their orders, and that at least is something in your favor. To whom did you speak there?"

"Major McLure."

"Angus McLure?" Blake said. "Luckily, I know him well. What did he tell you. Again I must ask you to be precise."

"He said that the tanks had passed through, that their orders were signed by General Gort personally and stated that the tanks were to proceed to Portsmouth without delay. McLure provided them with an escort."

"Major, are you aware of what you're saying? You just stated that McLure told you that the tanks had passed through. Am I to infer that you didn't place the call as soon as the sergeant had informed you that the tanks had passed through the roadblock? That you waited for what must have been the better part of an hour if not more? Am I wrong in suggesting that you never told Major McLure that the tanks had passed through your command with little more than a tip of the hat?"

Sancroft's face had drained of all color. Blake rushed to the telephone. "Connect me with Major Angus McLure in Brighton as quickly as you can." While he waited, Blake spoke to the Commander. "Where is the Dutch ship?"

"The *Van Hoorn* was sunk off Beachy Head," Whiting said.

"Sunk? When you said she had been lost, I assumed . . ." he paused. "Angus? Andrew Blake here. Pardon me if I seem abrupt, but something has come up here at Newhaven. Sorry, no time for explanations. Tell me all you can about the three tanks that passed through your command earlier tonight. From the beginning, and please be precise." Blake fell silent, listening. Whiting watched him intently, while Major Sancroft sat with his head in his hands.

After some time, Blake said, "That was to the point, Angus. Now listen, I want you to have your escort remain with the tanks. Do they have sufficient fuel? . . . Fine, then have your sergeant keep an eye on them—subtly. . . . No, Angus, I can only tell you that there's a possibility that they may not be what they seem to be. Tell me about Major Sancroft's call."

As he listened, Blake's eyes remained on Sancroft. Finally, he spoke. "I see. Listen carefully, Angus. When your escort sergeant reports in again, arrange a regular schedule for calls to you. I want to know if they should suddenly decide to change their plans. If they *are* proceeding to Portsmouth we have ample time to clear this up. I stress that under no circumstances are these tank fellows to know that they're under surveillance. It shouldn't be difficult for your man to keep well ahead and call in regularly since the tanks can't be moving much over ten miles an hour. . . . No, I can't tell you more just yet. This is merely a precaution we're taking until we can clear up some inconsistencies. I'll arrange for a line to be kept open between us. Keep me informed.

"One more thing, Angus. Please have some of your men cover the ground along the coast road between Kemp Town and Newhaven. They're to look for a Humber sedan that may have had an accident. A lieutenant, driver, and two or three troopers were on their way to Brighton and haven't been heard from. . . . No, as far as I know there's no link."

After a few more rapid orders Blake broke the connection, and then said to the operator, "Get me headquarters, coastal command. General Bryant. This is top priority."

He dropped the phone in its cradle and turned to Whiting. "May I ask you to find another telephone and arrange for an open line to McLure, Commander? I'll be busy on this one for the next few minutes, and HQ will want it kept free."

"Of course, Colonel," Whiting said. Glaring at Sancroft, he rushed from the room.

Blake moved to the table near the seated Sancroft. "In a few minutes you are going to be relieved of the command of this post, Major, and frankly, you may not be able to keep your dinner date with Major McLure. I can't begin to understand your actions, but we are now faced with the job of clearing up your blunders, when a simple call at the beginning. . . ." He walked back to stand near the phone, waiting for its ring, then added, "The frightening thing is that your self-serving foolishness may have put your country in serious danger."

Sancroft looked up. "I don't know what it is you're implying. The tanks are ours and the men are ours. Even that bloody fool of a sergeant could recognize that!" he shouted.

"Would you really expect the Germans to attempt to land three of their own tanks and man them with soldiers who couldn't speak credible English?" Blake said calmly.

"Germans?" Sancroft said, his face again draining of color.

The telephone rang shrilly. Blake reached for it. "Colonel Blake here. Good evening, General. Yes, sir, Newhaven. I've something of the utmost importance here. . . ."

CHAPTER 23

Major Angus McLure was beginning the second month of his twenty-second year in the British army and had known Andrew Blake long enough to realize that his telephone call from Newhaven had been more than just a simple surveillance request even before he had heard the operative sentence ". . . possibility that they may not be what they seem to be." The implications inherent in those words were frightening. Three heavy infantry tanks, possibly manned by the enemy; so thickly armored as to make them virtually immune to standard antitank weapons; loose in a country staggering under the effects of the evacuation of France; a country where a temporary uncertainty ruled the day, and even worse, the night. It was a dangerous situation indeed. These thoughts caused McLure to decide that he couldn't simply wait for Sergeant Clark to call in.

Captain Paige had been fully briefed and had just returned from ordering the search for the Humber and its occupants. He looked up expectantly as McLure spoke.

"What did you think of that young officer you brought up here, Paige? I would have said that he was as English as Yorkshire pudding."

"The only thing I'm certain about in any of this, sir, is that Parker *is* English. I know something about language, having taught it. English is his language. I've never heard a foreigner, no matter how well schooled, who isn't instantly recognizable as foreign."

"I agree. But our agreement doesn't alter the fact that I've been ordered to keep an eye on those tanks, and Colonel Blake is not a man to give such orders without reason. As you know, Sergeant Clark's brother was killed at Cassel only two days ago. Poor lad took it hard, and it would be foolish to assume that he will act naturally if I tell him too much. He hasn't your professorial expertise in language. To him, my order to keep an eye on the tanks because we're suspicious of their occupants will mean only one thing—Germans. So, I won't put it quite so bluntly. I'll tell him to continue the escort, to keep in touch regularly, and to report at once should they decide to turn off the main route to Portsmouth—since you will be on your way to join them."

"Me, sir?" Paige questioned. "If, as the colonel put it, they aren't what they seem to be, how am I to explain my sudden appearance without warning them and forcing some sort of action?"

"Tomorrow's joint Army-Navy conference in Portsmouth. You can say I've sent you along early and asked you to see that everything is going well with the escort."

"It's a gamble, sir. They're either genuine and this is simply some sort of misunderstanding created at Newhaven, or they're whatever it is Colonel Blake seems reluctant to specify and they'll be immediately put on their guard."

"You'll go alone in my car, with my driver. The two of you will hardly be a force to make them suspicious. Granted we don't know what they are—deserters, enemy, or whatever—but I don't want to risk our lads having any confrontation with twenty-six-ton tanks. The Mark 2 is a fortress and, if it should become necessary, it will take experts to flush them out. I want you to see to it that our men don't get in the way."

Captain Paige rose to his feet. "I'll leave at once, sir."

"Stop at Shoreham and ring me here," McLure said. "I may have some word from Blake to pass on by then. Remember, should those tanks turn off at any time after you arrive, for whatever reason they might give you, you and the men are to make no attempt to stop them. Keep them in sight if possible, without endangering yourselves, and notify me at once." McLure stood up and offered his hand, "Good luck, Captain."

"Thank you, sir."

Captain Paige left the office, moved through the busy main room, and out into the night.

As Paige started out, the tanks were moving ahead more than twenty miles to the west. Sergeant Clark's latest call, made before Blake's call to Major McLure, had resulted in orders to continue the escort to Bognor Regis and then return to Brighton. Dietrich had mixed feelings about the orders. They were moving steadily behind the escort, something that would have been impossible without them since Dietrich had found that he had underestimated the difficulties of moving heavy tanks through the streets of the fair-sized cities that lay in their path. There were also more check points, both military and civilian, than he had been led to believe in the briefings. It would have meant constant stop and go, and that was something to be avoided, both for their own safety and the danger of breakdown due to constant demands on the engines and clutches. But it was possible that the helpful major at Brighton might just order the escort to stay with them all the way to Portsmouth; then the motorcyclists would become a danger to them. Sergeant Clark's calls to Brighton would pinpoint their location.

If they aren't called back, he decided, we'll have to get rid of them, and that too could present a problem. Dietrich went over the route in his mind. After Worthing they would pass through Littlehampton, Bognor Regis, and then the swing away from the Channel northwest to Chichester. That was it—the rolling, largely deserted farmland that lay between Bognor and Chichester. It wouldn't be difficult to find a spot there. He hoped that it wouldn't prove necessary. Enough bodies could already be connected with their passing, even though so far no one seemed to have made the connection.

The motorcyclists were clearing the way, allowing them ample room to edge their way through the surprisingly crowded streets of Worthing. Dietrich's thoughts were driven from his mind by a glance over his shoulder. He couldn't believe what he saw! Siegler appeared to be answering the welcomes of enthusiastic civilians with what seemed to be a close approximation of the Nazi party salute! Only a slight waving movement of the extended arm kept the gesture from being unmistakable.

The bastard, Dietrich fumed, his anger rising. First he leaves his men alone at Brighton, and now he seems to think that because we've come this far without trouble these people are fools. He was forced to look away as Falck began a turn at the eastern end of a large park, back toward the sea and the clear, largely deserted road along the beach. When Dietrich was able to look back again, he saw Schiller gesturing agitatedly. The reason was clearly visible. Siegler had now abandoned even the slight arm movement. He stood in his cupola, arm outstretched above the thinning groups of civilians. Most seemed to think that the tank officer was joking. Many of them were laughing, but some, particularly the uniformed ones, didn't seem to find it amusing. They could be dangerous. He leaned down into the turret and called, "Schemke—get on the radio quickly and tell Siegler I want to talk to him." He raised up and looked worriedly to the rear. Soon he felt a tug on his leg. He hung his headset on the cupola rim and dropped down into the turret. Schemke handed him the microphone. Dietrich pressed the transmission lever. "Siegler, I'm going to tell you only once. Keep your goddamned hands at your sides."

"I don't know what you're talking about," Siegler said innocently. Even in the metallic response of the receiver, Dietrich could tell that Siegler was laughing at him.

"Forget the civilians and watch the road," Dietrich snapped. There was no mistaking his anger.

"I can't do that very well down here in the turret," Siegler answered calmly.

213

Dietrich cursed as he thrust the microphone back at the puzzled Schemke. He stood quietly for a moment, attempting to control his anger. Finally he said: "What's your opinion of Siegler?"

"Willi? I don't know," Schemke answered.

"Damn it, speak freely. I'm telling you, if anyone buggers up this mission it will be Siegler. He was just standing in his cupola giving a Party salute to the English civilians."

Schemke's brief smile faded when he saw that Dietrich's anger was real. "I thought you knew that Willi's a wild man. At Eben Emael everyone seemed to think that was a good thing to be. He saved my life twice up there on that Belgian fort, and he did his job." He shrugged. "He'll settle down."

"You'd better pray you're right," Dietrich said. "We have a good forty miles to go. If that son of a bitch does anything else to jeopardize this mission I'm going to relieve him of command. We don't have an advancing army to relieve us here as we did in Belgium. Siegler doesn't seem to realize that if he keeps up that childish crap, one of these civilians is liable to shoot his arm off—and then start on us."

Dietrich climbed back up into the cupola as Falck braked the tank to the right onto the road running along the shore west of Worthing. He looked over his shoulder at the tanks behind him. Schiller was leaning out over his cupola rim, his attention on his own tank's crablike turn. Siegler was watching the approaching corner, and Dietrich noted with relief that his hands weren't visible.

The escort waited until all three tanks were moving along the shore then returned to their position ahead. Dietrich looked to his left and studied the amusement pier stretching out into the Channel from the Worthing shore. He could see figures working among its support pilings. It was apparently being wired with explosive charges, just as the piers of Brighton must have been. It was another bit of information to add to the growing list of defense measures being taken by the British, which he would report when he returned to Germany. What he had seen thus far had been interesting but hardly impressive. It seemed impossible that so few precautions had been undertaken during the nine months they had been officially at war. Dietrich smiled at the thought of twelve Englishmen attempting to move seventy miles through the cities of Germany, even if they spoke better German than Goethe.

Ahead, the escort was struggling against the boredom of their assignment. Keeping the powerful motorcycles at the slow speed necessary to stay just ahead of the lumbering tanks was tiring. Ranging far ahead, Sergeant Clark was keeping checkpoints informed about the arrival of the armor, and the convoy was seldom forced to slow below ten miles an hour. Clark's proficiency left the others of the escort with little more to do than concentrate on remaining upright. Dietrich watched their taillights weave like busy insects in the darkness ahead. Their almost hypnotic effect was finally broken by a hooded headlight as it weaved through the phalanx of the escort. Sergeant Clark approached and fell in beside the tank.

"Bridge at Littlehampton coming up, sir. That's the last of them. It's rather narrow, but you won't have any trouble. They're clearing everything out of the way, so you can go straight across."

"Fine, Sergeant. You've been most helpful. I'll be sorry to see you leave," Dietrich said.

"I'm to call in again from Bognor, before we leave you. Never can tell, sir, if the transporters haven't shown by then, they might just let me continue on."

"I'm more than glad to have had you with us this far, Sergeant," Dietrich said, but he was thinking: For your own sake, sergeant, I hope your superiors decide you've gone far enough.

The bridge was behind them. It was nearly one in the morning, and there was little traffic. They passed numerous roadblocks manned by alert civilians armed with a remarkable assortment of weapons. Dietrich had seen naval cutlasses, axes, golf clubs, and even what he could have sworn seemed to be an ancient pike staff, and he could see that the civilians were taking their assignments very seriously indeed. General Kellner had been correct in his warnings about the existence of the civilian defense force, but obviously wrong in his estimation of their number. Dietrich again began to have some second thoughts about the efficiency of the Abwehr's resident agents and realized that the trip to the coast after the attack might not be the simple exercise that the commander—in his briefings aboard the *Van Hoorn*—had made it out to be.

And yet, the escape might not prove to be as difficult as it seemed. It would be daylight, and that could simplify things. Surely the civilian roadblocks wouldn't be so fully manned during the day. These men—an unpaid, ancillary army—must have jobs to do. Even patriots had to support their families, Dietrich mused.

Dietrich looked briefly at the tanks behind him. Schiller gave him a slight wave. Siegler was watching the road to the rear.

Dietrich removed his headset and dropped into the turret. He could see that both Richter and Schemke were beginning to show the effects of their confinement in the cramped interior of the fighting compartment.

"As soon as possible I'm going to stop," Dietrich said "You'll take over the driving for a while, Schemke. Falck must be getting pretty cramped by now, and I want him at his best when we get to the target."

"That's good news, Lieutenant," Schemke said. "I never thought I'd be spending my time on a mission to England sitting on my arse, being slowly bored to death."

Dietrich laughed. "Tell the others. They're to switch drivers too. The escort will probably be leaving us at Bognor. We'll stop as soon as possible after they've left. If they don't leave, you won't be bored much longer."

In another half hour they would be at Bognor Regis. Once past it, another seven miles would bring them to Chichester, a point more than halfway to the targets.

After his latest call to Brighton from Bognor Regis, Sergeant Clark sped back to the convoy with what he thought would be good news. He had been surprised when he had been connected with Major McLure, who had given him his orders personally. Despite the tiring ride he was glad to be told that he was to continue the escort. Clark liked the tank officers. They were friendly, and they also had been part of the force that had been opposing the bastards who had killed his brother.

Major McLure had been partly right. If he had told the sergeant too much, Clark would have been reacting quite differently. McLure's mistake lay in not telling the sergeant enough, thinking that Clark was maintaining the usual aloofness of the enlisted man with officers. He neglected to warn him not to discuss the orders with the tank commander. Instead, he made them sound almost casual, knowing that Captain Paige was on his way and would soon be able to take charge.

"Good news, sir," Clark called enthusiastically as he pulled alongside Dietrich's tank. "We're to continue on with you. Seems that Captain Paige is going to Portsmouth too. He's coming up somewhere behind us. We're to go back with him tomorrow."

Dietrich was immediately wary, but he forced a smile. "Glad to have you, sergeant. Odd time for the captain to be going to Portsmouth, wouldn't you say?"

"The major said something about a conference. Strange thing though, he said to ring him at once if you decided to turn off anywhere. You weren't thinking of doing that, were you, sir?"

"No, Sergeant. I'm just as anxious to get there as you and your men must be. Why on earth did your major tell you that?"

"I expect it's because of Captain Paige. Probably doesn't want him to miss us."

"When should we start looking for him?" Dietrich asked.

"Shouldn't be too long, sir. He'll be moving two or three times faster than we are. An hour or less, I'd guess."

"Right," Dietrich said. "Might as well cut his time a bit more, Sergeant. As soon as we get past Bognor, I want to stop and change my drivers. It will give your men a chance to get off those motorcycles for a few minutes as well. Look for a place well out in the farmland. I don't want civilians mucking about these tanks."

"Yes, sir, I'll find us a clear spot."

Dietrich watched the motorcycle speed off into the darkness. It was bound to come, he thought as he dropped down into the fighting compartment. "They're on to us," he said. He explained what Clark had told him and what they were going to do. Minutes later he had dropped off the rear of the tank and allowed Schiller's tank to overtake him.

"What's the matter?" Schiller called.

Dietrich climbed aboard the moving tank, made his way up to the turret, and told him.

Captain Paige settled back in the rear seat of the car as it moved across the Norfolk bridge. The call he had just completed to Major McLure had been inconclusive. Headquarters had asked for a list of the tank crews and offered nothing else. There had been no word from the Willard search party or from Colonel Blake. But then it had only been fifteen minutes since he had left McLure, hardly enough time to expect dramatic developments. Only Blake's involvement led him to believe that the whole thing was possibly more than just another foul up of Brian Sancroft's, but it had to be something less melodramatic than an enemy incursion. If the young tank lieutenant was a German, he thought, he himself was a Hungarian.

"Where do you think we'll catch up to them, Cooper?" he asked his driver.

"Somewhere near Havant, I'd say, sir. If I can speed it up a bit, perhaps sooner."

"Very well, Cooper. Forget the speed limit when possible."

CHAPTER 24

Bognor Regis was behind them. The tanks were now moving northwest into the rolling, virtually deserted farmland that would be perfect for the plan Dietrich had in mind. He would have preferred to follow the escort through the intricacies of Chichester, but now that was impossible.

Sergeant Clark ranged ahead, following the lieutenant's order to find a suitably quiet spot to change his drivers. Less than two miles out of Bognor, he found what he was looking for: an unfenced field, clear of obstructions, flat until it ended at a small stand of trees, two hundred yards from the road. It was an ideal place for the tanks. There were no visible houses and little likelihood of pedestrian traffic. Clark turned around on the dark, quiet road, and sped back toward the convoy.

Dietrich watched the sergeant approach, knowing it meant that they would soon have to act. Schiller had accepted the need for killing the British soldiers as unavoidable but, like Dietrich, not without a feeling of compunction. Siegler had reacted with a smiling and disconcerting intensity that worried Dietrich. It was becoming apparent to him that Siegler could easily prove as dangerous to his comrades as he was to an enemy. But Dietrich drove those thoughts from his mind.

After he had reported his find, Sergeant Clark roared ahead to inform the rest of the escort. Dietrich raised his hand in a prearranged signal to Schiller and watched him pass it along to Siegler. They were ready.

Within ten minutes the tanks moved off the road and followed the escort into the field. Dietrich could see that the sergeant had chosen well. The wooded area at the far edge of the field would be an ideal place to hide the bodies and the motorcycles, solving what he had thought might be a dangerous problem.

Ordering Falck to keep the engines idling, he climbed out of the cupola and watched all the others but Schiller leave their tanks, then he leaned into the turret and said, "Let's go, Schemke. Richter, stand by to traverse and cover us if we have any trouble. Stand in the turret hatch, and keep one eye on the road, too." Schemke joined him outside and the two men moved over the engine covers to the ground.

The escort had stopped well ahead of the tanks. Dietrich waited until Falck had climbed stiffly from the driver's compartment and then beckoned to the waiting sergeant Clark. As he approached, Dietrich said, "Well done, Sergeant. This is perfect."

"Thank you, sir," Clark replied. "Didn't think you'd be bothered by any civilians here."

"No, it doesn't seem likely," Dietrich agreed. "Have your men join us over here, Sergeant. I've arranged for a cup of tea before we move on."

"We can use it, sir," Clark said and hurried back to his waiting men. All of the men of the tanks' crews were grouped near the middle tank.

When the six men of the escort had joined them, Dietrich lead the way to Schiller's tank. A large thermos container sat on the superstructure behind the turret. The British soldiers were looking up expectantly. Schiller began to move the container, then said, "Give me a hand here, will you, Sergeant. This thing is rather heavy."

"Yes, sir," Clark said and began to climb up on the tank. Schiller leaned over and reached out a hand. Clark grasped it and was almost up when the heel of Schiller's right hand struck him on the neck. Schiller pulled the limp body up onto the superstructure, removed a knife from the hilt on his belt and plunged it into the stunned sergeant. The body fell to the ground. Schiller winced when he heard an arm bone snap loudly when Clark hit.

The men of the escort had no time to react, frozen by the incredibility of Schiller's first blow. The ready tank crews behind them struck quickly. Only one of the British soldiers had the time to cry out, and Siegler dropped to a knee and plunged his knife into the man's back again and again.

"Goddamn it, Siegler, that's enough!" Schiller yelled angrily.

Siegler looked up at him disdainfully, and calmly wiped the blood from the knife blade on the dead man's uniform.

"Let's move," Dietrich called. "Thyben, Priller, and Bohling, start bringing those motorcycles over here. Leave one, we can use it. Falck, you get over to the road and watch, both ways. Schemke, you go through their pockets, take anything that could help identify them. We'll bury whatever you find well away from here. Siegler, you use those motorcycles to take the bodies into those woods and hide them as well as you can. Don't take too long, we still have that captain to think about." Behind him, the motorcycle engines began to cough to life.

Sergeant Clark heard the voices faintly. He felt the ground against his face, and wondered why. He managed to move his head enough to focus on the tank towering above him. Had he fallen? Then he suddenly remembered, and as he did he gagged on the blood that was filling his mouth. He managed to spit it out. He lay quietly listening to Dietrich's orders. The names he heard were all German! It gave him strength to know that he was dealing with something he could finally understand. He heard Dietrich's mention of the captain and decided he would have to make a try at stopping the bastards. The pain in his left arm was almost unbearable, and he cried out when he tried to move it, but the noise of the motorcycles covered it. His right hand edged slowly to his holster. The pistol was still there! He managed to remove it and bring it up to his chin. He ignored the pain in his useless left arm and forced the pistol under his head to finally bear on the dim figures grouped around the motorcycles. Then something moved into his limited line of vision. He saw a figure bending over what he finally recognized as the body of one of his men, going through the pockets. The pain was causing his vision to blur, but he was thankful that there was at least one of them too close to miss and glad that he had taken the time to modify the pistol's normally stiff trigger action. A dying Sergeant Clark looked over the front sight at the crouching figure and fired.

The thirty-eight caliber bullet, traveling at six hundred feet a second, struck Schemke in the chest, flinging him backward with incredible force. Clark was moving the pistol unsteadily toward the blurred group near the motorcycles when Siegler's bullet hit him.

"Jesus!" Dietrich cried. "He hit Schemke!"

Pistol in hand, Falck moved forward cautiously and bent down alongside the spread-eagled body of Schemke. "He's dead," he said.

Siegler's pistol was still in his hand as he turned toward Schiller. "You did that," he said, raising the Enfield. "You're so worried about the Englishmen, you should stay with them."

Dietrich moved quickly. The muzzle of his own pistol was pressed against the back of Siegler's neck as he said, "Put that gun away, you damned fool, or I'll blow your head off."

Siegler said coldly, "So you're siding with this bastard. I should have known."

"These things happen, Siegler. Now put that gun away and get these bodies into the woods," Dietrich said angrily. "No more argument. Move or I shoot. A bit more noise won't make any difference now."

Siegler lowered his pistol. "I won't forget that this swine killed Schemke." He turned to look at the body. "What do we do with him?"

"Take him along with the others," Dietrich answered quietly.

"Leave him with these. . . ."

"No more argument, Siegler," Dietrich said.

Siegler slowly replaced his pistol in its holster. Dietrich waited until he had moved away before he turning to Schiller. "I'll need a loader-operator in the lead tank. Keller will move from Siegler's tank to mine. That will leave him one man short, so he'll take over the middle position."

"He's not going to like that," Schiller said.

"I don't give a damn what he likes!" Dietrich said sharply. "As for you, Willi may be right. Maybe in a way you did kill Schemke because you didn't really want to kill the Englishman. The next time you may manage to get us all killed because of your goddamned conscience. You and Siegler are both dangerous. You think too much, and he doesn't think at all."

"I think you'd better worry more about Siegler than me, Walther," Schiller said. He turned away and moved back toward his tank.

Dietrich watched him go. Now I've got two of them to watch, he thought. Behind him, figures trotted back across the field.

He waited for Siegler. It was best to keep him occupied, he had decided. He ordered the others back to the tanks, motioning for Siegler to wait.

"Take that motorcycle and move back over the road we've covered," he said, watching Siegler closely. "Make sure the captain from Brighton is alone. We'll find a place up ahead to wait for you. If he is alone we still have a chance to get to the targets before they get too worried about him or the escort. If not, and they know what we are, he'll have his own escort, and we'll have to fight. Don't let him see you and get back as fast as you can."

Siegler ran toward the motorcycle. Dietrich had no doubt that if Willi Siegler found that the captain was surrounded by an army escort, no one in the special force would ever see him again.

The tanks lay behind a ten-foot hedge that fronted the road for a quarter mile on either side of the narrow entrance when Priller waved Siegler to the side of the road and directed him to the waiting Dietrich.

"He's just behind us," Siegler said. "Alone. Just a driver."

"You're certain it was him?" Dietrich asked.

Siegler nodded. "They stopped where the tanks came out of the field. He got out and looked at the tracks."

"Did he go into the field?" Dietrich asked anxiously.

"No. He just looked at the tracks and got back in the car. You'd better get a move on, they aren't far behind me."

"Good work, Willi," Dietrich turned to Priller. "Get out in the road and flag him down. The rest of you, under cover on either side. We'll take them as soon as they stop. Willi, the driver is yours. Get the car off the road quickly."

The men faded into the darkness, and Priller stood in the middle of the road, waiting nervously. Soon, around a bend fifty yards from where he stood, moving pinpoints of light appeared; taped headlights directed weak beams on the dotted center line of the road. The driver reacted to the sudden appearance of the man standing in the road by standing on his brake heavily, causing the drowsing Captain Paige to be thrown forward against the front seat sharply. Before he could recover, the back door was pulled open and he found himself staring into the muzzle of a pistol, held only inches from his forehead. His belt was removed expertly, and with it his holster and pistol. No one had spoken. Paige didn't recognize the man whose gun remained aimed at his forehead, but a glance at the man's uniform left no doubt that Colonel Blake's guarded implications were fact. His driver had already been dragged from the front seat, another man taking his place. The car moved forward, then turned abruptly into a dirt road through high hedge. Then Paige saw the tanks, and knew that there was a good chance he would soon be dead. "What is the meaning of this?" he snapped. "Take that pistol out of my face. And where is Sergeant Clark?"

"You'll be seeing Sergeant Clark soon enough," the driver said, without turning.

The car stopped, and the door was opened by the man Paige knew as Lieutenant Parker. "What the bloody hell is going on here, Parker?" he said.

"I'll be glad to answer all of your questions, Captain, after you answer a few of my own." Dietrich smiled disarmingly. "Why did you come after us?"

Paige was pushed roughly from behind and stumbled out of the car. He would have fallen if Dietrich hadn't held him up.

"I didn't come after you. I'm on my way to Portsmouth," Paige managed.

"Why?" Dietrich persisted.

"I don't explain my actions to junior officers. I am not . . ." Paige began.

Siegler's fist hit him above the ear, and suddenly he found himself sprawled on the cold ground attempting to focus on the blurred group of men standing above him. Dietrich crouched down. "Why, Captain?"

"Command conference," Paige answered dazedly.

Dietrich smiled. "Thank you. Let me help you up. Now, would you mind telling me why Sergeant Clark was ordered to call your Major McLure if we decided on a detour?"

Paige's head was clearing. So that's it, he thought. "Major McLure didn't want me to miss you."

"Why would he think we might have any intentions of making a detour. Our orders are clear."

"I don't know."

"I think you do, Captain."

Again Paige was unprepared when Siegler hit him in the mouth. There was no move to help him up this time. Blood was streaming down his face as he struggled to his feet. "Who are you people?"

"I would like you to tell me who *you* think we are, Captain," Dietrich said.

"I don't know what you're driving at," Paige said. "I now see that we should have taken more interest in you, but you're a fool as well as a scoundrel if you believe Sergeant Clark would have told you his orders if we had suspected you of something."

The questioning continued until finally Paige lay unconcious on the ground.

"For God's sake, Willi, why'd you have to hit him so hard?" Dietrich said angrily. "The captain made a point. They would have warned Clark to keep quiet, even if they didn't tell him why. We seem to have gotten another reprieve. Willi, you put the captain back in the car and see if you can bring him around. Let him see your knife and then ask him one more time. If he sticks to his story, we can be as certain as we're going to be that he's telling the truth. Then kill him and move the car down the hedge to that far corner and hide it as well as you can. Bohling, you and Keller put that motorcycle in the back seat with the driver. It's too dangerous for us to use it anymore." Siegler grabbed the unconscious captain by the collar and began to drag him into the front seat of the car, as Dietrich added pointedly. "Make sure both of them are dead."

Dietrich and Schiller were studying a map under a hooded flashlight when, some five minutes later, Siegler loped out of the darkness and reported that Captain Paige had died without changing his story.

"He was either a very brave man or he was telling the truth," Dietrich said. "If he was telling the truth, we should have another hour or two before they're forced to piece it all together. Once we pass by the road to Portsmouth they won't be as undecided about us as they may be now. From now on we move as fast as we can. I'm going to avoid Chichester and use the secondary roads below it. Watch for my directions. Let's get moving." He began to climb onto the tank, pausing when Schiller said,

"Doesn't it seem unnaturally quiet to you, Walther? Nothing has passed us going either way for an hour."

Dietrich hid his own uneasiness. "I'll worry more when it isn't quiet," he said.

Earlier that evening, at the time when the *Van Hoorn* was dropping the tanks to the pier in Newhaven, Elizabeth Fitzroy waited patiently on the platform of the Hamble railroad station, happily anticipating the arrival of her husband.

She had been greeted pleasantly when she presented her platform ticket and passed through the gate. Few others waited on the platform, preferring the warmth of the dimly lighted canteen in the blacked-out station building, where hot, satisfying tea was still available; tea that somehow seemed to taste better in the stark, British railway mugs than in the finest bone china. Under other circumstances Elizabeth, too, would have sought its comforting warmth.

A brief wind blew across the platform, surprising in its chill. Elizabeth placed her hands under the large collar of her coat and shivered slightly. She began to pace, her smile hidden by the night. Ten minutes later she was beginning to feel the coolness and was thinking of moving into the station's waiting room, when she heard the train approaching. It was remarkable, she thought, that it could move through a blacked-out night and yet arrive only a few minutes behind schedule. It was the moon, she decided romantically.

The engine passed her, clothed in steam, and she watched each compartment door of the cars that followed it. The train stopped, but she still hadn't seen him. Then he was there, behind her. She smiled happily.

"Darling, what on earth are you doing here?" Edward Fitzroy said. "You must be frozen. I thought you'd be waiting at home." He held her tightly, brushing at the tears running down her cheeks.

People passed them, feeling somehow comforted for having seen the young couple's obvious happiness. It made the war seem remote, and life unchanging.

CHAPTER 25

Thirty minutes after Blake's initial call to Brighton, the only noise in the office at the Newhaven customs building was the impatient drumming of Commander Whiting's fingers on the table. Colonel Blake sat across from him studying an unfolded map of southern England. Finally, he looked up.

"It's incredible. A possible enemy in our midst, and I sit here attempting to trace their route on a petrol station map." Blake frowned. "If these men are enemy, they're certainly acting strangely. To have been able to land in this port with such ease is something of a remarkable feat in itself." Blake didn't see the commander wince. "Yet, once having gotten in, one would expect that they would start shooting, and not set blithely off on a joy ride along our coast . . . unless they have a specific target in mind somewhere west and simply chose to enter Newhaven because the opportunity presented itself."

"Portsmouth itself?" Whiting suggested.

Blake shook his head, "We may not believe German intelligence to be anything to worry about, but even they must know that tanks wouldn't be allowed within a mile of the naval base until their orders were checked and double checked. Portsmouth is well fortified. They would have to be fools to choose it as a target. If these men are enemy soldiers, they are well trained and dangerous and certainly not fools."

"I trust the army isn't sitting about waiting for them to reveal their plans," Whiting said blandly.

Blake frowned. "Those tanks are deadly, Commander. Their armor is heavier than that of any tank in any army, including the German. Plans are being made now, but we'll need more than the pitifully few antitank guns we have scattered in this vicinity, if it comes to that. They're being allowed to proceed unmolested for the moment. Hopefully we will have enough time to . . ."

The telephone's strident double ring interrupted him. Blake quickly picked up the receiver, identified himself, and listened while Whiting watched him expectantly. Finally Blake said: "Then he's on the way now, sir? . . . Fine, I'll get out there immediately." There was another period of silence as Blake listened. "I shall tell Brigadier Fox that you wish him to call from Brighton. . . . Yes, sir, we should be there thirty minutes after leaving this pier. Goodbye, sir."

Blake looked at Whiting. "I must leave now. Major Sancroft's replacement should be arriving shortly. Sancroft will be leaving for third division headquarters at Lancing College as soon as he has turned over his command. I don't envy him the trip."

"Good riddance," Whiting said bluntly.

Blake ignored the statement and continued, "It seems that Portsmouth knows nothing about the tanks and was not ordered to send transporters, as stated by the tank officer to McLure. General Gort is being contacted, but it's proving rather difficult due to the conditions in France." Blake rose and started to gather up his papers. "You will be glad to know, Commander, that steps are being taken now to isolate the tanks in the Farlington area, just above Langstone harbor, away from heavily populated civilian areas."

"Why wait till then?" Whiting asked.

"This is hardly the time to advertise a German invasion to the civilians, if indeed they are Germans. Actually, we're taking a page from the Germans' own book. They had their only successes against the Mark 2 in France by using 88s, flat trajectory antiaircraft guns. We intend to have these men in a cross fire of our own 3.7s. The guns are on their way from Portsmouth."

"You're assuming they will continue to move straight ahead," Whiting said.

"McLure's escort has been ordered to warn us if they attempt to turn off." Blake started to the door. "Now I really must be going. A patrol boat will arrive at the end of this pier shortly. My C.O., Lord Fox, will be aboard. We hope to have an interesting interview with these tank chaps when they're taken. We'll be making a brief stop at the Brighton pier before we continue on to Portsmouth. You can contact me there if anything further comes up, particularly if you get the autopsy reports on the bodies recovered in the fire."

"I'll come along to the pier and arrange for line handlers," Whiting said, following Blake out of the door.

They were proceeding down the pier when a voice called from behind them. "Colonel Blake, sir." Sergeant-Major Ryan rushed up to the two officers. "The reports, sir. Sorry it took so long, but they hadn't finished till ten minutes ago." He handed Blake a bulky envelope.

"Good work," Blake said. He took the envelope and asked, "Have you a flashlight you can let me have, Sergeant-Major?"

Ryan reached into his dispatch case and handed over a taped flashlight.

"Carry on, Ryan, and thank you," Blake said.

The commander hurried on ahead to arrange for the arrival of the MTB. Blake followed him slowly, reading the reports, under the carefully guarded beam of the flashlight. When he reached the end of the pier, Whiting was waiting.

"The boat's approaching the entrance now, Colonel." Whiting noticed that he was frowning. He looked at the colonel questioningly.

"It looks as though we're going to need those 3.7s, Commander. I've just looked through these autopsy reports. There seems to be no doubt that Colonel Collingwood was murdered before the fire started. His neck was broken by a blow, and they're quite certain the same thing is true of the others."

"Good God," Whiting said. "Then they are Germans."

"It would appear so," Blake answered.

The MTB lifted skyward and then dropped back with a shudder that caused Brigadier Fox to tighten his already desperate grip on the chair in the wardroom. The smell of petrol was overpowering in the small cabin.

"At this speed, we'll be there in no time, sir," Blake said encouragingly.

The wardroom door burst open, letting in both a blast of cool air and a respectful petty officer. Lord Fox and Blake watched with amazement as the sailor stood at attention, apparently unaware of the boat's bone-jarring motion.

"Captain's compliments, sir. We'll be at the Palace pier in five minutes."

"Thank you," Fox said weakly. He watched the man leave. "It boggles the mind. These chaps do this every day. Now you see why I didn't choose the senior service, Andrew."

Ten minutes later Blake stood talking to Major McLure on the lower stage of Brighton's Palace pier while he waited for the brigadier to complete his call to southern command headquarters. Blake felt somewhat better with the pier beneath his feet, but when he looked down at the pitching MTB tied up below him, he winced in expectation of the remainder of the trip to Portsmouth.

"Any luck in the search for Lieutenant Willard?" he asked.

McLure shook his head. "I'm afraid not, and from what you've just told me about those autopsy reports, I hate to think of what we'll find when we do locate him."

"So do I," Blake agreed. "Apparently these tank fellows have already killed at least ten men, counting Willard and his men, possibly more. I'm beginning to think I was hasty in having your escort remain with those tanks."

"They were still all right at Bognor, and by now Paige should have caught up with them. He'll see to it that they stay out of danger."

Blake's surprise showed. "What was that?" he said.

"I sent my aide, Captain Paige, after the tanks to take charge of the escort. The escort sergeant's brother was killed in France just a few days ago. No matter what orders I gave him, if he suspected that he was being told to keep an eye on men suspected to be the enemy, he would have most likely attempted to take them on himself."

"You may have put those men in a very dangerous position, Angus."

"The tank commander knows Paige. Met him at Brighton," McLure said. "He went alone, with only a driver and an excellent cover story. Why would they be suspicious?"

"I trust you've informed headquarters?"

"I have, and they concurred when I told them my reasons."

"I sincerely hope that you haven't made a dreadful mistake, Angus. The men in those tanks have proved they won't hesitate to kill. It seems now that they are enemy soldiers. They know that if they're taken in British uniform they will be executed. They have little to lose now."

Before McLure could answer, a dull explosion reverberated across the water. From where they stood, the two men could see a sudden spout of flame rise into the air above the high ground to the east. It was gone as quickly as it had appeared, to be replaced by an insistent and pulsating red glow. McLure rushed away without a word, leaving Blake standing alone at the pier's edge.

Brigadier Fox called from the top of the stairs to the upper level, "What was that explosion?" He descended with surprising swiftness. "McLure went by me at a run."

Blake pointed at the glow to the east.

In a surprisingly short time, McLure came back down the stairs.

"What is it, Major?" Brigadier Fox asked.

"Booby-trapped auto in a boarded up petrol station, sir. Two of my men were hurt rather badly. They were searching a shack behind the station, broke into the place, and the damned thing blew up. They found Willard and his men, at least what was left of them, in Sancroft's car. Those bastards are running up quite a score. I should be getting back, they'll need me at the office. Is there anything else I can do for you, sir?"

"Not just now, but I would suggest that you warn your escort to keep on their toes."

"I will, sir." A glance passed between McLure and Blake before he rushed back up the stairs.

Brigadier Fox backed down the ladder to the MTB's deck. Blake followed him. He glanced over his shoulder and saw that the glow of the fire was no longer visible. The boat was already turning to sea at high speed when he reached the door to the wardroom.

CHAPTER 26

The tanks moved out of the hedge-lined ambush they had prepared for Captain Paige and proceeded along the quiet road. Ever since Schiller's mention of the lack of traffic, Dietrich found himself more aware of it and his own growing uneasiness. But the civilians who patrolled the rail crossing at Drayton greeted the passing of the tanks enthusiastically, easing his anxiety somewhat.

His concentration was on the moonlit darkness ahead when he saw the automobile parked well to the left of the road. As he watched, the auto's headlights flashed on and off twice in an obvious signal. Dietrich's hand moved to the headset switch. "Something ahead, Falck. Close your hood. Keller, warn the others to close hatches and stand by the guns."

Falck closed the armored hood above him. His eye was now on the driver's periscope, and the limited view it afforded made him thankful that the road was straight and no intricate maneuvers were required—at least not yet. He followed Dietrich's directions and maintained speed toward whatever lay ahead, preparing himself for the shock of the first shell striking the tank's hull if it should prove to be the enemy. Then he heard Dietrich's metallic voice through his earphones: "Pull ahead twenty feet and stop, Falck. It's a car and a single civilian. The damn fool called out the code and my name in German! It must be one of the commander's agents."

The tanks moved into an arrowhead formation as they stopped, each turret covering a different section of the area around them. They had stopped well ahead of the car, and Dietrich watched the man look at the menacing guns and closed hatches of the tanks as he hurried toward him. Dietrich's pistol was in his hand, hidden below the cupola rim. He smiled in mild disgust, thinking of the commander's defense of his agents as soldiers. The approaching man was short and almost grossly fat, but as he drew nearer Dietrich was startled by the fat man's resemblance to General Kellner. Only the difference in height and his baldness convinced him he wasn't hallucinating.

When the man stood beneath the turret, Dietrich could see that he wore a suit of obvious quality and carried a bowler hat, giving the meeting a certain ludicrousness. But the fat man identified himself by code that left no doubt of his authenticity, and there was something about him that indicated a man of authority.

"Why did you stop us?" Dietrich asked.

"It wasn't in the Abwehr plan for me to contact you at all," the man said in flawless English. "I was to watch your progress from a distance. But there was no other way to warn you."

Dietrich tensed. "About what?"

"They're preparing an ambush for you some miles ahead. The road between Wymering and Brockhampton has been isolated, and luckily I saw that they were moving heavy guns and troops onto it. I can't begin to understand how you've managed to get this far, but if you expect to continue, I suggest you follow me to a detour I've located near Bosham station, not far ahead. Perhaps I can show you how to get around them, but you must get off this road at once. They'll be sending out scouts soon."

"Lead on, but don't get in the way if anyone starts shooting," Dietrich said.

The fat man seemed annoyed. "I am an army officer. A colonel of Storm Division IV, during the last war, so I'm not completely without experience in this sort of thing. Get ready, I'll turn the car. Watch my brake lights. I'll flash them three times if I see anything before we get to the detour."

"I'll be watching, Colonel. Thanks for the warning," Dietrich said, but the fat man was already running back to the automobile.

Within ten minutes the tanks followed the agent's automobile into an intersecting road. They edged ahead and turned, when the car turned, into a field and were soon well hidden by the trees that lined the road. When they had stopped, the agent left his car and rushed back to Dietrich. "We should be safe enough here for the time being, but I would suggest that you send a man back down to the road to keep an eye out both ways," he said.

"Get down there, Priller," Dietrich ordered. "If you see anything at all get back here as fast as you can." Priller loped away into the darkness.

The fat man unfolded a map he had carried with him from the car and spread it on the engine covers of Dietrich's tank. "I've spent the last fifteen years familiarizing myself with the roads of southern England, preparing for a day such as this," the agent began. "I thought it would be an invading army that I would eventually be assisting, but my orders seem to indicate that you men are just as important, so I will lead you first north and then west."

Dietrich followed the agent's tracing finger on the map. "It's a maze up there, Colonel. Can we make it before sunrise?"

"I don't know. The question is academic since we've no other choice."

"What sort of guns did you see, Colonel?" Dietrich asked.

"Antiaircraft, 3.7s I think, and that would seem to prove that they're on to you."

"Mobile guns, Colonel?"

"Yes, I see what you mean," the agent said. "Your slow speed gives them plenty of time to get ahead of us when they find we've foxed them. Perhaps you should move quickly to an alternate target?"

Priller came running up behind them. "Something moving toward us from the west. It's too far away for me to be sure, but I'd say it was a tracked vehicle; a light tank, or a Bren carrier, from the way their headlight's are bouncing."

"Only one?" Dietrich asked.

"Only one, and moving slowly."

"We're in bad trouble anyway, so why don't we stop them, and hold up the search a bit longer?" Dietrich asked.

"How can you do that?"

"Your car, Colonel. They'll stop for it," Dietrich answered and outlined his plan rapidly. It did not include the agent.

"An interesting plan, Lieutentant," the fat man said. "But it will have a much better chance of succeeding if I am in the car when they stop while your men wait nearby."

"Yes it would, Colonel." Dietrich realized that he had been wrong to suspect the agent's competence. "Are you sure you want to try it?"

"Quite sure, Lieutenant."

"Bring the car over here, Willi," Dietrich said. "You and Priller go with the colonel. Don't start anything you can't finish. If they won't stop, or if it does turn out to be a tank, wait until they're out of sight and get back here fast. If they stop, kill them and bring the vehicle back here. We'll find somewhere to hide it and then decide on an alternate target."

Siegler rushed away toward the car. The fat man turned to Dietrich. "Do you have an extra pistol, Lieutenant?" he asked. "I'd like to be in a position to protect myself if something should go wrong."

"My men won't be doing any shooting, Colonel, not here. But if it makes you feel better. . . ." Dietrich climbed up onto the tank and into the turret, reappearing moments later. He climbed out and crouched down, handing a pistol to the waiting agent. "I hope you're familiar with this weapon, Colonel," he said. "If not, and if you should have to use it, wait for the closest range possible, and aim for the middle of the body."

"Thank you for the advice, but I'm quite familiar with the Enfield, Lieutenant. I certainly won't attempt to use it unless I'm certain of success."

Dietrich stood up and reached down into the turret hatch, removing three Mills grenades from a small tray on the inner bulkhead. "That's fine, Colonel, but I'd feel better if you'd take these along too. They're rather noisy, but if it should come to your having to use them, don't hesitate. We'll have to assume that if it should come to the point where they're needed, the fat will be in the fire and a bit more noise won't matter. They should assure that you will be able to get away. If we are forced to fight here, I want you out of it. You'll be needed when the army you were expecting does land." He crouched down again and passed the grenades to the fat man, who pushed them into the pockets of his well-cut suit and smiled.

"I feel like a bloody cinema gangster," he said. "And not a respected employee of the British Foreign Office, which I happen to be." He was smiling as he entered the driver's seat of the waiting car. Siegler sat beside him, and Priller in the rear.

Dietrich watched the car edge through the trees and then speed down the road. He then walked over to Schiller and ordered him to have one of the men explore the perimeters of their hiding place.

Siegler and Priller waited in the ditch across the road from the agent's parked car. The fat man was playing the role of stranded motorist perfectly. He was leaning over the opened engine compartment, staring at the motor and ignoring the road.

Weak beams of hooded headlights glinted on the car as a vehicle approached. Siegler patted Priller's arm, and then gave a thumbs up gesture. It *was* a Bren carrier, open and easily taken if all went well. They watched the fat man turn away from the car and signal the tracked vehicle.

From his position below the level of the road it was impossible for Siegler to tell how many British soldiers they would have to deal with. He waited impatiently as the fat man began to speak.

"I'm certainly glad to see you chaps," he said to an officer standing in the carrier's bed.

"Having trouble, sir?" the officer answered.

"I stopped here for a bit of rest, and now I can't get the blasted thing started again. Where the devil is everyone? I've haven't seen a soul for at least an hour."

"Have you come far on this road, sir?" the officer asked.

"Up from Bognor Regis," the fat man replied, then added, "I say, perhaps one of you chaps could have a look at my motor?"

"Sorry, sir. I'm afraid we haven't the time." The officer paused for a moment. "Did you happen to pass any military convoys on the way up?"

"As a matter of fact, I did. Three tanks, near Bognor. Heading this way."

"How far behind you would you say they were, sir?"

"Miles, I should think. Slow, cumbersome beasts. Now, since you say you haven't the time to help me, perhaps you could use your wireless to let someone know I'm here."

"We'll see to it, sir. May I see your identification?"

The fat man knew the time had come to act, but there was one more thing the men waiting across the road should know. "Forgive me if I seem abrupt, young man, but you seem to have sufficient time for questions. You have four men with you, one of them could have seen to my car by now." He was reaching into the inner pocket of his open jacket, ostensibly for his identification.

"Sorry, sir," the officer said and then gasped when he looked into the muzzle of a pistol that had suddenly appeared in the fat man's hand.

"See to it that none of you move," the agent said.

Siegler and Priller had already moved out of the ditch and now stood behind the Bren carrier, their own guns drawn.

"Good work, Colonel," Siegler said. He leaned into the vehicle, his pistol on the stunned soldiers seated in the open bed of the carrier. "Stand up and keep your hands in sight. See to them, Priller." He climbed into the carrier to join Priller, then spoke to the fat man: "We'll take it from here. Move the car back to the tanks. We'll follow you in a minute."

The agent returned to the car. It was soon moving away.

Priller had removed all weapons from the reach of the British soldiers, and stood covering them with his pistol, his hand on the hilt of his sheathed knife. Siegler, gun in one hand and knife in the other, pulled the officer away from the rest of his men, and said, "You're not a very alert scout, Lieutenant. Where's the rest of your force?"

The officer looked at the weapons and swallowed nervously. "You'll be seeing them soon enough. There's no way for you to go ahead or behind, you bloody fool."

Siegler drove the knife into the officer's throat. The soldiers heard him fall and heard Siegler move up behind them. As one, they prepared to fight for their lives, but disarmed and stunned they were no match for the highly trained specialists. In seconds they had joined their officer on the bed of the carrier.

"You drive," Siegler said to Priller. "It's time we got out of here."

Priller moved into the driver's seat, and the Bren carrier lurched ahead. Siegler was checking to see that all of the soldiers were dead when he heard a muffled hum and crackle. His eyes moved to the radio, and he saw that the transmission lever was depressed. The set was live and transmitting! Siegler had no idea whether the radio had been live when the agent had been talking to the dead officer, or whether it was sensitive enough to have picked up the fat man's words—or his own. If it was being monitored somewhere ahead, it wouldn't take them long to try direction finders. But then, Siegler thought, that might just be useful.

He leaned over and whispered their predicament to a shocked Priller, who recovered quickly when he was told what they were going to do. That done, Siegler moved back over the bodies and stood near the radio.

"It looks like we've done it," he said loudly. "They think we're keeping to this road. They'll never suspect we've turned south."

"How far is Selsey? Priller asked, playing his part.

"I don't know for sure, but we'll be there before they catch on," Siegler answered.

"Once they close this road, we'll be trapped down there," Priller said.

"Not before we've done what we came here to do," Siegler answered.

The agent's car moved into the field where the tanks were hidden. Dietrich was beside him immediately. "Where are the others?" he asked. "No trouble?"

"None. The men should be just behind me." He and Dietrich walked to the opening in the trees and emerged onto the road just as Siegler ran out of the darkness. He quickly told them what had happened, and his plan to counteract it. As he listened, Dietrich had to admit a grudging admiration for Siegler's quick thinking.

". . . the point is to convince them we're moving south," Siegler was saying. Priller and I will take the carrier back about half a mile, then turn south. Fishbourne Channel isn't far, we'll run it into the water and get back here. By that time, if they fall for it, they should be convinced we're on our way to Selsey."

"It's a gamble, " Dietrich said. "There isn't anything at Selsey that could interest us, and they'll know it."

"There's bound to be something that close to Portsmouth. The colonel will have to come with us with the car. I don't fancy walking back."

"Is that all right with you, Colonel" Dietrich asked. The agent nodded. "Then get to it," Dietrich said. "As it is, they may seal the road before you can get back."

"Maybe," Siegler said. "But they won't have the time to move up the heavy guns. We found two American Thompson machine guns in the Bren carrier. If you hear firing, I wouldn't hang about here, if I were you." He turned to the agent. "We'll be moving east, look for the first turn-off south. When you catch up, take the lead and look for a good place to get rid of the Bren carrier." He ran back down the road.

Minutes later the car followed.

The agent kept well ahead of the Bren carrier, slowing only when he reached the waters of the Fishbourne Channel, off to his left. Finally, he stopped the car near a gate leading to a boarded-up yacht club. Beside the shuttered building, a wooden pier stretched out into the quiet waters. He left the car and waited for the Bren carrier to pull up behind him. "This looks like a good spot," he said to Siegler.

"Perfect, Colonel," Siegler agreed. He studied the wooden gate blocking the road in. "Do you have a tire iron, Colonel?" he asked.

The fat man moved quickly to the rear of the car, returning with an iron bar. Siegler took it and carefully pried the hasp from its flimsy wooden support. He pushed the gate open and waved Priller forward. When the Bren carrier was inside the fence, Siegler pushed it closed and said, "Get set to leave, Colonel. The sooner we get out of here the better."

"Amen," the fat man replied.

Siegler rejoined Priller in the Bren carrier. They moved cautiously ahead along the deserted pier to its end, where a boat loading ramp angled down into the water. Without pausing, Priller drove over the lip of the ramp, then he and Siegler jumped to the pier, each carrying one of the Thompson machine guns they had found in the carrier.

The vehicle moved steadily ahead into the murky water, carrying with it the bodies of the dead soldiers secured to the interior with their own belts. Soon, only a few bubbles broke the water's surface. Siegler could see that it was dimly visible in the shallow water, but he hoped that if the padlock was replaced when they left, it was unlikely to be discovered before high tide at daybreak.

Siegler and Priller were about to turn away when a voice came from behind them.

"Put those guns down slowly, then hands above yer heads. High! I'll cover 'em, John. You get the machine guns first, then the pistols."

"Right," another voice answered.

Siegler glanced over at Priller, nodded, and lowered his machine gun to the pier carefully, having made sure that the safety was off. Priller did the same. They turned around slowly. Two civilians stood covering them.

One held a shotgun with easy familiarity, the other a forty-five caliber automatic. Both men were elderly, but competent looking.

Siegler ignored the man with the handgun. He recognized it as a well-maintained American army weapon of the last war. The heavy gun was wavering slightly in the old man's hand, and Siegler knew that it took a strong wrist to fire it with any hope of accuracy. Not that it wasn't extremely dangerous; even a nick by a forty-five caliber bullet would break bones and shock anyone hit by it into unconsciousness. But, for the present, the man with the shotgun was the main problem. He was the one they would have to deal with before the other man got his hands on the machine guns. Once he had *them*, it would be suicide to try anything.

"What are you? Deserters?" the man with the shotgun questioned, looking at Siegler. "Watch 'em John. This big one looks like he's thinking of trying something. Get those big guns fast."

"We should've stopped them before they ran that Bren carrier into the water, Harry," the other man said, moving toward the guns.

"How could we know they'd do that."

Siegler, watching them, said, "You gentlemen are interfering with army business." He prepared himself to spring at the man approaching behind him, and with luck, to use him as a shield. What might happen to Priller never entered his mind.

"That didn't look like any army business I ever heard of," the man with the shotgun answered. "Spent four years in it myself and never once saw the like. You're a cheeky bastard, I'll say that." The shotgun remained aimed at Siegler's chest.

"At least they speak English," the other man said, moving warily behind Siegler. "Move forward a couple of paces," he ordered.

Siegler edged forward slightly, tensing himself to turn. Then something caught his eye, and he relaxed.

"Obliging bastard, I'll say that," the man behind him said, still cautious. Siegler's eyes were on the man with the shotgun, and he saw the hole blossom in the center of his forehead as the bullet struck him from behind. Siegler reacted quickly. He turned to the shocked man behind him, battered the forty-five aside, and struck the old man in the face with all his strength. He followed the old man to the ground, picked up the forty-five automatic, and smashed the butt into the man's face again and again until he felt himself being shaken by Priller.

"For Christ's sake, Willi. He's dead."

Siegler stood up and threw the automatic far out into the water. He turned to find the fat man watching him warily. "Sorry, Colonel," he said quickly. "I guess I lost my head for a bit. Nerves I guess." It was convincing in its ingenuousness.

"I admit you were in a nasty spot," the fat man said, "but I suggest you try to maintain better control of yourself in the future."

"I will, Colonel. That was quite a shot you made."

"It was luck. I couldn't wait to get closer. That man would soon have had the machine guns."

"It worked, that's all that counts. Now, let's get rid of this mess." He motioned to Priller. "I'll take care of the bodies, you roll some of those empty barrels over the blood." He picked up the shotgun and threw it into the water.

When they were moving back toward the car Siegler said, "I'm glad you kept an eye on us, Colonel."

"I'd turned the car and was coming inside the gate to wait when I saw them leave the building. Luckily they didn't see me. When they walked toward you, I followed."

"Let's hope their relief doesn't show up too soon," Siegler said.

Priller and the agent waited in the car while Siegler calmly hammered the padlock hasp back into the gate post.

Seconds later they were racing back to the north.

They were turning back into the cutoff road leading to the tanks when they saw the long line of lights approaching, far to the west. The attempt at misdirection had apparently worked. It seemed obvious that the British were moving toward them in force and had abandoned the ambush.

CHAPTER 27

Even in the protected water of Portsmouth's inner harbor, the MTB rolled drunkenly against the fenders protecting its thin mahogany hull.

"Thank God," murmured Brigadier Fox as he stepped up on the quay. He watched Colonel Blake move up the pier and shook off the arm of the young captain of the patrol boat rather more brusquely than he had intended. "Thank you, Lieutenant. I think I may just be able to manage by myself now. It was a most interesting trip."

"Sorry to have shaken you up, sir."

Lord Fox, his feet back on solid ground, was beginning to regain his usual good humor. "Forgive me, Lieutenant. As my stomach readjusts, my reason returns. I thank you for your assistance. Sorry we had to take you from your group. I shan't keep you any longer."

"Thank you, sir." The naval officer saluted smartly and moved back down the gangway calling rapid orders to the men standing by the lines fore and aft.

Colonel Blake, escorting two officers along the isolated pier toward the brigadier, waved briefly at the naval officer, no doubt with the same feeling of relief expressed by Lord Fox.

"I believe you already know Colonel Armstrong, sir?"

"Yes, of course. What's the latest, Hugh?"

"We've got them. They've turned south toward Bracklesham Bay."

"South? Why on earth would they turn south?"

"I haven't a clue, sir. It seems their destination is Selsey. They left the A27 near Chichester—we don't know exactly where yet—but it is certain that they're no longer on it. Captain Holt here can fill you in on a rather remarkable transmission from one of our Bren carriers, which I'm sorry to say, fell into their hands. Shall we go up to the car, sir?"

"Yes. I think we'd better get a move on. Selsey did you say?"

"Yes, sir. Then there is something important there?"

"Not that I know of, Colonel."

"Is it possible that there may be an RDF research center or some other installation connected with the radio direction finders situated there? Something of which you may not be aware, sir?"

243

"No, Colonel."

"Tell his Lordship, Captain Holt," Armstrong said.

The MTB roared away from the pier in a tight sweeping turn, and then settled, moving slowly past Fountain Lake dock, finally turning south toward the sea, as the four officers walked quickly up the pier to the waiting car. Captain Holt spoke rapidly, giving a precise report of the attack on the Bren carrier and the subsequent transmission of the open wireless. Brigadier Fox listened without interruption, glancing occasionally at Colonel Blake, who met the incredulous flickers in the general's eyes with unspoken assent.

At the car, the driver stood stiffly at attention by the open door. The brigadier climbed into the back seat, followed by Colonel Blake. Colonel Anderson and the captain took jump seats facing them. The brigadier waited until the driver had closed the door and was moving to the front seat before he spoke.

"Four more men. Blast! Hugh, please have your driver take us to signals as quickly as possible. I don't like the smell of this. Those damned Huns, or whatever they are, have been one step ahead of us for some time now. I sincerely hope that we haven't been had again."

"It's no good," Dietrich said. "We're getting behind our schedule. When they discover that we didn't turn south, they'll have the whole countryside watching for us. They probably have already."

"What can you suggest as an alternative, Lieutenant?" the agent asked. "If you can't come up with a miracle, I suggest you get on with it. You can't stay here."

"A miracle? Perhaps we can manage one. While we were waiting for you we heard a train out there. The railroad crosses the road less than a quarter mile from where we're standing. I sent one of the men ahead on foot to see what we could expect at the crossing. He reported only two men, civilians, and only one is armed."

"That would suggest that they haven't been alerted yet."

"The two men are unimportant. Something else he reported *is*. The train we heard is in a siding just east of the crossing, alongside a factory dock. An engine with steam up, two freight wagons, and six flat wagons being loaded. Does that suggest anything to you, Colonel?"

"Impossible! I admire your ingenuity, Lieutenant, but perhaps you don't remember that this branch runs through all of the cities you're trying to avoid. How could you take an unauthorized train through them?"

"I don't really know, but it's a better chance than the one we have now. We've come this far by convincing them that we're something we're not."

"How would you get the tanks onto the flat wagons?"

"From the factory dock. I've sent Lieutenant Schiller up to see if it can be done."

"Will they hold the weight?"

"As I remember, they can carry over forty tons. One tank to each flat, and there should be no problem. Luckily we brought the bivouac covers."

"I admire your enthusiasm, but how do you intend to get the tanks off the train? Can you depend on another convenient factory dock?"

"There are a number of ways, Colonel."

"One would reassure me."

"When I get to where I want to go, or at least as far as I think I can go, I'll . . ."

"Walther!" Lieutenant Schiller appeared out of the night behind the colonel. "It's perfect: a ramp leading up from the ground to the dock, both concrete. Two civilian guards, one at either end of the dock, three men on the train, engineer and fireman in the cab, and another man in the brakeman's van. Ten men loading heavy machinery from the look of it. The train crew haven't shut down the engine. It looks as though they're ready to leave as soon as they're loaded. We'll have to get a move on, they're beginning to load." He noticed the agent. "I'm glad to see you back safely, Colonel. How close are they?"

"Not far, but I think we may have fooled them for the time being."

Schiller didn't question him further. Siegler was standing near the fat man, and his expression told Schiller that it had been an interesting trip.

"Richter was right," Schiller said to Dietrich. "The ramp is at the eastern end, almost opposite where the tanks are now. I don't know if they heard them over the noise of the locomotive, but one way or the other we'd better do it quickly. It should be easy. The guards don't seem to be very alert. The man in the brake van is asleep, and the engineer and fireman are busy in the cab."

"Right," Dietrich said. "Get back to the tanks and move in. Take the guards first and then the workmen. Check inside the factory. Willi, you go with the colonel in his car and get rid of the two civilians at the crossing while Schiller's getting into position. No shooting if possible. We'll give you a head start. When you've done it, get back to this side of the locomotive. I'll be waiting for you near the cab. You and I will take the train. The factory is no more than two hundred yards from the crossing according to Richter." He looked at Schiller, who nodded in confirmation.

"But if you can manage it without being seen, make sure that the switch to the main track is locked in."

"Why don't I take the guard at that end of the dock? I'll be closest to him," Siegler said.

"You can operate the train. I want you with me."

"You're an engineer too? Remarkable," the fat man said to Siegler.

"Not an engineer, Colonel. I was trying to get into the railroad union before I left England. Some of the engineers were helping me. I learned enough."

"You may not have to do it straight away. I'm hoping we can persuade the crew to help us."

"This is all very encouraging, Lieutenant, but I still don't see how you intend to run that train through hundreds of switches, through the maze of tracks through the cities on the way?"

"I don't know myself until I try, Colonel. Havant is the first real barrier. It's open track till then. We can't be any worse off than we are now. Your trip south may throw the Englishmen off for an hour, but not much more. They have us pinpointed in this area. This is where they'll concentrate their search. They know how fast we can travel and the time of the attack on the Bren carrier. They'll be moving in to isolate us within the circle they'll be drawing on their maps, knowing we have to be somewhere inside it. We might just slip through on that train."

"You're right, of course, Lieutenant. What do you want me to do?"

"After we've taken the train, get to a telephone and tell your men to move into position at once. If this works we could be there much sooner than we thought."

"My men will be waiting, Lieutenant. Shouldn't I wait somewhere ahead to see if you've had to abandon the train?"

"No use pressing your luck, Colonel. If that happens we'll try to take the shortest route in. Something else, sir, if we should find that we can't get the tanks aboard that train, we'll have to try your detour. Keep well ahead of us if that happens because it won't be long before we're forced to fight."

Willi Siegler listened to the colloquy, his thoughts racing. He had to admit that Dietrich had surprised him with the audacity of his plan. It was the way *he* would have handled it. As far as he knew, he was the only man in the force who had even the remotest knowledge of the intricacies of a steam locomotive. Success or failure would lay largely in his hands. The Führer would be pleased when he told him how *he* had managed to save the mission.

"Willi! Wake up! Don't point that damned thing at me," Dietrich snapped.

Siegler was unaware that he had been pointing the Thompson machine gun directly at Dietrich's chest, his finger on the trigger.

"Sorry," he said.

"Leave that thing here. I don't want it used just yet. Remember, no signs of violence at the crossing."

"There won't be."

"How are they going to take the guards without shooting?" the agent asked.

"Our men will simply walk directly up to them. They're not apt to shoot at British soldiers if they haven't been warned. What about it, Schiller? Did it look as though they'd been warned about us?"

"No, and there would be more than one at each end if they had."

Dietrich shrugged. "So, no shooting unless it's absolutely necessary, and we'll really be in trouble if that happens. Listen."

The men heard a faint rumble of heavy equipment from the general direction of the coast road.

"Good God. We're no more than a quarter mile from the A27," the fat man said nervously. "Isn't it time we got started? They might send someone up here to reconnoiter. Do you think they'll hear your tanks?"

"Not with the noise they're making. What about tread marks where we turned in, Willi?"

"I didn't see any."

"Good, It's unlikely they'll take the time to inspect every minor road to the north, when they *know* we're heading south. But you're right, Colonel, it's time to get a move on."

The two men patrolling the rail crossing presented no problem to Siegler. When the car stopped at their signal, the two unsuspecting LDV men made the fatal mistake of approaching the automobile together. The colonel opened his window and called a greeting, extending his identity card. Siegler pretended to be asleep; his hand was poised on the handle of the back seat door.

"Good evening, gentlemen," the fat man said.

"More like morning it is, sir, I'm happy to say." The two men glanced briefly at Siegler and were reassured by his uniform.

"I can imagine," the fat man answered. "It must be rather tiring?"

Siegler stirred, smiled briefly at the two men, and stepped from the car.

"All in a good cause, sir," the LDV man was saying pleasantly.

The fat man was stunned. One moment the civilians were there at the window, and then Siegler was standing over their quiet bodies. It had happened so quickly, the colonel hadn't even seen how the young soldier had managed it.

For the last few hours he had convinced himself that the twenty years of exile had not changed him. Now he saw how wrong he had been. Despite his own downgrading of his marksmanship, he had thought that without his presence the two storm troopers would have been captured easily at the yacht club pier. Now he realized how foolish the self-deception had been. As he watched an unconcerned—and suddenly rather frightening— Siegler dragging the dead men into the heavy foliage alongside the tracks, he began to admit to himself how twenty years had changed Johann von Helmholtz; not simply into the quietly respectable, harmless, fat man known legally as John Helm, but also into a fool who thought he could suddenly regain the proficiency he had left on the battlefields of France two decades earlier.

Until now he had been bolstered by adrenaline and ego. He had killed a man impersonally, at a distance, by what he now had to admit had been sheer luck and not resurrected skill. The young soldier had just killed two men with his bare hands, no more than a foot from where he sat, with a deadly competence that underlined the futility of his own attempts to recapture a state of mind dulled by the long years of exile.

The colonel looked nervously over his shoulder into the deserted night. There was no sign of the huge soldier.

"You're out of practice, Colonel," Siegler said, leaning casually into the window to the fat man's right, on the opposite side of the car.

"Good God. How did you get over there?"

"It's best not to look for the obvious, Colonel. It helps you live longer. You'd better pull ahead, across the tracks, around that curve. And, Colonel, would you do something for me?"

"Of course."

"Have the car waiting at Eastleigh as planned. If this works, I might still be able to get to the secondary target."

The fat man looked at Siegler incredulously. "Very well, Lieutenant. The car will be waiting. I can't help but admire your persistence."

Siegler smiled. The colonel found it difficult to believe that this huge, disarming young man was the same person who had just killed two men and had brutalized the old civilian guard at the yacht club pier.

"Thank you, sir. I imagine I'll be seeing you again, after *our* army lands."

"I sincerely hope so."

"*Auf wiedersehein,* and good luck."

"*Vorsicht,* Herr Colonel."

Von Helmholtz waited until Siegler had disappeared into the field alongside the tracks and then drove over the crossing. Off to his right he could see the dim bulk of the factory building and, briefly, the glow of an opened firebox lighting the cab of the locomotive standing beside it.

Willi Siegler peered cautiously over the edge of the track embankment only long enough to see that it would be impossible to get to the siding switch without being seen by the factory guard if he was where Sergeant Richter and Schiller had reported him to be. Willi was uncomfortably aware that the darkness was beginning to seem less dense.

The locomotive sat well back from the Western end of the long loading dock, emitting reassuring puffs of steam. Siegler moved along the slope for another twenty yards, and then raised his head again to study it. He was gratified by what he saw: A 4-6-2 Britannia, designed to pull the heaviest loads. Willi continued on, crouching beneath the lip of the obscuring slope.

He noticed that the embankment was flattening as he moved farther east, indicating that another crossing lay somewhere ahead; a place where the tanks could cross without endangering their treads by rolling over exposed tracks. He paused, listening to the hiss of steam from the breathing locomotive and the occasional metallic clang as the fireman loaded fuel. The tanks must be in position ahead by now, he thought, and edged to the top of the slope again. Behind the locomotive's tender were two enclosed freight wagons, which Siegler's eyes passed over quickly to concentrate on the flat wagons and their relation to the loading dock. It was difficult for him to be certain, but it looked as though the beds of the flats were almost level with the platform edge.

Siegler heard movement behind him, and rolled over quickly, his hand on the butt of his pistol.

"Willi?" came a whisper.

"If it wasn't, you'd be dead now," Siegler answered dryly. "It looks perfect. When do we move in?" he added as Dietrich crouched beside him.

"Now. It looks as though it's going to be worth it."

"You'll have to forget about the switch until we have the train. I couldn't get to it. It seems to be getting lighter."

"Later then. Any trouble at the crossing?"

"No. Both men are dead and well hidden. The colonel is waiting on the other side. He'll leave as soon as we're set."

"Good. Ready?" Dietrich pressed the switch of his flashlight briefly. The two men heard the muffled whine of diesels as the tanks began to move in the darkness beyond the factory.

"Now, we're going to stand up and walk straight over to the locomotive. When we get there, or if we're challenged, let me do the talking. I want to find out as much as I can before we take them over."

"Can Schiller handle it? If any of them get away..." Siegler gestured at the train.

"Lieutenant Schiller will do his part."

"Will he? He got Schemke killed."

"Leave it, Willi. Let's go."

The two men stood up and stepped out onto the tracks, crossed over them, and stood beneath the cab of the locomotive. They stopped, listening.

"... so my missus doesn't mind me getting these night jobs. Says it keeps me out of the pub. No bloody sense in tryin' ter figure 'em out. Hates to see me enjoy myself with a few pints, but when I take 'er along, she damn near drinks the bleedin' place dry."

A second man's laughter came from the darkened cab.

Dietrich motioned to Siegler to move to the metal ladder leading to the catwalk alongside the boiler. When he stood with one hand on a rung, ready to climb, Dietrich called, "Hello up there."

There was an abrupt silence, and then a man's head and shoulders appeared at the cab window. A burly, red-faced man wearing an engineer's cap eyed them speculatively. "Who's that?" he asked.

"Lieutenant George Parker, Royal Tank Corps, sir. I'm embarrassed to say that I've gotten myself—and three tanks—hopelessly lost. It certainly was a relief to find you here. The roads are deserted."

The man glanced back into the cab. "It *was* tanks, Phil. I told yer I heard tanks." He looked back at Dietrich. "Did yer say you was lost? Hear that, Phil. This young feller and his tanks are lost. What's the bloody army comin to? How'd yer happen to get lost, son?"

"Some frightfully amusing chap seems to have turned most of the remaining road signs completely around," Dietrich said.

"I heard they was doin' that. And it worked, eh? Hear that, Phil. Young feller, I hope yer don't get lost on the way ter Berlin when the time comes. I don't know as we can help yer. Old Winnie says not to tell nobody nothing. Don't know as he meant lost lieutenants though." Laughter echoed in the locomotive cab. "What do yer think, Phil?"

"Better help 'em, Jack. Mum might be worried if they don't show up fer tea."

The engineer laughed heartily. Dietrich showed appropriate indignation, and waited until the laughter faded. "May we come up, sir? I have a map here. If you'll be good enough to show us our approximate position, we'll be on our way."

"Righty-o, lads. Come on up." The engineer shifted his attention to Siegler. "What's the matter with yer mate there, Lieutenant? Can't he talk?"

"It seemed a shame to interrupt you, sir. You were having such a good time." There was no trace of irritation in Siegler's voice.

Again the man laughed. "Up yer come, lads. Don't know as I can figure out yer map, but I guess I can tell yer about where yer are."

The two soldiers climbed the ladder and made their way into the cramped cab.

"Come in," the engineer said heartily. "I'm Jack Hall, and that dirty chap over there is Phil Clyde." He gestured at a short, wiry man who nodded pleasantly and then returned his attention to the flickering steam gauge.

"I'm Lieutenant Parker, and this is Lieutenant Wheatly," Dietrich said.

"Sorry we put the mickey to yer, lads." the engineer said.

"That's quite all right, sir. I imagine we do look somewhat foolish."

"Nonsense, son. It's easy enough ter get lost around here even when the bloody road signs are up."

"Still, it's lucky for us that we found you, Mr. Hall, but isn't it rather late for you gentlemen to be working?"

"How long yer been lost, lad? There's a war on. Ain't that right, Phil?" The fireman agreed. "We've been at it back and forth since yesterday afternoon. Finally on our last trip. Once we're loaded, we make our run and unload, then another crew'll bring her back again fer more."

"Not explosives, I hope?" Dietrich said.

"Dynamos. Don't sound too important, but they are, so we've been told. Ain't that right, Phil?"

"Right enough," the fireman answered, shaking his head in wonder at the muscular young officer standing beside him. "Move aside a bit, will yer, lad. I have to tend me fire."

"Certainly, sir," answered Siegler pleasantly.

Dietrich glanced briefly at Siegler. Dynamos meant heavy weight. Schiller had been right. He reached into his tunic and removed a clean, unmarked map. He opened it, and pointed vaguely to the area west of Chichester, saying, "I know we're somewhere here, sir."

The engineer squinted at the map in the dull glow of the open firebox. "I thought they had compasses in tanks, son?"

"They do. Not very trustworthy ones, I'm sorry to say. If we depended on ours, we most probably would end up in Berlin instead of Southampton."

The engineer chuckled. "Southampton? So you lads are heading there too? That's a good distance yer have ter go."

"You're going to Southampton?" Dietrich said.

"Straight to 'er, son."

Dietrich smiled. "You couldn't give us a lift, could you, sir? I've always said that southern rail was the best way to travel. I must say that this train looks as though it could handle heavy tanks with no trouble at all."

"She can handle 'em. Has in fact, but after we've loaded, the only space we'll have left is here in the cab, and yer can see that there ain't too much room fer us, much less three bloody tanks."

"Hardly," Dietrich agreed, laughing. "But you'll not blame me for trying. Well then, sir . . ."

"Name's Jack, son."

"Right, Jack, if you can point out the way to the A27, we'll be on our way."

"If it's the A27 you're lookin' fer, yer can put the map away. Just ahead of us there is a road crossing. If yer can make yer way to it, and turn that way"—he pointed to the south—"the road will lead yer straight to the A27, then turn right."

"Better show 'em which is their right hand, Jack, or they might get their feet wet," the fireman said slyly.

"And yer better mind yer tongue, Phil. That quiet young feller standin' by yer might just toss yer inter yer own fire."

The fireman looked up at Siegler. "Yer right, Jack. He might at that."

Siegler smiled.

Dietrich was refolding the map. "Straight ahead, left, then right. We're not as far off as I thought we might be."

"Not much more than a half mile, son."

"How long will it take you to get to Southampton?" Dietrich asked conversationally.

"No time at all hardly. We get clear track all the way."

"Aren't you held up by the cities?"

"We skirt the worst of 'em. This load is priority, son. They see us comin', we toot the whistle, and they clear the way. Last trip I made it in little over an hour."

"The bloody fool thinks he's runnin' one of yer tanks," the fireman said. "Can't see ten feet in front of 'im, and still he pushes this old girl like she was the Bournemouth Belle."

At that moment the four men were startled by a muffled, but unmistakable report of a shotgun being fired somewhere in the darkness ahead of the locomotive.

"What the bleedin' hell was that?" said the engineer.

"Someone fired a shot. See what it is, Wheatly," Dietrich said anxiously to Siegler.

The fireman leaned out of the cab window. "Can't see a damned thing. Are yer thinkin' what I am, Jack?"

Dietrich looked at the engineer, waiting for the answer.

"Yep. Must be that bloody guard. The worthless bastard most likely shot himself with 'is shotgun. I could see he didn't know the first thing about it."

Siegler dropped to the platform, and raced to its end. He glanced behind him to the east and saw the workmen being herded against the factory wall. Schiller was running toward him. Siegler gestured angrily, pointing to the workmen. Schiller stopped.

Siegler searched the end of the platform and found nothing. Then, a low moan came from the darkness below him. He jumped to the ground and raced toward the sound. Sergeant Bohling lay on the ground; dark, arterial blood gushed from a ruined leg.

"Keep quiet! Where did he go?" Siegler said, kneeling beside the wounded man, his pistol ready in his hand.

"Jesus, Willi. I came up in front of him like the lieutenant said. He had the gun slung with the barrels down. It went off when I grabbed him."

"You're a goddamned careless fool, Bohling."

"How bad is it?" Bohling asked weakly.

Siegler ignored the question. "Where did he go? Quick! If he gets away, we've all had it."

"The crossing. That way...."

Siegler leaped to his feet and ran along the tracks toward the road. He saw something move ahead to his right and angled across the field toward it. He slowed down, moving more quietly. It occurred to him that panic had most likely driven the guard to the crossing. When he didn't find the LDV men, he might come to his senses and return to the train. Willi didn't want to frighten him off.

Colonel von Helmholtz stood near his car, looking in the direction of the factory. At the sound of the gunshot he had managed to restrain his impulse to bolt. He concentrated on the night, and soon heard someone running in his direction and then an excited voice calling for the dead LDV men at the crossing. He reached into the car and turned on the lights. A man ran around the slight curve into their dim glow. Von Helmholtz saw that the man carried a shotgun. He held his own pistol behind his leg, out of sight.

"Quickly, sir. I'll need some help. I've just shot a man."

"Who are you?" the fat man asked suspiciously.

"Security guard—at Dentons—the factory over there. He came up on me suddenly. The gun went off. I bloody near shot his leg off."

"Are you alone over there?"

"God, I forgot. My mate is on the other side, and the others. I'd better get back. Have you seen the men at the crossing back there? The bastards picked a fine time to disappear."

"No, I haven't. Perhaps they're investigating your shot? What can I do to help?"

"We'd best get that man to hospital. I may have made a terrible mistake. It was an army sergeant I shot. Didn't say a word, just grabbed at me. . . ."

"Control yourself, sir. Is that gun still loaded?"

"One barrel." He leaned the gun against the car fender with disgust, and was wiping his forehead with a dirty handkerchief when von Helmholtz pushed his pistol into the shocked man's chest and pulled the trigger. He stared at the body lying at his feet for a moment, and then dragged it to the side of the road. Killing was getting easier, he thought wonderingly. As he straightened up he heard an indefinable movement. He raised the pistol unsteadily and attempted to get a bearing on it.

Siegler's voice came from behind him. "Saving our bacon is getting to be a habit with you, Colonel."

Von Helmholtz spun around. "You shouldn't depend on my lack of proficiency as a marksman, Sergeant. I might have shot you. I don't know if my heart can stand much more of your red Indian creeping about."

"The obvious, Colonel. Remember?"

"That man said he'd shot one of you."

"The bastard was carrying a slung shotgun with the safety off. You might say Sergeant Bohling shot himself."

"You don't seem very concerned. Is your man dead?"

"Not yet, but he hasn't a prayer."

"I'll get him to a hospital."

"And how do you intend to explain the wound, Colonel?"

"I don't know. We can't simply let a German soldier die."

"It's too late to help him. He wouldn't go with you anyway. He knew the risks. We have the train. I suggest you get out of here, Colonel. If anyone heard those shots . . ." he paused tellingly. "If not, we'll be away in fifteen minutes or less. There's no need for you to wait any longer."

"When the train leaves, I'll leave."

Siegler's tone changed. "No. From what we've learned from the train crew, we have a good chance of pulling this off. If you're found here, you'll have to answer questions and they'll start looking for the LDV. No, Colonel, the best thing for you to do is get to a telephone and make sure your men are ready. We may be there much sooner than we thought."

The fat man was glad to concede. "The odds are getting shorter," he said.

Siegler shrugged. "I have to get back now, Colonel."

"What about him?" von Helmholtz pointed to the dead guard.

"I'll see to that."

"Very well, Sergeant. Good luck." The fat man walked quickly to his car, adding under his breath, "I'm afraid you'll need it more than ever now." By the time he had turned across the road and was pointed north, Siegler and the body were gone.

Bohling was dead. His body was placed in the freight wagon behind the tender along with those of the factory guards. Dietrich felt the locomotive lurch as the last tank was eased from the loading dock onto a flat wagon bed. Willi Siegler held his pistol trained on the angry engineer and his fireman.

"What the bloody hell's going on here? Who are you?" the engineer asked. The two soldiers ignored him.

"Walther!" The voice came from the loading dock. Dietrich leaned out of the window.

"Are you finished? Did Becker set that switch?"

"We're ready," Schiller replied. "The switch is set."

"How about the prisoners?"

"In the second freight wagon."

"Right. Get back with the tanks, Friederich. Take command until we can get this thing moving. I have something to do to try and make our trip a bit easier. Put out two pickets and get the rest of the men busy covering those tanks. I saw tarps on that dock. They couldn't have done better for us if we'd written ahead and told them to prepare. The drivers and the gunners are to stay under the tarps while we're underway. I want them ready, no telling what we'll run into ahead.

"And Friederich, see if you can find something to wear in the brakeman's cabin, or take some clothes from the prisoners. You'll have to check the lashings while we're moving and I don't want you in uniform.

Get going, and make certain that all of the men get aboard when I blow the whistle. You have ten minutes at the most."

Schiller started off. "Wait," Dietrich yelled. "Send Priller up here. I want him in the tender with one of the machine guns."

Dietrich turned from the cab window: "All right, Jack," he said to the engineer: "We'll want to be getting underway in a few minutes, so do whatever it is you have to do."

"What the bloody hell are yer talkin' about? Val-ther, Freed-rish? Jesus! What's the big bastard's name—Adolph?"

"Save the comedy for the pub, Jack. I want you to get this train ready to move," Dietrich said flatly.

"Bugger off."

Ignoring him, Dietrich said to the fireman: "And you,—Phil, isn't it? Mind you don't let that fire go out."

"Mind it yerself, yer bleedin' bastard."

Dietrich watched calmly as Siegler smashed the barrel of his pistol into the fireman's cheek. It was done with remarkable restraint for Willi Siegler. The fireman dropped to his knees, shocked but conscious. There was a reason for Siegler's restraint.

"Jack here gave me a good idea a while ago," Siegler said. He passed the pistol to Dietrich, and then leaned over to open the firebox door. Sudden heat filled the cab. "You said I was liable to throw him into his own fire, Jack. You must be a fortune teller. That's just what I'm going to do." He reached down and grabbed the stunned man by his collar and belt, lifting him easily. A denture fell to the floor of the cab as the dazed fireman screamed with fright.

"God! Don't! I'll run the bloody thing," the engineer cried. He heard a machine gun being cocked by another man who now stood in the coal tender.

"Let him go, Willi," Dietrich ordered. "But if Jack here should look like he's changing his mind, put them both in."

Siegler released the fireman in midair. He fell heavily to the metal floor of the cab. The engineer ignored the gun trained on him, leaned over the moaning man, and helped him to his feet. "Tend the fire, Phil. There's nothing for us but ter do it. They'll get the bastards." After a questioning look at Dietrich, he reached for the shovel lying near the boiler. "Here, you lean on this till yer wind comes back. I'll get yer teeth."

"You can blow his nose later, Jack," Siegler said menacingly. "Get this thing moving."

"Not just yet, Willi," Dietrich said. "Are there any other trains due along this track in the next hour, Jack?" he asked the engineer.

"None till daylight."

"The truth, Jack."

"Not till daylight."

"Right then, One more thing. You told us that you were to leave as soon as the cargo was aboard. Now your cargo *is* aboard. What's your drill?"

"I don't get what yer mean." He knew very well what the German meant but continued to hope that he was wrong. His earlier confidence was based on the knowledge that the train could only proceed normally with the permission of the dispatcher at Havant.

"Don't you call ahead to let them know you're starting out?" Dietrich asked with a half smile.

"I only run the train. I don't . . ." he paused. The young officer was no longer smiling.

"Jack, I don't have the time for games." Dietrich looked at Siegler. The engineer shifted his glance to the huge German.

"Someone inside does it," the engineer said carefully, but knowing that it was hopeless.

"Who?"

"I don't know for sure."

Siegler began to move toward him. The engineer was about to tell them when Dietrich said, "Wait, Lieutenant. Ask Mr. Clyde."

The fireman watched the soldier turn and saw the knife in his hand. "Mr. Tyndall," the fireman said weakly.

Dietrich beckoned to the older man.

"Come along, Mr. Clyde. I want you to point the gentleman out. I'm certain he'll be greatful that you've saved all of your lives. You stay here, Willi, and keep your eye on Jack. We'll be back shortly."

Anxious minutes later the engineer watched the fireman climb back into the cab, followed by the German officer. He could only guess what happened. He had heard the door of the freight wagon being opened and Tyndall's name called. After that there was nothing but silence. They didn't seem to have had much trouble convincing Tyndall to make the call to Havant, the engineer mused angrily. But then I can't really blame him. He doesn't want to die any more than old Phil or I do. Worthless old men, all of us. I was going to tell them myself until they picked on Phil, so it's no use pretending I'm something I'm not. By making that call Tyndall's made it possible for them to go straight through. The only hope now is that somebody discovers the place deserted and asks some questions. That was it. These bloody Germans hadn't a prayer of getting the train far. He glanced over at the fireman, whose fear was obvious. Poor old Phil. When we're stopped there's likely to be shooting. I can't let him be killed. When we get to one of the flat stretches, I'll have to find a way to shove him out and hope he doesn't break his neck. At least he'll have a chance that way. Maybe I can get out too. As for now—I don't think they're anxious to kill us just yet, they need us to run the train. He watched as Siegler pushed the fireman aside and helped Dietrich into the cab.

"No problems?" Siegler asked.

"None at all. The gentleman was only too happy to cooperate after I'd explained things to him. He did a creditable job, considering Falck's knife was at his throat while he was talking. We're cleared to Havant. They in turn clear the next stretch of track, and so on down the line. It looks as though we may be able to go all the way. Now, Willi, go back and make sure the men are ready.

"I've got to see that the tanks are properly secured. If they're not we could lose them on the first good curve. The sooner we do it, the sooner we can get started. Let's go. Keep an eye on our friends, Priller."

Siegler dropped to the ground while Dietrich made his way back over the coal tender and climbed to the top of the first freight wagon. Moving to its rear, he jumped over the gap to the one behind it. He could hear the muffled voices of the captured workmen through the roof of the wagon as he walked cautiously along the catwalk to the far end. Below him, on the first flat wagon, Lieutenant Schiller was alone, making a final adjustment to the canvas now covering the lead tank. Dietrich could see that Schiller had done well. The propped canvas cover effectively disguised the tank's silhouette. Farther back, the next two flats held similarly covered shapes. Huge wooden crates were vaguely visible on the remaining flats. Dietrich was satisfied: The dynamos were what the English expected so their minds would register the familiar while they saw but didn't really see.

Dietrich climbed down the ladder from the catwalk and stepped over onto the flat wagon.

"You've done a damned good job, Friederich," he called. "I wouldn't suspect that there were tanks under that canvas, even standing this close."

He looked around him. "Where are the men?"

"All around us," Schiller answered. "Some deployed around the train, one in front of the building, another inside. There's that telephone. I thought it would be best to have someone in there to answer it if they decided they wanted to talk to Tyndall again. The others will take care of any unexpected visitors."

"Good. Did you make sure that the treads are well braced?"

"No problem there. We found plenty of timber on the dock. Braces for the dynamo crates. Incidentally, I inspected them, too. It wouldn't do for one of them to fall off. They're all tied down."

"You seem to have thought of everything. A few more minutes and we'll be on our way. Where the hell did Willi go?"

"Back there," Schiller answered, gesturing toward the rear of the train.

"That man moves like an animal. One minute he's in sight, the next he's gone."

"Like an animal," Schiller echoed dryly.

"Don't start that bloody nonsense again, Friederich. Accept him for what he is, a good soldier. That's all I care about. Actually, there's only a shade of difference between Willi and me. We're not here to play the bloody game. It's going to take an animal to survive this."

"Don't patronize me, Walther. I'm a German officer, despite what you and Siegler seem to think. I tried my damndest to kill that British escort sergeant," Schiller said evenly.

"But your damndest wasn't good enough, was it? I wasn't being patronizing. I haven't the time for that kind of subtlety. I'm not questioning your ability. You'll be a good officer with an infantry company, where the killing happens so quickly you haven't the time to debate the morality of it. In this sort of job there's no time for debate. Forget Siegler and do your job. I need Willi more than I need a moralist."

Dietrich turned away abruptly. Edging past the covered tank, he crossed the gap to the next flat.

"Willi?" he called softly. He waited, then tensed at a noise from the ground below him. Siegler pulled himself up to the bed of the flat. "What the hell were you doing out there? You could have gotten shot. Schiller has the men all around the train."

"I wanted to see for myself that everything was secure."

"And are you satisfied?"

"I am now."

"What does that mean?"

"I just killed the Englishman in the brakeman's cabin. He was halfway through his ropes. Another few minutes and he'd have been away and had the whole British army down on us."

"He couldn't have gotten past our sentries."

"Why not? I did."

"Why wasn't he put in with the other prisoners?"

"Ask Schiller."

"I will. Get back to the engine. We have four minutes to leave on the schedule from Havant. If we don't, they'll be ringing here to ask why."

The two men passed back across the coupling to the first flat wagon. Schiller was on the opposite side of the covered tank. Dietrich motioned Siegler ahead and moved over to Schiller. He waited until Siegler had disappeared over the top of the freight wagon, then asked, "Why wasn't the man in the brakeman's cabin put in with the other prisoners?"

"There wasn't time. Why?"

"Why? If he had gotten away. . . ."

"What the hell are you talking about? There wasn't any danger of his getting away."

"Not now. Siegler just killed him. He was almost through his ropes."

Dietrich was momentarily stunned when Schiller laughed. "You find that funny, Schiller?"

"What has that madman been telling you, Walther? No, don't bother telling me. Listen. I went back there fifteen or twenty minutes ago to take that brakeman up to the other prisoners. I untied him and he tried to attack me. I had to kill him. This time I made certain I'd done the job. I don't know what Siegler told you, but it would seem he's gotten to the point where he's knifing corpses. I assume that's what he did, since I didn't hear a shot. Or did he just break the man's neck for the second time?"

"Jesus," Dietrich said.

"Watch him, Walther. He'll be after the other prisoners next."

"Goddamn it! Two hours at the outside. That's all we need. Are you certain the man was dead?"

"He was dead. I suggest you get this train moving before your fellow animal does something else."

"In two hours we can do it," Dietrich said quietly.

"Right. We'll both forget Siegler for now, Walther."

The engineer watched the young officer clamber down over the coal in the tender after giving muffled orders to the soldier with the machine gun. Strangely, the engineer was almost glad to see him. He hadn't liked the way the other one—the big brute—had been staring at him. Apart from his size, there was something in the man's eyes that was totally frightening. The engineer had avoided Siegler's stares and continued to plan ahead.

"We're ready to go then," Dietrich said. "That leaves only the problem of Jack here."

At the mention of his name the engineer moved backward without thinking and for the first time in twenty years backed into the firedoor. He cried out in pain and jumped forward almost into Dietrich's arms.

"Not to worry, Jack . . . yet," Dietrich said reassuringly as he turned to Siegler. "Take this train up that switch to the main line, Lieutenant. I want Jack here to stop depending on what he thinks is his indispensability. There are times to be a hero, Jack. This isn't one of them."

Siegler shouldered his way past them to the engineer's seat. Glancing briefly at the dials above him, he made a few unhesitating passes over faucet-like valves, and then moved a vertical bar that projected down from the cab roof forward, as he advanced the horizontal throttle bar. The train began to move ahead slowly. When they neared the switch, Siegler reversed his earlier motions casually. The train stopped.

"Now, make sure that the switch is set."

Siegler dropped to the ground and ran forward. He was back in seconds.

"It's set."

"Then it's time we were on our way," Dietrich said, after a glance at his watch. "Take over, Jack. You've seen that this train can be run without you. Be thankful that I should prefer to have you at the window during the trip, but it's not absolutely necessary. My admiration for a brave man has its limits. The next time you hesitate to follow orders, you'll be killed. Now move."

Jack Hall said nothing. He moved into his seat and leaned out into the night air, breathing deeply to quiet his racing heart. His hand, on the throttle, was shaking visibly.

The locomotive edged slowly ahead into the switch onto the main line as Dietrich said to the still groggy fireman, "Don't you think that you should see to the firebox, Mr. Clyde? There's a good chap."

Colonel Blake found himself only half listening to Colonel Armstrong's attempt at subtle probing, which was leading up to the inevitable questions that he knew he would be unable to answer. Blake was aware that his eyes were moving with increasing regularity to the door, behind which Lord Fox sat talking to London. The brigadier had been alone in the communications room for nearly ten minutes; Blake verified the time again by yet another glance at his watch. He mused disgustedly on how ultimate action seemed to depend on words. During those ten minutes the tank force at their top speed might have moved two and a half miles nearer to their mysterious objective.

What on earth could their target be, Blake wondered. It was always

261

possible that Whitehall, in its infinite wisdom, had set up some sort of secret installation, neglecting to inform the men eventually responsible for its protection and that the Germans had learned of it before the intelligence section of the British army. God! Lord Fox would certainly bring that to their attention.

"Colonel Blake?"

"Yes, Colonel Armstrong?"

"I'm sure that it's been a difficult day for you, but can you explain how these killers happen to be moving along our coast in three British tanks and why? Can you tell me who and what they are?"

"No, Colonel. Sorry. I'm certain that you will understand when I say that I should prefer to leave the explanations to Lord Fox."

"I see," Colonel Armstrong bristled slightly. "Perhaps that sort of hesitancy to confide has allowed them to remain free to roam about at will and helped cause the loss of four of my best men." Colonel Blake's expression hadn't changed visibly, but there was something that caused Colonel Armstrong to reconsider. "Sorry, that was uncalled for."

"No need to apologize, Colonel. Your comment is quite understandable. Knowing Lord Fox as I do, I can assure you that the sentiments you've just expressed are being passed along to London at this very moment. I can't tell you how sorry we are about the loss of your men—and the others who have lost their lives this night."

"Others, you say?"

Blake nodded. The score of dead was mounting: the escort, and Captain Paige and his driver had obviously been killed. Blake shuddered slightly as Colonel Armstrong continued.

"And yet headquarters had me send a single Bren carrier to look for those brutes? Have they gone mad?"

"It was a matter of timing, Colonel. Inconsistencies began coming to our attention only a short while ago. The tanks were making no threatening moves and were ostensibly proceeding under the orders of one of our most respected ranking officers, one whom it is difficult to contact at this time for reasons that are classified. When the inconsistencies I've mentioned came to the attention of Lord Fox, he acted immediately. It was, and still is, a delicate situation. Those tanks are virtually impregnable. If they were what we were beginning to suspect they were, it became more than a simple matter of rushing to confront them. A pitched battle on our home shores, in a place not of our choosing, is something command wants to avoid. Thus your orders to set up the ambush at Langstone harbor and the order for the reconnaissance of your Bren carrier. We have no idea how they became aware of it. Since a civilian motor car was involved in the attack on your men, I can guess that the occupant, or occupants, of that vehicle saw the preparations, put two and two together, and warned them. I suspect they risked the attack on the Bren carrier in order to get confirmation of their suspicions."

"You had no idea that they were going to turn south?"

"No. We had every reason to believe that they were proceeding to Portsmouth."

"Since I'm not to be told officially, I shall have to guess that they are Huns, and that is rather frightening."

"Frightening, Colonel?"

"In the sense that we are so unprepared for war that an enemy force can land unopposed and make damn fools of us in the process. I assume that they took advantage of the evacuation to get in. I can even understand how they might have been able to get the armor on a pier, but what I do not understand is why they were allowed to leave it. I shall have to revise my opinion of our fellow officers of the senior service."

"Unfortunately, Colonel, the ultimate blame lies with the army. It was the initial dereliction of one of *our* fellow officers that led to all this. In all fairness, I should also add that were it not for the suspicions of a naval officer, they might just have done their dirty work with us none the wiser until it was finished."

"My God, Colonel. I believe that I've heard more than I wish to. Let us hope that another mistake isn't being made in removing my guns from their naval base emplacements. I'm certain that you are aware of how few 3.7s still remain in this country? Until we get some of the three inch back from France . . ."

"Forgive me, Colonel, but we shall have to do with what we have for the present. Nothing is being brought over from France other than the troops. Thankfully we are doing quite well in that respect, but all heavy equipment is being abandoned. Again—classified information."

"Thank you for telling me that much. If the expeditionary force's equipment is being abandoned, it's worse than I thought. That makes me more anxious than ever about risking my guns in a confrontation with heavy infantry tanks."

"We've no other choice, Colonel."

"I must say that I'm concerned about civilian lives and property. I'm sure that you are aware of the dangers involved in firing the 3.7 at ground targets. I have some of the better trained crews left in this country, but they've never been trained to fire at ground targets."

"We're hoping to avoid that. When the tanks are located, we shall attempt to disable them in a place that will offer the least danger to civilians, if they allow us that courtesy."

"Wasn't it Bernard Shaw," Brigadier Fox asked from the door, "who said, 'We learn from experience that we never learn from experience,' or was it Hegel? Colonel Armstrong, would you please have the car brought 'round and get the latest from Fishbourne, will you? I'll brief you on the way up."

Brigadier Fox waited until Colonel Armstrong had left the room before he said to Blake, "Well, Andrew, this mess is hitting closer to us than either of us imagined. The motor car involved in the attack on Armstrong's Bren carrier is owned by our old friend Johann von Helmholtz. We never learn. Once a Prussian and all that. The Foreign Office chaps will waste no time in making it known that we gave the damnable man a clean bill some years ago."

"Von Helmholtz? Good Lord, sir, he's been a model citizen for nearly twenty years."

"A careful citizen, Andrew. Until now. The fool must be well aware of the treachery bill since it was passed only a bit more than a week ago. He's led himself to a death penalty by this night's work. There is no doubt that the car is his. It fits. There was some reference to a colonel during that attack as I remember?"

"Yes, sir, and von Helmholtz was a colonel."

"Still is, I should imagine. Hardly a recommendation for a career in the German army," Lord Fox said as he examined his notes. "He left his home in London early yesterday morning, telling his wife that he had business in Southampton and intended to spend the night there. He drove down in the car in question, having arranged for a long weekend's leave unknown to his wife. He's not checked into any of the hotels, but an alert constable has been found there who is familiar with the car. He's seen it often, parked in the Albert Road; a residential block near the Itchen, rather away from the town center, I gather."

"Remarkably fast work there, sir."

"Not really. Local constables are apt to take notice of London number plates and jot them down. It appears that von Helmholtz has been spending a great deal of time in Southampton lately. That's not all of it. Just before dusk yesterday evening, that same constable actually saw him enter the car and then cross on the floating bridge to Woolston."

"The Portsmouth Road!"

"Precisely."

"Have they picked him up yet, sir?"

"We don't want him just yet, Andrew. We'll give him a bit of rope. All of the key roadblocks, and as many others in the area as it has been possible to contact, have been ordered to watch for his motorcar and report its passage immediately. He has no reason to believe that we're on to him, and I have an idea he'll take the fastest route back to Southampton. Why Southampton? Call it a hunch. No one at the foreign office can explain why he's been spending so much time there. Actually they were completely unaware of his visits. We've been lax, Andrew."

"A woman perhaps?"

"That possibility is being gone into. I rather doubt it. He's hardly the sort, and there's never been a hint of that kind of activity through the years. The alternative possibility is one I'm reluctant to entertain."

"An organized cell?"

"Exactly. If he has confederates—and it would now seem likely that he does—I want them. I want all of them."

"Would you like me to get up there, sir?"

"Not just yet, Andrew. I want you here with me until we round up these raiders. I've rung Major Fitzroy. As you know, he's in Hamble. He can be in Southampton within the hour. Our mobile force will be there to meet him. Time is important. We'll go up there together as soon as this tank business is taken care of."

"I've more here that you should know. One Alfred Billings of Haven Road, Eastleigh—a stone's throw from Southampton—received a call last evening. A man, identifying himself as a Mr. Crawford of Liberty's Stores, London, inquired about a neighbor of Mister Billings. It seems that the neighbor, Otto Siegler, was one of the resident aliens interned earlier this month. The caller seemed shocked. Both Mr. Billings and his wife, who also spoke to the caller, believe that the man who called was Mr. Siegler's son, Wilhelm, who left the Country in 1938 for Germany! Billings notified the local police. Needless to say, Liberty's knew nothing about the call or the caller."

"I don't quite understand the connection, sir?"

"The call was traced to a kiosk on the Brighton promenade and was placed approximately at the time the tanks were lying alongside Chichester Terrace, waiting for the obliging Major McLure to provide them with an escort. The telephone kiosk used is just down the road from Chichester Terrace. I believe that the man who rang this man Billings was one of the tank force. So it's quite possible that we have our first name: Wilhelm Siegler."

"That could explain why McLure and the others all agreed that the officers are British. Suppose they are all like this man Siegler, raised in this country, and who—for reasons I can't begin to fathom—left the country and joined Hitler's bully boys. It might be worth our while to look into emigration during the past few years. Legal and otherwise."

"It is being worked on at this moment."

"The ports, sir . . ."

"They've been informed. Screening is as tight as possible under the circumstances. When we clear this up, I want to get back to London and look into our entire security setup. I want it to come from us, rather than wait for the inevitable overreaction of the bureaucrats. I'm also going to do what I can to have this entire incident kept from the public as much as possible, even though it may smack a bit of Hitler's methods. We've hundreds of foreigners in this country and are allowing more in every day. We've already been inundated with reports of fifth columnists, parachutists, mysterious lights, and all sorts of nonsense. I don't fear panic. I'm more inclined to worry about misdirected patriotism."

"I certainly agree, sir."

"Thank you, Andrew. I shall need all of the support I can muster."

"Surely the Prime Minister . . ."

"Winston is that rare combination of politican and soldier, and that can be a rather frightening dichotomy. I shall make my recommendations and hope for the best. The sooner we clear this up the better I'll feel."

"A moment more, sir? I've been thinking about something you said earlier. Perhaps it is just coincidence, but since you mentioned the floating bridge it has struck me that it does indeed cross the Itchen to Woolston and connect with the Portsmouth road. Von Helmholtz's car has been seen on the Albert Road, which I've just remembered roughly parallels the river no more than a stone's throw from the bridge approach. It may be coincidence, but it's a frightening one. I don't like the idea of von Helmholtz and his cohorts lurking about in that particular area. since the Woolston landing lies between the Vickers-Supermarine plant and Thornycrofts. May I suggest that we have security at both of those sites increased, sir? And another coincidence: Eastleigh airport happens to be the assembly and flight test location for Supermarine. The Spitfire, Sir!"

CHAPTER 28

Colonel von Helmholtz was almost hypnotized by the glow of the headlights dull, deflected gleam, which flashed over the dotted white line in the center of the road. He suddenly became aware of the roadblock some distance ahead and braked, approaching it carefully. The barrier was unexpected in this area of downland. Even more surprising to the colonel was the efficiency of its construction. Rather than the haphazard jumble of farm carts he was used to, he saw sandbags piled nearly 30-feet high barring the traffic lane to his right, leaving only a narrow gap ahead of him. To his left the wall stretched out into a cleared field, turning abruptly north at the edge of a nearly completed, concrete blockhouse. He had arrived at the crossroad he had been watching for.

He glanced with nervous inadvertence at the dashboard glove compartment. He realized that it was something he had been doing with increasing regularity now that he was moving away from his thrust into violence. He knew that he must get rid of the pistol and the grenades, but he was reluctant to. The weapons were reassuring to the frightened man.

The imposing roadblock showed the influence of a military mind in its construction, von Helmholtz mused. Perhaps this was one of the civil defense units led by retired senior officers. He remembered having read of one such group in which no less than five retired generals not only patrolled isolated posts, but by vigorous training programs were turning the initial fumblings of old men and boys into what could soon be viable fighting units.

Three armed men appeared dimly at the opening of the barrier. One of them motioned him to stop some distance from the block. The colonel stepped on the brake nervously; the motor stalled. If one of those men decided to search the car . . . He shuddered, realizing that his fear was another all too apparent example of the incongruity of his involvement. He clutched the steering wheel tightly as the men approached him. Had it been imagination or did it really seem that the civilians were showing more than usual interest in his car? The Bren carrier's open transmitter worried him. But there had been no mention of his name during the attack.

Foolishness. There was no way in which he could be connected with the storm troopers. He forced himself to relax as one of the men reached his window:

"Good morning," he said.

"Morning, sir. Your identity card please. Is this your car, sir?" the LDV man asked, as he accepted the card.

"Yes it is."

"May I see the papers?"

Von Helmholtz searched through his wallet carefully, attempting to control what he thought must be the obvious tremor in his hands. Was this something new? He couldn't remember having been asked for the registration before. He passed the folder to the LDV man.

"Thank you, sir. Now, wait here please."

The man turned away and vanished through the opening in the barrier. The other two men made no attempt at conversation and remained at some distance from the car.

Von Helmholtz suppressed the urge to open the glove compartment and remove the pistol. He decided that it would be foolish. If they were on to him, he had assisted them admirably by stalling his motor. He settled back in the seat fatalistically, angered further by the guilt feelings that were causing him to react to everything with unreasoning suspicion. His eyes moved to the remaining men. They were talking animatedly, paying no attention to him. The colonel breathed deeply attempting to control his racing heart. By the time the man he had spoken to reappeared, von Helmholtz's collar was wet with sweat. He looked up expectantly.

"You can move along now, sir. Sorry for the delay," the LDV man said, returning the papers.

"Thank you," the relieved colonel answered. "Can you tell me what's going on? I was ordered off the A27 by the army."

"Maneuvers, I should think, sir. Good time for it usually. Very little civilian traffic at this time of night."

"I daresay," von Helmholtz agreed. "I can tell you that I should much prefer to be home in bed myself. Perhaps you can help me? Would the crossing road beyond your barrier be the best way for me to get to Southampton? If I'm not completely turned around, I should guess that it was heading east and west. I'm on Foreign Office business and should prefer not to spend the rest of the night going around in circles."

"Southampton, you said, sir? Well now, yes, I'd say that if you turn left here you'll certainly be heading in the right direction. These roads can be confusing to a gentleman like yourself who's not used to them, so rather than trying to direct you further, I'd suggest that you take it a step at a time. You'll find other roadblocks as you move on. They'll be able to tell you when you can move back to the A27. That would be best, I should think, sir."

"Yes, thank you. Left, you said. Well, I may as well get on with it. Incidentally, one other thing. Perhaps you can tell me where I might find a telephone kiosk?"

"After you've turned, you'll find one about a mile down the road. But wait, since you are with the Foreign Office, I suppose I could ring in and get permission for you to use ours if it's government business."

"No, no. That won't be necessary, thank you. It's not that pressing. I'll use the one ahead," von Helmholtz said quickly.

"Right-o then, sir." The LDV man called, "Tim, use your flashlight and direct this gentleman through the block. Mind you're careful with it."

"Bit of a maze there, sir," he said to von Helmholtz.

"Thank you for your assistance."

The colonel was relieved to find that the car's motor started immediately. He engaged the gears and edged through the roadblock. Once through he turned slowly left, waved, and was lost to sight behind roadside trees.

The LDV man waited until the car was gone and then spoke to the boy who had led the car through the block. "Follow him, Tim. As far as Higgin's block. You shouldn't have any trouble if he keeps to the speed limit."

"That bike of mine isn't in the best of shape. Brakes are just about gone."

"Do what you can."

"What's so important about that bloke?"

"I don't know. You heard the questions he asked. Just what we were told to watch for. It's a test, plain and simple. They knew who he was. Had me describe him. Rather obese gentleman I told them. Well put, they said, Mister Holmes or Ham or some such name is not a man easily lost in a crowd, but have one of your chaps follow him for a bit, and we'll see if you're right. Bloody toffs. They said the army will take over before he gets to Funtington, so we aren't the only ones in this drill. Now get on with it or you'll lose him. I'd better ring back and tell them about that telephone business. It might just be part of it."

After some minutes of hard pedaling, young Tim Conroy saw the dim pinpoints of red light in the distance and increased his already dangerous speed. The darkness of the road was complete, but he pumped furiously in an attempt to narrow the gap between himself and the car. Showing no light himself, he was forced to divide his attention between quick glances at the automobile's tail lights and the road directly in front of him.

As Tim's eyes were concentrated on the road below his front wheel, the colonel stopped at the telephone kiosk. When the boy looked up and saw that he was overtaking the car and realized that it had stopped, he applied his faulty brake urgently. It locked. The bicycle swerved toward the road's edge. Tim struggled to regain control, but the darkness was disorienting. He went off the road and ran headlong into one of the substantial oaks lining it with the precision of a manmade fence.

Ahead, Colonel von Helmholtz struggled out of the driver's seat and moved stiffly to the kiosk. The grenades and the Enfield pistol were in the pockets of his jacket. He had finally decided to get rid of them in the dense woods lining the road after he made his call. He entered the kiosk and was about to deposit a coin when something broke the stillness of the road behind the car. The noise was sudden and undecipherable. He stepped out of the kiosk, listening intently, but heard nothing more. The colonel remained unmoving, his hand on the butt of the revolver for a full minute, searching the silence. Nothing. He finally decided that it had been an animal of some sort. The colonel was surprised at the calm he had felt with his hand on the butt of the reassuring Enfield. It was then he changed his mind and decided to keep the weapons. It was now quite obvious that he wasn't under suspicion, and each mile took him farther away from the storm troopers. It was foolish to worry about a personal search by the LDV. There was no reason to search a harmless middle-aged man with Foreign Office credentials. And the weapons might just come in handy in the next few weeks—when the Wehrmacht landed. Having made the decision, he reentered the kiosk, deposited the coin, and began to dial.

Tim Conroy lay on the ground for some time, stunned. His head had struck the tree as he was flung over the handlebars of the bicycle. Finally he stirred. After a confusing moment or two, he remembered what had happened. He put his hand to his head, feeling the tender spot just above the left eye. It felt damp; sticky damp. Actually it was a minor scrape, but the boy's imagination began working furiously. He had the sudden thought that he might be bleeding to death. The thought forced him to his feet. He was amazed to find that apart from the throbbing of his head he seemed to be unhurt. The bicycle lay nearby. He got it upright and discovered angrily that the front tire and rim had been bent almost double by the force of the collision. Dragging it back to the road, he looked west, somewhat thankful to find that the fat man's car was gone.

The boy touched his wound gingerly. The minor blood flow was already coagulating, but he wasn't greatly reassured. He secured the front wheel under his armpit and, dragging the rear wheel behind him, began walking back toward the roadblock. He was more than a little worried about what his mum would say when she saw the blood on his shirt.

At the next major roadblock, the colonel's rapidly returning self confidence was further reinforced by the cursory examination of his papers by a polite, apparently bored, civilian. The colonel noticed that the man seemed impressed by the Foreign Office credentials. In answer to his request for routing to Southampton, the LDV man surprised him by asking why he didn't simply turn south and join up with the easily followed A27.

"But the A27 is closed to traffic," the colonel said. "I was diverted up here by the army."

"It's open now, sir. Drill's over, I suppose. We've just gotten the word."

"That *is* good news. Thank you," the colonel beamed.

"Are you familiar with these roads, sir?"

"No. Not at all."

"Then careful's the word in this blackout. There's a rather nasty curve halfway down that one." He pointed to the south fork.

"Oh?" the colonel said.

"No matter, sir. You've come along just at the right time. You can follow Archie Powell's lorry down. That's him over there, talking the ear off my men as usual." He leaned closer to the colonel. "Quite a talker, Archie, but he does know the road. You can follow him as far as Havant if you like."

"If the gentleman doesn't mind, I shall be most happy to follow him. I must admit that I'm not the best of drivers. You are certainly most helpful."

The LDV man seemed embarrassed. "Glad to help, sir."

"Here, Archie!" he called. "This gentleman is going to follow you to Havant. Doesn't know the road, so mind you keep to the speed limit."

The man waved a hand casually and then returned to his animated conversation with the LDV men.

"I'll have him get a move on, sir," said the helpful LDV man.

Von Helmholtz watched him walk over to the group of men and speak to the one identified as Archie Powell. He saw the man glance briefly at him, then wave as he made his way to the cab of his lorry. Once there, he called, "Ready, sir? Just follow my lights, but mind you don't get too close."

Von Helmholtz acknowledged that he was ready. Putting his car in gear, he again thanked the LDV man and followed the lorry around the barrier into the road leading to the south.

"And that should do it nicely," the LDV man said under his breath. Walking quickly to the center of the crossroad, he watched von Helmholtz's taillights fade, and then made a beckoning gesture.

A black Rover sedan pulled out of the darkness of the northern leg of the road, and disappeared in the wake of the colonel's car. Behind the sedan, a Bren carrier followed noisily into the middle of the road and stopped. The LDV man said a few rapid words to its occupants and then pulled himself up over the treads. He spoke briefly into a microphone and then, at his order, the Bren carrier lurched forward, braked, and turned into the road leading west.

Colonel Andrew Blake stepped through the door of the roadside pub that had been hastily commandeered as the Fishbourne command post. Across the road, one of the 3.7 antiaircraft guns brought up from Portsmouth stood, still hooked up to an oddly shaped artillery tractor. The colonel looked to his left and was just able to make out the second gun, huge and menacing, its barrel pointed skyward. As he watched, it began to lower as its crew completed a drill under the direction of an impatient gun commander. Blake watched the barrel drop until it seemed to center directly on him. He stepped out into the road, smiling at the vague sense of unease he felt at knowing what sort of damage a gun designed to fling its shell more than six miles into the air could do when fired at a ground target, its shell fused to explode on contact.

"I can imagine what you're thinking, Andrew." Brigadier Fox stood behind the colonel, who hadn't heard his approach.

"Sir?"

"Those guns. Let us hope that we catch the Huns with the water at their backs."

"I must admit I was thinking somewhat along those lines, sir."

"Unfortunately, we've no other option. I do have some positive news for a change. We've got von Helmholtz—under surveillance to be precise. He just passed through a roadblock north of Bosham station. Captain West had the prescience to have one of our undercover surveillance units at that very spot. West actually spoke to our Prussian. It seems that von Helmholtz asked directions to Southampton, so the captain obligingly directed him back to the A27."

"That was a quick piece of work, sir."

"That's not all of it. West even provided him with Sergeant-Major Powell in one of our civilian lorries, ostensibly a farmer who was asked by our good captain to kindly direct this gentleman to the A27. Von Helmholtz was most appreciative, and off he went, no doubt quite pleased with himself. So Powell is leading in the signals lorry, with the backup car bringing up the rear while Captain West parallels them on a road to the north. The other cars are moving into position ahead and will take over at Havant. Actually, it's little more than an exercise, since we know exactly where he's going."

"Albert Road?"

"Albert Road. Thanks to one of our alert local defense volunteers, our people were able to intercept a telephone call von Helmholtz made from a roadside kiosk."

"Did he say anything we might use here, sir?"

"No. It was apparently innocent conversation but quite contrived. Code of some sort. However, he is heading directly for the Albert Road. He said that clearly enough."

"Any hint as to how many others we're dealing with, sir?"

"More than a hint. The telephone is listed under the name of William Smith. A guest house with eight permanent residents, all men. At least they pay for permanent residency, but the neighbors state that they only see them occasionally, and all at the same time usually. The owners are an elderly couple, both of whom were born in Southampton. They haven't been questioned yet. I don't want anyone near the house until we're ready to move in. Questioning the neighbors was risky enough. The lodgers are all there now, and as soon as von Helmholtz arrives and they're all together, they'll be taken in charge. Until then, we've little more than suspicion to charge them with. We can leave the Prussian and his cohorts to others for the present and concentrate on the puzzle we're faced with here. The search must have penetrated at least a mile down there by now."

"About that, sir. There are literally scores of possible places large enough to hide the tanks."

"Despite the testimony of those civilians, I'm beginning to suspect that they're not down there, Andrew. I don't know why, but I feel it. I've missed something somewhere."

Colonel Blake hesitated briefly. "While you were talking to headquarters I've had some time to study Major Blythe's report, sir, and I must admit to some doubts of my own. Both of the civilians he's uncovered thus far who heard something pass spoke in the singular. One said: a treaded vehicle, and the other spoke of 'a rather nasty clanking,' which he took to be a tank. *A* tank, sir. We've both heard heavy infantry tanks moving over concrete roads. With all the talk about invasion, the noise made by three infantry tanks should have aroused the interest of the entire countryside

273

to put it mildly, and yet, our three apparently disturbed only two rather elderly insomniacs."

"I knew I'd missed something. That's it! A treaded vehicle. The Bren carrier! They *were* on to us. I found it difficult to believe from the start that highly trained assault troops wouldn't have discovered that the Bren carrier's wireless was live. We swallowed their bait. Damn it! They disposed of the Bren carrier down there, used von Helmholtz's automobile to return to the tanks, and then moved north."

"It's quite possible, sir, and yet I frankly don't see how. All the roads are covered by the army or the LDV. There hasn't been a hint of the tanks' passage. Home forces now have this area encircled, and von Helmholtz was obviously alone when Captain West spoke to him."

"Then they have gone to ground up there."

"I should think so, sir. They certainly haven't passed through the outer surveillance perimeter, so they must be somewhere within, say, two or three miles of this point. That is rather a bit of countryside to cover."

"We may be able to narrow it down a bit further. Von Helmholtz was first reported passing through a roadblock approximately one half mile north of the A27, between Fishbourne and Old Fishbourne. He was directed west, moving on to the roadblock at the B2146, where our chaps took over. It was between the two roadblocks that he stopped to make his call to Southampton. I would hazard a guess that he had left the tanks only shortly before he arrived at that first roadblock." Brigadier Fox shook his head impatiently. "We're doing little good here, Andrew. Come along. I'll pass our suspicions on to Bryce-Morton, and then we'll do a bit of snooping on our own, starting at that roadblock above the Fishbournes."

"Von Helmholtz has the answers, sir."

"And you think I should have him picked up at once, eh?"

"Sorry, sir. I wasn't questioning your judgment. But knowing that he does have the answers makes the waiting somewhat difficult."

"No less difficult for me, Andrew. He should be in Southampton within the hour, and I should prefer to make it a clean sweep."

"Yes, sir."

"While I'm getting through to Bryce-Morton, I'd like you to arrange for a signals vehicle to accompany us while we're retracing the Prussian's movements."

"I'll have it waiting, sir." Colonel Blake said as the two men entered the command post.

Some minutes later, Blake was waiting at the door of the general's car when he noticed the sudden increase in the activity around him. He was moving toward the command post, when Brigadier Fox burst through the entrance.

"They've found the Bren carrier," he said grimly.

Colonel Armstrong stared into the darkness beyond, the dark water lapping gently over his carefully polished shoes. Even though he was expecting it, Armstrong was startled when the surface of the quiet water broke, and a head appeared about ten yeards out from the lower end of the yacht club ramp. He watched the man swim to the ramp and stand up. The swimmer wore only bathing trunks. Once out of the water, he stood shivering, his teeth chattering audibly as he spoke.

"Wires hooked on, sir, and I've managed to get it out of gear. It's only just under the surface."

"Good work, lad. Are they there?"

"Felt like it, sir. Too dark to see anything down there though." The man shuddered.

"You've done well, Corporal. Now you'd best get out of there and into some warm clothing."

"Yes, sir. It is a bit chilly."

The colonel waited until the corporal had moved over the upper end of the ramp and then said, "Get it moving, Sergeant."

"Ready, sir, but you'd better stand clear, Colonel. No telling how she'll come up."

Armstrong stepped over the tow wire and walked quickly up the ramp to join Brigadier Fox and Colonel Blake on the pier. He paused, looking at the body covered with a greatcoat and lying in a pool of water on the pier.

"Bloody savages!" Colonel Anderson said vehemently.

The engine of the heavy Scammel transporter roared as it began to inch forward. The tow wire stretched and tightened, throwing spray into the air. Shielded lights shone on the water lapping against the base of the ramp. The transporter was straining against the tow wire. Then the Bren carrier broke through the surface of the water and began edging backward up the incline. As it cleared the water, it began to slue toward the ramp's edge. The sergeant directing the tow ran down the ramp and climbed aboard the vehicle. The officers saw him pause, pointing his flashlight down into the rapidly draining open compartment. They heard the fury in his voice.

"Looks like at least three more men, sir. Tied to the bloody fittings like animals." The sergeant averted his eyes abruptly. He dropped into the cramped, water-filled compartment, forced his way into the driver's seat, and straightened the vehicle until it passed over the upper end of the ramp. He then raised a dripping arm and the Scammel stopped. The sergeant climbed down and moved away without saying a word.

The three officers approached the Bren carrier through the rapidly growing pool of water on the pier. They leaned over the tread, following Colonel Armstrong's flashlight beam as it passed over the interior. The light steadied on one corpse: a young noncom. His eyes were open, staring at them reproachfully. The water dropped in the compartment, and the head fell forward, straining against the belt tied around the swollen neck.

"My God!" Brigadier Fox said.

"I suppose I should have been prepared for this when my men found Lieutenant Thompson, also tied by the neck, floating out there. If he hadn't floated free, we should probably have missed finding them until the next low tide."

A young lieutenant spoke from behind the three horrified men. "Colonel Armstrong?"

Armstrong snapped off the light. "What is it, Lieutenant?"

"I'm afraid we've just found another body, sir, floating just alongside the pier—a civilian, rather badly damaged. It could have been the pilings, but I rather doubt it. It looks as if he was beaten to death with a blunt instrument of some sort."

Colonel Armstrong, after an agonized glance at Brigadier Fox, hurried across the pier followed by the Lieutenant.

"That settles it." Brigadier Fox said, his voice quivering in anger. "You were right, Andrew. Contact the mobile force. I want von Helmholtz picked up at once. Have him brought to the command post in Fishbourne as quickly as possible. Then get through to Major Fitzroy in Southampton. Have him prepare to move in on that house in Albert Road as soon as we've taken von Helmholtz. Tell him what we've seen here and that he's to take no chances. Tell him we want some answers."

Von Helmholtz was thankful for the guiding taillights of the farmer's lorry. He was tired to the point of total exhaustion. The physical and psychological demands on his body during the past few hours had drained him completely. The LDV man had been right; the road south to the A27 had been somewhat treacherous in the darkness. The colonel was forced to stay alert by the demands of the road. After what had seemed an interminable ride, he sensed the sea ahead. He watched the lights of the lorry carefully, applying his own brakes when the man ahead slowed and then crossed the railroad tracks, which told the colonel that the A27 lay just ahead. He was surprised when neither the lorry nor his car were stopped by the LDV men in evidence at the crossing. Von Helmholtz looked to his left, his mind turning to the storm troopers. Had they passed yet? No, probably not. Siegler had said at least fifteen minutes. The colonel sighed tiredly. For an instant he toyed with the idea of turning the car back to the north and making directly for the familiar sanctuary of his flat in Chelsea. The thought passed quickly.

Ahead, the lorry braked again and turned right onto the A27. Von Helmholtz found himself back on familiar ground. It made him feel better. Traffic was sparse. What there was seemed to be largely military, moving to the east. Von Helmholtz smiled at the audacity of the storm troopers. His doubts were fading. The seizure of the train might just work. Siegler had said that it most likely would not be missed before daylight. Obviously all of the British attention was being directed to the area of the attack on the Bren carrier. Von Helmholtz glanced to his right at the rail line now running parallel to the A27, then brought his eyes back to the road ahead, and as he did, noticed the dim headlights showing in his rear view mirror. He sighed with satisfaction. Traffic behind him, and the lack of any military checkpoints on the road reinforced his opinion that the foolish Englishmen had decided that all danger lay to the east.

He began to see signs of life as he followed the lorry through Southbourne and Emsworth. ARP men and an occasional white-coated constable patrolled the streets purposefully, but without the urgency the colonel would have expected had there been a general alert. Actually, he could understand the dilemma facing the British military command. It was hardly the time to admit to an uneasy populace that an enemy force was loose in their midst, if indeed they believed it to be an enemy force.

At that moment Colonel Blake had just finished talking to the lorry guiding von Helmholtz along the quiet road. The unmarked car behind him had already begun closing in.

CHAPTER 29

The dim reflections in the rear-view mirror were growing steadily larger. Colonel von Helmholtz was surprised since the twenty-mile-an-hour speed limit was seldom broken by British motorists, at least on major roads. But it was obvious that the car that was overtaking him was coming on at well above that speed. He glanced nervously at his own speedometer. The needle hovered just below the twenty mark. He began to feel uneasy.

The farmer's lorry was well ahead and, as far as he could see, there was nothing else on the road. The feeling of isolation accentuated his anxiety. There was, he knew, no logical explanation for it, but he decided that he must stop and let the speeding car pass him before he could continue.

He drove through the deserted streets of Warblington and moved into the easy curve to the north. Ahead the road curved back to the west, into the outlying buildings of Havant. The lorry had entered the western curve and was hidden from view. Buildings fronting the road obscured the overtaking car. Von Helmholtz switched off his lights and was pulling over to the curb when he saw a street directly in front of him, branching off to the north between low buildings.

He shifted gears, drove ahead, and turned into it, continuing on for fifty yards, then edging to the curb. When he had stopped, he turned to watch the road behind him through the rear window. He hadn't long to wait. It seemed that he had hardly turned when something flashed across his view, traveling at high speed.

Even though von Helmholtz hadn't been able to see more than a vague blur, he was now convinced that the automobile was an official vehicle of some sort. No civilian would have been foolish enough to maintain such speed through a built up area. Von Helmholtz continued to stare through the window, reluctant to make the decision to move.

"Good evening, sir."

The voice came from behind him. Von Helmholtz was frozen, cursing his carelessness. The pistol was in his coat pocket, pressed against the back seat and impossible to get at quickly. He turned to the driver's window reluctantly.

A slight, elderly civilian, wearing an incredibly dirty raincoat and threadbare cap, leaned over and stared into the colonel's face. He touched his cap respectfully in a half salute: "Sorry, sir. I didn't mean to frighten you."

"Where on earth did you . . ." von Helmholtz croaked, unable to continue.

"Patrolling my post, sir. ARP," the man said proudly.

Von Helmholtz did his best to control his shaking hands. The old man eyed him with interest "Are you ill, sir?"

"No, no." von Helmholtz said quickly. "It's just that the streets seemed deserted. You gave me quite a turn."

"Sorry, sir. Having trouble with your auto, are you? I see you have no lights."

Von Helmholtz thought quickly.

"I turned them off. No trouble with the automobile. It's me, I'm afraid."

"Sir?"

"I was looking for—a public facility."

The old man laughed. "Caught a bit short, are you? I can understand how you feel. I have a bit of a problem there myself. Well, sir. If it's urgent I'll just be getting out of your way, so to speak. Although a gentleman such as yourself isn't likely to be wanting to pee in the street," he smiled slyly.

Von Helmholtz noticed that the old man had only one front tooth, but that it seemed perfect and startlingly white. The colonel couldn't help but be fascinated by it as the man continued. "But if you think you can make it, Denville's station is just ahead. Rather nice loo there. Wouldn't sit down though, if I was you, begging your pardon. You can't miss it. Keep on straight ahead. No one there now except old Quill the gate tender. Looks like an old pirate, one leg and all. Wooden it is. Lost it in the last war. For what its worth, I wouldn't get him started on the Boche. He'll talk you deaf until you have an accident for sure."

"I shall take your advice, sir. Thank you." Von Helmholtz reached over and switched on his lights, and put the car in gear. The old man seemed reluctant to leave. Von Helmholtz smiled, saying, "My problem is not critically urgent, but it is pressing."

The old man laughed loudly, the glistening tooth breaking into the darkness like daylight at the end of a tunnel. "Hope you make it, sir. I'll say goodnight to you." He walked away.

Nothing showed in the rear view mirror. Even the ARP man had blended into the buildings lining the road. Now von Helmholtz knew exactly where he was. This road led eventually to Southleigh Forest and was one he had no intention of following. Turning west up there meant entering the maze of upper Havant. He would have to stop starting at shadows and return to the A27. But not until he had made a brief stop at Denville's station. The need to relieve himself was no longer imaginary. When he had tended to that, a telephone call to Southampton would reassure him and calm his foolish reactions to almost everything in the night.

Colonel von Helmholtz arrived at the grade crossing after having traveled no more than a quarter of a mile. He pulled into the isolated parking space in front of the station, left the car, and entered the station's single, unlocked door. The narrow interior was deserted as the ARP man had warned. A single oil lamp burned dimly on a shelf beneath a peeling British railway map and seemed to intensify the darkness beyond its weak illumination. Von Helmholtz noticed the telephone kiosk near the small tea counter.

"Mr. Quill?" the colonel called softly, not wanting to have an unexpected encounter with a peg-legged pirate. He doubted that his overtaxed heart could stand it. "Mr. Quill?" he repeated. There was no answer.

Von Helmholtz walked over to the lamp. With it at his back, he was soon able to discover the door to the toilet in the corner of the room. His nose helped. When he entered the cramped cubicle, he saw that there was no seat on the single bowl, and in the brief light of a struck match, he also saw the ample evidence that many of those who had used the facility previously had obviously depended on memory. He soon discovered personally how disorienting complete darkness could be.

The acrid smell of the cramped interior was beginning to sicken him. He backed out and closed the door thankfully, moving back to the lamp. The simple act of relieving his bladder had made him feel much better. He paused at the lamp to search his pocket for coins and then moved to the telephone kiosk with renewed confidence.

He was about to dial when he heard the loud screech of the crossing gates. The train! At first it was nothing more than a subtle trembling of the floor beneath his feet. Soon there was no doubt; a distant whistle sounded urgently. The colonel dropped the receiver back into its cradle and made his way to the platform gate. Discovering that it was securely padlocked, he turned back to the main door. Once outside he hurried toward the crossing.

Von Helmholtz paused at the corner of the station building when he saw that the crossing gates were down. The guard must be nearby. He decided to avoid the man if possible. He had already come into contact with far too many people. Again the whistle shrieked behind him, and the building creaked as the heavy locomotive entered the crossing. He caught a brief glimpse of the engineer leaning from the cab window; enough of a glimpse to be certain that it hadn't been the huge Siegler. Freight wagons followed the tender and then flats. There was no suggestion that tanks were hidden beneath the formless canvas covering the loads on the first three. Then he saw the huge uncovered, lashed wooden crates on the last wagons. Von Helmholtz turned away before the brakeman's cabin passed through the crossing and faded into the darkness. It had struck him as he watched that it couldn't possibly be the train, since the crossing gates were down and had been before the first whistle of the locomotive. This one was expected. Even those German soldiers couldn't have arranged for that sort of cooperation.

The colonel decided to forget the telephone call until he could find an isolated kiosk somewhere nearer Southampton and was making his way back to the car when he heard the crossing gates being raised. He was about to open the car door when he became aware of dim light at the crossing and the unmistakable sound of a treaded vehicle moving across the tracks. He was frozen into frightened immobility. He had recognized the characteristic clanking of a Bren carrier, even though it was still hidden by the station building.

The colonel forced himself to move when he saw other lights approaching along the road leading back to the A27. He reached into the glove compartment and fumbled for the grenades. When he had found two, he pushed them into his pockets, closed the door and made his way quickly to the station. The Enfield pistol was in his hand. He remembered the locked platform gate and having noticed a large bolt on the inner jamb of the main door. Damn it! he reassured himself, there can be no reason for anyone to be after me. I'm more likely to give myself away by acting like a bloody fool.

He opened the station door halfway, peering around its edge toward the crossing. He couldn't understand why the vehicle hadn't come into view. He heard it idling out of sight, behind the corner of the station. The other vehicles were almost at the crossing. The first, a black civilian sedan, stopped at the end of the station building. Von Helmholtz pushed back farther into the shadows. He had the uneasy feeling that he had seen the car before, passing at high speed along the A27 after he had turned north. He began to sweat freely when the lorry pulled up behind the sedan. It was the same one he had been following from the roadblock!

The colonel looked at his car longingly. But even if he could manage to get back to it without being seen, there was no way out of the parking area. It was enclosed by a high fence on its eastern end, and a smaller but no less impassable one on the south. He had foolishly trapped himself in a hopeless cul-de-sac.

He looked at the eastern end of the station building, deciding to skirt it, cross over the tracks, and lose himself in the fields on the other side. The colonel began to steel himself for the move when he heard the familiar voice of the farmer who had been driving the lorry and turned again to watch the men exiting through the now opened rear doors. At that moment he heard the Bren carrier begin to move and lost his chance to make it to the end of the station unseen. The vehicle clanked noisily into his view and turned toward him before it stopped. Its lights made it impossible to leave the protection of the doorway.

Frightened as he was, the colonel risked another look and saw the men from the sedan and the lorry grouped near the new arrival. A man jumped lightly to the ground from the bed of the Bren carrier and passed in front of its lights. The colonel's palpitating heart almost stopped when he recognized the helpful LDV man from the last roadblock he had passed to the north. So intent was he on the crossing, he hadn't noticed the man whose voice called from directly in front of him. "Here's his motor, sir."

Von Helmholtz no longer had any doubts that they were looking for him. He backed into the station, closed the door, and barely managed to control his shaking hands as he slid the heavy bolt home. Hurrying to the oil lamp, he shut it off and edged over to the opposite wall as he heard the main door's knob being rattled. He knew they'd try the platform gate next. Hopefully, when they found that it too was locked, they would carry on their search elsewhere. Von Helmholtz tried to reason calmly. Could the storm troopers have been taken? No. Even if they had, he couldn't imagine any of them implicating him. What could it be? The only reason he could think of was that he had been reported passing one of the roadblocks and had been checked through the Foreign Office and found to have no official reason for being in the area. No, it was more than that. Why had they gone to the trouble of setting him up to follow? Why hadn't they simply taken him in charge? Good God! Perhaps they'd picked up his men in Southampton—or suspected that they were there—and were hoping that he would lead them to the Albert Road.

For a moment he considered surrender. Impossible. The treachery bill had made that virtual suicide. He would be tried and hung long before the German army landed. The Wehrmacht would want to occupy Paris before turning on England with an invasion force. After all, there was little need for haste for them. He would have to get to a telephone. If he found that the others had been taken, he would have to make his way to

London and hope that the Italians could get him out of the country, or he could try the storm troopers' escape route. The thought of the waiting submarines made him feel slightly better. He had the pistol and two grenades. He would commandeer another automobile and . . .

Von Helmholtz pressed his back against the wall as the platform gate rattled softly. He heard the whispering voices less than two feet away.

"This one's locked too, sir."

"I can see that, Sergeant. Go and get the crossing guard. He'll have a key."

Quill! Von Helmholtz had completely forgotten about the crossing guard. He was now hopelessly trapped, unless . . . He tried to remember how many men he had seen at the crossing: three or four in the Bren carrier; another three from the sedan, and at least four from the lorry. Ten or more men, and signals out for more if the Bren carrier was radio equipped, and he had no doubt that that it was. If he was to get out at all, it would have to be soon. His main asset was the grenades. They had no way of knowing he had them. If they had, they wouldn't be moving about so freely. He planned his next moves with more confidence.

While backing carefully to the toilet door, he removed the pistol from his jacket pocket and transferred it to his belt. Pushing the door open slowly and noiselessly, he stepped into the soggy interior. The colonel's bulk filled the small cubicle; he was forced to turn sideways as he searched for the grenades. When he managed to get them out, one went into his jacket pocket, the other he held in his hand.

The air in the cubicle was stifling. Von Helmholtz was breathing heavily, adding to his discomfort. He leaned cautiously out of the door to watch the area of the platform gate. He ignored the main door, since the heavy bolt should give him plenty of warning should they attempt to break in. The silence was oppressive, broken only by the gurgling of the toilet's ancient plumbing.

The colonel pressed back into the cubicle as a powerful flashlight beam cut across the darkness of the station interior and began to move slowly across the inner walls. Despite his fear, the colonel knew that its beam couldn't reach him, and yet his hand moved to the butt of the pistol, pausing only when he remembered that he must arm the grenade.

The flashlight beam moved to the main door and steadied on the bolt. The colonel fought to control his shaking when he heard the unmistakable sound of a padlock being opened, and the screech of the gate as it was drawn back carefully.

"Mr. Helm?" a voice called.

The bloody LDV man, the colonel decided. He waited tensely,

wanting as many of them inside as possible before he acted. The gate was open; he now had a way out. When they had moved into the station he would roll the grenade into their midst, wait out the explosion in the safety of the cubicle, and then make his way out through the open gate before the men covering the front of the building had a chance to react. The pistol would take care of anyone who might still be alive—and he still had the other grenade.

The voice startled him. "Helm? We know you're in here. I want you to walk to the center of the room with your hands on top of your head. Please do it at once."

Von Helmholtz heard the sounds of men moving stealthily into the station interior. He held the grenade in his right hand, with his fingers closed firmly over the striker, and pulled the retaining pin. As soon as the tension he maintained on the striker lever was released, the striker would contact the detonator cap and fuse the detonator. Seven seconds later the grenade would explode.

"Mr. Helm, please don't be foolish. There's no way for you to get out of here."

Von Helmholtz peered around the door's edge. The beams of two unhooded flashlights were now moving over the station's narrow interior. He saw at least six men in their reflected light. One of the beams was moving slowly toward him. He leaned against the door to open it wider and allow freer movement of his right arm. With his left hand he reached for the butt of the pistol. He was concentrating on the flashlight beam and the deadly grenade when he found the pistol butt and pulled it from his belt.

In his fear, Colonel von Helmholtz had forgotten how dangerous a revolver can be to a frightened man. His hand closed around the butt, and his forefinger moved naturally to the trigger. As he pulled the gun free, the raised blade sight on the front of the barrel caught in his belt. The upward motion of his hand didn't stop as the cocked gun did. His finger tightened on the trigger and the gun fired.

The bullet tore into the colonel's right groin. He was thrown backward and fell across the toilet bowl, coming to rest between it and the wall. His right hand clutched feebly at the wound and then, even in his shock, he realized that the hand was empty. He had hardly begun to scream when the grenade exploded.

At that same moment, seven miles to the east, Colonel Andrew Blake was saying, "There it is, sir."

"Just look at it, Andrew," Brigadier Fox replied, as fascinated by the roadblock as von Helmholtz had been. "It took more than a bit of hard work to build that. But I don't understand it. Not a hint of the LDV at the rail crossing, and yet here at a comparatively minor road crossing, we find this—fortress."

"Rail crossings are top priority, sir," Colonel Blake said. "There must have been men there. We did pass rather quickly."

"I don't like it one bit. Complacency, doing half the job, just won't wash. Something moving ahead."

"They're waving us down, sir."

"I should hope so. Stop here, Sergeant."

Three armed civilians approached the car and gathered near the brigadier's open window. One man leaned over and said, "Good morning, sir."

"Good morning," Brigadier Fox replied.

The civilian looked puzzled when the general said nothing further and simply sat staring at him expressionlessly. He glanced at the other officer, a colonel, and found him equally unresponsive.

"Have you ever been in the forces, Mister . . ." Fox asked.

"Trent—Bill Trent. In the forces? Yes, sir, from '17 to the finish."

"Then I must say that I'm disappointed in you."

The civilian looked at the brigadier in questioning astonishment, then smiled briefly and said, "Your identification please, gentlemen."

"Good man," Lord Fox said, reaching for his papers. Colonel Blake followed his example.

"And you, son," Trent said to the driver. "Check the lorry, George," he ordered one of the men behind him.

"Now, Mr. Trent," the brigadier said, "I shan't keep you from your post for long. . . ."

"Just a moment, sir," the LDV man interrupted. He inspected the papers carefully in his flashlight beam. Colonel Blake was about to speak when the general raised his hand slightly in a forestalling gesture.

Mr. Trent had been chastened subtly and was enjoying his revenge, but he began to feel foolish when neither officer showed any visible reaction. He handed the papers back through the window.

"Now, sir. How can I help?"

"Tell me what preceded your excellent report to army headquarters," Brigadier Fox said. "I refer to the motor car that you had been ordered to keep an eye out for and that passed within the hour."

"Right, sir." The log, if you please, Ted," Trent said to the remaining civilian, who had obviously been enjoying the exchange between the two men. "I thought you might just be in a hurry, so I brought it along, sir. It's all in there." He handed a heavy book to the brigadier who in turn passed it to Colonel Blake.

286

"See what you can make of that, Andrew. Notes, please." He returned his attention to the civilian. "How did the driver seem? Nervous? Anxious to be on his way?"

Trent considered the question. "No, sir. Not that I noticed. He just sat there. It must have been nearly five minutes before I got back with his papers after reporting in. I handed him back his papers, he thanked me, and went on his way."

"He asked you for directions, I believe?"

"Right, sir. Asked how to get to Southampton. I told him to turn left and ask for directions farther on, as I was ordered to do. Oh yes, he asked where he could find a telephone kiosk. I told him about ours and said that I could ring in and ask for permission for him to use it. Come to think of it, he wasn't too anxious for me to do that. So, I told him about the one down the road there, and off he went. I sent a boy to follow him. He saw the man stop at the kiosk, but then he managed to run his bicycle into a tree and knock himself unconscious. When he came to, the motor car was gone."

"You sent a boy to follow him? On a bicycle?"

"Orders, sir."

"Do you happen to remember the name of the officer who gave you that order, Mr. Trent?"

"It's in the log there."

"Jot that officer's name down please, Colonel," the brigadier said. Returning his attention to the civilian, he said, "I trust the boy wasn't hurt badly?"

"Young Tim? No, sir. He's fine now. I sent him home. He's more worried about his bicycle than the bump on his head. He bent the front wheel almost double."

"What's the lad's name, Mr. Trent?"

"Conroy. Tim Conroy."

"Tim Conroy. Mark that down, will you, colonel? I'll see to it that his bicycle is replaced, Mr. Trent."

"Will you? That's mighty nice of you, sir," Trent said, not really believing. "I shouldn't ask, I suppose, but can you tell me what this is all about, General? The fat gentleman had Foreign Office credentials...."

"A rather special drill, Mr. Trent," Lord Fox said smoothly, leaving no doubt that he had no intention of saying anything further on that subject. "One more thing. Did you see or hear anything out of the ordinary either before or after the man's car passed? Another motor car perhaps, a tractor, a heavy lorry, anything?"

"None of those, sir. We're a bit off the beaten track here. We seldom have more than two or three autos pass through on most nights. There hadn't been one for hours before the fat gentleman came up. Not likely we'd see any tractors at this time of night, and there hasn't been a lorry of any kind come through since I came on duty at midnight. Noise of any sort is an event. No, the only thing I heard before or after the fat gent came through was a train passing down below there, and that's something happens every night."

"I see," Brigadier Fox said. "Not much chance of your missing anything, is there?"

"I don't know how familiar you are with this area, sir, but the road up beyond the block begins to curve down to Fishbourne just out there," Trent pointed past the driver, to the east. "A quarter mile that way," he pointed west, "there's another road that runs straight up from Old Fishbourne. We're smack in the middle, at the top of a rough sort of pyramid." Trent straightened up abruptly. "Half a second, sir. Nothing like an example to prove a point. Just lean out here a bit, will you, sir?"

Brigadier Fox complied as Trent stepped back and pointed to his ear, gesturing with his head.

"Hear that?" Trent asked. "That's a lorry, coming up from Old Fishbourne. Army, I'd say. You get so you can tell from the sound of them. I'd say it was like the one you brought with you. There's another point, sir. We could hear *you* coming before you crossed the rail line."

"I can see what you mean about the silence," Brigadier Fox agreed. Trent spoke to the man standing patiently behind him. The man started toward the roadblock.

"Sorry, sir. I was just sending Ted up to take some men over there to see what's coming. We're covering that road too. Now wait, sir. Now that I think of it we did hear lorries earlier, that one out there reminded me. Down there to the south. On the A27, I should think. Tanks, too."

"Tanks!" Brigadier Fox said.

"George said there were tanks with the rest. I didn't hear them myself, but I was on the phone with my regular report at the time."

"Is that man still on duty, Mr. Trent?"

"George? Yes, sir."

"Would you mind asking him to step back here?"

"Not at all, sir. George!" he bellowed. The brigadier glanced briefly at Colonel Blake, then turned as the man approached.

The brigadier greeted George and said, "Mr. Trent tells me that you heard tanks moving to the south of here." His eyes shifted to Trent. "How long ago would you say?"

"About an hour, I'd judge. Wouldn't you say, George?"

"A bit less," the man answered briefly. He seemed preoccupied.

"Could they have been nearby?"

"I doubt it. They were down on the A27. Moving east with the rest."

"It was a distant noise, then?"

"Near half a mile."

"Then you're quite certain that they were on the A27?"

"I wouldn't swear to it, if that's what you mean, but I heard them moving east with the rest. That means the A27. Nowhere else for 'em to be."

"Your impressions are important to me, so I trust you will forgive my persistence. It's your judgment that the tanks moved to the east?"

"No doubt about it."

"How many would you say there were?"

"I couldn't say for sure, General. More than one or two. Four or five maybe? I heard the lorries first, then the tanks. After they faded out, I could still hear the rest, so there must have been four or five in the middle of the convoy, or whatever it was."

"Do you hear anything now?"

Root looked at the brigadier quizzically. Then after a moment's hesitation, he said, "No tanks, but there is a lorry."

"Where would you say it was?"

"Out there on the Fishbourne Road."

"That's east, isn't it? Mr. Trent seems to think that the lorry is approaching on the Old Fishbourne road to the west."

"Does he now?" The man straightened up and stood silently, holding the general's gaze.

"Thank you," the brigadier said, "I shan't keep you any longer."

George's face was expressionless as he turned away and walked toward the roadblock. Trent waited until he was out of earshot, then said, "You'll have to forgive him if he seemed a bit rude, sir. His only son's in France. Just a few days ago he learned that the boy was wounded. Hasn't heard a thing since. Worried sick, poor chap, and now the news seems none too good. How are things going in France, sir?"

"We're holding our own," the brigadier answered carefully.

"I can understand that you can't talk about it, sir, but I'd surely like to have something hopeful to tell George there. He wouldn't ask for himself."

"Give me the lad's name, Mr. Trent. I shall make inquiries, and get back to you."

Trent beamed. "Thank you, sir. He'll want to know, whatever it is. Private George Root. R-o-o-t. Second Corps, Third Division. I don't know his number."

"That won't be necessary. I trust that I shall have some news for you later today. You have the particulars, Colonel?"

"Yes, sir," Blake answered.

"Then I shan't keep you any longer, Mr. Trent. Thank you for your assistance. Is there anything you wished to ask Mr. Trent, Colonel?"

"You did mention the unguarded crossing, sir."

"Ah yes. Are you gentlemen at this post also responsible for the rail crossing just south of here?"

"Yes, sir."

"Why isn't it manned now?"

"It is. Two men."

The general shook his head negatively.

"Not there? That's odd, sir. They aren't the sort to dog it."

"Look into it, will you?"

"I'll send someone down straight away, sir." Trent said, somewhat angered at the officers happening to have passed the isolated post at that particular time. He knew that the men usually took a few minutes to have tea with the men at the factory near their post. At no time would they be out of sight of the crossing.

"Thank you, Mr. Trent," the Brigadier said.

"You won't forget about young George Root, will you, sir?" Trent asked.

"Of course not, Mr. Trent."

Trent touched his cap and walked back to the roadblock.

The brigadier watched the receding figure for a moment, then said, "Stop at the signals lorry, Sergeant."

When the staff car had pulled to a stop, Brigadier Fox leaned out of the window and spoke to the officer waiting alongside the idling lorry. "I take it you've heard nothing from Fishbourne, Lieutenant?"

"No, sir. We've been monitoring their transmissions. The search has penetrated down below Bosham, but they've found nothing. Units are now moving west from Chichester and north from the A27. If we're heading back now, sir, we should meet one of those units on this road."

"I trust they've been keeping to the special frequencies?"

"Yes, sir."

"Good. I should prefer to know that our raiders aren't listening to our preparations to deal with them. Did you notice any civilian sentries at that rail crossing south of us as we came up, Lieutenant?"

"No, sir."

"I shall want to stop at that crossing before we continue on to Fishbourne. Inform Colonel Black at the command post."

Brigadier Fox began to lean back in the seat, but stopped midway and added, "On second thought, inform Colonel Black that we shall join the search up here for the time being. Ask him to keep me informed."

"Yes, sir."

"Do it quickly. I have the feeling that we're getting close to an answer. We'll pull just ahead and wait for you."

"I can transmit while we're under way, sir."

"Fine, then let's get on with it. Move out of their way, Sergeant."

The staff car pulled well ahead. Brigadier Fox and Colonel Blake watched while the heavy lorry turned expertly in the narrow road and fell in behind them.

"Move on, Sergeant," said the brigadier. "Forget the speed limit. Get us down to the rail line as quickly as you can."

The staff car made a sudden leap ahead as Brigadier Fox settled back in the seat. "Try to get us there alive, Sergeant."

The car slowed almost imperceptibly. The brigadier sighed. Ignoring the road ahead, he fastened his attention on Colonel Blake.

"I've no doubt that they're wasting their time south of the A27, Andrew. Three tanks simply couldn't have moved far down there without being seen.

"I also have no doubt that Mr. Root heard tanks, but I do not believe that they were moving on the A27; certain of it, in fact. There are no tanks with our force. Root himself demonstrated how confusing auditory perception can be in open country in the darkness. Could you tell exactly where that lorry was?"

"Frankly, no, sir. I accepted Mr. Trent's evaluation at first, but when the other chap contradicted him, I'm dashed if I didn't agree with him when I listened carefully."

"Precisely. I couldn't tell either. You see what I'm getting at?"

"I think I do, sir. I suspect that you're thinking that the tanks are somewhere between that roadblock and the A27."

"I'd bet on it, Andrew. They couldn't be anywhere else. Trent said that the men assigned to the rail crossing aren't the sort to dog it, and I've no reason to doubt him. Frankly, I'm very worried about those men. I hope that I'm wrong and that we find them there when we arrive. If we don't, I shall order the search intensified up here. As I remember, it seemed an ideal spot. Weren't there two east-west roads at the rail line?"

"Yes, sir. One on either side."

"One of them may hold the answer."

"Rail crossing ahead, sir," the driver said.

"Cross the tracks and stop near the tree line, Sergeant," the brigadier ordered. "Any signs of LDV ahead?"

"No, sir. Looks deserted." The sergeant braked suddenly as the car approached the tracks. The interior of the car filled with light as the signals lorry closed dangerously with the slowing car; then it too slowed and dropped behind. The two vehicles crossed over the tracks and stopped on the southern side. The brigadier was stepping from the back seat, his attention on the crossing behind him, when Colonel Blake said, "Lights to the south, sir. Quite a few on either side of the road."

"I want this crossing checked over thoroughly, Andrew. Please take the car and have the man in charge down there send a few of his men up here. Those civilian guards may have simply packed up and gone home. . . ." He studied the crossings. "I want that area gone over inch by inch."

"Right, sir. I'll bring some back with me. Save some time. Plenty of room in the car."

"Get to it, will you? Pass me your flashlight, Sergeant."

The driver handed a large flashlight to the general as Colonel Blake closed the door. The staff car moved away toward the distant lights. Brigadier Fox swung back toward the crossing and the signals lorry, shining the beam over the road. He crossed and recrossed it, covering the ground carefully, but saw nothing out of the ordinary. Arriving at the signals lorry, he said to the waiting lieutenant:

"As soon as Colonel Blake returns with a few of those men, I want you to leave the wireless in the charge of your best man and take command of a search party. Cover the area of the crossing thoroughly. Look for any signs of tank tread marks and for the two LDV who are supposed to be covering the crossing."

"Yes, sir."

"While we wait, put me through to Fishbourne. I shall want to speak to Colonel Black."

The brigadier was about to follow the lieutenant into the lorry when he glanced down the road. The distant light seemed to be converging at one spot on the eastern side of the road. He then saw a number of them break off and move out into the fields where he lost sight of them behind the intervening trees. I was right! he thought, as he pulled himself up.

A metallic, disembodied voice was crackling as he entered the interior of the lorry:

"—inform Brigadier Fox that Captain West reports that the suspect ordered detained is dead. He either blew himself up intentionally or accidentally. Set off a grenade in the water closet of the Denvilles railway station. Good place for him. Minor injuries to four of Captain West's men. No fatalities other than the suspect. Major damage to the station building. It's still afire, but under control. The suspect's body has not yet been recovered, if there's anything left to recover."

Brigadier Fox picked up the microphone. "This is Brigadier Fox. To whom am I speaking?"

There was a slight hesitation. "Sergeant-Major Carling, sir."

"Repeat what you just reported, Carling, and omit the asides."

"Yes, sir." The voice assumed a formal tone and repeated the details of Colonel von Helmholtz's death.

The brigadier listened quietly until the report ended, then asked, "Is Colonel Black available?"

"Yes, sir."

"Have him told that I wish to speak to him at once."

While he waited, the brigadier could hear the sounds of activity through the open line and the breathing of the sergeant-major.

"Brigadier Fox? Lieutenant Thoday here, sir. I've sent for the colonel. He's down with the guns, but I thought that you'd want to know that we've just now gotten word that one of the search units has found tread marks leading into a field to the north of us. We're getting the coordinates now, sir."

"Thank you, Thoday. If I'm not mistaken, I already know the coordinates."

"Here's Colonel Black now, sir."

"Good morning, sir. Colonel Black here. Sorry to have lost von Helmholtz. Of course we had no way of knowing that the man was armed with grenades."

"There's nothing we can do about that now, Colonel. I shall want Captain West's full report as soon as possible. See to it, please. Lieutenant Thoday has just informed me that one of the search parties has discovered tread marks north of the A27. It seems that I was watching them when they made their discovery. The unit is just south of my present position. I'm on the north-south road lying between Fishbourne and Old Fishbourne, just south of the rail line. There are two other north-south roads to the east and the west of me. Send one of the 3.7s up here to my location immediately. As for the other two, move one to the road leading up from Fishbourne. Have it wait just above the town. Keep the other at the command post ready to move until I get a clearer picture. The raiders have apparently turned back to the east. Inform General Twining that it is my considered opinion that we've found our quarry, and I would like to speak to him. Do that now, Colonel, and get back to me as soon as you can."

"It won't take a minute, sir. We're in constant touch with the general. He has just been informed of the search unit's find, but I'll get back to him at once."

"Quickly, Colonel."

Brigadier Fox waited impatiently until the voice broke into his thoughts. "It's done, sir. The general's aide has gone to get him. We'll link you up as soon as he arrives."

"Fine, Colonel. Now, get through to Major Fitzroy at Southampton. I want him to move in on the house on Albert Road immediately. Tell him about von Helmholtz. He is to use the utmost caution. I want those men alive, but not at the expense of the major or any of his men. Report back to me as soon as he's done it. Inform General Ironside at HQ, and tell him that I shall be standing by this wireless to report personally." The brigadier paused as the screech of brakes outside told him that Colonel Blake had returned. "I'll be getting a report from Colonel Blake momentarily. Get me linked with General Twining as soon as you can."

The brigadier handed the microphone to the lieutenant. "Stand by here, Lieutenant. I'll be just outside."

Brigadier Fox dropped from the lorry as Colonel Blake rushed toward him. The brigadier was able to make out at least six men leaving the staff car and beginning to line up under the shouted orders of a noncom.

"You were right, sir," Blake said. "There were tread marks all over the edge of the road. Apparently they stopped down there for some reason and then turned off into the fields to the east. The search unit is following the trail.

"But east? Why east?" Blake asked.

"I don't know, Andrew. They may have tried to double back to the road leading north to Sennicot, and then turn west between East and West Ashling, hoping to get by us."

"They would have been seen, sir."

The brigadier rubbed a hand across the stubble beginning to show on his face and was faintly annoyed by it. "Perhaps they've seen the futility of continuing and have simply abandoned the tanks somewhere out there. If they have, we've a job cut out for us. Von Helmholtz may have supplied them with the wherewithal to elude us for a while."

"We can get the answers from him, I'm sure, sir."

"I'm afraid not, Andrew. Von Helmholtz is dead."

"Dead, sir? How. . . ."

"Killed himself, either by accident or design, at the Denvilles station. I've given orders for Edward to move in on the house in Southampton. Perhaps we'll have better luck there."

"It hasn't been going well till now, has it, sir?"

"Hopefully we'll muddle through. Now, I'd like you to get back with the search unit and see to it that they don't try anything foolish. I'll join you as soon as I've spoken to General Twining and HQ. Tell the officer in charge down there that he's to follow their tracks with caution. When he discovers where they're holed up, he's to await further orders. See to it, Andrew. There have been quite enough dead men already. I've ordered one of the guns brought up. If I'm not mistaken, I can see it now."

The lieutenant leaned out of the lorry. "General Twining is on the wireless, sir."

"Thank you, Lieutenant. And Lieutenant, you can take charge of the men Colonel Blake has brought us and get on with your search of the crossing. We seem to have found the armor, so have the men concentrate on the missing civilians. You have ten minutes. If you've found nothing in that time, report back here, and I'll have the command post ring through to the roadblock and their men can take over. They are sending someone down at any rate."

The brigadier waited until the lieutenant had moved away toward the waiting soldiers, then said, "You'd best go now, Andrew. I'll join you as soon as possible."

The lieutenant had the soldiers fan out to the four corners of the rail crossing. He was angry. He had forgotten to bring a flashlight, and it made his contribution to the search almost useless unless he kept close to one of the soldiers, each of whom was equipped with a large one. It seemed a wasteful duplication of effort considering the general's time limit. He decided to inspect the large factory building lying close to the northeastern side of the crossing.

He made his way over the tracks and began to pick his way carefully through heavy weeds toward the ramp leading up to the deserted, crate-covered loading platform. The lieutenant was unaware that he had crossed directly over the spot where Sergeant Bohling had bled to death. He had reached the base of the ramp when, behind him, he heard one of the soldiers calling excitedly. He ran back toward the crossing.

It had taken them less than five minutes to discover the bodies of the LDV men, hidden casually in a culvert to the west of the crossing.

CHAPTER 30

The engineer knew that it was a desperate gamble. The hand on the throttle bar was trembling visibly. He leaned out into the wind to clear his head. Jack Hall didn't want to die, but Siegler's cold, satanic stare reflected in the glow of the open fire box gave him little hope that they wouldn't be killed eventually. He thought of the others, locked in the cramped darkness of the freight wagon, and knew that dangerous or not he would have to try it.

The efficiency of the rail workers in setting the switches ahead of them had given him little excuse to more than slow the heavy train. They had moved steadily west over open farmland, through local stations. Earlier, at Denvilles, he had tested Siegler. His hand had gone to the whistle cord. One long blast, then a second. As he was beginning to pull down for the third he felt the cold muzzle of the pistol at his temple and heard the paralyzing click as it was cocked.

"What is it?" Dietrich asked.

"He was about to give the backing signal," Siegler answered. "The whistle, three long blasts means danger, I'm backing. The bloody fool wasn't smart enough to wait for a less deserted place to try it. If he had, we could have been in trouble."

"I wasn't going to . . ." the engineer protested weakly.

"Put the gun away, Willi. He won't try it again. I want him at that window when we move through Havant. He blew the damned thing twice. What does that mean?"

"Acknowledging a signal."

"There's a station ahead, so that shouldn't seem out of place. I'm afraid we've picked ourselves a brave man in old Jack here. Is there anything else he might try?"

"He's trying it now."

"What? For Christ's sake, Willi. . . ."

Siegler replaced the pistol in his holster, then reached over to pull on a lever jutting out among what, to Dietrich, was an incomprehensible maze of controls in front of the engineer.

"You're right. He is a brave man. So even if he breathes too heavy from now on I'm going to kill him whether you want him at the window or not. This lever injects water into the boiler. If the water level drops below a lead core inside the boiler the core melts and the boiler blows. We'd be spread out over five miles of the countryside. I've been waiting to see if he had the guts to let it happen. Now I think he has: That makes him dangerous."

"You heard what he said, Mr. Hall," Dietrich said. "If you even look like you're thinking of trying something else, both you and your fireman will be killed instantly. And this time you can be positive that it's more than just an idle warning."

The train crept over the preset switches at the junction with the main line from the north, through the rim of the blacked-out city of Havant, and finally into the long curve to the southwest. Just ahead lay the grade crossing over the A27. The engineer could see a military convoy lined up on either side of the crossing, waiting for him to pass. His thoughts raced as his hand went to the brake control and the train slowed. Dietrich leaned out briefly behind the engineer's shoulder, then ducked back inside and gave rapid orders to the man standing in the tender.

"Carefully now, Mr. Hall," Dietrich said as the two German officers crouched down in the cab.

Jack Hall glanced over at the fireman. The older man's expression of fear strengthened his resolve. They wouldn't be expecting him to try anything else so soon after the warning he had received. He would apply the emergency brakes at the crossing and hope that the sudden change in the train's forward motion would throw the crouching Germans to the floor of the cab. He would push himself out of the engineer's window before they could react, and risk breaking his neck, hoping that Phil had the presence of mind to jump from the cab door during their momentary advantage. He had seen that the armed soldier was no longer in the tender.

"There must be two hundred soldiers up ahead," he said pointedly, glancing at the fireman.

Siegler had crouched at his feet, watching him steadily, but he moved over to the window on the far side of the cab to look out as they neared the crossing.

Dietrich's eyes had followed Siegler as he moved to the window. The engineer looked at the fireman, who was watching him with frightened intensity. Hall nodded briefly at the brake control, and then at the open door of the cab. He saw a brief nod of understanding.

Dietrich, on one knee in the far corner of the cab, had resumed watching the fireman. The old man's glance kept moving from the engineer to the open door of the cab. Dietrich watched carefully as the fireman threw a shovel full of coal into the firebox. He felt a sudden awareness of danger. The fireman had not withdrawn the shovel, but seemed to be leaning against it as if bracing himself. His eyes moved to the engineer, whose hand was clutched tightly over the brake.

"Willi!" Dietrich shouted above the noise of the locomotive. "The brake! He's going to. . . ."

Siegler moved quickly. The knife in his hand flashed upward into the stomach of the shocked engineer. Wrenching the knife free, Siegler reached up and dragged him from the seat to the floor of the cab. He grabbed the cap from the head of the fallen man, and pulled it low over his eyes. The engineer began to moan, until Siegler's heel struck him viciously in the temple, and he lay quiet.

Siegler sat behind the controls and calmly slowed the train further as they entered the grade crossing. He waved casually to the troops seated in idling lorries beyond the crossing gate. The soldiers returned his wave, and then the crossing was behind them. Siegler edged the throttle bar ahead slightly and felt the huge engine respond. "Start shoveling," he growled at the stunned fireman.

Phil Clyde stared down at the unmoving engineer. Jack was dead! His old mate was dead. The open eyes stared at him. It was my fault, he thought. I gave it away. Suddenly his fear was replaced by anger. His shovel still rested on the rim of the firebox. His muscles tensed as he pushed the blade deep into the roaring fire. He found that he was surprisingly calm as he withdrew the shovel filled with blazing coal—and turned to throw it into the face of the still crouching Dietrich. Without pausing, he began to swing the now empty shovel in an arc toward Siegler's head. Behind him, Dietrich was a screaming torch.

At that moment Siegler's eyes were on the track behind. As the last car cleared the crossing, he advanced the throttle. The locomotive lurched ahead. The fireman, off balance and well into his turn, slipped on the crushed coal covering the cab floor. The momentum of his swing was lost as he fought to keep his footing.

Siegler acted reflexively. He twisted out of the seat and ducked low as the shovel blade passed just above his head. He hit the fireman in the stomach with all his strength. The old man doubled up and fell forward until Siegler's knee caught him below the chin. He was already dead as he fell against the boiler with the back of his neck against the lip of the open firebox. His sparse hair flared and was gone in an instant, then the lurching of the train flung him to the floor.

Dietrich was unconscious, lying on his back. The front of his uniform had burned away. A few red-hot coals still burned into the exposed flesh of his upper body. Siegler looked down at him expressionlessly. Dietrich moaned. Still alive, are you? thought Siegler. He heard a voice calling from beyond the tender as he leaned over to pick up the shovel. He moved so that his back was to the tender and then jabbed the shovel blade with a short, powerful thrust into Dietrich's larynx.

He laid the shovel down carefully and hurried back to the engineer's seat as Sergeant Priller scrambled down over the shifting coal.

"Jesus!" Priller said, staring down at the bodies. "What happened?"

He bent down to brush futilely at the coals burning deeper into Dietrich's body, but stopped when Siegler growled, "Leave him alone. He's dead. There's nothing you can do for him now. Shovel the rest of that hot coal back into the firebox and then go back and get Schiller. Tell him to bring the map."

Priller continued to stare down at the body.

"Move your ass, goddamn it!" Siegler shouted. "There's water out there. We're heading south. Somewhere ahead we've got to turn west or we *will* end up in Portsmouth."

When Sergeant Priller was moving back over the tender, Siegler began to slow the train. He leaned out into the rushing air and breathed deeply. He was smiling.

The bodies had been moved to a corner of the tender and covered with coal, and the smell of burning flesh was beginning to clear as the train moved ahead. Lieutenant Schiller shuddered involuntarily. He could imagine how Dietrich had felt during that split second when he had seen the shovel coming at him. Thank God he was dead before he burned. He had no doubt that the shovel blade had killed him instantly.

"How far before we turn, damn it?" Siegler asked, watching him closely. Looking down at the map, close to the light of the open firebox, Schiller could still see the charred, contorted face of Lieutenant Dietrich.

"Use your flashlight. You're in Priller's way."

Schiller moved aside to let Priller throw a shovelful of coal into the fire.

"For Christ's sake, you can have a good cry later. When do we turn?" Siegler persisted.

Schiller shook his head angrily. The son of a bitch was right. There was nothing to be done for Dietrich now. "Shut your goddamned mouth, and keep your eyes on the track, Siegler."

Siegler laughed. Play the officer while you can, he thought. This mission is mine now. "I can't see the water any more," he said.

"It was the upper reaches of Langstone harbor," Schiller said, referring to the map. "We should be passing Farlington now, and then Drayton. At the southern edge of Drayton we'll come to the switch area. From the look of it we're on the right track to make the turn west. Those outer ones must be the through line to Portsmouth. We'd better slow it well down. The switch can't be too far ahead."

Siegler worked the brake valves, and the locomotive responded smoothly.

"Priller, you get back and tell the men to stay under cover and warn those prisoners again that if you hear one sound, you'll drop a grenade in on top of them. And, Priller, have the guns manned, just in case."

Sergeant Priller threw the shovel down and made his way to the top of the tender.

"There it is. I can see a signal lantern ahead," said Siegler.

"Hurry it up, Priller," Schiller yelled, "and keep low."

"He's waving us on."

"Good. I'll keep low at the other door, Willi. If we pass anything that looks like the main line west and we don't switch over, I'll sing out. Stop immediately and do whatever it is you have to do to make this thing move backward. If they're waiting for us, that would be the perfect place to do it. Once we pass those points and don't turn west, we may have had it." Schiller leaned down, picked up the shovel, and began transferring coal into the firebox hurriedly. "Is that enough for a while?" he asked.

"Plenty. It looks as though the switch is set. I can just about make it out. There's only one man that I can see, and he looks friendly enough. Close that firedoor and get out of sight."

Schiller used the shovel to shut the door and then crouched near the far door.

The cab's interior was now dark. The locomotive crept slowly up to the man on the tracks. Siegler waved once and then ducked his head back into the cab, pulling the engineer's cap down lower over his face, apparently intent on the dials in front of him.

"You're early tonight, Jack," he heard the man below him shout. He again waved his arm out the window. Siegler felt the locomotive lurch into the switch, and begin to cross over the westbound tracks. The man with the lantern was behind him now, hidden by the locomotive's bulk. Siegler eased the throttle ahead slightly, resisting the urge to push it forward to its limit. He looked back. The first freight wagon was now entering the switch.

Wilfred Tyndall sat apart from the others at the forward end of the freight wagon. His isolation was actually in deference to his position as night manager and not, as he thought, rejection by the other men. He listened nervously to their whispering as the lurching darkness steadied and the train slowed. They were quiet as they heard Sergeant Priller's footsteps on the roof above them and listened as he repeated Schiller's warning. They were then able to follow his progress down the metal ladder at the end of the wagon. No one spoke until they were as certain as they could be that the man had moved back onto the car behind. Finally a voice whispered, "How's it coming, Jock?"

"I'm through. Not much of a hole though. It's only a bloody wee pen knife. The blade isn't going to last much longer."

"It's better than nothing. If it was any bigger they wouldn't have missed it in the search. Can you tell where we are yet?"

"I've a pretty guid idea. There's water out there. Looks like we're doon to the Portsmouth line. The last turn must have been Havant."

"That's why they're slowing then. Let me look, Jock. I've made this run ten or twelve times in the last week. I might be able to tell for sure."

The man pressed his eye to the small hole cut roughly through the wooden side of the wagon on a seam.

"You're right. That's Langstone harbor. Is this train cleared through the points ahead, Mr. Tyndall?"

Wilfred Tyndall didn't answer. He sat with his ear pressed to the forward wall. He hadn't told the others of the brief, but absolutely chilling, scream he had heard only moments earlier. His heart was pounding erratically; the heart that had kept him from service with the forces during the last war. But experience in the forces wasn't necessary for him to imagine what the effect of a grenade dropped into the crowded interior of the wagon would be. He concentrated, but there had been no other sound, only the clacking of the wheels beneath him.

He was badly frightened and had been since he had been forced to make the call to Havant. Sweat poured down his face even though he was shivering with cold. He winced as the sweat ran across the slight cut on his throat. He could still feel the blade the soldier had used to insure his cooperation.

"Mr. Tyndall!" The urgent voice coming from the darkness of the wagon startled him out of his introspection.

"What is it?" he whispered.

"We're coming to the points below Drayton. This train is still cleared to Southampton, isn't it?"

"Yes," Tyndall answered, adding, "keep your voice down. That guard must be listening."

"Sod the bastard. This is our chance. Old Bill Potter will be standing out there with his lantern. If Jack can't get word to him, it's up to us."

"What are you going to do?'

"What the bloody hell do you think we're going to do? Try to tell him we're in here."

"You heard what that guard said." Tyndall's voice rose.

"I heard him and I'm bloody well damned if I'm going to wait for them to do it sooner or later."

"You'll get us all killed."

"The bastards are most probably going to kill us anyway."

"Oh God," Tyndall said.

"Hurry it up, Jock. Make the hole as big as you can."

"The bloody blade just broke."

"Then it will have to do. Let me in there." He pressed his eye to the ragged hole. "No more than five hundred yards now, near as I can figure."

Bill Potter waved his signal lantern and watched the heavy locomotive approach. Steam exausted in great gusts from beneath the locomotive as it slowed and began to move into the switch. The cab passed above him. "You're early tonight, Jack," he called through the swirling steam. The engineer didn't answer; Potter saw only an acknowledging wave. He must really be in a hurry, thought Potter.

Jack usually stopped briefly at the switch to inquire about Potter's ailing wife and to trade speculations about the war. Potter looked forward to the exchange. His was a lonely job. He shrugged stoically and stepped back as the tender followed the locomotive into the turn. The freight wagons followed. Potter was looking down the length of the train when he heard a muffled voice.

"Bill! Bill Potter!" His name was being called from—somewhere? He looked up at the freight wagons as they rumbled past. "Bill!" Again his name was repeated. "This is John Walling. Twelve of us prisoners! Germans have taken this train! Call . . ." By then the wagons had passed, and the voice faded into the noise of the wheels.

Potter couldn't believe what he had heard. Germans? The familiar voice had said Germans. He backed over into the center of the main line tracks and looked up at the passing flat wagons carefully. He felt suddenly exposed on the open track, expecting to see the flats filled with Huns. But there was nothing that he could see other than the familiar tarpaulin-covered cargo. The train was moving faster now, and the flats passed quickly. Finally, as the brakeman's cabin clanked past, he was convinced that the disembodied voice hadn't been imaginary. For the weeks of the regularly scheduled run of this train, Pitt, the brakeman, had been standing at the open door of the cabin. He had never missed his few words of greeting, or at least a friendly wave as the last car of the train passed through the switch. Tonight the door was closed.

Potter waited until the train was through the switch, and then hurried across the tracks toward his hut and the telephone.

Sergeant Priller was crouched beneath the tarpaulin covering the lead tank, watching the man with the lantern on the track ahead from a carefully lifted corner of the canvas. He saw the man's startled turn of head as a muffled shout came from the freight wagon ahead.

"Get forward and tell Schiller that the prisoners contacted that man out there," Priller said to the soldier kneeling beside him. "He can decide whether to stop and wait for me. Tell him I think he'd better chance stopping. I'm going after the man, but he might get by me somehow. If he does, we've had it."

"Jesus," Sergeant Becker said as they pushed their way out from under the canvas. "Get him, Ernst. For Christ's sake, get him."

"I will."

When Becker saw that Priller had dropped safely to the tracks, he climbed quickly to the top of the rear freight wagon and ran along the catwalk on its top. The prisoners heard his passage.

"Must have heard me," John Walling said nervously.

"Oh God," Wilfred Tyndall said, flattening himself against the wood at his back, waiting for the explosion.

Siegler leaned out of the window and looked back toward the switch, and then ahead, satisfied that the train was well across the north-south tracks. His hand went to the brakes. The train had stopped before Becker had finished his anxious report.

"It was a mistake to bring those civilians with us," Siegler said angrily.

"We wouldn't have gotten this far if we'd left them behind," Schiller said.

"No. *If* they were alive. Take that machine gun," Siegler said to Sergeant Becker, "and get back and cover Ernst. We can't sit here long."

Becker dropped from sight through the cab door.

"We can't let them get away with it. They'll be yelling their heads off at every crossing," Siegler said.

"Leave them alone, Willi," Schiller said. "We're going to abandon the train anyway. We can't hope to go all the way. They'll have discovered that we didn't move south by now. It's only a matter of time until they learn about this train. We'll have to take our chances overland. I want to get the tanks off those flats while we still have the chance."

Siegler's pistol was pointed at Schiller's stomach. "Did I hear you say that you want to abandon the tanks?"

"No, you fool. Why don't you listen and stop thinking with that gun. I said we'll take our chances overland. If Becker manages to do the job quickly, we can still chance going through Fareham. It's the last city of any size before Southampton. The country after Fareham is too good for an ambush for us to stay with the train. If our luck holds, it's also a good quiet area to get the tanks down."

Siegler lowered the gun to his side. "How the hell do we get them off?"

"You were at Wunstorf, Siegler, you should know how. I'm going back to talk to the prisoners. You stay here and watch the track, and be ready to move as soon as the men get back. And Siegler, don't point that pistol at me again. Shoot me and you may as well surrender to the British. I'll get the tanks down, but we'll be finished if you start firing that gun either at me or at the prisoners. That's a city above us. You'll be happy to know that you're going to get your wish about the prisoners, there's no other way, but I'll tell you when and how."

He backed down the ladder, watching Siegler as he replaced the pistol in its holster. Siegler opened the firebox door as Schiller dropped to the ground. Above him he heard Siegler shoveling coal into the firebox.

Sergeant Priller ran across the tracks to the right of the train and stood hidden behind a stack of piled ties. He waited impatiently for the remainder of the flats to pass him. It had been a gamble. If the man had walked the other way, he would have had a good start and he might elude him in the darkness. But it had been a calculated risk; he had seen the hut before he had dropped to the tracks, and the telephone wires leading to it.

The train was past. Priller searched the track as well as he could in the darkness. He couldn't see the man, but he did hear him kicking the gravel ballast between the ties. The man was heading directly for the hut. Priller moved quickly over to it. He found the door open and entered. A small coal stove burned redly in one corner. In its glow, Priller saw the remains of a sandwich and a half-full mug of tea on a small table standing against the far wall. A chair was the only other piece of furniture in the hut. The telephone hung on the wall opposite the stove. Priller crossed to it and used his knife to cut the wire above the box. The door opened behind him.

"Cor, Sergeant. You gave me quite a turn. Where did . . ."

"Sorry I broke in," Priller said. "My motor car broke down. I figured that there had to be a telephone down here I could use."

"You'll have to wait a bit, son. I don't know if anyone will believe me, but there were Germans that train that just passed through."

"Germans? Come now, sir . . ."

"That's what I said, Germans. Now let me at that phone."

"How could Germans . . . ?"

"I'll have enough trouble trying to convince the guvnor, without taking the time to try it out on you." He brushed past.

Potter's mind had barely registered the fact that the soldier's arm had suddenly moved around him, when the knife was thrust expertly into his throat.

Priller stepped back quickly to avoid the sudden gush of blood. The body fell to the floor heavily. Priller crossed to the door, stepped outside, and closed it behind him. A padlock hung on its ring. He removed it, closed the shackle over the ring, and locked it. Unless someone else had a key, they would have to break the door in. Every minute gained was an advantage.

Priller ran back toward the waiting train. He met Becker on the way.

Siegler watched impatiently from the cab window. Try as he might, he could think of no way to get the tanks off the flat wagons. His first thought had been to back them off, but then he realized that the wagon beds were more than four feet from the ground. Even if they managed to get one end down without tipping the tank over, the other end would drop four feet—heavily. The engines would never stand up under such a drop.

Schiller and four of the men were at the second freight wagon talking to the prisoners when Siegler saw Priller and Becker run up. He watched as they spoke hurriedly to Schiller, who in turn gave muffled orders to the waiting men. The door to the freight wagon was closed, and the men began to climb back aboard the flats.

Schiller ran forward to stand below the cab. "Priller stopped him before he could get to a phone, so there's still a chance to gain a few miles."

"What about those prisoners?"

"I think I've convinced them that they'll be foolish to try that again. We're past the worst part of it. Portchester and Fareham ahead, and then we've got two or three miles of open track. That's where we'll unload. Then it's only about eight miles to the target. I'm going back to get things ready. Get moving."

"What about Dietrich's tank? We haven't enough men to handle it. And you said something about the prisoners before . . ."

"I've got an idea about those problems that should please you, Willi. I'll tell you about it after I get the tanks ready. Now, get this train underway."

The bodies lay on the ground near the signals lorry.

"At least those poor chaps weren't butchered," Brigadier Fox said.

The lieutenant moved into the beam of the brigadiers flashlight and leaned over the dead men. "Not a mark on them, sir."

"Good Lord!"

The lieutenant followed the brigadier's shocked downcast eyes. The lieutenant's shoes and the bottom of his trousers were soaking with blood.

"Have you cut yourself?"

The young officer fought nausea. "I don't think so, sir." He raised his trousers gingerly, while the brigadier shone the flashlight over his legs.

"You must have walked through literally a pool of blood. Where were you searching?"

"Near that factory across the tracks, sir. I was about to check it over when the sergeant discovered the bodies."

"And you didn't notice that you had walked through . . . that?"

"No, sir, I had no light."

"I see. Keep the men away from that building, although the precaution is a bit late, I'm afraid. I'll contact Colonel Blake."

Brigadier Fox listened to his suspicions being confirmed as Colonel Blake's voice came metallically from the speaker. ". . . they moved over the fields to the road along the southern side of the rail line, then crossed the tracks at an access just below the large factory building above your position, sir. We're moving cautiously. It looks as though they've turned into the factory grounds. Not much doubt that we've found them."

"Any idea what they manufacture there, Andrew?"

"Heavy machinery, sir. Dynamos and such."

"Then there would be guards. That would seem to explain the blood. Have the officer in command deploy the men. Get the 3.7 down in a place where it covers both the front and back of the building. I'll have the others brought up. He's to make no moves until the other guns are in position. No chance of holding them if they should decide to move out on my side before those other guns get here. Have your signals inform General Twining about the guns, and have this area sealed. I'll contact HQ and ask them to inform the owners of this place and the railroad. We don't want a train blundering through at the wrong time. When you're finished, I'd like you to join me up here."

"Yes, sir."

Brigadier Fox handed the microphone back to the sergeant. "Get me headquarters, immediately," he ordered.

Twenty minutes later, Brigadier Fox and Colonel Blake stood in the trees near the track's edge, looking over at the dim bulk of the factory building. They knew that units now surrounded the factory, but they had seen no movement. The brigadier spoke softly, "They're doing a creditable job for comparatively untrained troops. I haven't been able to spot a single trooper."

"Neither have I, sir."

"And all of it wasted effort, I'm afraid."

"Sir?"

"They're not in there. Our precautions are proper, but I dare say we'll find that they've been gone for some time. Even if they're all deaf, they couldn't have missed the activity of our search unit. I could hear them, so it's unlikely the Huns didn't. Add that to the men I so foolishly sent to search for the LDV. No, they wouldn't wait about in there while we surround them. They would have broken out as soon as they saw our interest in the crossing."

Before Colonel Blake could answer, the signals lieutenant rushed up behind them.

"What is it, Lieutenant?"

"All units and guns are in position. They're beginning to move in now."

"Thank you, Lieutenant. That was quick work."

"And, sir," the lieutenant continued, "I've just received a rather puzzling signal from HQ. They contacted the owners of that building and were told that there should be a crew of at least fifteen men at work there now, a loading crew. When southern rail was contacted and informed to stop all rail traffic in this area, they immediately asked about the status of the train that is loading at the factory. They're worried about damage to it should we start firing. I told HQ that there was no train here that I could see. Is there another spur on the other side of the building, sir? I was told to check on it and report back immediately."

"Heavy machinery—loading crews. What does that suggest, Andrew?" The brigadier was already walking away.

"Flat wagons, sir."

"Precisely. Back to the signals lorry, we've been had again."

CHAPTER 31

The last of Fareham was behind them. The train moved through the maze of switches across the Gosport branch line without incident and was now moving steadily, slightly north of west.

"Why can't we go straight through?" Siegler asked. "They don't know anything about us."

"They may or may not. We can't be certain of that," Schiller answered.

"It's been easy."

"Too easy. I don't like it. Early as it is, people are starting to move about. Didn't you notice that as we passed through Fareham?"

"I saw a few civilians . . ."

"Willi, there's no open country beyond the Hamble River suitable for what we have to do. We might be able to take this train straight through to the embankment just above the Hazel Road, but what would we do once we were there? What good are the tanks to us on the flats? It will take the better part of thirty minutes—if we're lucky—to get them down on the ground. Do you think the people at that factory will simply stand about and watch us while we unload?"

"What about this train once we're off it? And Dietrich's tank?"

"I'm going to destroy the train . . . and Dietrich's tank."

"How?"

They passed over the River Moen as Schiller told him. For the first time Willi looked at the lieutenant with something approaching respect. It was a fleeting expression.

Schiller glanced at his watch, and then at the map. "Stop here, Willi. This is as good a spot as any. There should be a road just ahead."

Siegler brought the locomotive to a stop. Schiller watched, then continued, "You know what you have to do, Willi. Watch for my signals."

Schiller backed down the ladder to the ground. Willi studied the empty fields to the left and then repeated his inspection on the other side. Satisfied, he settled himself in the engineer's seat and looked to the rear. Schiller's flashlight waved weakly in the darkness. Siegler advanced the throttle, easing the train ahead slowly. He felt a slight lurch and knew that the flat wagons, behind those on which the tanks rested, had been uncoupled. He stopped at Schiller's signal, and at the same moment heard the comforting sound of the tank's engines. The train swayed as one of them began to move.

Schiller had explained the procedure. Willi was angered by its simplicity and angered more by his own inadequacy. He would never have thought of the solution supplied so easily by Lieutenant Schiller. He leaned out of the cab window. If it didn't work—the mission was over.

The uncoupled flats lay fifty yards to the rear. Schiller and Sergeant Priller stood on either side of the flat wagon and called corrections to Sergeant Becker who watched from the wagon bed and transmitted the instructions to the driver. The tank backed slowly to the far end of the flat wagon and stopped. Schiller and the others ran forward and repeated the procedure with the tank on the flat ahead; this time they didn't stop it at the end of the flat. It continued to back across the narrow gap between the cars until it, too, was on the rearmost flat with the other, one at either end. Again Schiller and the others ran ahead and directed the remaining tank back onto the now empty flat behind it. The rear flat creaked ominously, but Schiller was satisfied. They now had two tanks on the end flat and one on the second. At Schiller's signal the remaining men climbed up to the bed of the rear flat, between the two idling tanks. They waited, having already been given instructions, while Schiller inspected the couplings of the heavy towing hawsers attached to the eyes on either side of the turret. One coupled hawser ran back over the engine compartment and down beneath the tank. The other ran around the turret and down over the front superstructure. At Schiller's signal, Corporal Knoedler ran to the front of the forward tank and pulled another hawser, already attached to the towing eye on the front edge of the superstructure, down to the bed of the flat, where it was pulled back beneath the tank body by means of a preattached rope. It was then attached to the joined couplings of the hawser that lay beneath the rear tank. The two tanks were now joined by the coupled hawsers.

Schiller dropped to the bed of the flat "Remember to keep your head low, Falck," he said to the driver of the rear tank. "That wire could cut your head off when it goes taut."

"Have you ever seen this done before, Lieutenant?"

"Yes, Sergeant."

"Good. I was afraid that I was going to be the first to try it."

"In a way, you will be, Reinhold." Falck looked at Schiller warily as he continued. "I saw this done with Mark 3s. This thing weighs twenty-six tons."

"Jesus!" Falck said.

"Not to worry, Sergeant. Those towing hawsers are made to take this weight."

"If it drops, both my legs will go, unless the explosives go first."

"It will work. Let's go over it again quickly. When the rear of the treads reach the track bed, stop. Thyben will hold you in position with the other tank until we attach the other wire. Then Siegler will move the train ahead slowly. When I give the signal, start backing down as slowly as you can . . . at the same rate as the train, if possible. I don't want to tear up the tracks down there. When your front end is clear of the flat, both you and the train will stop. Then August will back his tank and lower you down."

"What about those bumpers and the coupling? If I get the treads caught up in one of them . . ."

"The treads should clear them. You only have to worry about them coming through the bottom." Schiller saw Falck's pained expression. "The armor's angled beneath you. You'll slide right over them."

"Let's get it over with," Falck said fatalistically.

"Back up . . . slowly," Schiller ordered. "Do it right and I'll let you take the other one down." Schiller dropped from the flat wagon to the ground. "Now!" he called.

The tank backed slowly over the rear of the flat. Near its center of gravity, Schiller signaled and Falck stopped. At another signal, the tank ahead of it edged forward until the towing wire was taut near Falck's head, then stopped. Schiller waited until the tank ahead had been shifted back into reverse, and then motioned for Falck to continue backing.

The treads bit into the flat's wooden bed as the tank tilted backward and hung for a moment at a forty-five degree angle, held only by the wire stretching from its turret to the one rising from beneath the tank ahead. The underside of the tank ground noisily over the flat's coupling as it started down, then the rear of the treads touched the track bed lightly. Falck stopped the tank with relief. One end was down. He looked out to his left and saw Schiller smiling at him.

"You'll be down in a minute, Sergeant. Get ready. The wire is attached. Remember, back slowly until your front end clears the flat, then stop. Willi and Thyben will do the rest. Wait for my signal."

"Take your time," Falck said wryly as Schiller walked away.

"Now!" Schiller called.

Sergeant Falck eased out the clutch and the treads began to bite into the track bed. He felt a jolt as the train began to inch ahead. The turret of the tank ahead of him rose into his view, and he knew that he was near the end of the flat. The tank lurched suddenly as its front end left the wagon bed. The treads behind him were firmly on the ground now and he had no fear of tipping over, but as he stopped his backward movement he also knew that the entire weight of his tank now rested on the towing wire running beneath his tank to the one ahead. He began to drop slowly as Thyben backed along the flat wagon above him. The towing wire rasped over the edge of the flat. Falck ducked his head to avoid splinters being flung from the wooden bed as his eyes came level with it. Another lurch and the wire stretched upward directly in front of him. His breath exploded in relief. He was down. Schiller and the others were removing the wires before his heartbeat had returned to normal.

"You did it, Falck. Ready to try again?"

Sergeant Falck stood up, framed by the driver's hatch. "There's nothing to it, Lieutenant. But don't you want me to move this one off the tracks first."

"No. Leave it there until we get the other one off."

"Come on, Falck," Priller said. "Give us a hand with these wires. The damned things are heavy. You can congratulate yourself later."

"You take the next one down, Ernst," Falck called good naturedly. "A child could do it."

"Then you should have no trouble."

"Pay attention," Schiller ordered. "I'm having Siegler move the train ahead again."

After the train had been moved forward for the second time, Siegler dropped to the ground and walked quickly around the front of the locomotive. Nothing disturbed the quiet night. He made his way rapidly past the freight wagons, pausing at the end of the first flat where he climbed up to its bed. The tarpaulin had been replaced over the tank that was to be abandoned. Willi crawled under the canvas and up over the superstructure to the turret. The hatch was open. He dropped into the fighting compartment and felt along the mostly empty racks. His foot struck the assembled 110-pound charge now secured to the rear of the fighting compartment. He recoiled involuntarily.

They had already removed the twenty-five pounders, he soon discovered. He climbed back up and out of the turret to the flat bed and out beneath the tarpaulin. The other men were busy with the two tanks on the ground and none looked in his direction. He then saw the familiar bell-shaped forms lined up on the ground beside the wagon. Crouching low, he reached out for the leather handle of one of the devices, picked it up, and then retraced his way to the locomotive.

Once in the cab, he leaned out of the window. There was no sign that he had been missed. After the explosive charge had been hidden beneath the coal at the rear of the tender, Willi busied himself with the shovel, spreading coal evenly over the fire. When he was satisfied that the engine was ready for its last trip, he moved back to the engineer's seat.

The second tank was on the ground. Schiller, despite his outward confidence, was as surprised as the others at how easily it had been accomplished.

"Remember," he said to the drivers, "slowly along the track until you get to the crossing. Then and only then move onto the road. This train has to blow on the other side of that river we crossed earlier to make this work. If the treads tear up the track, we'll have to destroy the train here, and it wouldn't be wise. They'd know where we are within a few miles. If it goes up back there it will take them hours to figure out what happened. I'm hoping they'll think we were all aboard. But no matter what they think, we should be at the target in less than an hour even with the detour above the Hamble. We're no more than ten miles from Woolston. Any questions?"

There were none. He had covered everything during the preparations to remove the tanks. Schiller gave the signal for Siegler to move the train ahead.

After stopping well beyond the road crossing, Willi waited impatiently. Finally he climbed down to the track and walked back to the end of the flat wagons.

The two tanks were creeping along the track bed, their drivers directed by Schiller and the troopers. The treads of each tank straddled the two rails. To have turned the heavy, lumbering machines where they had been unloaded would have surely destroyed the tracks, isolating the two sections of the train on either side of the break. Willi shook his head angrily; again the unaccustomed self-doubt. Would he have thought of that? The nagging certainty that he would not have, further added to his hatred of Lieutenant Schiller and his quiet efficiency.

When the two tanks were turned safely onto the road, Schiller walked back along the track inspecting it carefully, then moved back to the cross road.

"We were lucky. It's still in one piece." He saw Siegler looking at him. "What the hell are you doing here, Willi? You're supposed to be watching ahead. No matter how deserted it looks, there may have been guards at this crossing. Are you ready to roll?"

Siegler glared at Schiller but nodded acknowledgement.

"Prime your fuses as soon as Willi joins up with the other cars, Priller. He'll set the speed and jump. He'll signal you just before he leaves the cab. Set them fast and get off fast. The ten-minute fuse should bring the train well back on the other side of the river before it goes up. Be careful, both of you. This is no time to break a leg. Make sure you're off before it picks up too much speed."

Siegler turned without a word and ran back to the locomotive. Schiller waited until he saw him climb into the cab and Sergeant Priller pull back the tarpaulin from the tank remaining on the flat. Then he said, "The rest of you into the tanks. We'll move as soon as they get back. I want to be as far away as possible from this rail line before the explosion. Even here, it's going to make a hell of a noise."

While the troopers ran to the tanks, Lieutenant Schiller stood at the edge of the tracks watching the train back slowly past him. Sergeant Keller, now the extra man, watched with him.

"As you said, Lieutenant. It's going to make a hell of a noise."

The two men saw the train move into the darkness beyond the crossroad.

"Jesus," Keller said, looking at the wagon holding the prisoners, "I'm glad I'm not in there."

Schiller's eyes followed the freight wagon. There was nothing he could do about it, he thought, trying desperately to rationalize his barbarism. The prisoners had to remain with the train. Perhaps a few would survive, but no amount of rationalization could erase the fact that they were confined in a wooden box no more than fifty feet from what would be a devastating explosion. He had joined the other animals. He stepped back as the locomotive backed past, obscuring itself in billowing steam.

He soon heard the sound of the contact as the train reached the uncoupled freight wagons.

Willi left the controls untended as he retrieved the hollow charge from the tender and strapped it against the boiler below the firebox. He was back at the throttle in time to slow the train and creep up on the dim shape of the uncoupled wagons. When contact was made he slowed the train until it was barely moving and signaled to Sergeant Priller. Seconds later he watched him drop to the ground. Willi knelt and set the fuse on the hollow charge then moved back to the throttle. He pushed the bar ahead then backed out of the door and down the external ladder. Priller was waiting for him. They watched the huge driver wheels spin briefly against the track, then catch. The locomotive was already moving faster as it backed into the darkness. Willi and Priller watched it briefly, then ran back toward the crossroad.

"I told the Englishmen we were backing down a few miles and would leave them there. That should keep them quiet until it goes up," Priller said as they ran.

"It doesn't matter much whether they're quiet or not . . . now," Siegler said.

Wilfred Tyndall remained huddled at the end of the freight wagon and listened to the others discuss what the German had said.

"It sounded like they took the tanks off."

"They did. I reckon they're hoping we have no idea where. That's why they're backing down."

"Do we know?"

"Just about. We crossed the Meon. That puts where they stopped this side of Park Gate."

"It's lucky we have that hole you made, Jock. Knowing where they stopped will make it easier for our own lads."

Their relief at their apparent reprieve lasted until the wagon began to lurch violently as the train picked up speed. Tyndall was thrown sideways to the floor; another man landed on top of him.

"Get to work on the door!" Tyndall heard the Scot shout. "The bluidy bastards led us doon the garden path. They've abandoned the train. Thank God there's all those cars behind us. We might have a chance when she hits something."

"It's no use! Can't budge it!" another voice shouted.

"We'll go off the track," a voice screamed as the wagon lurched with even greater violence.

"Most likely. We'd all best get back to the far end. Keep close together. Hang on—and pray."

Tyndall felt a vague reassurance as the others huddled around him. He wasn't alone in his fear. It was palpable.

The tank exploded one half mile from the western edge of Fareham.

The two charges fused by Sergeant Priller went off simultaneously, the jet effect blowing gaping holes through the heavy armor as the main explosives detonated the remaining unfused charges. In that split second of detonation the flat wagon beneath the tank simply stopped, then disintegrated, driven down into the tracks by the incredible force of the explosion. The still thrusting locomotive drove what was left of the freight wagons, and itself, into an accordian effect. The prisoners had all died at the instant of the explosion, huddled together against the crumbling wall and crushed by the wagon behind them.

The uncoupled cars were flung from the track by the continuing detonations as the tank's turret tumbled in a slow-motion arc above them. The locomotive was leaving the tracks as the twenty-five-pound charge exploded against its boiler. In one terrifying blast the huge bulk of the locomotive was reduced to bits and pieces of flying metal, some of which rained down on the rooftops of Portchester, five miles to the east.

Seconds later the shock wave passed over the tanks now moving at top speed nearly four miles to the northwest. Lieutenant Schiller was unprepared for the incredible violence of the distant explosions, even though he and the others had trained to the point of exhaustion with the highly secret hollow-charge explosives along an isolated stretch of the imposing Benes line of Czechoslovakia, an Allied gift obtained by Hitler at Munich. The few that they had been allowed to detonate during fuse familiarity training had been set off on open ground and had given little hint of their astonishing effects when strapped to a firm base of metal or concrete.

The air was quiet again as he turned to see Priller in the open hatch below the cupola.

"They *do* make a bit of noise, don't they, Lieutenant?" He had seen Schiller flinch.

"There were two separate explosions back there," Schiller said. "The locomotive must have gone up too. Dammit! I may have made a mistake leaving so much explosive in that tank. A noise like that will wake everyone for miles."

"No reason for anyone to connect us with it, Lieutenant. We must be five miles away by now."

"I hope you're right, Ernst." Schiller's hand tightened on the cupola rim. He pointed ahead. "Look," he said. The two men concentrated on the lights rising and dipping on the road far ahead. "Looks like only one. Can you make it out?"

"A lorry from the look of it," Priller replied calmly.

"Get below and stand by the guns." His hand went to the microphone. "Slow down, Thyben. Close your hood. There's something ahead."

He signaled to Siegler. The second tank began to close the gap between them. "Lights off!" he shouted into the intercom, angry at having forgotten.

The lorry approached slowly. Then its lights began to move to the left. Schiller sighed with relief as he watched the vehicle turn into a converging road far ahead. It moved without any sign of urgency. Schiller watched until it had disappeared behind the trees.

He spoke into the headset. "They've turned off. Stop here, Thyben. I want to talk to Siegler. We're coming close to Botley. It's about seven miles to the target, so start preparing the weapons, Priller." He climbed out onto the superstructure. Siegler was already on the ground, coming toward him.

"I have the extra man, Willi, so when we force the main gate, you'll cover us while we plant the charges in the first building. You keep close to the fence once you're inside, just in case one of our charges should go off prematurely. If that should happen, some of my crew may be hurt or killed, and the other buildings will be up to you. After we take care of the hangars, we'll cover you while you fire the main building. Then we crash the fence, back onto Hazel Road."

He shone his flashlight on the section map of Woolston. "The colonel's man should be waiting just about . . . here, and then we'll be on our way home. You'll be responsible for setting the demolition fuses in your tank, so watch for my signal. Five minutes is all we can allow safely. Let's make sure we set them at the same time."

Schiller looked at Siegler inquiringly. "Anything you want to go over, Willi? We won't have the chance to stop again. From now on we move at top speed to the target."

"No questions," Siegler answered. "I know what I have to do."

"Then let's get moving. Good luck, Willi."

Siegler ignored Schiller's outstretched hand and walked toward his tank. Schiller watched him swing easily up on the superstructure, then shrugged and ran back to his own tank.

Otto Wirth was still frightened, but his fear had been receding somewhat since he had been chosen to drive the pick-up car to Eastleigh. The alteration in the original plans simplified his own. Despite his apparent zeal, Otto Wirth had no intention of allowing himself to be shot at, and perhaps killed, by trigger-happy Englishmen.

He pulled the blackout curtains open slightly and peered out through the tape-crossed windows at the Albert Road. The street was deserted. His eyes moved to the darkened buildings on the opposite side of the street, knowing that less than four hundred yards beyond them lay the Itchen River and, across its narrow reach, the Vickers-Supermarine buildings. Death was out there. He was glad that he couldn't see the river.

Like many other transplanted Germans, Wirth had come to admire Adolf Hitler. In 1935, when a representative of the new government of Germany had approached him, flattering him into joining Colonel von Helmholtz's group, he had looked upon his acceptance as a harmless if somewhat foolish decision. More of an excuse to escape the monotonous reality of his day to day existence and the increasing irascibility of a climacteric frau.

He knew why he had been chosen: The Iron Cross, second class, awarded after the first British tank attack on Arras. Wounded in action; bravery in the face of the enemy; Otto Wirth smiled in remembrance.

He had seen no reason—since all of the others had been killed—to confess that he had been shot by his own officer when he had bolted his station on the gun as the huge British AV6s lumbered frighteningly toward them over the dead. His was the only gun of six still firing. The officer's bullet tore through his shoulder. He lay on the ground watching his own blood spreading beneath him, hoping that the lieutenant wouldn't notice that he was still alive. He glanced toward the gun just as the shell struck it and then heard the metal monsters turn away. He thought fast in those days. Crawling back to the gun over the headless corpse of the lieutenant, he lay near his station and waited.

He was unconscious when they found him and was carried carefully to the field hospital under the personal direction of the company commander, who had decided that the private's bravery should not go unnoticed; an example to the swine who were showing an increasing tendency to panic at the sight of the new British weapon. The lieutenant's bullet, which had fortunately passed through his flesh, kept Private Wirth uncomfortable but safe in Germany for the next three months. When he had fully recovered, promoted and decorated, he was assigned to a gunnery school in Bavaria where he served as an example of what was expected of German artillery troops. He remained there until the end of the war.

Now his luck seemed to be holding. He was the one assigned to drive the car to Eastleigh, where he was to wait for Siegler and his crew after their attack on the airfield. It had been a reprieve for Wirth. He had had no intention of bobbing about on the Itchen in a small boat waiting for the storm troopers to attack the Supermarine plant. It was obvious suicide, and he had been wondering how best to sneak away from the others before they were killed. He hadn't the slightest doubt that they *would* be killed, and he had no desire to join them. Now he could be back in London when it happened. If the attack should succeed, he would think of some excuse for not being in the place assigned to him. Driving about the blacked-out, aroused, English countryside with German storm troopers was absolute madness. Wirth started guiltily at the voice behind him.

"Otto, get away from that window. Do you want the ARP pounding on our door?"

Wirth stepped back and adjusted the blackout curtains carefully.

"The street is deserted," he answered defensively. "Even that old warden won't be prowling about at this time of the morning." He yawned.

"I wouldn't be too sure of that."

Wirth shrugged. "When do you want me to leave?"

"Give it another three quarters of an hour. You can be in position in less than half an hour. It wouldn't be wise for you to get there too early. The longer you have to wait in a parked car, the more chance that someone will see you."

Wirth controlled the urge to plead, and settled for argument. "I don't know, Josef. You're not allowing for any emergencies. Suppose I should have a blowout?" Otto was pleased at his own cleverness. He was planting the possibility of a breakdown in their minds.

Another man spoke. "Otto's right, Josef. We don't know exactly when the troops will arrive now. It might be worth the risk for him to leave early. We can be in position in a few minutes. He has the blackout and the roads to contend with."

Otto blessed him, as the other man answered, "Perhaps you're right. Do you want to chance it, Otto?"

"No one will see me. The trooper who chose that spot knew what he was about."

"I should have preferred it to be the colonel's decision, but . . . very well, I suppose it is best that you leave now. It *is* less than two hours to sunrise, and the troops would be in a bad spot if you weren't there to pick them up after the attack."

Otto Wirth walked quickly to the door.

"Be careful, Otto. Four German soldiers are depending on you. Heil Hitler."

"I would much prefer going along with you," Wirth lied happily. "You have the difficult job. Good luck to all of you. Heil Hitler." He stepped out into the narrow hall, and closed the door.

The room was on the second story of the three-story house. The lower floor was occupied by the owners, while the upper floors each consisted of three guest bedrooms, permanently occupied by the members of von Helmholtz's cell. The elderly owners found nothing strange in the fact that their guests were seldom in residence and appeared altogether only on certain days of the month. They paid regularly, in advance, and were singularly undemanding, refusing even the modest breakfast that was included in the rental. They were ideal tenants, and the elderly couple blessed their good fortune. Having the benefits of a fully rented house without the inconvenience of permanent, demanding guests was an uncommon boon.

As Otto Wirth was stepping out into the upper hall, the owner was explaining all of this to Major Fitzroy. His wife busied herself at the stove, clucking occasionally at the early hour and the sight of armed men in her kitchen.

"How do they explain their irregular occupancy, sir?" Major Fitzroy asked, keeping his voice low.

"Specialists. They've something to do with machinery and move about from factory to factory when they're needed. Don't know much more than that, none of my business."

"Have they mentioned any factory in particular, Mr. Smith? Vickers-Supermarine for instance?"

"Tea, Major?" Tea had seen the elderly woman through many a crisis.

"No, Ma'am. Thank you very much."

"I think they do work at Vickers, Major."

"Why, Ma'am?"

"Well, it was one day last week. I'd gone over to Woolston to shop. I'd just gotten off the ferry when I saw Mr. Temple and Mr. Prince turning into the Hazel Road, just alongside Vickers, you know."

"I do indeed, Ma'am. Temple and Prince, you said? I take it that you've never taken a look at their identity cards or ration books, Mr. Smith?"

"No, Major, I can't say that I have. They don't take their food here, never have. I don't take to those blasted cards. Bloody interference in a man's private life, as I see it. Englishmen not able to walk about without being asked to show the damned things to any Tom, Dick, or Harry who asks to see them."

"A necessary interference, Mr. Smith."

"I suppose so. War! We haven't gotten over the last one yet and we're at it again."

"We didn't attack Poland, sir," said Fitzroy.

"Might as well have. Why didn't we slap that Hitler fellow down before he got big enough to. We must be bloody blind."

"Sir?" came a voice from behind them.

Major Fitzroy turned to face an officer who had stepped quietly into the kitchen.

"The men are in position, sir."

"Very well, Lieutenant. Have them get on with it."

"What did he mean, Major?" the old man asked, worry in his voice. "Are you intending to start some sort of battle in my house?"

320

"No, sir. Of course not. We shall be out of your way shortly. Thank you for your cooperation."

Otto Wirth stopped at the head of the narrow stairs. The building shuddered momentarily, and he heard the hollow reverberation of what he sensed must have been a distant, massive explosion. He waited a moment. He was about to continue on down when another thud, even louder than the first, echoed through the house. Wirth's first thought was of the mysterious new explosives carried by the Storm troopers. Had they been discovered? He heard the excited muffled voices of the others through the closed door behind him. Even if the explosions had no relation to the raiders, Otto Wirth was even further resolved to get away from the madness he had become involved in. He began to walk down the stairs, then heard the click of the front door latch. Pressing back into the darkness, he watched as the door was opened and a man holding a taped flashlight hurried silently through it and entered the door of the front parlor.

In that brief instant, Wirth knew that they had been discovered and that the distant explosions that had caused him to pause had saved him. The man he had seen below him had been a fully armed army officer, and in the glow of the flashlight Otto had seen him glance up the stairs meaningfully.

Fear prodded Otto into movement. He crept back along the hall to the stairs leading to the top floor and climbed them quickly. He had not paused at the door to the front bedroom. There was no thought of sharing the ladder to the roof with the others. One man could make it. Otto intended that it be him. Perhaps it had been premonition that had prompted him—unseen by the others—to inspect the ladder and the roof weeks earlier. He could move across the roofs of the attached houses to the edge of the school grounds at the north end of the street, where he had—providentially—parked the car. He should be able to tell if anyone was watching it. It was unlikely, since not even the colonel knew which of the group's cars would be used for the pickup at Eastleigh.

He must move quickly. Once the street was sealed off, he would be trapped. Wirth tiptoed silently to the closet near the rear bedroom and entered it, closing the door behind him. The air was stifling. He felt for the ladder, and began to climb.

At the top, he reached above his head and pushed up on the heavy box-like cover over the exit. He edged it slowly over the raised frame that held it snugly in place and moved it away from the opening, thankful for the rush of cool air. With both hands on the frame, he climbed up another rung and peered over the edge. Something moved behind him; he froze in fear as he felt something cold and metallic thrust into the hollow behind his right ear and the vibration run through it as the pistol was cocked. A voice behind him whispered, "He's alone, sir."

Otto Wirth felt the gun barrel move upward slightly against his ear.

"Up you come now, and be quick about it."

Otto's hands remained frozen to the frame, until he felt the hands on his collar dragging him bodily up into the darkness.

Major Fitzroy looked at the silent men lined up against the wall of the front bedroom as they were searched by thorough troopers. None of them had said a word. Fitzroy heard the bedroom door open behind him, turned, and followed the beckoning lieutenant into the hall.

"We've caught the missing one, sir. He was trying to get away over the roof."

"Why him? How did *he* know we were here and not the others?" Fitzroy said.

"I don't know, sir. He most likely heard or saw us and made no attempt to warn the others, simply bolted."

"Let's ask him, shall we? However he knew, it was run and the devil take his confederates. I've the feeling he could be their weak link."

"I don't think that we shall have any trouble in getting that one to talk, sir. Lieutenant Caine tells me that the prisoner almost fainted when he was reminded of the treachery bill."

Ten minutes later, Major Fitzroy hurried down the front steps to the Albert Road and ran toward the waiting signals vehicle.

Half a mile south of Botley the tanks turned west and followed a deserted road, fringed by ancient trees, to a bisecting road where they again turned north. Within minutes they had again turned to the west. The target now lay five miles to the southwest. They were traveling at top speed along the class A road, which they found was also deserted. Schiller pressed the microphone button. "Slow down, Thyben. Siegler's too far behind us. The road south should be just ahead."

As the tank slowed, Schiller waited until Siegler had closed to within thirty yards and then gestured vigorously to the left. Siegler raised an arm in acknowledgement. Schiller returned his eyes to the road ahead. "There it is," he said into the intercom.

Sergeant Thyben braked the tank expertly into the connecting road and began to increase speed. Schiller's attention was focused on the ground ahead during the turn. When he finally looked behind him, the road was empty. There was no sign of Siegler's tank.

"Stop, Thyben," he shouted into the intercom. "Willi's missed the turn. Come up here, Priller."

Sergeant Priller pushed the hatch cover back and looked up at Schiller.

"Willi missed the turn. Get back up to that road and find him. He must be blind as well as deaf. How could he have missed seeing us turn?"

"He's not blind, Lieutenant. I hear him. Way off there." He pointed to the west.

"What the hell is he doing?"

"Does that road lead to Eastleigh?" Priller asked.

"That son of a bitch!" Schiller exploded.

"Listen to it. He's going flat out, Lieutenant. Is that what we sound like? He must be half a mile away by now. Shall I try to contact him?"

"No," Schiller answered angrily, his knuckles whitening against the cupola rim. "That ties it. We're on our own now."

"We can do our job without Siegler, Lieutenant, and maybe his attacking that airfield will take some of the attention off of us after we've hit the factory?"

"Or add to it. The idea was to be well on our way to the coast before they could react. If he attacks first, the entire southern command will be alerted before we crash the gate."

"He'll follow the original plan."

"Will he? I doubt it. He hasn't followed anything else."

"Then we'd best hop to it, shouldn't we, Lieutenant?"

Schiller punched the microphone button. "Move out, Thyben. Willi's taken off on his own. It's up to you to get us to Woolston before he gets to the airfield. If he beats us, we may have more on our plate than we expected."

The tank lurched ahead as Schiller leaned closer to the sergeant. "Get below and tell the others that we'll follow the single tank attack plan." Priller began to back down into the fighting compartment. "Wait," Schiller said. "Connect up one of the 110s and have it ready to pass up when I give the word. When we're almost there I'll lash it to the turret and drop it as soon as we crash the first hangar."

Priller looked at him in surprise. "What if they *are* waiting for us? Those bloody explosives are dangerous enough inside the tank, but at least there's seventy millimeters of armor between them and the British antitank guns."

"Just have it ready. They wouldn't have let us come this far if they

323

knew what we were up to. Once we get down to the Portsmouth Road we'll be in the eastern end of Woolston, buildings on either side of us. They won't use antitank guns there."

"No?" Priller was not convinced. "It's too bloody deserted. I don't like it, lieutenant."

"I won't put the damn thing out unless everything looks clear. We'll have all the company you want if we don't get a move on. Look at that sky. It won't be long before first light."

Willi Siegler smiled smugly as he spoke into the microphone. "Get ready to turn right, Hans. The next crossroad will be the A27. Once we're on it, it's only three and a half miles to go. We'll cross a bridge about a mile from the airfield. Once we're over it, we'll stop and go over the attack. There's a cemetery there, so it should be quiet enough."

Sergeant Falck, in the turret hatch, watched him nervously.

"Are the explosives ready?" Siegler asked.

"Everything's ready."

"We'll use the twenty-five pounders and the cannon in the first two hangars. No incendiaries until we're on our way out the far wall. I'm changing the plan. We'll be better off moving to the car on foot. No use letting them know which way we've gone. We'll fuse two of the 110s in the tank and leave it in the third hangar. On the way out we'll set whatever twenty-five pounders we have left and scatter them around and fire the building. That should keep them away from the tank until it goes. We'll cross to the other side of Wide Lane and put as much ground as possible between us and that hangar. When the tank goes up, it will be a twenty-six-ton grenade. I'll go over it again when we stop."

"Looks as if we're going to do it, Willi," Falck said.

"There was never any doubt," Siegler said as Falck dropped out of sight.

Siegler returned his attention to the road. The darkness was no longer impenetrable, and Corporal Knoedler had no trouble in keeping up speed toward the outlying buildings of Bitterne. Siegler smiled again in smug self-satisfaction. Schiller had made it easier by his stop some minutes earlier. Willi had made certain that their conversation had been held out of earshot of his own tank. None of his crew had questioned his statement that Schiller had decided that they were to proceed to Eastleigh as originally planned. Actually, the men were relieved. The open fields of an airport were much better suited to the defense of a tank, should it come to that. They had all had unspoken thoughts about the attack on the factory at Woolston. Hemmed in, surrounded on two sides by town buildings, and on a third by the river, they would be confined to the eastern extension of Hazel Road after the attack, depending on unknown civilians for their ultimate escape. They all knew that the civilians were the weak link. If they weren't there—or bolted at the sound of the first explosion, leaving the attackers isolated in British tank corp uniforms—capture or death was almost a certainty. None of these points had escaped Willi Siegler either. He was still smiling as he ordered the turn into the A27. There was no roadblock.

"I'm at Goodwood now, Edward. We have only minutes, and then I must leave. I'm sorry I wasn't available for your first report, but when we discovered that they had made off with the train we had to get things moving. We seem to have been one step behind them again, unfortunately. Still, with what you've discovered, we finally have something to work with. We've got them now, but they've done a lot of damage."

"You say that the explosions we heard was the train blowing up, sir?"

"It was."

"Then I don't understand, sir. Weren't they with the train?"

"No, Edward. They apparently abandoned one of the tanks after they removed the others. How they did that, and why they abandoned one is a puzzle we shall have to wait to get the answer to when we pick them up. The one they abandoned was obviously full of fused explosives. They set the locomotive's throttle and left it backing toward Fareham."

"Good Lord, sir. It didn't . . . ?"

"No. It went up less than a quarter mile from the outskirts. The force of the explosion was tremendous, as you no doubt gathered. They found a Mark 2 turret, intact, half a mile from the center of the blast. There was enough evidence to make an educated guess that only one exploding tank caused that holocaust. That can be the only way to describe it, from what I've heard."

"We heard two separate explosions some seconds apart, sir."

"The other seems to have been the locomotive. Picture something that large virtually disintegrating."

"Then two of them are still on the loose, sir?"

"Yes, but thanks to you, we know where they're heading, don't we."

"Yes, sir. But surely we aren't going to wait . . ."

"They will be allowed to proceed to Woolston."

"But, sir, if they've some new explosive, wouldn't it be better to keep them as far away from Vickers as possible?"

"They've been under direct observation for the past twenty minutes. They are less than ten miles from where you are now standing. Unfortunately, we haven't the time or a suitable gun near enough to make the preparations to stop them; however, steps are being taken. They've turned north—that gave us a turn—but your information proved to be correct. They were simply skirting the upper reaches of the Hamble, below Botley. The last information had them turning back to the south into the 3033, toward the Portsmouth Road. Precisely where we want them."

"Then an ambush *has* been arranged, sir?"

"They will be allowed to continue on to the floating bridge."

"Forgive me, sir, but if they're engaged there they might still get at Vickers."

"We're counting on the navy to see to it that they don't get the opportunity."

"Did you say the navy, sir . . . ?" He heard muffled noises at the other end of the line. "Sir?" he said.

"Hold on for a moment, Edward."

Major Fitzroy waited, pondering on what the brigadier had said. What on earth could the navy . . . ?

"Edward? Are you there?"

"Yes, sir."

"We've just gotten word that the tanks have split up. It would seem that your information was right on the money. One of them is moving to the Portsmouth Road, and the other apparently proceeding to Eastleigh. They are certainly confident beggars, although I must say we've given them little reason to be otherwise as yet. Still, splitting their force doesn't seem logical even for Huns. But whatever their logic, it simplifies things for us. We do have the firepower at Eastleigh, and now, with only one to deal with at Woolston, we seem to have things under control at last."

"You mentioned the navy, sir."

"Where are you, Edward? Your precise location."

"At the west end of the Albert Road, sir."

"Near the floating bridge?" the brigadier asked.

"It's just behind me, sir," the puzzled Fitzroy answered.

"Then take a good look at Thornycroft's when you get the chance. I must ring off now. The aircraft is ready. I've changed plans. Colonel Blake and I are being flown to Eastleigh. I want to be there when the Huns arrive. I'd like you to be there too. Have your prisoners been removed?"

"Just now, sir."

"Fine. Headquarters will take care of them. There's nothing for you there. Start at once, if you will. Once they're over the Hamble we'll close the net at Eastleigh. You've done remarkably well, Edward."

"I shall leave at once, sir. But what if they should manage to get the tank crew here to surrender? Shouldn't one of us be here?"

"I'm afraid that is very unlikely, Edward. I've been receiving reports for the last half hour. Bodies, English bodies, are being found all along their route from Newhaven. That might have been put down to the fortunes of war under other circumstances, but these Huns are in British uniform. None of our lads had a chance, and there may have been as many as ten or twelve civilians locked aboard that train when they blew it up. It's doubtful, knowing the extent of what they've done, that they will be anxious to surrender only to be hanged.

"Add to that the indisputable fact that Vickers-Supermarine is absolutely vital to the survival of this country. No, the tank will be destroyed before it can lay its sights on that factory. I shall expect you at Eastleigh. Goodbye, Edward."

Major Fitzroy left the signals lorry and hurried toward the ferry slip. The darkness seemed less intense. It was beginning to brighten perceptibly in the east. He moved past the sentries onto the ferry, walking quickly along the uncovered center vehicle platform to its far end. The Itchen flowed sluggishly below him. Across the river, the Woolston slip was dimly visible; to its left lay the buildings of Vickers-Supermarine; to its right, Thornycroft's shipyard. Fitzroy watched the tug's screws thrashing the water as they edged the destroyer's bows dangerously close to the pilings of the ferry slip.

Major Fitzroy now guessed what the brigadier had meant. He made his way back to the landing. Once ashore he went quickly to his car.

Twenty minutes after he had spoken to Major Fitzroy, the twin-engined airplane carrying Brigadier Fox and Colonel Blake touched lightly down on the grass field at Eastleigh.

As the aircraft settled, the brigadier called at the open door of the flight deck, "Get us over to the hangars as quickly as you can, Lieutenant."

The young officer grinned excitedly. "Yes, sir."

His grin faded when the brigadier added, "And then take this aircraft back to your base at once. This airfield has been cleared. There will be no aircraft of any sort remaining on this post until this is over."

At that same moment Major Fitzroy, on the Portswood Road two miles below the airfield, was removing his tunic, angrily preparing to help his driver repair a flat tire. The driver was removing the spare from the trunk.

"This one's a bit flat too, sir."
"Dammit, Sergeant . . ."
"I think it's just low on air, sir."
"Do you have a pump?"
"Yes, sir."
"Then for God's sake, get on with it."
"It's in here someplace, sir."

CHAPTER 32

The junction with the Portsmouth Road was dimly visible ahead. Sergeant Thyben slowed at Schiller's order and they approached cautiously. Schiller, feeling uncomfortably exposed in the cupola, watched the barrier and spoke rapidly into the intercom.

"If we get by the block ahead I'd say we're in the clear. Stand by the guns, Richter, but don't get edgy. You're not to fire unless I give the order or something should happen to me. If it does, Priller will take command. The target is approximately two miles to our right. No more turn-offs once we're on that road beyond the block. Close your hood, Thyben."

The ally of darkness was deserting them rapidly. The roadblock, Schiller could see, was another jumble of farm carts. But there was a difference: there was clear passage through the center! As they drew closer Schiller could discern only one man near the barrier, and soon saw that it was a uniformed constable leaning casually against his bicycle. A tin hat hung from its strap on the handlebars.

Schiller's hand held the cocked Enfield pistol out of sight below the cupola rim. He spoke again into his headset.

"Only one man ahead that I can see, a constable. It looks as though our luck is still with us. Keep going, Thyben." Schiller laughed nervously, his free hand still on the microphone button. "He's yawning. Too bad we interrupted his nap. Come left a bit. That's it. Hold it there and keep moving straight through."

The tank lumbered slowly through the barrier.

"Good morning, constable," Schiller called above the tread noise.

"Good morning to you, sir." The constable reached hurriedly to the handlebars, removed the tin hat and placed it on his head as if surprised in some dereliction. Schiller gripped the pistol tighter at the sudden movement, but nothing happened. He glanced behind him; the road was clear, and he relaxed.

"Quite a lonely post for you to be standing alone, isn't it?" Schiller said.

"Not mine, sir. The LDV leave at first light. They're supposed to remove these bloody carts before they go, but it looks as though it's up to me today."

"Like some help?"

"No, sir. Ta. Gives me something to do. Can't blame them really, they put in a long night."

Schiller waved, then pressed the intercom button. "Hard right, Thyben. You can open your hood again for a few minutes. Keep your eyes open. There's bound to be some traffic on this road. In half an hour we should be on our way home." He replaced the pistol in the holster.

Captain Basil Whitten undid the confining button at the neck of the badly fitting constable's uniform. He watched the tank turn into the Portsmouth Road. When it was out of sight behind the buildings lining the road, he raised his arm. Seconds later the command post at Vickers-Supermarine transmitted another signal to *H.M.S. Vengeance.*

After the turn into the Portsmouth Road, Lieutenant Schiller forced himself to stand upright in the cupola. He found that he had been unconsciously assuming a half crouch in expectation of the first shot from some unseen ambush ahead. The constable's friendly greeting had eased the growing sense of foreboding somewhat, but the prickling sensation at the back of his neck remained. He looked back as casually as he could and studied the road behind him. It was empty. Damned foolishness, he thought. Nothing could stop them now. Another mile and they would be at the Itchen.

He glanced momentarily at the headstones, aligned in neat rows and reflecting the pale light of predawn, as the tank rumbled past the cemetery to his right. His eyes returned quickly to the road ahead. Man is a superstitious animal.

Approximately four miles to the north, Siegler and his tank were also passing a cemetery, and he, too, glanced at the stark headstones, but no superstition clouded Willi's elation. Mansbridge, spanning the upper reaches of the Itchen, had been crossed uneventfully. Willi returned the hearty greeting of the lone constable who had been leaning against the rail of the otherwise deserted bridge with barely disguised contempt. Once over the bridge, a sharp turn to the north obscured the signal given by the apparently bored policeman.

In the second of the three hangars on the western rim of Eastleigh airport, Brigadier Fox sat in the empty engineers' office fighting the drowsiness he was beginning to feel. He glanced at his watch. The back-up troops were on the way and should arrive at any moment. But until they did arrive he, as senior officer, was in command. It could be worse, he mused. There were two 3.7s with trained men to man them, and Colonel Evans and his officers. There was a knock on the door. The brigadier rose and opened it.

"Ah, Colonel, come in," he said to the tall, immaculate, angry looking officer who followed the brigadier into the room, shutting the door firmly.

"Our lot have crossed the bridge, sir. They've stopped just west of Stoneham cemetery road."

"Stopped? Do you think they smell a rat?"

"I doubt it, sir. Going over their plans most likely. It gives me the opportunity to speak to you . . . frankly, if I may."

"Certainly, Colonel Evans."

"Two points, sir. This is a difficult position we're in here. A pocket surrounded by civilians. As you know, one gun is set up at the eastern corner of the southernmost hangar. We must consider it as a last resort since it is trained south. The other is sited just this side of the crematorium at the north end of the cemetery road, or to be more precise, on the southern edge of the field. That gun is approximately four hundred yards from Wide Lane, giving us a comparatively clear field of fire of perhaps fifteen degrees beyond the road. If they move along Wide Lane they will see the gun as soon as they pass the building. If I don't shoot to kill and get her quickly—within that fifteen degree arc—shells will be landing in southern Eastleigh. I simply wanted you to know that my men are trained regulars, but engaging tanks was not part of that training. If we should miss in an attempt to disable, and they turn away to the west, it will leave only ten men and a single 37-mm. antitank gun dug in on the fields to the west to stop them. Highly unlikely with a Mark 2. If the Germans stick to it—and having gotten this far they strike me as the sort who will—they might move down into the fields to the west, below the road, and come in on the western side of the hangars. Once they did that, both guns would be useless—unless we intend to help them do their job."

"My intelligence capacity prompted my rather hasty order to attempt to take them alive," Brigadier Fox said. "Consider it rescinded, Colonel."

"Thank you, sir. That will simplify things somewhat."

"What was your other point, Colonel?"

"Simply that they might decide to come up Stoneham cemetery road behind the crematorium gun."

"You said that they had stopped to the west of the cemetery road."

"Yes, sir. Stopped. No reason why they can't backtrack once they think about it. Call it a hunch if you will. If I were in command of that tank, and it was still dark, I'd use Wide Lane. Now that it is light enough—or soon will be light enough for fighters to take off; they haven't been out of the tank and haven't seen the field yet, so I must assume that they believe that the fighters are still here—I would come in the back door, and as I crossed the field to the hangars I would make certain that I took the precaution of destroying any aircraft that might come after me. You did say that they intend to abandon the tank after the attack?"

The brigadier nodded, and the colonel continued. "If they should come up the cemetery road, they have a fifty-fifty choice as to which side of the crematorium they use to enter the field. I've opted for the western side, but should they choose the eastern side they'll be behind my gun with no time for me to turn it. So, I've taken the liberty of mining the ground on either side of the building. I should like your permission to train the hangar gun on the crematorium. The mines should disable the tank, but they will still have their cannon. The hangar gun should be ready to fire immediately."

"Won't they see the hangar gun as soon as they pass the building? It could be chancy, Colonel Evans. If they should fire first and put that gun out of action, we'll have had it."

"The hangar gun has been hidden behind a Vickers lorry, its motor running, with one of our best drivers in the seat ready to pull it out of the way. I'll need to have your decision immediately, sir. We haven't much time."

"You're prepared to retrain the gun immediately should they follow the original plan?"

"Yes, sir. It will be done as soon as they move onto Wide Lane."

"Do it then, Colonel."

"Thank you, sir. With your permission, I'll give the order and get down to the gun."

"Down? Are you taking command of the southern gun yourself?"

"Yes, sir."

"You realize, Colonel, that should your hunch prove to be correct, and the hangar gun is fired, it will be firing toward you and your men as well as at the tank. I can't vouch for the stability of the explosives they're carrying."

"I realize it, sir. With luck we'll be able to move around to the western side of the building before they fire. I have a man on the upper floor of the crematorium. If he sees that they've decided to come in to the east, we shan't hang about, I can assure you."

"Thank you, Colonel Evans. You'd best do what you have to do. I don't mind saying that I'm damned glad you're here." Brigadier Fox returned the officer's salute and followed him to the office door.

The brigadier watched the colonel hurry through the deserted hangar, past the rows of partially assembled Spitfires, to the door where he paused momentarily to allow Colonel Blake to enter. Brigadier Fox began to walk toward Blake, his tiredness forgotten.

"Any word of Edward?" he called.

"No, sir. He left Southampton shortly after he spoke to you. He hadn't passed the block above Swathling station before it was closed. I'm afraid he'll have to wait it out. I shouldn't worry, sir."

"No, but I hope that he has indeed been held up at the roadblock. It wouldn't do to have him driving up Wide Lane now, particularly after my chat with Colonel Evans."

"Quite, sir. A car is just outside the door. Will you come along now? It's rather an uncomfortable feeling to be standing in the bull's eye of their target."

"After my talk with the estimable Evans, I've an idea that this may be the safest place on this post, but lead on." The two men walked to the door as the brigadier continued, "What's the latest on the other tank?"

"It should be in the box any moment now, sir. No doubt about Edward's information now. They had just passed Station Road as I came in here."

"Then we should know soon whether Admiral Trevor's remarkable innovation works out in practice."

"I don't see how it can fail, sir. Once they're in range, they've little room to maneuver."

"Ironic, isn't it, Andrew. We can thank the Germans for the damage they inflicted on the *Vengeance* at Dunkirk. She wouldn't have been at Thornycroft's otherwise, the only destroyer available north of the Solent."

"Divine justice, sir."

"Quite so." The brigadier stepped through the door. It was now light enough for him to see the intense expression on the face of the officer who hurried toward him.

"Sir. Colonel Evans reports that the tank has begun to move again. He suggests that you and Colonel Blake proceed to the field HQ. He asked me to tell you that the tank is continuing west."

CHAPTER 33

Admiral Sir James Trevor raised his binoculars and focused on the Portsmouth Road beyond the floating bridge landing.

"Nothing yet, Captain," he said to the officer beside him.

"They're passing Oak Road, sir," a voice called from the wheelhouse behind them.

"Any moment now, sir," the captain said to the admiral.

"We'll stop this lot, Captain, but if it comes to bombing from the air, we shall have our job cut out for us protecting that setup. Just look at it." The admiral's glasses moved down past the angled confluence of Oakbank and Hazel Roads to settle on the buildings of Vickers-Supermarine. "Civilian buildings and the river framing it like a bull's eye."

The admiral shook his head slowly as he passed the lenses over the row of buildings perched so precariously on the edge of the Itchen. "You're quite certain that all of the civilians are clear?"

"Yes, sir."

The glasses moved to the men on the sidewalks of Portsmouth Road. "And those men?"

"Army volunteers, sir. to calm the nerves and trigger fingers of our visitors."

"I trust that they aren't foolish enough to hang about down there too long? I feel badly enough about firing on British soil, without killing some of her citizens."

"They've had their orders, sir."

"Where are the antitank teams?"

"One at the end of Wharf Road, and one behind the buildings of Oakbank Road, sir."

"The army isn't putting much faith in our gunnery."

"If they should turn off for some reason, and we can't get a shot at them, it will be up to those men, sir."

"My remark was uncalled for, Captain. But we shall have to see to it that their participation will not be necessary."

"Passing Coopers Lane, sir," came the voice from the wheelhouse.

"Very well. Inform Guns," the captain said, his own binoculars steady on the road. "I see them, sir."

The admiral had seen them too. He whispered encouragement to the tank, "Steady as you go. That's it. Directly down the center. Cheeky bastards."

"One minute to fire, sir."

"Very well. Sound the siren." The whoop-whoop of the powerful siren shattered the stillness. "Hand me those phones, Quartermaster," the captain ordered.

The quartermaster passed the headset to the captain, who spoke hurriedly to the gunnery officer. The quartermaster stared in fascination at the easily visible front silhouette of the infantry tank. Its two-pounder cannon seemed to be pointed directly at him.

"Inside everyone," the admiral ordered. "Tell Guns to get on with it, Captain."

"Ready to fire, sir."

"Very well. Sound the final warning. Clear the decks," the captain ordered.

The curved armored hood was closed above Sergeant Thyben's head. He squinted through the thick glass of the driving slit at the road ahead. He had no difficulty in keeping on the center line. The darkness he had cursed earlier had lifted with startling suddenness. Thyben shook his head angrily when he realized that all of his muscles were tensed. He forced himself to relax; this was no time for a leg cramp. God! he thought, I'll be glad to get out of this bloody box. He glanced up at the hood above his head and felt the damp darkness of the driver's compartment, fighting the recurrent thought of how like a coffin it was. Sweat poured down his chest and he was disgusted by the smell of his own fear. He forced himself to listen to Schiller's running commentary. The lieutenant had kept at it since ordering the tank closed up. To the driver, and the three men in the fighting compartment, it was both reassuring and infuriating. They were all beginning to feel the preattack tension, which would ease only when they crashed the gate and the body took over, pumping reserve adrenaline into the bloodstream.

"Everything quiet." Schiller's voice came to them metallically. "We're passing a pond to our right. Railroad viaduct just ahead. Slow turn to the right coming up, Thyben."

"He must think I've gone blind," Thyben growled unreasonably. He readjusted his earphones. They were beginning to annoy him almost unbearably. He crabbed the tank into the turn. Ahead, the road—now a building-lined canyon—reversed its curve flatly to the left.

"Station to the right," Schiller said. "Shoaling."

In the fighting compartment, Priller repeated what had been said to Keller, who had no headset.

Keller laughed mirthlessly. "He sounds like a bloody tour guide. Ask him to stop. I'd like to pick up a souvenir pillow for my gran."

"People moving about on the sidewalk, waving at us," Schiller continued. Priller could hear the relief in his voice, and in his own as he repeated Schiller's words.

"Three quarters of a mile to go. Pass up the charge and then the bren."

Priller, glad for something to do, removed the headset and handed it to Keller. Schiller had climbed out onto the superstructure, and now leaned into the cupola to drag the charge up and out of the interior. He strapped it quickly behind the turret and then climbed back into the cupola. He reached down for the waiting bren machine gun; after attaching it to the Lakeman mounting he leaned into the interior.

"I'm going to fuse the charge now," he said to Priller.

"Jesus! Be careful. Don't set the fuse too short."

"Don't worry," Schiller said. "Once we're through the gate we'll go straight through the end door of the first building. As soon as we crash the fence, Richter will traverse the turret to the rear and cover that area. I'll cover the front with the Bren. The traverse will bring the charge around with it. You get it down fast. Once you've pulled the lanyard, we have three minutes on this fuse, so don't hang about."

Priller looked at him with disgust, as Schiller continued, "You'll have to get it down yourself, Ernst."

"I'll do my bit. Just make sure Thyben doesn't stall the engines."

"He won't. Once you've armed the fuse, get back up into the turret, and we'll go out the side wall before the building comes down on top of us. Don't forget to close the bloody hatch."

Schiller straightened up and looked ahead. Satisfied, he leaned down once again. "When the first one goes, we'll go back in, so have the first charge ready. Keller will handle the incendiaries."

"Right," Priller answered. "A piece of cake, Lieutenant."

Schiller straightened up again in the cupola and leaned over the strapped explosive. It was safe enough—until the lanyard was pulled activating the fuse. He pressed the microphone button.

"Police station to the right. Four coppers in front." One of the policemen called a greeting. Schiller smiled broadly, pointing to the head set and shaking his head negatively as he returned the waves of the others. "Wished us good morning," he said.

Schiller visualized the German uniforms, Wehrmacht and S.S., who would soon replace those friendly constables. He felt somehow cheated. It was apparently inevitable. He had expected more of the English. He glanced back over his shoulder; the constables were gone.

Ahead, the road now ran straight to the river. He studied it through his binoculars, then related what he saw to the others. "The river's just ahead. A quiet morning from the look of it. Too bad we're going to wake them so early. A few tradesmen cleaning their sidewalks. The ferry isn't in the slip on this side. There's a ship backing down toward the dock at Thornycroft's. Just blew her siren."

He decided not to tell the others that the ship was a destroyer. He ran the glasses over the damage plainly visible on its upper decks, past her shattered bridge, down over the front turrets apparently out of action, their guns pointed skyward. Schiller considered waiting until the ship was in its berth. No. They would be inside before the ship could man any of their secondary armament if it was still operable. He dropped the glasses to his chest and pressed the intercom button.

"Check everything again—and then get ready to hold on when we crash the fence. I'm closing up now. Priller you get on the periscope and keep an all around watch. Slow down a bit, Thyben. We'll attract too much attention going full out."

Schiller leaned over for another brief inspection of the lashings of the hollow charge then cocked the Bren. After a last look ahead, he dropped into the turret and pulled the cupola hatch closed. He couldn't shake off the nagging feeling that he had missed something—something that was wrong—and yet obviously everything was right.

Schiller's eyes ran over the dimly lighted interior. Sergeant Richter sat in the gunner's seat tensely, his knuckles white on the trigger of the two pounder. Sergeant Keller crouched beside him, one hand on the leather handle of a twenty-five-pound charge. Priller looked at Schiller from behind the periscope. "I thought you said that there were civilians on the street, Lieutenant? Bloody place looks deserted to me," he said uneasily.

Again Schiller felt the hair on the back of his neck tingling. He moved over to the periscope, motioning Priller aside. The buildings themselves seemed to be moving in slow motion as he passed the lens over the deserted road behind the tank. Suddenly he knew what he had just seen and not assimilated. "My God!" he said aloud. Swinging around, he pointed the lens toward the river, shouldering the anxious Priller roughly as he turned.

"What . . . ?" Priller began.

Schiller focused on the destroyer. It remained where it had been when he had first seen it. The decks were empty! If it were docking, there should be line handling parties! That was what he had seen and not noticed, and he knew that it could kill them.

The lens moved quickly over the forecastle and settled on the forward turrets. Both were now pointed directly at him! Schiller reached over and snatched the headset from the startled Priller. He punched the microphone button.

"They're on to us!" he shouted. "Full speed, Thyben. Turn into the nearest street, either side. Now! For Christ's sake, now!"

Sergeant Thyben reacted instantly. Schiller felt the tank surge forward and begin to lurch as Thyben braked heavily on the left tread.

"What is it?" Richter cried, genuine fear in his voice, as Priller started toward the commander's periscope in the cupola. Keller still crouched behind the gunner, frozen into immobility.

Schiller had no time to answer. He saw the muzzle flash from the lower turret and died a microsecond later knowing that he had failed.

The single steel-jacketed shell penetrated the tank just behind Sergeant Thyben at the base of the turret, passing through Sergeant Richter as the time fuse in its base took over, and it exploded instantly detonating the hollow charge explosives crowding the interior. The human occupants disintegrated into blood and tissue and then nothing.

The heavy cast turret blew backward and downward into the engines where the jet of flame, metal, and hot gas of an exploding hollow charge struck the undetonated charge strapped to the outer facing of the turret. The ensuing explosion threw what remained of the turret into the upper floor of a building that shuddered opposite the holocaust.

Shattered glass from the providentially evacuated buildings was sucked into the vacuum created by the unbelievable explosion and, caught up in the cyclone of inrushing and outrushing air, became a lethal hail peppering the side of the destroyer as it heeled over under the shock wave, over onto the tugs. The smaller one, at right angles to the larger ship's bow, was driven beneath the water of the Itchen where it remained as the destroyer began to recover. The other tug at the stern remained barely afloat.

Admiral Trevor was watching through a bridge window when the 4.7 fired. He woke up three hours later in the ship's sick bay and stared in wonder at his own leg suspended in traction above the bed. The architect of the cataclysm had no memory of how he happened to be there. The captain sustained only a mild concussion, having managed to grab the compass binnacle as he was thrown casually across the bridge. The quartermaster was unhurt, having had the presence of mind to hold onto the wire leading to his headset, knowing that it was screwed firmly into its outlet. Twenty-three members of the crew had been injured by the sudden heeling of the ship.

Only one man was killed: a sentry, impaled by flying glass a quarter of a mile below the explosion, whose curiosity had caused him to be foolish enough to ignore the destroyer's final warning.

The explosion at Woolston echoed thunderingly behind the staff car. Major Fitzroy saw his driver's eyes glance at him questioningly in the rear view mirror.

One down, thought the major. It was the second time that night that he had gotten indication of the fearsome power of the unknown devices brought in by the raiders.

"What was it, sir?"

Fitzroy ignored the question. "How far to the airfield, Sergeant?"

"A mile more or less, sir."

"Speed it up a bit. We've lost enough time as it is."

"Yes, sir, but it looks as though we're going to be stopped ahead. Look, sir, the road's sealed off just above Swathling Station."

"Damn!" the Major said.

The single, flat crack of the naval gun had been inseparable from the ensuing blast. Siegler hadn't heard it. He ordered Corporal Knoedler to stop for the second time and listened intently, hearing nothing but the continuing echoes of the explosion. He spoke into the intercom. "That damned fool Schiller has managed to blow himself up."

Sergeant Falck appeared in the turret hatch. "We heard it, even inside. What do you think happened?"

"Only one thing could have happened. All the charges went up at once. One of them got careless with a fuse."

"Jesus!" Falck said nervously as he looked at the empty road. "How far do we have to go, Willi? It's too quiet here. I don't like it."

Siegler followed his gaze to the buildings lining the road ahead. "Those houses have been evacuated. Would you want to live on the edge of a military airfield? The hangars are about one thousand yards behind those houses, that's how far we have to go."

"Then we made it?"

"Don't be too sure. That noise will wake everyone for miles, including the airmen on this field. I don't know why I didn't think of it before. This is a fighter base."

"Think of what?"

"The aircraft. They'll have fighters in the air before we finish with the first hangar. It's lighter than I thought it would be."

"What can we do, Willi? We can't just sit here."

"According to the map, the road through that cemetery leads straight up to the edge of the field. It's a good straight road. I could see all the way up when we passed. There's a stone wall to the left of the road, and the cemetery to the right. There's a crematorium at the far end, so there shouldn't be anyone about at this time of the morning. We can go up to it easily without being seen. Once we pass it, we're on the field about four or five hundred yards from the hangars. The planes will be on the field near the airmen's tents. We'll use the cannon on them as we cross the field. Tell Becker we're going back. And Falk, on the way up to the field check over all the fuses—carefully."

Knoedler eased the tank into Stoneham Cemetery road.

Siegler, in the cupola, glanced briefly over the rows of headstones and then concentrated on the road. Behind him, well hidden by the monuments, a nervous British soldier spoke softly and rapidly into a field telephone.

Halfway to the crematorium, Siegler spoke into the microphone. "Knoedler. Pull alongside the wall and stop. I want to look at the ground on the other side."

Sergeant Knoedler edged the skirting plate against the wall, grinding to a slow stop.

"Easy, Knoedler! Don't knock the bastard down yet."

Knoedler moved the steering levers, cursing his inability to answer Siegler on the one-way intercom. Fucking bloody field marshall!

Siegler removed the headset, climbed out onto the superstructure, and pulled himself easily to the top of the wall. He was smiling as he dropped back and returned to the cupola. Replacing the headset, he said, "It's perfect. Same level on the other side. I didn't see any planes on the field, but the building is in the way. Move up to it, Knoedler. We'll go through the wall to the right of the building. That should bring us just below the tents. When I give the word, Becker, traverse the turret to the rear. I don't want to damage the guns going through. Turn it back the minute we're on the other side."

The tank lurched ahead.

"One of them just looked over the wall, sir."

"Good," Colonel Evans replied. "Hopefully that means they'll be coming through on this side. Inform Captain Harper to prepare to move the lorry." He turned to the gun crew. The 3.7, its transport wheels raised, rested on its adjustable pads, the long barrel pointed toward the fields to the west of the crematorium. The ten-man crew looked at the colonel expectantly.

"The mines should stop them just out there." Evans pointed along the barrel. "Don't fire until I give the order. Once they're disabled they will see the gun. It should give them second thoughts. But, should they be foolish enough to attempt to fight—if their turret moves toward us one inch—I shall give the order to fire. One round in the turret will do it at this range." He smiled briefly at the understatement. "Understood?" The gunners chorused their understanding.

"Now, if they try to come through behind us, and they strike one of the mines, we shall do our best to turn the gun. If they should miss the mines, you are to abandon the gun and move out around the west side of the building. Remember the mines. Keep close to the wall. Make it snappy *if* I give the order to abandon the gun. Captain Harper has orders to fire immediately *if* they should manage to get by the mines, or *if* they should attempt to fire. Any questions?" There were none.

"They've stopped in front of the building, sir."

"Heads up, lads," the colonel said.

The road turned sharply in front of the crematorium. Siegler looked up carefully at the tape-crossed windows. Nothing moved.

Knoedler maneuvered the tank to the beginning of the turn and stopped at Siegler's order. Willi dropped down into the fighting compartment. "Ready?" he asked. Becker and Falck nodded. Siegler removed the Bren gun from its tray and moved back up into the cupola. He held it by the barrel alongside his leg and spoke to the driver.

"Move to the other side of the building, Knoedler, and go through the wall. Once we're clear, make for any planes you see on the field. Once we take care of them, turn for the hangars. Becker, you concentrate on the planes, I'll take care of any troopers with the Bren. Move it, Knoedler."

Knoedler edged the tank to the wall on the east side of the crematorium and stopped. He shifted down to emergency low gear, then pressed the accelerator and eased out the clutch. The wall crumbled easily before him, raining debris down over his armored hood. He was now looking at the fields ahead and then at the lightening sky as the tank began to climb over the rubble. He changed into high gear when the nose began to drop to the field. He could see the tents, but no aircraft! He felt a sudden uneasiness. He maneuvered the tank closer to the side of the building and began to accelerate. He heard the turret traversing behind him.

Siegler threw the hatch open as soon as the wall had fallen and mounted the Bren as the tank dropped into the field. He was leaning back to the outside of the turret for a cartridge drum when the tank struck two of the closely planted mines simultaneously. The front of the heavy machine was lifted almost casually into the air and then fell back heavily, leaning over to the right on ruined bogies. The turret stopped in midtraverse and the guns were now pointed upward at the building to its left. Siegler was pitched out of the cupola. He fell heavily to the ground beside the shattered tread. He forced himself to his knees and listened. Nothing moved in the tank.

Pulling himself up, Siegler was about to climb back up on the tilting superstructure when he heard Colonel Evans's shouted orders. He peered around the edge of the turret and saw the soldiers struggling to turn the heavy antiaircraft gun. He dropped to the ground and ran, crouching, to the shattered wall. He paused, looking quickly to the right and left, and then crossed the road to the cemetery where he flung himself down behind the first row of headstones. They hadn't seen him! He watched British troopers moving cautiously around the corner of the crematorium; their attention was on the tank. None looked in his direction. Siegler dropped back into a crouch and ran through the rows of stones. His only thought was to get as far away as possible before that gun fired.

Sergeant Falck got to his feet groggily in the tilting fighting compartment. He looked up at the light entering the open cupola hatch. Siegler was gone, maybe lying hurt outside, he thought. He reached for the Thompson submachine gun, which Siegler had kept close at hand just below the cupola hatch and cocked it. After a brief glance at the crumpled form of Sergeant Becker, he climbed up into the cupola. Three British soldiers looked up at him in shocked surprise from the ground. He forgot the basic dictum for automatic weapons and emptied the clip into the soldiers. Tossing the empty gun aside, he turned to the Bren gun, assuming that it had been loaded by Siegler. His hand was on the cocking bar when he realized that it was unarmed. His hand was moving to his holster when he was hit by massed fire from the corner of the building. His body hung for a moment on the cupola rim and then fell back into the fighting compartment.

Siegler slowed at the sound of the machine gun. One of them was still alive. Good, he thought, that should keep the British occupied. He saw movement far to his right and dropped behind a headstone. Four British troopers were running from the cemetery grounds toward the break in the wall. None of them looked in his direction. When they had passed, Siegler ran deeper into the cemetery, pausing occasionally to study the ground ahead. He reached the iron fence fronting Mansbridge Road without seeing any more troops. The road, too, was deserted. He began to edge to the west, toward the entrance. As he neared it he heard the motors of heavy lorries beyond the curve in the road to the east. Others seemed to be approaching from the west.

Thankful for the blind curves at either end of the road fronting the cemetery, Siegler didn't hesitate. Reaching the entrance he ran across the road into the intersecting southbound street directly opposite it. He continued to run down the deserted pavement until the motor noises grew louder, then went into the nearest front garden and dropped behind a low hedge.

He watched the troop lorries turn at high speed into the cemetery; the last one stopped, blocking the entrance. Armed soldiers were dropping from it when Siegler moved back to the sidewalk and walked casually toward the corner, fighting the impulse to run. No one on Mansbridge Road looked in his direction.

At the corner he turned west, looking back over his shoulder; the street behind him was empty. He walked rapidly, not breaking his stride even when he saw the lone constable approaching from the far end of the block.

Good thing they pick the biggest ones for coppers, Siegler thought. He looks near enough to the right size.

He turned into the front garden of the nearest house and knocked loudly on the front door. The constable was now trotting toward him. Siegler knocked again. Nothing stirred in the house. So they've evacuated this lot too, he reasoned. He waved the puzzled constable forward and then kicked the door open.

The constable was as interested as he was puzzled. What the bloody hell? He must know that there's no one there. "Here, sir. What is it?" he yelled. He heard the man answer, "Follow me, Constable. Hurry!" as he disappeared into the house. The constable followed him.

CHAPTER 34

Ten minutes later Siegler crossed the footbridge over Monk's Brook and walked toward Swathling station. He had decided on the direct approach. He would simply wait for a train.

He abandoned the idea quickly when he saw soldiers patrolling the platform and a constable talking to the ticket taker. When the constable had gone back into the building, he crossed over the tracks boldly and skirted the edge of the station up to High Road. He stopped when he saw the roadblock at the junction to his right and the staff car parked well below it. He watched manned troop lorries moving through the roadblock and then his eyes returned to the staff car. He saw an officer leave its back seat and begin walking toward the barrier.

Siegler crossed the road without a trace of furtiveness and approached the car. The driver, a young sergeant, glanced at him casually. Siegler saw that there was no one else in the car. He looked to his right; the officer was returning.

"Not the best place to be standing, Sergeant," Siegler said.

"Tell it to him, Constable," the soldier replied, gesturing at the approaching Major Fitzroy. "What was that shooting we heard?" the sergeant asked.

"I was going to ask you," Siegler answered. He looked down at the young soldier: thin, pink cheeked, and obviously short. Too bad. Still, his luck had been phenomenal so far. No use expecting too much. He looked at the major: a tight fit, but it would have to do. At least I'm on the right side of the roadblock. And it seems a fine car.

Siegler backed out of the way as the driver opened his door and stepped out. Willi almost laughed when he saw how correct his assessment of the sergeant had been. He towered over the noncom, who moved around him gingerly, hurrying to open the back door. Siegler followed him.

"What is it, Constable?" Major Fitzroy asked.

"Just asking your sergeant how long you intend to be here, sir."

"I've been asking the same question for the last twenty minutes, Constable. I've just been told that it will be only a matter of minutes now."

"That's fine then, sir." Siegler stepped back as the sergeant closed the door. He waited until the driver had returned to his seat, then reached into the constable's gas mask bag and withdrew the Enfield pistol. He held it low, close against his leg. A glance at the roadblock told him that no one was looking in his direction. He leaned over and opened the door. Both Major Fitzroy and the driver turned toward him.

"Yes, Constable?" Fitzroy asked.

"I'd like to ask you something, Major, confidentially." Siegler looked meaningfully at the sergeant, who turned away. Siegler beckoned to the puzzled Fitzroy, who leaned closer.

Siegler hit him carefully and pushed him back into the far corner of the seat. The driver spun around to find the pistol pointed at his face as Siegler settled himself in the seat beside the unconscious officer.

"Start the car, Sergeant. This is official business." He punctuated the command by cocking the pistol. The sergeant started the motor.

"Now turn around and head south carefully," Siegler said. Conditioned not only by training, but by inclination, the driver made a careful U-turn and started down the southbound lane. He looked into the rear view mirror. "Eyes on the road, Sergeant. Keep to the left at the fork."

"What . . . ?" The sergeant had found his voice.

"Not now, Sergeant," Siegler said easily. "I'll explain when we get to Bitterne."

"Bitterne?"

"Right. Slow down and turn left at the road just ahead. You've done well, Sergeant. Sorry about the pistol, but I couldn't take any chances."

The driver was relieved by Siegler's tone. He turned left, his confidence returning. "Is it something about Major Fitzroy?"

"It is," Siegler said as he studied his map.

"But he's . . ."

Later, Sergeant. Once you're over the river and through Riverside Park, we'll turn south to Bitterne proper. I'll tell you when."

"Is it something to do with that explosion we heard earlier?" the driver persisted.

"Eyes on the road, and no more questions."

"Yes, sir."

Siegler searched for, and found, Major Fitzroy's wallet. A letter was folded in it. Siegler glanced at the envelope. A return address in Hamble. He dropped it on the seat beside him and went through the wallet. The usual amateurish pictures: a girl, smiling, pretty, standing alongside the major; another of the girl alone, standing on the bow of a large sailing boat; another of the girl standing self-consciously on a pier with an obviously isolated house in the background. The photographs were new, showing no signs of having been carried for long. He picked up the letter and read it through quickly. The photographs had been sent to the major in that envelope. Siegler smiled as he studied the postmark. The letter had been mailed three days earlier.

"Do you know Major Fitzroy's house in Hamble, Sergeant?"

"Yes, sir. I picked him up there earlier this morning."

"Good. As soon as you cross the river we'll find a place to stop. I'll need your help in finding our best route there."

"Hamble, sir? You said Bitterne—"

"He has a boat there, I understand."

"Yes, sir. I think so. There is a dock and a boathouse. Why, sir?"

Siegler ignored the question. He leaned forward and showed the sergeant one of the photographs. "Is this it?"

"Yes, sir."

Siegler leaned back contentedly.

They crossed the Itchen half a mile below Mansbridge where the tank had crossed such a short time earlier. The car was now moving through a large, wooded park fronting the eastern side of the river. Siegler looked out of the rear window and then ahead.

"Pull over here, Sergeant," he ordered.

Brigadier Fox watched the troopers lower the body of Sergeant Becker to the ground and place it alongside that of Falck. A sergeant appeared in the turret hatch, holding an oddly shaped object by its leather handle.

"Crammed full of these, sir, and four big ones."

"Put that thing back where you found it ... carefully, Sergeant. And clear the interior immediately," the brigadier ordered.

The sergeant acknowledged and dropped back into the turret.

"Thank goodness Evans didn't have to fire, Andrew. I think it would be best to clear the men from this area until the explosives team arrives."

"I certainly agree, sir. What about the man in the driver's compartment?"

"Are they quite certain he's dead?"

"No doubt of it, sir. From what we can see through the driving slit, he was thrown upward against the hood by the mine blasts. Cracked his head like an egg."

"Then leave him. There's nothing we can do for him now. Someone else will have to figure out how to get that hood open."

The infantry sergeant climbed from the hatch and dropped to the ground. He approached at the brigadier's summons.

"Is that all of them, Sergeant?" he gestured at the bodies.

"Yes, sir."

"Strange—what do you think about those explosives, Sergeant? None of them fused, I trust."

"No, sir. Not much chance of us still being here if they were. They'd have to be crazy to fuse anything that big inside. And only one of them was alive after the mines got them. He wouldn't have had the time what with shooting that bloody machine gun, sir." He paused to look at the covered bodies of the British soldiers lying apart from the Germans. He was about to continue, then thought better of it.

"I don't want anyone near that tank until the bomb squad arrives, Sergeant," the brigadier said.

The sergeant saluted and moved off shouting orders at the soldiers. Brigadier Fox and Colonel Blake turned the corner of the crematorium just as the quad transporter began to pull the heavy 3.7 across the field back to its emplacement. Colonel Evans was hurrying toward them.

"Bad news, sir. The man I had on the top floor has just reported that he thinks he saw a man running into the cemetery grounds shortly after the tank struck the mines. He said he only had a brief glimpse of him and isn't certain that it wasn't one of our own men. He had been signaling me at the back, so he didn't actually see where the man came from. By the time he got back to the window after the blasts, whoever it was was just disappearing behind one of the mausoleums."

"How could someone get in there without being seen by the men you had in the cemetery?"

"I'm afraid it would have been possible, sir. I had ordered those men to keep well to the west behind the building, out of the line of fire in the event that the hangar gun had to shoot."

"Then it's possible that one of them is still alive and on the loose. I was wondering why there were only three men in that tank. They abandoned one tank, and we know there were twelve of them. Nine men in the one at Woolston? Impossible."

"Perhaps they were whittled down a bit on the way up, sir. I can't think of any other reason for destroying that other tank." Colonel Evans said.

"Unless they have something else in mind and dropped the abandoned tank's crew off somewhere along the way," Colonel Blake said.

"Damn!" said the brigadier. "What have you done about this, Colonel?"

"I've ordered every available man to search the cemetery, stone by stone. He's got to be in there. The area was sealed only minutes after the tank struck the mines. I gave the word the moment the tank was secured."

"Find him, Colonel. I want him alive. What about those houses down along Mansbridge Road?"

"They're being searched now, sir."

"Good, but don't stop there. All houses around and near this post are to be searched. If he did get out, he should be easy to spot in that tank corps uniform. Knowing that, he's certain to try for a change of clothes. The roadblocks will remain fully manned until we find him. You've informed them, I trust?"

"Yes, sir. Sorry about all of this."

"It couldn't be helped, I suppose. Why didn't your man report what he had seen immediately?"

"He did, sir. He reported the man as one of ours and asked why he was running the wrong way. My man on the field telephone didn't report it to me until we had secured the tank. It was only minutes ago that I got the whole story and began the search. Dammit, sir. I thought we had done a good clean job."

"And so you did, Colonel. You saved the post. I'm sorry that we lost those men in the process, but . . . Keep me informed. I shall be at the signals lorry."

The brigadier and Colonel Blake watched the harried colonel walk away.

"We're in for a long day if they don't find him, sir."

"Blast! I thought it was finally over. Perhaps the man was mistaken?"

"Possibly."

"But you doubt it, eh?"

"Yes, sir."

"So do I. We'll be hearing from Winston soon, and then the fireworks will really start. Come along, I want to put a call through. I think that Edward has been cooling his heels at that roadblock long enough."

CHAPTER 35

The explosion at Woolston rattled the heavily curtained windows of the house in Hamble, waking Elizabeth Fitzroy. She lay listening to the echoes rumbling around her, and when they died away she listened to the silence. Her hand moved to the empty place beside her in the bed. Edward's sudden summons during the night worried her even though she knew that little could prove dangerous to him here in England, unless the Germans had begun to bomb. That had been her first thought earlier after the first sound of distant thunder across the quiet river, but then, too, there had been nothing but silence.

Elizabeth left the bed and crossed to the window. She was surprised when dim light brightened the room as she opened the blackout curtains. She must have fallen asleep soon after Edward had left. Poor Edward must be exhausted, she thought guiltily. Their lovemaking had been tender and prolonged, and they had talked for what had seemed hours until he had fallen asleep in midsentence. She had lain watching him until she had heard the telephone's insistent ring. Later, when he had gone, she had returned to bed expecting to spend the remainder of the night in sleepless worry and had fallen asleep instantly.

Elizabeth pulled the curtains open fully and looked out over the river at the cloudless sky. It was going to be a beautiful day and Edward had promised to return to her as quickly as possible. She was humming as she turned the taps of the bath.

When she had dressed, she busied herself straightening up the bedroom, and then went downstairs looking forward to the first cup of tea. She felt wonderful.

The inevitable lag between issuance of an order and its execution had allowed Willi Siegler to recross the Itchen unnoticed well before the cordon had been tightened around the Eastleigh area. The troops searching the cemetery and the surrounding fields had found no trace of a fourth man. The lookout was questioned again and again. He remained firm in his insistence that he had seen a man running into the cemetery. The men who had been stationed near the cemetery road were just as firm in their insistence that they had seen no one.

Brigadier Fox took no chances. He ordered an intensified search of the evacuated houses to the south of the airfield, knowing that if there had been another man who had managed to slip by the soldiers closing in behind the tank, his only possible route would have been back to Mansbridge Road. Open fields and tightly spaced British troops blocked all other possibilities. Troopers had already completed a house-to-house search of the civilian homes fronting Mansbridge Road whose back gardens faced the fringes of the airfield. Others had been moved quickly by lorry into the surrounding streets to complete an impassable net around the field, but by that time Willi Siegler was gone.

By the time they had discovered the body of the constable in the house on the deserted street south of the Mansbridge Road—and the discarded uniform of a British tank officer—Siegler was five miles to the south, nearing Hamble. He wore an officer's trench coat and hat. He drove the staff car carefully. A casual observer would have said that he was alone.

Brigadier Fox waited impatiently while Colonel Blake spoke to the officer in charge at the roadblock above Swathling station. As the brigadier watched, Colonel Blake suddenly began to run toward him.

"What now, Andrew?" the brigadier called through the open window.

"Bad news, sir. Very bad, I'm afraid. I've ordered the lieutenant back there to pass the word."

"What, Andrew? What?"

"Edward's car was parked just below the block waiting to be passed through. According to the lieutenant he left more than half an hour ago. His driver made a U-turn and drove off to the south. The lieutenant seems to think that Edward received a message of some sort; another man entered the car and drove off with him."

"For God's sake, Andrew. You can't mean our German?"

"I'm afraid that it would seem so, sir. The lieutenant said that the man who left with Edward was a constable."

Tom Peters was tired. He pedaled his bicycle into the long driveway of the Fitzroy house. Only fifteen minutes earlier he had been preparing to leave LDV headquarters on the Hamble foreshore, having completed his night's patrol along the river, when he read the general alert, a carefully worded order to all army, police, and LDV units to stop and hold the occupants of a military staff car. There was a description of the occupants:

Major Edward Fitzroy; Sergeant Ian Goodall, driver; and a third, unidentified man, possibly in constable's uniform and considered armed and dangerous. The officer and his driver were considered to be hostages. There was no further information on the third man. As he read, Mr. Peters thought immediately of the young Mrs. Fitzroy alone in the isolated house on the river.

"I'm going up to the Fitzroy house, Alf," Peters had said to the only other man in the headquarters. "That young woman shouldn't be alone up there, just in case something should happen. A constable's uniform? What do you suppose it's all about?"

"I haven't the foggiest. As usual they tell us as little as possible. Maybe it's a deserter? Why don't you ring the Fitzroy house from here? Might save yourself the trip."

"No," Tom Peters said after some consideration. "If the army's already rung through, I don't want to frighten her into thinking I've heard something. I'd rather be there if I have to tell her myself. I'm usually struck dumb on the damned telephone anyway."

"Nice of you to be thinking about her, Tom. I'd come along with you, but you know I can't leave the phone."

"Not the time for a bloody convention anyway, Alf."

"Want me to keep an eye on your gun, Tom?" Alf said as Peters walked toward the door. As he expected, he got no answer. Tom Peters' shotgun was his prize possession. No one in the LDV group had ever been allowed to handle the weapon. Alf was smiling as he looked out the window at the old man pedaling off toward the winding hill of the narrow High Street.

As he approached the Fitzroy house, Tom Peters was wondering how to tell the young woman, if it should be necessary. He got off the bicycle, readjusted the shotgun slung across his back, and walked toward the house. He stopped when the front door opened and Elizabeth Fitzroy ran down the front steps.

"Oh, Mr. Peters, have you heard anything about Edward?"

So they had called her. He was glad he had come.

"No, Ma'am," he said softly. "I just heard about it myself. I didn't like to think that you were up here all alone." He stood helpless as tears streamed down the young woman's face.

"Thank you," she said and suddenly buried her face in his shoulder. Peters' embarrassment faded quickly as he comforted her.

"There, there," he said. "Nothing will happen to the major, Ma'am."

Elizabeth looked up into the old man's face. He forced a smile and dabbed clumsily at her eyes with a spotless, carefully ironed handkerchief.

"Thank you," Elizabeth said, and stepped back. "I'm sorry."

"Nonsense," the old man said, attempting to control the tears he could feel welling up in his own eyes.

Elizabeth took his hand. "Please come inside. I'll make some tea."

"That would be nice," he replied.

Siegler had gotten specific directions from the sergeant before he killed him. At first he had toyed with the idea of allowing the soldier to drive him to Hamble but soon abandoned it as foolish. The issue was decided for him when, after stopping the car in Shoreside Park on the east bank of the Itchen, the sergeant had begun to recover from the shock of Siegler's takeover and to have second thoughts about the constable's status. They went over the map and then, completely forgetting about the pistol, the sergeant demanded to see some identification. Seconds later he was dead.

Siegler worked quickly. He knew that it wouldn't be long before the major was reported missing and that even the British fools might connect that disappearance with the abortive attack on the airfield. Willi had no idea whether he had been seen when the tank struck the mines. To play it safe, he would assume he had been and plan accordingly. He would also assume that he had been seen entering the major's car. If he had been seen, and their search turned up the constable's body, they would put two and two together.

He glanced at his watch and then at the map. He was depending on that very thing that had allowed the storm group to get as far as the targets—the time lag between suspicion and action.

The English had obviously known about the attacks both at Woolston and Eastleigh. Either the colonel or his men had been captured and had talked. Willi knew that he should also assume that they knew about the routes and means planned for the escape. He would have to find his own way back to France.

After disposing of the driver's body in the deserted wood he had removed Major Fitzroy's jacket, tie, and shirt. By slitting the back seam of the jacket, the collar of the shirt, and the hat band, he managed to make them fit acceptably. He struggled into the officer's trench coat and felt that he was effectively disguised to all but close inspection. Major Fitzroy, now gagged and tied tightly with strips torn from the constable's discarded shirt, lay on the floor below the back seat, covered partially by the constable's tunic. The major was still unconscious.

Siegler drove carefully along quiet, secondary roads. Traffic was sparse and no one passing paid any attention to him. On the outskirts of Lowford, he turned south. While passing through the quiet town of

Hound, he heard the first signs of Major Fitzroy's return to consciousness. He risked speeding up slightly and soon turned into what he hoped was the road marked on the map by the sergeant, Satchell Lane. When he crossed above the rail line, he knew that he had been right. According to the map he was now less than three-quarters of a mile from the major's house and his means of escape to France, if the boat was really there. He began looking for a secluded spot to stop the car. It was time for a talk with the major.

Major Fitzroy's uncomprehending eyes were open when Siegler pulled the constable's tunic away from the bound officer's face.

"Good morning, Major," Siegler said pleasantly. "Sorry about all of this, but I'm afraid it was necessary. I'm going to remove the gag, but first I want you to understand something. You are to talk only when I say so and then quietly. Should you forget, you won't get a second chance." Leaning over, Siegler touched the major's throat lightly with his knife. "Nod if you agree." The major nodded. "Good," Siegler said. He slipped the blade under the gag and cut. Major Fitzroy winced as the sharp blade cut into his cheek.

"Nothing to worry about, Major. It's only a scratch."

Fitzroy looked up at the smiling man. God, he thought, I'll have to be careful. This one is a sadist. He's actually hoping I'll call out. Who in blazes is he? He kept quiet, feeling the blood trickling down his cheek.

"Now, Major, we haven't time for a long chat, so I'll get on with it. We're not far from your home in Hamble." He saw the major's reaction as he continued. "Remember, this is no time for heroism. You may as well answer since I'll be going there with you or without you. Is your wife there?"

Oh, God, Elizabeth, thought Fitzroy. He nodded.

"Any servants?"

Fitzroy shook his head negatively. Siegler reached down on the seat beside him and picked up one of the photographs, showing it to the major. "Is this boat there?"

Major Fitzroy hesitated. It had come to him suddenly. This man was one of the raiders! He forced himself to nod again. He would have to appear to cooperate for Elizabeth's sake. He couldn't leave her to this desperate man. He saw immediately what the German had in mind. He wanted the *Seraph* to escape to France. With the evacuation going on he had a good chance of making it if he ever got it to sea. He now knew the reason why *he* was still alive: The bastard needed help with the boat, and in order for him to give it, he would eventually have to be untied. The thought calmed him.

Above him, Siegler sighed in obvious relief. The next question was now the most important. "Is it seaworthy? Speak out."

"There's no auxiliary motor."

"Is it in the water?"

"Yes."

"You have sails?"

"Yes."

"Good. Can it be sailed to France?"

"France? It could. Not alone, of course. And you'd be crazy to try it in the daylight. You'd most likely be blown out of the water by your own air force."

"My own . . . so you've guessed." Siegler's face darkened. "How did you learn about us?"

"I heard about some sort of raid when I spoke to the officer at the roadblock. Did you parachute in?" Fitzroy hoped the German would accept the lie and was relieved when the man shrugged.

"Perhaps, Major. I take it that you would suggest that I wait until dark?"

"I don't suggest anything. You have the knife."

"And this." Siegler reached down for the Enfield pistol and placed the barrel between the major's eyes. "I can almost hear you thinking, Major. We both know that they'll send someone down here to inquire when they discover you're missing. We'll be well on our way by then. Where were you going?"

"London."

"Then it's not likely that anyone they send down will think about the boat. It may be risky, but I'll have to chance it. We'll have to chance it. All of us."

"You can't handle a boat of that size by yourself. It would be doubtful even if you knew how to sail her, and you obviously don't. If you lay one finger on my wife, you'll have to kill me."

"Don't be a bloody fool, Major. As you've already guessed, I'm a German officer. She won't be harmed as long as you both follow orders. I take it that she is an accomplished sailor?"

"Better than I."

"Fine. You don't seem to be listening. I said all of us were going, that includes the woman."

"And what happens to us in the unlikely event that we get to France?"

"That won't be up to me, Major, but at least you'll be alive. Settle for that. I have the knife and the gun, but I could kill you easily without either, so forget your plans. If you should try anything, perhaps you'll live long enough to watch me kill the woman."

"She's going to have a child. Leave her here."

"Is she? Congratulations, Major, if what you say is true. All the more reason for you to be careful."

I'll be careful, you bastard, thought Major Fitzroy, and one of us will be dead before we reach the Channel. The German was confident. Confident men get careless.

Siegler smiled down at him. "I think that I shall have to watch you carefully, Major. You're thinking again." He put the car in gear.

Tom Peters sought for some way to reassure Elizabeth Fitzroy and was angry with himself for not being able to find the right words. He watched her as she busied herself at the stove and he sat self-consciously at the table near the kitchen window.

"Will you have milk, Mr. Peters?"

"Yes, Ta."

"Please don't feel uncomfortable, Mr. Peters. I can't tell you how grateful I am that you were thoughtful enough to come all the way out here and allow me to cry on your shoulder."

"I didn't come here to worry you half to death, Ma'am. I just didn't like to think of you being here all alone imagining all sorts of things."

"Elizabeth," she said, placing a steaming cup in front of him. "My name is Elizabeth. Please don't feel that you must be so formal. I think that you are a truly wonderful man. You remind me of my own father." She was smiling at him gratefully.

Suddenly she turned away. "Listen," she said.

"What is it?"

"I hear a car. It's coming up the driveway."

The old man rose and followed as Elizabeth rushed toward the front door.

"It's Edward's car!" she said excitedly.

The old man followed when she opened the front door and rushed out. He watched her speak to the man in the driver's seat and then open the back door and climb inside the car. The driver was not the major, Peters noted, but at least he was an army officer—but the back seemed to be empty and he could no longer see the young woman. Puzzled, he walked toward the car. As he neared it, the front door opened, and the officer stepped out, a huge man in an ill-fitting uniform. Peters hesitated, thinking about the shotgun leaning against the wall near the kitchen door, but he knew that it was too late to go back and get it when he saw the man walking toward him. He saw the trousers as the man approached: black, too short; a constable's trousers. When his eyes moved back up to the man's face, Tom Peters saw the pistol pointed at him.

"Help the woman with the major. He's still a bit groggy." Willi Siegler was disturbed by the old man's calm appraisal of him. "Move!" he added angrily.

"What are you son? A deserter? This isn't going to help you. . . ."

"Get a move on, Grandad. Do what I told you. Get the major and the woman inside."

Peters said nothing else. He brushed past Siegler to the car. Major Fitzroy sat on the floor below the seat, his hands tied behind him. Elizabeth was sobbing against his bare shoulder. The major was about to speak when the old man whispered, "Does he know that they're looking for you . . . and him?"

The major answered, "No."

"Good. I think it's best he doesn't find out. I have a shotgun in the kitchen. We shall have to try and keep him out of there."

The old man helped Elizabeth out of the car and then reached in to help the bound officer. "He has a knife as well as the gun," Fitzroy whispered as he stepped unsteadily to the ground.

"Won't help him a bit if . . ."

"Stop the bloody nattering and move," Willi said from behind them. "Wait." He turned and studied the driveway. "Can you drive, Grandad?"

"Yes."

"Then get in and drive us around to the back of the house. You two get back inside."

The old man hesitated. That would bring them near the kitchen door.

"Do what he says, Mr. Peters," Fitzroy said. He had no doubt that the German would kill the old man if he hesitated too long. Peters shrugged and got into the driver's seat while Elizabeth helped the major into the back. Willi climbed in beside the old man, handing him the ignition key. "Slowly, Grandad," he said.

When the car was hidden from the main road, Siegler pocketed the keys and ordered them out.

"Inside," he said, after a careful inspection of the grounds and the dock.

Elizabeth was no longer crying. She moved quickly ahead of them and opened the back door, standing beside it when the others entered. She pushed the door closed at Siegler's order, not moving. Her body hid the shotgun.

"Into the front," Siegler motioned with the pistol. Major Fitzroy and the old man obeyed instantly. Siegler's attention was on them as Elizabeth followed. He hadn't seen the shotgun. He herded them into the middle of the parlor and then closed the front door.

"Do you know anything about boats, Grandad?"

"More than some."

"Then you're a lucky old man. Upstairs, all of you." Siegler followed them. He saw the telephone but decided against cutting the wire. Someone might try to call the girl and report that they had been unable to get through.

"Can I untie my husband's hands?" Elizabeth asked.

"Not just yet. This is a nice house, Major. I hope you have as good taste in clothing."

"Most of it is packed," Fitzroy said.

"You won't be needing dinner clothes. Just show me what you wear on the boat. But first, are there any weapons in this house?"

"Of course not," Elizabeth answered quickly. Too quickly, Major Fitzroy thought, but Siegler didn't pursue it. She opened the door of the master bedroom.

"Over to the bed and sit down." Siegler gestured with the pistol. When they had obeyed, he said, "Where?"

The major indicated a closet door. Siegler opened it. "Just what I was looking for, Major." He began to shrug his way out of the trench coat. "Start undressing, Major." He reached into the closet and removed a pair of well-worn trousers and a roll neck sweater. "Put these on."

"My hands are tied," Fitzroy said.

"So they are. Help him with it, Grandad. He can put the sweater on later. You're in luck too, old man. This place is like a bloody department store. When you've finished with him you put this on." Another sweater was caught by the old man as Willi added. "Keep you warm on the way over."

"The way over where?" Peters asked.

"France, Grandad, France."

"Why would a deserter want to be going to France?"

"He's not a deserter, Mr. Peters. He's a German officer," Fitzroy said.

The old man looked at Siegler with obvious surprise: "A German. How . . . ?"

"Get on with it," Siegler snapped.

"Acts like one," Mr. Peters said.

Willi Siegler was pleased by the major's unquestioning acceptance of his officer status. He laughed at the old man. "It's too bad that this one isn't over there with your army, Major. A few more like him, and you might have made a fight of it."

As the old man removed the major's shoes and then began to remove his trousers, Siegler pulled the tie from his collar and removed his shirt. He saw Elizabeth watching him as he pulled the sweater over his head. He smiled at her. She could make the trip a pleasant one.

"Now you, Liebchen," he said "Come over here and pick out what you need. I want you to keep warm. Particularly you."

Elizabeth didn't hesitate. She walked past Siegler and took her sailing gear from their hangers. She felt the man's eyes boring into her. "Where can I change?" she asked.

"Where can you change?" Siegler laughed loudly. "What do you think you have that that I haven't seen before?" He reached over and fondled her breast. Elizabeth jumped back, startled. A new element was being introduced that she hadn't allowed herself to think of before.

The old man had turned, his body hiding the major's view, and he had seen Elizabeth's reaction. He stared angrily at the German. Siegler looked back at the old man, amused. "All right. I'll go along with it for now." He glanced at his watch. "In the closet, Liebchen. You stay out of there, Grandad. The major wouldn't mind, but I would."

Elizabeth entered the closet warily and shut the door firmly. Siegler smiled. "When she's finished, you put all of this into the closet neatly.' He indicated the discarded clothing. "It might help you keep your mind on business."

When they were dressed, Siegler ordered them back down the stairs.

"We'll need food. I'm sick of British field rations. If that's the sort of stuff you feed your soldiers, Major, I'm surprised they have the strength to run."

"We haven't . . ." Elizabeth began.

"Into the kitchen," Siegler ordered.

Elizabeth moved quickly ahead of them, keeping her body between Siegler and the shotgun. He looked past her at the table and asked, "What were you doing here, Grandad?"

"Inspecting blackout preparations."

"Hear that, Major? Looks as if they were having a nice cozy cuppa. You'd better watch out for Grandad. I've got the feeling he's a better man than you are. I've also got the feeling that if I have to kill anyone it's going to be him."

"I could use a drink," Major Fitzroy said, attempting to keep the man's attention away from the side of the room where the shotgun stood.

Siegler looked at the major. "Where?" he asked.

The major nodded at a cupboard well away from Elizabeth and the door. Siegler walked over to it and removed a full bottle of whiskey, standing among numerous tins of food. "Good idea, Major. A drink might help you find your balls, but it will have to wait."

He looked at Elizabeth. "Sorry, Liebchen, that was rather crude. Still, considering the major, you may not even know what I was talking about.

"You, Grandad," he said to the old man, "put some of those tins of food in that wash basin. Mind you take enough."

Elizabeth backed closer to the wall as Peters filled the wash basin. When he had finished, Siegler walked to the door. Pulling Elizabeth out of the way, he opened it. The prisoners expected the shotgun to fall when the base of the door struck the butt. It didn't.

"Out," Siegler ordered.

They moved out ahead of him and stopped as the German walked to the edge of the house and studied the road.

"As soon as I can," the old man whispered rapidly to the major, "I'll try for the shotgun."

"Wait until he unties my hands," Fitzroy said.

"Lead the way, Major," Siegler said. "You go ahead. The old man and the woman right behind you. You won't mind that, will you, Grandad?" He watched as Peters fell in alongside Elizabeth. "Blackout preparations?" Again Siegler laughed loudly. "Sorry, old boy, but now you'll have to share her with me."

Peters felt Elizabeth shudder and saw the major tense angrily. Something would have to be done quickly. He squeezed her arm reassuringly as they moved onto the wooden pier.

"Step aside," Siegler ordered when the old man had opened the door to the boathouse. He looked inside and was at the same time elated and vaguely angry at the evidence of privilege. The well-kept yacht gleamed in the light of the reflecting river flowing beyond the open end of the boathouse. Siegler glanced up at the slotted roof through which the masts thrust up into a rapidly lightening sky, the topmost fittings rocking against the shining wood.

The foreshortened photographs he had taken from the major's wallet had given him no real indication of the boat's size. Siegler's eyes followed its trim lines from the bow to the stern. It filled the entire slip, and Siegler had judged the boathouse to be at least fifty feet long.

"How far is it to Boulogne?" he asked Major Fitzroy.

"I'm not certain. I'll have to check the chart," Fitzroy lied.

"Inside," Siegler ordered. They walked ahead of him through the door. Siegler closed it and came up behind the major, his knife now in his hand. "Stand still, Major, or you might lose a hand. You're going to need both of them. You have work to do," he said as he cut through the tightly knotted cloth binding the officer. "Change into that sweater and then get the chart. . . ."

As soon as his fands fell free, Major Fitzroy pivoted around and hit Siegler. He was already committed to the attempt when he realized that he was foolishly premature. After having been bound so long, there was little feeling in his hands or arms. He could hardly raise them.

Siegler was more surprised than hurt, and the knife dropped from his hands. He stepped back and hit the major without real anger, and then again, carefully. Fitzroy fell heavily, striking his head on the pier with a violence that made the German look down at him with disgusted anxiety until he began to stir. He needed the man.

Siegler had been expecting the major to try. The insults had been planned to make the British officer angry enough to try, to get it over with so that he could establish his own physical superiority. But he hadn't expected it to happen so soon. The major lay at his feet. Elizabeth knelt beside him crying softly. Siegler leaned down and picked up the knife; the pistol was in his other hand. The major's eyes opened, looking at him dazedly. Siegler hadn't realized that he was pointing the pistol at the stunned man.

"Please don't . . ." Elizabeth began.

Siegler looked down at the girl as if in indecision.

"Please," she repeated.

Siegler replaced the knife in his belt and lowered the pistol. He had no intention of killing the officer just yet.

"Very well, Liebchen, but it will be up to you to see to it that he doesn't try any of that sort of foolishness again. If he does . . ."

Siegler motioned to the old man, "Help him up, Grandad."

Tom Peters had watched the exchange tensely, ready to fling himself at the huge German in what he knew would be a futile attempt to help the major. He relaxed slightly when he noticed that the pistol had never been cocked; that the German obviously had no intention of shooting. He was simply playing on the young woman's terror. Someone had to handle the yacht, and the major was a known quantity.

He watched Siegler lean down and retrieve the knife while his own thoughts returned to the shotgun lying against the wall of the kitchen in the main house. The German was acting rationally enough now, but when he finally realized that the sails had been stowed, that it would take at least an hour of steady work by a crew of fit men to make the boat ready, he might . . . Damn!

Peters knew that his one chance would be to move quickly through the door and up to the obscuring shrubbery lining the shore. If he could then make it across the narrow stretch of lawn to the house—if he could make it to the kitchen—the shotgun would equalize things. Peters also knew that even if he were killed and the two young people managed somehow to get the yacht under way, even then the German would have no chance of getting to France. The yacht would be recognized and reported by the coast watch before it reached the Hamble foreshore. Two and two would be put together and the navy would be waiting at the mouth of the Hamble. Thank God the German seemed to be unaware that he and the major were the subjects of an intensive search.

But Peters had no doubt how the German would react when he realized that he was trapped. He looked at the girl and made his decision.

Siegler interrupted his racing thoughts. "Wake up, Grandad. I told you to help him to his feet."

Tom Peters started toward the major and Elizabeth. Satisfied, Siegler turned his attention back to the yacht. The old man didn't hesitate. He ran with surprising swiftness to the door. Reaching it, he was forced to pause; the door opened inward and was slightly warped. He pulled at the knob desperately, and it sprang free. As he moved behind the open door, Siegler, only momentarily caught unaware, fired the pistol once. He smiled satanically at the stunned girl as they both heard the unmistakable sound of a body falling to the wooden planking of the narrow pier beyond the door. Elizabeth began to sob convulsively and buried her face in her husband's shoulder, shielding his body with her own.

Siegler ran toward the door. "Stay where you are," he said to the girl with unmistakable menace.

Siegler had fired calmly and deliberately at the door just as the old man had moved behind it. He knew that he couldn't miss. Exiting the narrow door kept the man, seen or unseen, in the center of a virtual bull's eye. He'd fired low.

Peters had glanced over his shoulder just as he moved behind the door and had seen the pistol beginning to line up on it. He crouched down. The bullet, slowed and deflected by its passage through the wood, creased across his forehead as he ducked into it. An inch more and it would have entered his left temple. Incredibly, he remained conscious as he fell onto the planks of the pier. Blood streamed into his eyes as, fighting unconsciousness and terror, he dragged himself across the pier and unhesitatingly dived over its edge into the shallow water. The cold water cleared his head somewhat. He felt no pain, only a sort of disembodied vagueness, a difficulty in concentrating. He was aware that he was as much in danger of drowning as he was from the German's bullets.

He heard Siegler pause at the door of the boathouse. Forcing himself into movement, he pushed his way beneath the pier. He was concerned with the weakness of his limbs as he grasped one of the slippery pilings. Blood continued to run from his wound, darkening the sluggish water. He washed his eyes clear and listened to Siegler's heavy tread as he crossed the planking. Peters waited as he fought the growing acceptance of the inevitability of death. There was one chance, and he preferred death by drowning to a thirty-eight-caliber bullet. Peters inhaled deeply and let go of the piling. He lay in the water face down, his arms floating loosely in front of him. The dead man's float, he thought fatalistically, as he closed his eyes and the cold water bit into his head wound.

Siegler had been surprised to find the pier empty, but the trail of blood on the planking made it evident what had happened. The old man had been hit badly from the look of it but had managed somehow to regain his feet only to fall over the edge of the narrow pier. Siegler glanced back into the boathouse; Elizabeth still lay sobbing over the major.

He looked down at the water. Blood drifting from beneath the pier covered it. He dropped to his knees and leaned over the edge. Steadying himself with one hand, with the pistol in the other, he lowered his upper body down and looked cautiously beneath the pier.

He saw the body immediately, floating face down in the bloody water. Siegler aimed the pistol and then paused as the old man began to sink from sight. He pulled himself back up onto the planking, thankful that there had been no need for another shot. Inside the boathouse, the report had been muffled by the walls. Outside, in the quiet morning, it might be heard despite the isolation of the house.

There was a possibility that even the one muffled shot had been heard. Siegler glanced around him; nothing stirred. He rose, and ran back to the boathouse.

The old man held his breath until the last possible moment. He felt himself beginning to sink. He could wait no longer. He still had the presence of mind to break the water quietly as he surfaced.

Peters opened his eyes expecting to see the pistol, but nothing showed between the pier's lower edge and the water. He clung to the piling thankfully and listened to the German running back toward the boathouse. The old man fought unsuccessfully to control his gasping, but he knew that he hadn't been heard when the door of the boathouse slammed shut.

His head throbbed painfully now. Touching the wound gingerly, he followed the furrow across his forehead. It didn't seem too deep despite the copious bleeding, but he was weakening rapidly. He had to get to the house as quickly as he could to dress the wound before attempting to take on the German. There should be enough time. Even if the German didn't notice the lack of sails, it would still take considerable time to warp the yacht out of its slip without the assistance of an auxiliary motor. Suddenly he thought of the telephone which both he—and apparently the German—had forgotten. He forced himself into movement.

The muffled voice of the German soldier came from the boathouse and Peters heard a splash behind him as a mooring line was dropped into the water beside the yacht's hull, rocking against its slip less than ten feet from him. He kept to the protection of the pier, struggled as quietly as he could to its landward end, and crawled up the sloping bank to the low bushes lining the shore.

When he was certain that he could no longer be seen from the boathouse, he stood up and ran at a stumbling crouch across the rear lawn to the house and through the kitchen door.

Fighting the urge to sit down, Peters reached for the shotgun and released the safety after checking the load. He then crossed to the sink, leaned over it and let cold water run across the wound. It was still bleeding dangerously. He found clean towels stacked neatly in a cupboard above the sink. He tore one lengthwise and folded it double. Pressing it gingerly against the wound, he used the other half to secure it in place by tying it tightly at the back of his head.

Fighting a sudden dizziness, Tom Peters stumbled into the parlor and picked up the telephone.

CHAPTER 36

"Well?" Brigadier Fox said with more sharpness than he had intended.

"No word yet, sir," Colonel Blake answered.

"Sorry, Andrew. I didn't mean to snap." The brigadier shook his head exasperatedly. "These Germans have made us look like fools. First they cross seventy miles of this country unhindered, and now one of them simply walks casually through a cordon of troops, kills a constable, drives away in one of our staff cars with my aide as a hostage, and disappears. Damn it, Andrew, the man who's taken Edward won't hesitate to kill him, if he hasn't already. The body count along their route is becoming frightening. Were you able to get through to Elizabeth? I don't like her insistence on remaining in Hamble alone. I'm going to send someone down there."

"The line was occupied, sir."

"What? Who could she be calling at a time like this?"

"Her mother, perhaps?"

"Perhaps, but you did say that you had asked her to keep the line open?"

"I did, sir."

"I don't like the smell of it, Andrew. Elizabeth wouldn't disregard... Have them break into the connection at once as subtly as possible. I want to be certain that it *is* Elizabeth using that telephone."

The two men's eyes met. "Do you think that it might be the German, sir?" Colonel Blake asked.

"It sounds farfetched, and I hope to God that it is that, but it is conceivable. Edward was carrying photographs of Elizabeth and the house. He showed them to me in Dover. Good Lord! The *Seraph* was also in the pictures."

"Sir?"

"Edward's yacht. If the Hun has discovered that Edward has that boat, and has learned or suspects that he can expect no help from those men in the Albert Road... Get through to southern command. Have them order the nearest forces available to move in on that house. Explain my reasoning. It should be enough to get them moving. And for God's sake, Andrew, make it clear that they are to approach quietly. Have them inform the navy. The Hamble River should be locked at once. When you've done that, meet me at the car. We're going down there ourselves. Even if I'm wrong, I don't want that child alone in that isolated place and we're certainly doing no good mucking about up here."

Minutes later Colonel Blake rushed up to the brigadier, who was waiting impatiently in the staff car.

"I'm sorry to say that you were right, sir. The German is at the Fitzroy house now. Elizabeth and Edward are both with him. They're still alive, thank the Lord. The telephone was being used by a civilian the first time I called. An LDV man who had been shot and left for dead by the German. It isn't clear to me how he was able to get to the telephone, but he did, and managed to ring his local defense volunteer headquarters. They in turn alerted Southern command. Units from air service training—a pilot training center not far from the house—are moving in. The navy has detached a picket destroyer to cover the Hamble, and an MTB is moving from Southampton water and should be starting up the river now."

"Thank God they're still alive."

"There's more, sir. The civilian had a hidden shotgun and is now armed with it. He intends to try to take the German."

"The damned fool will get all of them killed."

"Forgive me for being blunt, sir, but it seems that the man gave a rather convincing argument that they will most certainly be killed if he doesn't try. The German needs Elizabeth and Edward to help him sail the boat. Apparently he knows little if anything about sailing. The LDV man said that Edward is going to warp the boat out into the river without the sails being bent on. Without an auxiliary, which I understand is dismantled, they will most certainly go aground. When that happens . . ."

"I'm all for him trying, sir. The man is a retired sergeant-major of the Royal Sussex, and no stranger to firearms. Our troops will have to move in cautiously or risk the German panicking. The sergeant-major thinks that the filthy Hun won't hesitate to kill them when he finds he's trapped."

"But you said that he'd been shot."

"He described it as a minor head wound. Apparently the German only grazed him. I had no time to get the details. All I can say is thank God he's there and armed. As he said, the German believes him to be dead. If he's careful, he has the element of surprise on his side. A shotgun is a deadly weapon in the hands of an experienced man . . ." Colonel Blake paused.

The brigadier had turned away, his hand covering his eyes. "Are you all right, sir?" the colonel asked anxiously.

The brigadier looked at Blake. "A retired sergeant-major, not back in the service now that we're at war, therefore an elderly man—with a head wound—up against a young, brutal, highly trained storm trooper. A wounded old man who is the only one at present who might prevent the deaths of my niece and her husband. I don't mind admitting that I was saying a silent prayer."

"I've already said mine, sir."

"Thank you, Andrew. Now . . . please have signals clear the road to Northam Bridge. Arrange for an escort and see to it that we're kept informed of anything that happens; anything. If that Hun harms either of those two young people, I shall personally put the rope around his neck when he's hung."

Peters hung up the telephone and left the house through the front door. His head now throbbed painfully and the loss of blood left him with a trembling weakness that had begun to worry him. But the familiar shotgun felt reassuring in his hand as he moved at a crouch toward the boathouse, even though his legs shook with the effort.

He approached on the side opposite the pier, where he knew that a narrow catwalk stretched along the entire length of the outer wall of the boathouse. His plan was to make his way along the catwalk to the open river end of the boathouse and work his way back inside behind the yacht. He had dismissed the idea of a frontal assault through the pierside door. He had to get close to the German. The shotgun was a devastating weapon at close range and he had no desire to be framed in that doorway again as a backlighted target for an obviously proficient marksman. He would have to move into position and wait for a time when both Elizabeth and the major would be clear of the spreading shot.

He climbed unsteadily up to the catwalk. Pressing his back against the wall, he peered cautiously around the corner, and then, after slinging the shotgun over his outer shoulder and holding it carefully against his body, began to edge along the narrow platform. He soon found that his frowning concentration was making him dizzy and he felt the beginnings of nausea. He stopped, flattening himself against the wood. Beyond the wall he heard Siegler giving curt orders. He gathered that they were preparing to start the petrol winch at the river end of the interior to warp the boat out o its shelter. Peters hadn't much time.

The nausea passed. Keeping his eyes down he continued to the end of the catwalk where he paused to unsling the shotgun. With his finger on the forward trigger he turned unsteadily around the corner of the building. The river lapped at the piling below him. Nothing moved on the water or on the opposite shore.

Peters dropped to his knees as he came to the entrance, almost falling from the catwalk as the dizziness returned. When he had steadied himself he peered into the boathouse cautiously. The interior was lighted brilliantly by the low sun hanging just above the opposite shore. The yacht, now free of its mooring lines, moved restlessly in the slip. There was no one on her decks. He heard Siegler shout an order from behind the yacht and now knew that the German was on the pier somewhere near the bows.

Peters moved quickly into the interior, behind the protecting bulk of the boat. He raised his head slowly until he could see across the stern. Major Fitzroy, obviously unsteady on his feet, fumbled with the starting lanyard of the petrol winch motor near the edge of the pier directly opposite from where Peters crouched. The old man rejected the idea of attempting to attract the major's attention. In the officer's dazed condition, he might inadvertently give it away. Elizabeth was somewhere out of sight, probably somewhere near the watchful eye of the German.

After several attempts the winch motor caught and whined noisily. The major then began to wind a line around the winch haltingly. As Peters watched, Elizabeth came into his view and, after a word to the major, bent down and picked up a heavy coil of line. The old man could see the expression of anguished concern on her face. With good reason, Peters realized. The major was moving with the uncoordinated, robot-like slowness of a man suffering from the effects of concussion.

There was no sign of the German, who was somewhere at the other end of the boathouse. Peters knew that it was time for him to move. He reached down and attempted to remove his shoes, but his earlier immersion in the water had made the laces impossible to remove. He gave up the attempt when the dizziness returned and his wound throbbed painfully. He crawled along the pier, keeping below the bulk of the yacht, toward its inner end.

He stopped beneath the bows and cursed under his breath. The unsecured boat, floating free in the slip, had ridden forward. The long bowsprit was now almost touching the inner facing of the landward wall of the boathouse, effectively blocking the way to the other side of the slip. It would have been a dangerously exposed passage even if the yacht had been securely moored; now it was impossible. There was no way, Peters realized, for him to climb over the bobbing bowsprit without being seen and heard.

He began to edge backward, knowing that he would have to cross over the boat itself. It was something that he had wanted to avoid. There was a two-foot gap between the pier and the yacht, and its deck level was another two or three above that of the pier. Still, the noise of the winch motor should cover the noise he would make, so there was nothing for it but to try.

Amidships, he paused, wondering if he still had the strength to make it. He decided fatalistically that there was only one way to find out and reslung the shotgun across his back. As he prepared to make the leap, the yacht stirred and began to move toward him! If Tom Peters had never been a true believer, he became one at that instant. The yacht, urged by the restless river, bumped against the pier, and he simply stepped up, steadying himself with the lifeline running along the boat's side. He was congratulating himself prematurely when his dizziness returned just as the yacht began to move back into the center of the slip. He was halfway over the lifeline when he found himself falling heavily to the boat's deck. Blood ran down into his eyes from the reopened wound. He reached into his pocket with difficulty and finally found his soggy handkerchief. He used it to wipe his eyes clear and then reached up to tighten the knot of the makeshift bandage.

Peters lay quietly for a moment until his head settled back into its now familiar, painful throb. He was thankful for the noise of the winch, but even more thankful that the shotgun had survived the fall and that he was still alive. It had come to him as he lay there that, for the first time he could remember, he had forgotten that the safety was off. He wondered how he had managed not only to survive the fall, but to do so without blowing his own head off.

He began to crawl along the deck. When he reached the end of the cabin, he looked across the forward deck. Seeing nothing, he continued to crawl across the deck and looked back along the pier.

Siegler stood near the winch with the major and Elizabeth. The pistol was in his hand. The old man couldn't hear what was being said, but apparently the major was being ordered to stand by the winch, and Peters saw him nod when the German gestured at Elizabeth with the pistol. Peters noted angrily that Siegler was smiling as the young woman, struggling under the weight of the heavy coil of rope, stumbled along behind him, a look of stunned resignation on her face.

Peters moved back to the opposite side of the cabin and waited, his finger on the trigger. He urged them on silently, beginning to worry about his condition. The fall had caused the pain in his head to increase, and he found that he was having difficulty in seeing clearly.

Elizabeth stepped up onto the deck. Peters saw her turn and look back toward her husband. Siegler was close behind her.

"Please," she said, "he's hurt. He doesn't seem to know where he is. Let me handle the winch."

Siegler ignored her plea. "Is this going to work?"

"I don't know. It should. We brought it in this way once. It has to be done slowly. . . ."

"Where does this rope go?"

"On the bitt near the bows."

As the old man listened he glanced up at the masts. Elizabeth had pluck. She and the major were going through with it. The German still hadn't caught on. He seemed unaware that once the yacht left the protection of the boathouse and got into the river current it would be helpless.

"Where are the sails?" Siegler asked as if he had read the old man's thoughts.

Peters held his breath.

"In the sail locker over there," Elizabeth answered calmly.

"When will you put them up?"

"Once we get outside."

The German was apparently satisfied by the answer. "Do what you have to do with that rope," he ordered.

Elizabeth uncoiled the line as she hurried to the bow. The German watched as she secured the line around the bitt. He was too close to her for Peters to act.

"Well?" Siegler demanded "Are we ready to move?"

Elizabeth nodded. Siegler gestured at the major. The winch motor whined at a higher pitch, and the boat began to move backward. Mentally, Peters urged Elizabeth to move away from the German. He knew what was going to happen. He admired the Fitzroys' bravery, but he was afraid that it might cause Elizabeth's death before he could do anything about it.

There was no one at the wheel. As the line became taut, the bow of the yacht swung toward the pier while the stern moved toward the opposite side. Peters watched helplessly as Siegler finally caught on to what was happening and grabbed Elizabeth by the hair. The pistol was against her temple as he shouted, "Stop that winch, Major, or I'll kill her."

The whine died instantly. The stern bumped lightly against the fenders alongside the pier as the line slackened.

"What happened?" Siegler growled. The frightened woman didn't answer. Major Fitzroy was starting toward them as Siegler yelled, "Stay where you are, Major. Tell me why that happened."

"The wheel, you damned fool. The rudder, the tiller, whatever you bastards call it. It has to be manned. Take your hands off of her. Without both of us, you won't even get this boat out of the slip, much less to France. She was frightened. She forgot. Take the wheel, Elizabeth."

The major sounded stronger, Peters noted.

Siegler released his grip. "Yes, take the wheel, Liebchen. Do it right this time. One more of your tricks and I'll take my chances with the car without you and the major. Now, is that rope in the right place?"

"Yes," Elizabeth breathed.

"Then get back there and do what has to be done. This is the last chance for both of you." Roughly, Siegler pushed Elizabeth ahead of him along the narrow deck alongside the cabin.

Tom Peters knew that he must act now. He waited until Elizabeth had passed across his blurring vision. The German was only a foot or two behind her, but he would have to risk it even though it would be dangerous. Once the German passed, he would be firing at her as well as the man.

As Siegler moved opposite him, the old man rose to his feet. In his anxiety for Elizabeth, and with his rapidly failing reflexes he lost his clear advantage. As he brought the shotgun up, it struck the overhang of the cabin roof briefly. Siegler heard and then saw Peters as he turned and fired instinctively just as the old man's finger tightened on his own trigger. Both guns seemed to fire simultaneously, but the thirty-eight-caliber bullet from Siegler's pistol struck the old man's right shoulder just as the shot left his barrel, forcing his gun slightly to the right. The main force of the spread passed by Siegler, while the fringes peppered his left arm and face. He was thrown over the lifeline onto the pier.

Tom Peters lay on the narrow deck, the shotgun still clutched in his hand. He heard Elizabeth scream as a shot was fired from somewhere beyond the cabin. Peters lay filled with anger at his failure. The shot meant that the German was still able to function. They would both soon be dead. Elizabeth's scream meant that the first shot had been for the major. He watched the blood spreading beneath him and waited helplessly.

Again the pistol was fired, but he heard the bullet strike high on the boathouse wall behind him. He was able to see blurred movement at the end of the cabin toward the stern. He no longer feared the death he knew was coming; only anger that he was unable to move the shotgun still in his hand. Then he heard Elizabeth sobbing softly. She was crouched behind the cabin, no more than six feet from where he lay, looking at him.

"Come here, Elizabeth," he called hoarsely. He could see that she was terrified. "Elizabeth! Come here!" he ordered. She hesitated, and then began to crawl toward him. "Quickly!" he urged. She crawled faster, but stopped at the edge of the spreading blood. The color drained from her face. "Don't look at the blood, girl," Peters said weakly. "I'm much better than I look. Listen to me!"

Elizabeth reacted to the tone of his voice, and moved closer. "This is no time to faint, Elizabeth. Where is he?"

She pointed beyond the cabin.

"Is he coming?"

"I don't know. His arm . . . and his eye . . . He shot Edward."

"Listen to me, girl. Reach down here and pick up this gun. Close your eyes if you must, but get it now!" Elizabeth hesitated. "Now!" the old man ordered. She reached across him and took the gun from his hand.

"Did he kill the major? I'm sorry, dear, but I have to know."

"I don't think so. I saw him move just before that man shot at me."

"Fine, dear, that is good news. Have you ever fired a gun like this before?"

"Yes," she answered.

"Thank the Lord for that. Put your finger on the back trigger and wait for him to come to you. When you can see him clearly, fire."

"I couldn't. . . ."

"You must. That man won't hesitate to kill you. It's your only chance and the major's. We'll need a doctor. Be careful . . . don't try to . . ." The old man slipped into unconsciousness.

Elizabeth was stunned. At first she thought he had died, but then she saw the pulse flickering beneath the blood-soaked beard.

"Liebchen!" Siegler's voice came from the pier beyond the cabin. "Liebchen!" he called again. "Do you hear me? I'll give you one minute to come down here. That old bastard managed to wound me. Do you hear me? The major is still alive. I'll kill him now if you don't come out. Help me and I'll leave in the car. Then you can get help for him. He's bleeding to death. Do you hear me?"

"I hear you," Elizabeth said.

"Come down here and help me to the house. All I want is some help with these wounds, then I'll leave, and you can get help for your husband." He paused, listening. There was no answer. His voice rose. "Come out now. I'm going to kill him!"

"Don't!" Elizabeth shouted. "I'm coming."

Willi Siegler had managed to struggle to his feet. He watched the deck of the yacht waiting for Elizabeth to appear. He now knew that she was behind the forward end of the cabin and would cross the deck at the bow. He raised the pistol.

The pain in his head was terrible. He could feel his left eye hanging from its socket against his cheek. His left arm hung uselessly against his side, shattered by shotgun pellets. He turned painfully to focus his remaining eye onto the forward deck and cocked the pistol. He had underestimated the old man. Where did he get that shotgun? How did he...? It was too late for that now, he thought angrily, but there was still a chance. As long as he remained on his feet there was a chance. First, he must kill the woman and the English officer. Then he would find something in the house to patch himself up temporarily. There was still the colonel. It had come to him suddenly that it hadn't been the colonel or his men who had given away the mission. It had been von Maussner! It had been doomed to failure from the start, but he would live to see the swine hang. When he was finished with these English and had tended his wounds, he would drive to a deserted telephone kiosk and call the colonel. Luckily the telephone number was still clear in his memory. The colonel would find a way to get him to the submarine.

Behind him, the major stirred. Siegler ignored him and called, "Hurry it up, Liebchen."

Elizabeth stepped carefully over the old man. She held the shotgun pointed downward at her side. No matter what the man had done she knew that she could not simply walk out and shoot him. She would disarm him, force him to help her husband and Mr. Peters. There was a medical kit just below in the cabin. She was moving across the forward deck when she heard Edward's voice. "Stay back, Elizabeth! He's going to kill you!"

At the same time she saw the German. Siegler had turned angrily toward the prone man, aiming the pistol carefully. He hadn't seen Elizabeth. He had begun to squeeze the trigger when he paused for a fraction of a second as he heard the sudden roar of a powerful engine from somewhere beyond the boathouse door. Whatever it was, its noise would cover the sound of the shot. Siegler was no longer thinking rationally; he realigned the pistol.

Siegler was less than six feet away and slightly below her when Elizabeth raised the shotgun and carefully squeezed the trigger.

Willi Siegler's pistol fired into the planking as his lifeless body was propelled in a tumbling pinwheel of blood across the boathouse. The mission was over.

Elizabeth Fitzroy dropped the shotgun to the deck and stared in horror at the crumpled mass against the wall as the MTB's bow nosed into the slip behind the yacht.

At that moment the sun rose above the level of the boathouse entrance, bringing for Elizabeth a sudden and merciful half darkness to the interior.

CHAPTER 37

Colonel Blake waited anxiously for Brigadier Fox in the corridor of the Victoria Hospital. It was difficult for him to believe that the events of the morning had taken place less than a mile to the east, on the banks of the quiet Hamble.

The motor patrol boat had preceded the troops by minutes, caution having been thrown aside by the sounds of gunfire from the boathouse. The naval landing party had jumped to the pier seconds after Elizabeth had fired. Major Fitzroy had struggled to a sitting position and waved away immediate assistance, pointing to his wife, who stood rigidly on the deck of the yacht, and then to the body of Willi Siegler. The naval officer understood at once. He gave rapid orders to cover the body, and then ran to the yacht, leaving the major to the medics.

"Mrs. Fitzroy?" he said tentatively from the pier. "Are you all right? Your husband is being looked after. He's not wounded badly."

For a moment Elizabeth didn't answer, then she began to cry softly. "Mr. Peters," she said.

The naval officer climbed to the yacht's deck. "I'm sorry, Ma'am. You said?"

"Mr. Peters . . . back there."

The officer walked quickly around the cabin, hesitating briefly when he saw the old man lying in a pool of spreading blood. Then he saw the eyes open beneath a bloodsoaked towel wrapped around his forehead. He knelt beside the old man when he saw the lips moving.

"She did it! Damned plucky girl, that one," the old man gasped.

"Yes, sir," the naval officer answered. He felt for a pulse and found it surprisingly strong. He called orders to the men helping Elizabeth Fitzroy to the pier and then said reassuringly to the old man, "Our doctor is coming, sir, and we'll have you in hospital in no time."

"Fine, son, but as I told the girl, I'm better than I look."

The naval officer smiled in admiration. "That's the spirit, sir."

"One thing, son."

"Yes, sir?"

"Bring me my shotgun, will you? There's a good lad."

Brigadier Fox was smiling. "Elizabeth is quite all right now that she knows that Edward will be up and about in a few days."

"Thank the Lord for that, sir. And Peters?" Colonel Blake asked.

"Touch and go, but the doctors seem to feel that he will make it. That man is a marvel—even for an Englishman. I'm eternally in his debt, Andrew. If he hadn't managed to telephone, that Hun might have conceivably gotten away with it."

"It's been quite a night, sir," Colonel Blake said.

"Unfortunately it promises to be quite a day as well. A car is waiting to take us to the Air College where an airplane is waiting to fly us to London. The Prime Minister is back in Downing Street hopping mad at the French for their failures, at the Huns for their successes, and at intelligence. It won't be easy to explain that with the assistance of the navy, an elderly retired sergeant-major, and my niece, we've managed to muddle through this night. We're going to need all of our wits about us this morning if I'm to be allowed to apply what we've learned in the future. Hopefully, Winston has managed to catch a few winks on the aircraft back from France. I'd say we're in for a difficult morning."

"Luckily, sir, apart from the explosion of the tank at Woolston, few civilians are aware of what really occurred last night. If I may, it might be best if they didn't learn the full story at this particular time. But I do suggest that we should see to it that Hitler knows of their failure."

The brigadier interrupted. "Winston has already seen to it that Hitler will have no doubts that he's failed and would be foolish indeed to attempt it again."

Hitler had indeed been informed.

Later that afternoon General Heinz von Maussner entered the staff car waiting below the Fellsnest and was driven through the quiet streets of Rodert to the waiting train. The driver glanced in the rear view mirror and noticed that the general was smiling. He wondered why.